DUSK *to* DAWN SERIES

YOU'LL COME TO ME

TINA MARIE NICHOLS

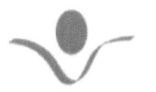

DocUmeant *Publishing*
244 5th Avenue
Suite G-200
NY, NY 10001
646-233-4366
www.DocUmeantPublishing.com

Published by
DocUmeant Publishing
244 5th Avenue, Suite G-200
NY, NY 10001
Phone: 6462334366

http://www.DocUmeantPublishing.com

Disclaimer: All characters appearing in this work are fictitious. Any resemblance to real persons, living or dead, is purely coincidental.

Library of Congress Control Number: 2017940937
ISBN: 978-1-9378-0182-3

DEDICATION

To my wonderful family, my love and appreciation go to each of you for the patience and understanding and never-ending support you've given me. Your love and confidence mean the world to me. Without you it wouldn't be worth doing.

ACKNOWLEDGMENTS

I've heard it said it takes a village to raise a child. Well it definitely takes one to publish a book. My sincerest gratitude belongs to my DocUmeant Publishing village. Thank you: Ginger Marks, Phil Marks, Chris Gibson, Wendy VanHatten, and Patti Knoles. Without all of you taking a chance on me this book would still be a pile of paper.

CHAPTER ONE

Raine Andrews gritted her teeth as the offending arm clamped tight around her waist, reminding her of a snake squeezing the life out of its prey. Blunt-edged fingers dug deeper into her already throbbing ribs. Her hate mixed with pain but she refused to utter a sound—instead she sought the safe haven she'd created in her head. When the pain receded, the coppery taste of blood filled her mouth. She'd gnawed her cheek ragged.

Evil-tainted pleasure coursed through her husband, gloating that she wouldn't dare make a peep, but just to emphasize his warning he dug in again. It was the hatred sparking in her angry blue eyes that revealed her feelings—she wanted to kill him. That wasn't happening! She'd meet her maker long before he did. However, as long as she kept her mouth shut, he mightn't hurt her—too badly. His evil-eyed stare dared her to open her mouth.

She ignored the dare, absolutely no way was she unleashing the still simmering rage from their earlier altercation. Besides, no one would believe him to be a crazed monster.

The consummate actor, he'd lied, telling their hosts she'd taken a nasty fall but refused to stay home. Solicitous, they'd made her comfortable amongst the activity, and doing so had certainly worked in Addison's favor, enabling him to watch her while enjoying the free-flowing alcohol and the cocaine supplied by another guest. Brazen but not stupid, Addison made sure his best foot was forward around Eric Sanderson. Out of several competitors, he'd been selected by Sanderson Real Estate to build their newest high-end subdivision.

Thinking of the earlier attack, his glittering eyes should have alerted her he was spoiling for a fight. What set him off? Was it her choice of dress? Normally, Addison couldn't have cared less, but not tonight. Tonight, he'd wanted her to wear something that fit her like a gunny sack. Instead, she made her own choice. Infuriated, he'd ripped the dress to shreds then started hitting her. Despite her pleading and begging, the hitting went on until, for the briefest moment, he'd stopped and seizing the opportunity, she ran but he caught her and slammed her to the floor. The impact stunned her and he'd kicked her again and again before ordering, "Get up! You're going to that damned party! Any hint of this, and so help me I'll finish what I started. I'm tired of you defying me and I'm damned tired of you sleeping with Katy. You're my wife and you'll start acting like it. From here on out you sleep in that bed and if you try otherwise, I'll drag your ass back here. And you do not want me doing that!"

In that moment, she'd vowed his threats would never be carried out. She'd never lie in that bed again and this was the last time he'd ever lay a hand on her.

Pulling herself together, she'd put on the too-large emerald green sheath. Heavy makeup covered the ravages of tears. At least he hadn't struck her in the face. Explaining why she looked like a Mack truck had run over her would have been difficult. He'd wanted to show her he was in control, that she couldn't say, do, or wear anything without his okay. Wrong! As far as she was concerned the dress was history, just like their marriage. So far, she'd pulled off the loving-wife-act. Slipping up even once would mean more hell to pay.

The hatred in her eyes excited the evil part of Addison, the part without feelings that relished hurting her. If not under the last hit of coke and double-shots of the superb single malt Scotch, perhaps a bit of conscious might have broken through but that part of him had disappeared as his use of drugs and alcohol intensified. Now, he intended showing her again who was in control. He couldn't wait to get her home, to inflict more pain, more punishment. He dug deeper. "Sweetheart, I think it's time to go home."

Though she swallowed back a scream, what she really wanted was to take each pain-inflicting finger and crush it. Then he'd never be able to hurt her again. Satan had nothing on Addison; he could have been Satan's teacher.

She knew the many faces of his personalities—how he could change from Dr. Jekyll to Mr. Hyde in seconds, and this evening was one of those times. He kept switching between the two personas—the loving husband around others, then to the pain-inflicting-monster when they were alone. She was certain the evil Addison was about to appear again.

A familiar prickling crept up her neck that screamed "run," and that's exactly what she intended. She was through taking the angry fists that left her bruised and bleeding, and fighting back made it worse. It was only a matter of time before something deadly happened, and the odds were definitely not in her favor. She'd tried leaving once, making the stupid mistake of going to her in-laws. She should have known they'd rat her out. Of course, Addison had lied then, blaming her for starting a petty argument, then blowing it out of proportion. He even convinced them she'd inflicted her own injuries. Later, back home, he'd given her an even worse beating.

She should have left again but his threats concerning Katy convinced her to stay. Should-haves. She had a whole pocket full, but that was soon to end. However, if Addison had any clue what she planned, what happened earlier would be horseplay. This time he'd kill her.

Addison hadn't always been like this, but the alcohol and drugs had warped his mind, fed his rage, and eventually destroyed her love for him and their family.

Addison was in no shape to drive. Snatching the keys, she hurried to the Lamborghini and with a flick of the wrist the powerful machine roared to life. She wanted to leave him in the dust to explain why the outrageously expensive car was missing right along with his wife and daughter.

Wanting to put on the dog, he'd leased the extravagant vehicle for the party. "That shindig's for me and I'm riding in style." Another sign he wasn't the same man she'd married. At one time, and not so very long ago, he'd been a caring husband and father. But that Addison had turned into the narcissist he was now.

Suddenly, he started rocking in his seat. Inside Addison's brain a rotten seed had taken root, its diseased tendrils quickly spreading, making his head buzz with imagined wrongs she had committed against him. He'd warned her, but had she listened? No! Instead she'd deliberately defied him.

"I saw you flirting with Sanderson. Haven't I warned you if you ever gave me reason to even think you were cheating, you'd be sorry?"

The Lamborghini's high-beams cut a bright swath through the inky black of the lonely stretch of highway. On another wave of terror, it was becoming clear she had to turn the tide of his thoughts and calm him before things escalated out of control.

"Honey," she gagged on the endearment, "I wasn't flirting with Mr. Sanderson. He was telling me he loves your ideas for his subdivision." She sounded calm but inside she was quaking right off the Richter scale and from the spewing curses he didn't believe her. All hope vanished like a ghost in daylight as she prayed to get home before he erupted into another raging fit. If Addison went off on her in the car she didn't stand a chance.

"You're lying! Even with his wife right there you flirted with him!" Each word was punctuated by a fist pounding on the dashboard. "Just wait until I get you home, you little bitch. This will be the sorriest night of your life."

Glancing over at him she half-expected to see him frothing at the mouth. "For the love of God, Addison, I haven't done anything wrong!" There was no getting through to him and his intentions were all too clear. Suddenly he dove across the seat, wrenching the steering wheel, sending the Lamborghini careening off the pavement toward the ditch. The tires grabbed at the loose gravel and pinging noises sounded on the low-slung undercarriage.

She slapped his hands. "Are you trying to kill us?" Anger obliterating her fear, she pounded the steering wheel wishing it were his face. She'd pound it into a bloody pulp. "You're crazy! You're drunk and high and you don't know a damn thing! You're hooked on the drugs and booze and if you'd lay off the stuff, you'd see how wrong you are."

"I'm not high, or drunk, and I'm not crazy!" Slurring bellows resonated around her. "You're the one who's changed, Miss High and Mighty, thinking you're too damned good for me to touch. You want all the money I can give you but when it comes to a little husband-loving you won't let me get near you!"

A full-blown body-shiver rocked her that his train of thought headed into dangerous territory; territory she wanted to stay far away from. And he was wrong. She didn't want his money any more than she wanted his hands on her. The very idea made her skin crawl.

Seeing their driveway, hope blossomed. All she had to do was get inside and lock the lunatic out! If need be she'd call the police. After all, she bore proof of his earlier attack. She hit the seatbelt release before the car jerked to a stop. Having kicked off her neck-breaking stilettos he'd insisted on, barefoot, she sped across the carpet-like lawn toward the house but despite his inebriated state, Addison was faster than she'd given him credit for. His speed increased her terror.

Pounding steps grew closer. Run! Run! Her frenzied brain screamed even as one hand anchored in her hair, the other around her aching ribs. The overpowering stench of alcohol gagged her. "Let me go! Stop it! Stop it, Addison! Let me go! You're hurting me."

He shook her hard. "You need hurting and I'll stop when I'm damn good and ready!"

Despite her kicking and struggling, he dragged her across the lawn. The front door loomed large in the glow of the porch light, now she didn't want inside. The house was her prison without bars, her personal torture chamber and it was about to get worse, once inside she might never come out alive. Intuition screamed this time was far different than any other. Nothing would ever be the same again. Holding her clamped to his chest, Addison unlocked the lock. Raine tried latching onto the doorframe with her feet but her attempts were futile against his brute strength as he carried her inside. If I could just get my hands on something, he'd get a taste of his own medicine. But he didn't give her the chance. He delivered several vicious slaps across the face.

"Stop it! Stop it!" The salty blood in her mouth increased her fury; she refused to go down easy. A fighter, a survivor, raised in an orphanage she'd learned to stand up for herself. So, she did. Things crashed to the floor. Glass shattered. Then his grip loosened and not missing a beat, she fisted her right hand and followed through with a resounding punch, then another, and another. Each blow seared fire in her fist when it connected with Addison's nose but the feel of bone hitting solid bone cheered her on.

Red-hot pain gushed up Addison's nose setting his face afire and he bellowed. For a split second, furious eyes locked with furious eyes then Raine lunged around him but he caught her, tangling one beefy hand in her long hair, the other gripped her ribs. It infuriated him further that she dared to fight. Drawing back, the last thing she saw was his massive fist coming at her. A resounding crack echoed even as pain exploded in her face then she was plummeting down a well of darkness.

When consciousness returned, she couldn't remember lying down and instinct said something wasn't right. Then, clarity hit her like a ton of bricks. Addison! He'd knocked her out! She tried moving but her limbs wouldn't budge and there were a million bees stinging her back and legs. But that didn't make sense. There were no bees in the house.

It was then she found herself bound so tight to the bed's head and foot posts she could barely move. God in heaven! He'd staked her out and trussed her up like some wild animal.

Not only that, but while unconscious he'd stripped her bare and done something to hurt her. On that thought the harsh breathing penetrated, sending hair-raising fear rifling through her. What did he plan to do to her? In her next breath, she got the answer.

"I warned you what would happen if you defied me! You're always testing me, pushing me until I have to punish you. Sometimes I think you enjoy making me angry." He sounded positively gloating.

"You're wrong. I've done everything to please you and I didn't do anything wrong tonight." She gritted. Her lips were split and swollen, blood staining the lace-trimmed pillow-case beneath her head. She was still shocked that while unconscious he had stripped her, meted out his punishment then waited for her to come to.

As Addison hulked over her, her attention landed on the leather belt in his hands. Doubling it up, he snapped the ends apart, the sharp cracks echoing like fireworks. Realizing the fiery stinging was because he'd already whipped her once and was going to do it again, she started struggling, but trussed-up it was no use.

"Don't, Addison. Don't do this." She begged the man who five years ago, had pledged to love her. But this man wasn't him. This was an evil monster hell-bent on punishing her, inflicting punishment was the only thing in his crazed mind.

He raised the belt and she tensed for the blow. The first lash sent a burning fire streaking across her already ragged flesh. Sharp cries flew from her as another and another lash bit into her but no amount of begging helped.

"I told you, I told you," he ranted in time with the strapping of the belt. Mindlessly out of control, spurred on by the demons in his head, Addison kept lashing, the blows landing anywhere and everywhere until she couldn't take it any longer and blacked out.

Chapter Two

While Raine sought blessed oblivion, several hundred miles away retired Sargent Major Jess Harper laid a crisp twenty-dollar bill on the bar. Smoothing his hand across the worn surface, he contemplated how many war stories the old bar had heard. A lot, he figured. A career Marine, Jess appreciated the establishment for men and women of the armed forces. He and his best friend, Cooper Michaels, were part of that esteemed group and whenever the words Semper Fi met their ears their blood ran proud.

Charlie Hooper, a Navy veteran and part-time bartender, rang up the tab then laid the change on the bar. "Keep it, Charlie." Jess said then grinned at the man beside him. "So, how long's the little troublemaker gone for?"

Earlier, Cooper had called Jess about meeting up for a beer after work. Normally he'd have gone straight home but Belle, his wife, was out of town and not wanting to face an empty house had hit his old buddy up for some company.

Cooper's brown eyes crinkled with humor. "Awe, come on. Admit it, pal. You love the hell my sweet little bride dishes out to you. Besides, it gives me a break from the doghouse, and Belle does love picking on you."

"Sweet little bride? Are we talking about the same woman?" Jess grunted. "Yeah, I love it all right. About as much as I love a toothache. If I wanted to be picked on, nagged at, or ragged on like she does me I'd get another wife," he tossed back. Though he loved Belle like a sister, she was a royal pain-in-the-ass, always telling him he should find a nice girl, get married, and have a house full of kids.

"Anyway, weather permitting, tomorrow. That's some hurricane whipping up on Florida and as much as I miss her, I don't want her taking any chances." A shadow flickered in Cooper's eyes.

Jess understood. It wasn't that long ago that Belle had been severely injured. Those had been some long and god-awful hours with Cooper going nearly berserk in his fury, and his guilt. Just one more reason, Jess decided cynically, not to get hitched to any one woman again.

He sure didn't need any more of those emotional ties that bind, then rip your heart out.

Taking one last pull from his beer bottle, he stood up. "See you in a couple of days. It's my turn to spring for dinner. Tell the little troublemaker she can pick the place this time."

Cooper shot him a "you're in trouble look." "You do know she'll go for that new sushi place, don't you? Ever since you said you can't stand the stuff she's been dying to go."

Jess grimaced. "Yeah, I know. I had to open my big fat mouth, so I'll have to pay the price. But, I figure they've got to have something I can choke down."

Jess climbed into his brand-new pickup, gleaming huge and black in the brightly lighted parking lot. It still had the tangy showroom-floor smell. Turning the key, country music streamed loud from the speakers. This time of night the station played oldies. Being strongly opinionated, he thought some of the crap played these days wasn't worth listening to and that the newbies should take a page from more seasoned singers' examples. They should quit swallowing the mike, turn down the amps and see if they really could carry a tune. Give him a good old George Jones, George Straight, or Ray Price song any day.

Driving the darkened blacktop, Jess thought about Cooper and Belle. Despite his teasing, Belle was a sweetheart and perfectly suited for Cooper. Not that their relationship had always been a bed of roses. It'd definitely hit a rough patch, but Belle's near-fatal run-in with her dead husband's assailant had brought Cooper to his senses. Now they were happy as two little clams keeping house together. But, he conceded, tapping the steering wheel in time to the music, what they had wasn't for him. He loved women, loved having them around, but only on his terms. Overly protective of his bachelorhood, he was a no-strings kind of guy. The women he dated knew the score because he made sure in no uncertain terms. There'd been a few along the way who'd tried breaking his steadfast rule, but he'd nipped it in the bud immediately. Having trekked the marriage road once, he wasn't about to make the trip again. His ex-wife was a nice girl, but early on they'd figured out they weren't meant to be together for the long haul. Thankfully, the break had come before any kids had arrived. The idea of being a part-time dad was not for him and was a situation he had thankfully avoided.

Harmonizing with George Jones' White Lightening, Jess pulled between the lit lamp posts and parked beside the cabin. Yes sir, he thought, he loved his little piece of female-free heaven. If he wanted to walk around buck naked he could and in fact did just that, stripping down as he headed for the shower.

CHAPTER THREE

While Jess Harper was enjoying his buck-naked freedom, Raine returned to consciousness and an intense all-over burning that had her clutching the bloodied pillow to muffle her moans. That's when she realized she was loose. Instantly, her brain screamed to run and though she wanted to, her battered body wasn't able. However, she refused to be a passive target for another of Addison's attacks. It was imperative she get Katy and prayed it wasn't already too late. Cora and Ethel, unaware the situation, would let Addison take her. No one knew this side—the dark side, of Addison. Fearing his threats, she'd kept the sordid secrets of her marriage to herself. Not even her best friends, Molly and Gordon Hanson, knew the awful things that went on behind the Andrews' closed doors. Had Molly known, she'd have gone gunning for Addison with a double-barreled shotgun. In hindsight, she should have called Addison's bluff, but that didn't matter anymore. Getting away was what mattered.

Through blurred vision she saw it was a couple of minutes past two; she'd been at Addison's mercy for three hours. A surreptitious glance around the room showed him gone. Had he left? Given his state of mind, he'd think it cause for celebration—the keeping-the-little-wife-in-line kind. Sometimes he left after hurting her then returned all sorry, making empty promises it would never happen again. Then, even those promises ceased. But, this time was far worse than ever before. This time, just as earlier, he'd been hell-bent on inflicting serious injury, and from the feel of it, he may have succeeded.

Easing off the bed, she swallowed a groan. If still in the house, she didn't want him hearing her. Grasping the foot post, she swayed and staggered like a drunken sailor. The plush carpet muffled her unsteady steps but seeing her image in the full-length mirror a gasp escaped before she could stop it. The reflection staring back had a face that was swollen, a mixture of mottled reds and purples and eyes blacked and nearly swollen shut. No wonder her vision was blurry.

Rummaging in the closet she found an oversized shirt, one of Addison's. As long as it was roomy and buttoned, it could've belonged to King Kong for all she cared. The material, though silky-soft, chafed the bleeding and ragged flesh of her back. A bra was definitely out, but no way would she go without panties. Pulling them on, she thought rubbing sandpaper down her backside couldn't have hurt any worse. Shoving her feet into the first shoes she came to; ironically they were her running shoes—an omen perhaps?

Her purse lay in the doorway and to her relief both keys and cellphone were in it. Looping the thin cross-over strap across her body sent fire needling across her back but she ignored it. Escaping was priority. She eased down the hallway and was nearing the front door when a large shadow loomed out of the darkened living room, scaring her so badly her heart jumped from her chest into her throat before plunging to the pit of her stomach. Instead of leaving, he'd waited for her to wake up, no doubt plotting more punishment and getting drunker.

"Un-unh, I don't think so. You're not going anywhere until I say so," Addison bellowed. In the darkness, a shiny glint in his left hand grabbed her attention. It was the pistol normally kept locked in the gun safe. Instinctively, she shrank back even as a backhand sent her sprawling. On the way down she crashed into something. There was the sound of shattering glass. It had to be the china tea service his folks had given them as a wedding gift. Good! She hated it, anyway.

Beyond all rational thought, somehow she had to convince him she wasn't leaving, and rid him of the gun. "I wasn't going anywhere. I was looking for you." She made her voice a sleepy whisper. "I woke up and you weren't there. I was worried." Lie! Lie for all you're worth. Thinking of Katy gave her the strength to get up but only for seconds as his fist slammed her cheekbone. Showers of black and white dots danced before her eyes but she fought the blackness, staying on her feet.

Enraged that she wouldn't stay down—wrath, deep and dark swirled inside him. "You're lying! You're sneaking out to meet your lover. Well, I'll make damn sure you never go anywhere. I'll kill you!" He ranted over and over.

A fresh wave of terror ripped through her when he grabbed her hair, his intentions abundantly clear when he dragged her to the couch. Fury overcame her fear and she started prying at the fingers tearing her hair out by the roots. No! No way was he forcing himself on her! Kicking out, a hard blow caught his shin but it only infuriated him more. Grabbing a fistful of shirt, he ripped it and the strap of the cross-over off as though they were nothing more than paper, leaving her bare from the waist up. But he wasn't finished. Now he was pawing at her shorts. With all her strength, she bucked like a wild bronco throwing off an unwanted rider but it was more like a gnat tossing an elephant. And one very important factor stayed—in her mind—the gun.

"Addison, stop! For God's sake put the gun down before you shoot one of us!" The words were barely out when a loud blast filled the room. Stunned, Raine took a shuddering breath waiting for the pain to come. But as seconds passed she realized Addison hadn't shot her. Then it sank in he wasn't moving, and the grip on her hair was gone and he was lying limp on top of her.

She frantically shoved his dead weight off her, and he hit the floor with a heavy thud. Scrambling up on shaky legs, she stared at the spreading red stain across the front of his shirt and giggled. Oh lordy, the crazy fool shot himself! It was so hilarious she laughed as tears ran down her cheeks.

Taking a deep calming breath, she muttered, "This is great! Just great! How ironic could it get? He tries to kill me and I have to save his sorry ass." Swollen eyes narrowed to barely discernible slits. "I ought to let him die," but she felt for a pulse. Did it make her a vengeful person that she hoped he was dead? Nope. It made her an honest one, and anyone who said otherwise was flipping crazy. Unfortunately, he had a pulse and needed help. Turning on the lights, she stared at the chaos around her; furniture was overturned, lamps and knick-knacks had been knocked from the end tables and shattered glass lay twinkling in the light.

Still scowling, she noted the blood stain had grown larger and debated whether to call for help. Conscious finally decided she would. However, she didn't see the phone. Okay. . . no phone, never mind her cell, then she couldn't call and he could bleed out . . . God please forgive me, she prayed, for being tempted to let him die.

The phone was under the couch, probably knocked there during their struggles. A female dispatcher answered. After explaining the situation, the dispatched told her to stay on the line until the ambulance arrived. As they waited, she asked Raine questions. Answering them, she detected anger from the dispatcher as she learned what he'd done. Well sister, join the club, you can't feel any angrier than I do.

Raine didn't mention her injuries figuring a bullet wound went to the top of the priority list. Though still half-wishing he'd die, instincts to save a life kicked in, so while waiting she used the shirt Addison had torn off her to staunch the blood.

She explained what she was doing but it wasn't helping. "The blood just keeps coming."

"Just keep pressure on the wound, help is on the way." And it was. Hearing the sirens, her conscious clear, Raine hung up. It was more than Addison could say. Another comical thought flitted into her head. Well actually, he can't say anything right now. A sputtering sound, half-hysterical laughter, half-hysterical sob burst out as she went to let the paramedics in.

Raine was totally unaware the shocking sight she made in the porch light with no top, her battered form and covered in blood. "He's in there." She pointed.

"Let's get her covered," Pop, the senior paramedic, nodded at another EMT.

Focused on the EMTs tending Addison, Raine didn't see the man and woman approaching the house—Detectives David Green and Nancy Collins of the Phoenix Victims' Crime Unit.

"Pretty snazzy spread, from what I can see in the dark. And would you look at that beauty," Det. David Green whistled, admiring the gleaming Lamborghini before looking at the lone figure bathed in the porch light. "And I have a feeling that is our Ms. Andrews."

"That's pretty astute of you," Nancy Collins, his partner of five years quipped.

"That's what Marti says I am." He grinned.

Nancy rolled her eyes. "Marti probably meant stupid."

"I heard that!" He feigned insult but his gray eyes crinkled. "You're probably right, though."

He noted the house was a rambling hacienda style in earthen tones of adobe and trimmed in western wood. It made a pretty picture nestled in the stand of native pines, and the soft glow from the dusk-to-dawn lights not only lit up the area for security purposes, they also provided an ethereal ambiance—all fairy-tale and candy-land happy. Inside it apparently held a different story. Just goes to show, he thought cynically, domestic abuse is a dirty little secret living in the best of neighborhoods.

Drawing closer, David's all-seeing eyes again zeroed in on the woman at the open door and his stomached pitched. "Son of a bitch!"

In the bright light her injuries stood out in garish detail and there was a dazed look about her, as though she had just awakened from a bad nightmare. But, it was her appearance from the waist up that raised his hackles right along with his blood pressure. It didn't take a rocket scientist to figure out what happened here.

Nancy was doing her own survey of the battered woman with the mass of tangled blond hair hanging to her waist. Proper protocol meant not picking sides until all the evidence had been evaluated but gut-instinct screamed, "To hell with protocol!" Her temper was sizzling; she wouldn't have been a bit surprised if steam shot out from every orifice. She opened her mouth but her hot-tempered partner cut her off.

"Son of a bitch!" he repeated, his stomach queasy imagining angry fists slamming into the woman. "Nance, she looks like she's been in a war and come out on the losing side."

Nancy snorted in agreement, not a good sign. Anyone who knew her even the tiniest bit headed for the hills when she made that god-awful sound. Any second she'd explode and from experience David knew it wouldn't be a pretty sight.

"Uh-huh! Since she's still standing I'm thinking she's the victor, but you're right about the war. Anyway, we're about to find out. It ought to be dandy tale."

"Want to bet she shot him in self-defense?" Always up for a good bet, David threw out the challenge.

"If not, I'll shoot him for her," Nancy said, patting her gun.

"Tsk. Tsk, Det. Collins! You've already formed an opinion before you even know the details."

"Tsk. Tsk, yourself!" She snorted again, making him laugh.

Then the laughter disappeared. "Get her covered up, Nance. I bet she has no clue she's missing a top. I'll take the husband. If what I suspect is true, I just might beat you to the punch and have the pleasure of shooting him myself."

She couldn't resist mocking him. "Tsk-tsk, Det. Green, you've already formed an opinion without knowing the facts first."

The easy banter helped lighten some oft-times very unpleasant cases and he thought this one might be the worst one yet. It was a well-known fact throughout the precinct that Green and Collins were the best of the best at handling domestic abuse situations. Each had worked in other divisions, but the Victims Unit was their calling. They'd become partners five years ago when circumstances had thrown them together. Not only were they partners, they were friends, too. Their families—David Green's wife Marti, twin daughters Shay and Shanna—and Sarah, Nancy Collins' mother, often spent time together. Not having grand-children of her own, Sarah Collins considered the Green kids her surrogate grandchildren and she loved spoiling them!

Raine watched the paramedics through blurred vision. Touching one eye, she winced then became aware of the man and woman standing beside her. She hadn't even heard them. The man was tall, broad-shouldered, his dark hair crisply trimmed. Steely-gray eyes were set in a rugged face. At the moment, they were flinty and forbidding. On the other hand, the compassionate smile of the woman offered kindness and under-standing, of which she could use a healthy dose. Both radiated official business. Both presented badges.

"Ms. Andrews, I'm Det. Green. This is my partner, Det. Collins."

In the porch light Raine Andrews looked as if she'd been hit over and over with a battering ram, or used as one. What else, Nancy Collins wondered with a curl in her stomach, had she endured this night? When the call came in they'd instantly recognized the Andrews name. Everyone knew Andrews Construction and wheeler-dealer Addison Andrews. And he was no small man, either.

Raine Andrews was on the petite side. Nancy pegged her at five-foot-three, maybe one-twenty at the most. So why, she wondered, after shooting him, hadn't she high-tailed it instead of sticking around? Something didn't smell right and instincts screamed Mr. Andrews was the rotten ingredient. "We need to ask you some questions, but maybe you'd like to cover up first?" she suggested gently.

Raine stared blankly then Nancy's words sank in. Looking down at her bare chest, an embarrassed "oh . . ." slid out. In a feeble attempt at coverage she crossed her arms over her breasts; the movement elicited a hiss of pain. "I used it, the shirt," she said, "to stop the bleeding."

Nancy slipped off her navy blazer to lay it over Raine's shoulders then caught a glimpse of her back. Fury welled so thick it fogged her brain. Now she really wanted to kick the bastard in his wound. It'd feel damned good giving him a taste of his own medicine! See how he liked being kicked like a dog.

"This'll be better." One of the EMTs gently enclosed Raine in a sheet.

Beneath veiled lashes Nancy looked at her partner. He was making notes on a small spiral pad. As if by radar, he glanced up. Their eyes caught, sharing a look that said more was going on here than met the eye.

"Come on, Ms. Andrews," Nancy said.

Chapter Four

Seeing Addison's unconscious form, Raine wondered if she were nuts being happy he was bleeding all over the place. If she didn't hurt so damn bad she'd dance an Irish jig in celebration. But her whole body was a river of pain and a new ache had come to life in her side. Even blinking made her head throb. Addison had used her as a punching bag and tossed her around like a rag doll for hours. Maybe that's why her brain wasn't firing on all cylinders.

"That little girl needs checking out," Pop, the senior paramedic said. He had a daughter about her age and heaven help any man who laid anything but a loving hand on her. He scowled at the man he was putting an IV in. To his way of thinking the bastard deserved shooting.

David's frosty-eyed gaze trailing them, he knew his partner possessed a special ability to connect with the abused woman better than any male officer ever could. Raine Andrews was in capable, caring hands.

Raine found another loose-fitting shirt, again one of Addison's, and another round of glee made her chuckle. His mother had given him the shirt for his birthday just last week. Good! By the time she was done with it, it could be tossed in the rag bin right along with the dresses he'd ripped to shreds. Slipping it on, little hisses slid from between gritted teeth.

Perusing the room, the sound drew Nancy Collins' attention. "Would you like some help?"

Raine grimaced. "I . . . think . . . I've . . . got . . . . it."

What a plucky and independent little thing, Nancy thought, turning her attention back to the master suite. Large and airy with floor to ceiling windows, its walls were a soft ivory. The furniture, some kind of light wood, looked expensive but knowing beans about furniture, she hadn't a clue. Shoot! She hadn't even decorated her own little bungalow. Bless Mom for taking on that task or she'd still be sleeping on a pallet on the floor. Standing in the middle of the room she closed her eyes letting her senses take over. Immediately, she shivered at the iciness enfolding her. A lot of abuse had occurred in this room and not just tonight. An evil aura hung in the air making goose bumps pebble her arms. When she opened her eyes, she expected to see a red devil, pitch fork in hand, and glowing eyes.

She took in more details. In a crumpled heap on the cream-colored carpet lay the tattered remnants of a green dress. At some point in their fight it'd been ripped to shreds. Finally, her gaze rested on the king-size bed and her eyes narrowed seeing the bindings still tied to the corner-posts. That was bad enough, but the droplets of blood spattered up and down the white bedspread heartily sickened her knowing exactly how those bloody welts had gotten on Raine Andrews' body. It was time to hear the details, horrible as they may be.

"Ms. Andrews, are you up to talking about what happened tonight?" Nancy removed a small note pad and a pen from her jacket pocket then nodded at the chair by the window. "Do you want to sit?"

Raine cringed. "Right now I can barely stand the clothes I'm wearing. I'm better off standing."

"We should get the paramedics to take a look at you, too. Now tell me what happened tonight."

Over the next few minutes Raine detailed Addison's earlier rage over the dress and the ensuing attack, the party, the explosive drive home, and his accusations of flirting with another man.

"Were you? Flirting with this man?" Cop instincts said no.

"No. Tonight's the first time I ever met the man. He hosted the party for Addison. All we discussed was how pleased he was with Addison's ideas. And his wife was there the whole time. She was sweet. I liked her." Raine gave a short derisive laugh. "Addison on the other hand, was anything but sweet, at least with me. I knew he was well into his cups and his nose." At the detective's questioning look, Raine made a sniffing sound.

Ah . . . cocaine. She pursed her lips, jotting a couple of notes on the pad. "I take it these incidents have happened before? Before tonight, that is, and you've never reported them?"

Raine dropped her eyes. "I had reasons for not reporting them." Nancy nodded, wondering what they were. Raine told how once home, Addison forced her inside then of the ensuing physical altercation, of being knocked out, bound to the bed, and whipped with the belt.

The fast-moving pen stopped writing. Staring at Raine, Nancy's heart went out to the woman so obviously the victim here tonight.

Hearing the sickening details from her own mouth made Raine mad. Never in her entire twenty-six years had she ever felt as helpless as finding herself bound to the bed. How could she have let things go so far? She should have been stronger, stood up to Addison instead of enabling him to exact his control over her. His threats had shackled her to him with invisible chains. Yes, she should have been stronger, should have taken her chances and run again but she couldn't dwell on the should-haves. She had to look forward and ensure this never happened again. Swollen eyes strayed to the ropes still tied to each bedpost. "He'll never do it again." The angry vow came out vehemently.

"I hope not, Ms. Andrews." Nancy's cool green eyes glittered and for a moment Raine thought she might go shoot Addison herself. "As far as I'm concerned he won't ever do it again. If what you say is true, he'll be sitting behind bars for a very long time. Between you and me and these walls, shooting him was too good for him!"

Raine's swollen lips curved faintly. "That's just it. I didn't shoot him." This was just getting better and better, the astounded detective thought. "I blacked out while he was whipping me. When I came to, he was gone and I was loose. I thought he'd left. I was almost out the door when he caught me. We fought, and the whole time he had the gun waving it around and threatening to shoot me. When he started ripping my clothes I knew I couldn't go through that again. I was trying to get him off me when the gun went off. I really thought he'd shot me."

Nancy Collins' head jerked up. Again! Raine Andrews had been raped by her husband in the past? She hadn't thought she could become any more incensed. If she could get away with it she'd march right back down the hall and finish off the bastard herself. Her green eyes gleamed; he wasn't to the hospital yet. Maybe she could convince the paramedics to lose him along the way—like maybe in some deep, dark hole out in the desert. "Ms. Andrews, I'd say a guardian angel was with you tonight. It could very well have been you being shot instead of him. If he's as drunk and high as you say, he might have let you die. He might be sorry after he sobered up but it would've been entirely too late by then."

Raine shook her head. "He wouldn't be sorry. He's way past that stage. But thank God he didn't shoot me or my little girl would be left to his mercy." And that wasn't happening.

At the mention of a child, Nancy frowned. "Please tell me your little girl's not in the house?"

"No, she's at the sitters."

"Good. That's good. Had she been here she could have been hurt." Nancy tucked the pen and note book away. "This is all for now. They should be close to transporting your husband. I wonder if he's regained consciousness yet." The telling look on Raine's face said she didn't care if he ever woke up again.

They returned to the living room to find Addison, hooked up to an IV, an oxygen mask over his face, being hefted onto a gurney. Raine stared at him in disgust while massaging the ache attacking her lower back. Conscious now, he was groaning pathetically. As full of booze and drugs as he was, how on earth could he feel anything?

From above the mask Addison caught sight of her. Immediately, his whole demeanor changed. No longer the pity-mongering victim, he became the aggressor, trying to lurch off the gurney to get to her, obvious to all that his agonizing pain was completely forgotten in the moment.

Pop, the senior EMT, made a note of it for the transport records. If ever that little lady should need it, they'd have a record on file.

Addison's face scrunched up in rage. "She shot me!" he tried shouting but his voice was muffled by the mask over his mouth. He ripped it off. When he spoke again even a deaf person could've heard every slurring word. "That crazy bitch shot me for no reason at all. So, we had a little argument. So I roughed her up a little bit. She didn't need to blast me to kingdom come."

The lurching movements sent pain slicing through him. Gasping and cussing, he collapsed back on the gurney. "She shot me! I want her arrested! The crazy bitch tried to kill me! You'll pay for this, you bitch."

Pop took the opportunity to shut him up—he replaced the mask and held it firmly in place.

Hearing the tirade, they all shared a single thought—not for a second did they believe Raine Andrews shot her husband, but had she, it was too damned bad the bullet hadn't put him out of her misery.

"Don't you worry, Mr. Andrews," David assured Addison. "We'll gather all the evidence and I guarantee we'll make an arrest." He only hoped his hunch was right and they'd be arresting Mr. Andrews. "Now let the paramedics do their job and get you to the hospital. We'll get your statement later."

Yes indeed, Mr. Andrews, David thought, we'll get your statement, all right, wondering how much spin he'd put on his version of tonight's events. It should be a doozy. Like the others, if Raine Andrews had shot him, he thought it too damned bad she hadn't succeeded in killing him. As for him, it was taking every ounce of willpower he possessed not to disregard all protocol and finish off the bastard. Huffing in disgust, he headed back to the house to find his partner and Pops trying to convince Raine she needed medical treatment.

"Ma'am, you could be hurt internally. You need a proper exam. Let us take you in and have the docs check you out."

Through swollen slits Raine stared at them. Lord, even her eyeballs hurt. "Okay, but first you have to do something for me." She looked at the two detectives.

Nancy gently cradled Raine's right hand in hers. The knuckles were bruised and swollen. Good for her, at least she'd gotten in a few good licks. "You name it, we'll do it."

"Cora Grey and her sister are watching my little girl. They can't let Addison take her if he gets out of the hospital. If he gets his hands on Katy, I'll never see her again."

"Trust me," David said, "you don't have to worry about him being released tonight. They'll operate to remove the bullet so he'll be there a while. And," he gave her an encouraging smile, "if my gut instinct is right, and it usually is in these matters, he'll have another set of accommodations waiting when he's released. Tell you what, you go get checked out and I'll personally let them know what's happened. What's the address?" Raine rattled it off. "What about your little girl?" He helped her up.

"One will keep Katy while the other comes to the hospital. Both are very protective and wouldn't want her seeing me like this. I'll need to clean up before I see her, too." Suddenly her throat constricted. Why did Addison have to do this?

Sensing her distress, David's strong, yet gentle hand gave her a slight nudge. "Let's get you into the ambulance."

They eased her face down onto the gurney, not that it made any difference what position she lay in, something was going to hurt. "You promise to tell them what's happened?" Raine looked over her shoulder.

Holding up two fingers, David stepped into view. "Scouts honor. And I'll make sure your husband doesn't get your daughter even if I have to take her to headquarters for safe keeping."

He turned then stopped. "Ms. Andrews, just so you know, we don't believe you tried to kill your husband but we still have to do our investigation."

Relief filled her. "I didn't shoot him, didn't try to kill him, but I believe before the night was over he'd have killed me. I've seen him angry but nothing like this. And believe me I try very hard not to do anything to provoke him."

"I'm sure you do." Anger edged his voice. "Anyway, I'll finish up here and head over to the sitters." David eyes sought Nancy's, sending a message.

She nodded as the ambulance driver closed the double doors. David was telling her to take care of their girl while he dug some more. Both wanted Addison Andrews locked away.

Watching the ambulance disappear, a burning settled in the pit of his stomach that no amount of antacids could help. Gut instinct told him a lot more went on in the Andrews household than just tonight's incident. Glad they'd been at the station when the call came in, it would give him the greatest pleasure putting the slime-ball away.

After a walk-through of the rest of the house he returned to the living room. Using the years-old digital camera he always carried he started snapping away. Closing his eyes, he recreated the fight. Immediately images of brawny fists hitting fragile bones appeared. He even heard the sickening sound of bone connecting with bone and unconsciously winced. No matter how many cases he worked he'd never get used to it. When he did, it would be time to get out.

On the mantel sat several framed photos of what was once a happy family. In the high-backed rocking chair sat a scruffy pink and white teddy bear. If only that bear could talk he'd bet it would back up Raine Andrews' story. For the life of him he'd never understand what perverted satisfaction a man got out of beating a woman and he'd heard all the lame excuses—she cheated on him, she smarted off to him, or dinner wasn't ready when he got home from work. The list went on and on and on. It had to be a power trip. Lording control over someone, it had to fatten the ego.

A bloodied shirt lay on the carpet. Stooping to pick it, a glint of metal beneath the sofa caught his eye. Well, well, look here. The gun must have been shoved there when the paramedics worked on Andrews. Taking pictures of both, he sealed them in evidence bags before heading to the room Nancy and Raine Andrews had entered. It was the master-suite. He did the same perusal as his partner; saw the bindings on the bed still attached to the bedposts and took pictures of them. Knowing what they'd been used for made him furious. And where was the belt he'd beaten her with? Then he spied it on the floor on the far side of the bed. Finished using it, the bastard had carelessly discarded it assuming no one would ever know what he'd done to her.

Hands still glove-covered, he examined the darkened stains on it, knowing it was Raine Andrews' blood. In his book of rules this could be called attempted murder. And the more evidence collected the better the chances of sending the wife-beating bastard to jail. They'd prove what a vicious monster Andrews was and by the time they finished a judge would lock him up and throw away the key.

Then a grim reminder surfaced. They'd lock him up and throw away the key, as long as Raine Andrews didn't back down from her husband. It wouldn't be the first time a woman let her heart overrule her common sense. Nor, he imagined, the last. "Just give me five minutes alone with the creep; he'd never lift a hand against another woman." Having seen some pretty rough sights, heard some outlandish excuses, this had to be the worst case yet. "I'm sure Mr. Andrews will come up with something stupendous." He continued muttering aloud as he locked up.

CHAPTER FIVE

Cora Grey raced through the door to the nurses' station. Breathless, she asked the nurse behind the counter. "Raine Andrews. Where is she?"

The shrewd-eyed nurse gave her a quick once-over. "You Ms. Grey or Ms. Ellison?" "Grey," Cora answered.

The nurse smiled. "Down the hall, last room on the right."

"Thank you," Cora stepped away then turned back. "Mr. Andrews?"

"Surgery. Not dead." Her dead-pan expression belied her opinion, that Mr. Andrews should just bite the dust and leave the poor girl alone.

"I feel the same way," Cora agreed.

The first thing Cora saw was the back of Raine's head. She thought it odd she was on her stomach. Then she glimpsed the exposed back and expanse of bloody red welts and understood why.

"Young lady why on earth didn't you tell us what he was doing?" Then her stomach bottomed-out when Raine looked over her shoulder. A strong urge to storm the operating room and finish Addison off overwhelmed her. And that reminded her. "In case you're wondering, he's still in surgery. Maybe he won't make it."

"I wasn't wondering, and he's too mean to die. Ouch! Ouch! Ouch!" Raine hissed as the doctor applied soothing ointment on the wounds.

"You'll feel better in a couple of minutes," he promised, lightly smoothing cream over the welts. "You'll even be able to lie on your back. Now let's take care of the rest of you." He flashed a meaningful look at Cora.

"I'll be outside."

While waiting, Cora recalled the past hour. It was the urgent ringing of the doorbell that had brought her and Ethel scrambling from their beds. Thank goodness Katy slept like a rock; the little cutie-pie hadn't moved so much as an eyelash. Peering through the security peephole at the big man holding up a badge had scared them both.

The nurse interrupted her musings. "You can come back in now."

Raine was sitting up now affording Cora a good look at her battered face. "That son of a . . . he should just bite the dust. How could he do something like this? He's been acting strange for a while, but I never expected something like this."

Holy cow! For Cora to nearly cuss was a sure sign of how upset she was. In the years she'd known the sisters she couldn't remember either saying even one mild swear word. It made her smile and considering how swollen her lips were, that was no easy feat. She rubbed her tongue over her teeth. At least she didn't need any dental work.

"I couldn't tell anyone what was happening." She picked non-existent lint from the white sheet covering her. "It wasn't safe confiding what Addison was doing. You can't imagine what it's been like to come and go, see everyone, yet have invisible bars surrounding me. Addison held the trump card, too. He used Katy to keep me under his thumb knowing I wouldn't dare force his hand."

Cora carefully patted her swollen hand. "You must have felt so helpless. No wonder you stayed quiet, never attempting to leave," assuming Raine had never tried. She couldn't have been more wrong.

Raine shook her head, "I did leave once. Took Katy and went to his folks for help. Big mistake! They ratted me out."

"What happened?" Cora asked, though figuring she knew.

"Just what you're thinking happened. Addison lied, made out like it was just a little tiff I blew out of proportion. Even said I inflicted my own injuries."

Cora stared in disbelief. "They believed him? Just how stupid could two people be? They always were a sorry snooty bunch, always thinking themselves better than anyone else, especially if you had less green stuff in the bank than them."

Cora's opinion was right on target about her in-laws. The Andrews were old-money rich but through various grapevines she'd heard tales about old man Andrews, Addison's grandfather, having been into bootlegging and speakeasies and owning several whorehouses back in the heydays of the twenties and thirties. Rumor even had it he'd had some questionable partners back in the day. Raine could only imagine the trench-coated, machine-gun-toting partners squiring their ten-cent-a-dance girls. She bet those long ago but not forgotten rumors didn't sit well with Addison's hoity-toity mother, either.

Shifting on the bed, she groaned. Her entire body was one humongous ache but at least she could lie on her back now. That was some awesome magic medicine. Catching Cora's worried frown, she assured her. "Don't worry. I'll be fine. It could be a lot worse, you know."

"No kidding." Cora agreed. "Just to ease your mind, Katy-bug was sound asleep when I left the house and Ethel's loaded-for-bear should your in-laws show up. They'll have a battle on their hands getting her away from Ethel. She's never cared for them, either."

That was something Raine hadn't thought of—Addison's mother and dad trying to get Katy. "Gosh, I hadn't even considered that. Thank heavens you two did. Right now, I can't seem to add two and two together."

Cora patted her hand. "That's because you've had your brain scrambled a little bit."

"Tell me about it. Addison batted me around like I was a badminton shuttle-cock." She fingered her bruised and swollen knuckles with a burst of pride. "But I got a few good licks in. I hope I broke his nose."

"Honey, I doubt his nose is top priority right now." Cora chuckled then sobered. "You did what you thought was right keeping him from taking off with Katy. Never doubt yourself for a moment."

Raine made a disparaging sound. "That's easier said than done. Though I stayed don't think I haven't second-guessed myself every second. I just didn't trust him, or his folks. Come to think of it, I wonder if they know he's been shot."

"Don't know." Cora shrugged. "You being his wife, the police might not let them know."

"No, they'll let them know and I can just hear them, especially Addison's mother, insisting it's my fault he was shot. She'll swear up and down I shot him but that won't fly. I never touched the gun. The detectives don't believe I shot him. Anyway, I don't care what they think about me. I quit that a long time ago. After they wouldn't help me I've kept my distance, only going around them when absolutely necessary."

"They're a real piece of work. No wonder Addison's the way he is." Cora peered closer at her eyes. How on earth could the girl see? "You've had quite a time shouldering all this alone." Gently she traced Raine's swollen and battered face, "You poor thing."

And the tears she'd been holding back fell, their saltiness stinging her cuts. Cora carefully gathered her in her arms; crying helped a soul to mend. Stroking her hair, she felt a tug of maternal love. If she'd been blessed with children, she hoped they'd have been just like Raine.

Quieting, Raine wiped the tears away with the back of her hand. Snatching a couple of tissues from the box on the bedside tray, Cora dried them.

"When that nice Detective Green showed up on our doorstep, Ethel and I nearly had heart attacks. We thought you'd had a car wreck. The crazy way people drive, you just never know. Anyway, you sure could've knocked us over with a feather when he told us what had happened. There are a lot of things I could picture Addison doing, but not this. But like I said, something hasn't seemed right with him for a long time."

Sadness filled Raine's eyes. "Addison hasn't always been like this but he hasn't been the man I fell in love with for quite a while." Seeing Cora's doubt, she raked a hand through the tangle of golden hair, wincing at encountering a knot. Cora noted the tinge of red on the roots and her lips pursed into a fine line. "I'm not defending him. I'll never do that again, but before the alcohol and drugs took control, he was different. I'd never in a million years believe he'd do these things."

"Maybe so, but there are no excuses for ever hitting a woman," Cora's eyes glittered, "but I'd sure like to give him a taste of his own medicine. He'd think twice before doing it again."

"I'm with you there, Cora." David Green and Nancy Collins stepped into the room. He stared at Raine, his stomach curling. He bet she was one hurting mess. "Ms. Andrews, your house is locked up and here's your purse. It was under the hall table."

Raine reached for it but Cora was quicker. "I'll take it. When she leaves, she's going home with me."

Raine stared at David Green's scrutinizing eyes. They were a mixture of cold steel and turbulent skies. She bet they'd seen a lot of evil and was infinitely glad he was on her side. She'd hate crossing paths with him when he was on the hunt. A smile played about her mouth knowing Addison had met his match in this man and his partner.

David knew exactly what Raine was thinking and nodded. He liked her, liked her spunk, her spirit, and toughness. Another spiral of anger zipped up his spine knowing she was trying hard to put up a brave front but there was no disguising the pain she was in—both physical and mental. He'd heard what she'd said about Andrews not always being the sadistic abuser. The initial pain in her heart would have long faded. He figured about right now she was kicking herself to hell and back for not leaving sooner. There was a reason she'd stayed, enduring the abuse, his hunch—the kid. "If you're up to it we've a few more questions."

Before leaving them to their questioning, Cora adjusted Raine's pillows. "I'll be in the waiting room. Come get me when you're finished."

Raine shook her head. "Stay. There's nothing you can't hear now that you're not going to sooner or later. Just know it's not a very pretty story." Cora didn't think anything about Addison would ever surprise her again. Raine gave the detectives a determined look. "Just so you know I'll do anything in my power to make Addison pay for what this, including walking Niagara Falls on a tightrope if it will help."

"That's what we wanted to hear but I don't think you'll have to go that far," Nancy chuckled. "We just checked and he's still in surgery. His folks are in the waiting room. We spoke to them and I'm sure you know they hold you completely responsible for this whole mess."

Raine shot Cora an "I told you so" look. "No surprise there. In their rose-colored world, their baby boy can do no wrong. Believe me, I know first-hand what they think of me. Everything bad that happens to Addison is my fault."

"We got that impression in the couple of minutes we spoke to them," Nancy said dourly.

Raine liked the opinionated Detective Collins. She'd been a big comfort on the ride to the hospital, staying with her, leaving only long enough to check on Addison. When she'd returned, she had two cups of coffee—one for Raine liberally laced with sugar and cooled with cream.

David, spiral notebook in hand, again took second string. He leaned his large frame against the only solid wall available, at the head of the bed. His partner, in her sincere and easy manner, led Raine through the events again.

Once started, the words poured out like water gushing from a geyser and Raine spoke of every violent episode she could recall. By the end both detectives' notebooks bulged and they were positive who the real trigger-pulling culprit was.

Nancy forcefully closed her note pad. Every ounce of retribution she possessed said march into that operating room and put another bullet in Addison Andrews. And that was after giving him a gigantic taste of the beating he'd given his wife.

Seeing the yearning, David cheered her on. He'd buy Nancy coffee for a year if she'd let him join in on the fun. He wanted to mete out some serious punishment, too. And in the end, they would—the justice kind—when the slimy scumbag was put away.

Raine shifted on the bed. "I tried leaving once, but made the mistake of going to his folks for help. They didn't believe Addison could do the things I described. You can probably imagine what happened after we got home." From the grim expressions, they figured she'd paid double for daring to leave. "That was when he started using Katy to keep me in my place, as he put it. After that, I tried to make sure she never stayed alone with him and when I couldn't I was a nervous wreck until I got back."

"I'd like to do some wrecking myself!" Cora huffed. Both detectives echoed their "so would we" sentiments as a smiling orderly appeared in the doorway.

"I'm here to take you to x-ray. Stay there. Doctor said take bed and all."

David straightened from the wall. "We're done here for the time being. We're going home for a few hours shut-eye but if you need us, just call. And we've posted a guard to your husband just in case he tries anything." Both detectives handed Cora their cards.

Starting out the door, Nancy stopped. "Wait! We need pictures."

"Good idea. We'll stick around until you get back. Come on Ms. Grey; let's get some of that wonderful hospital coffee," David quipped, tongue-in-cheek.

By the time everyone was finished Raine was exhausted. A battery of scans was taken starting at the top of her head before she was returned to her cubicle. Then it was the detectives' turn.

33

About the only thing they didn't have her do was stand on her head. On top of the scans and picture taking, she had a go-round with the doctor. He intended keeping her overnight but she wasn't having it. Understanding her desire not to share space with the husband who'd beaten her so severely, he released her.

Dawn was streaking the sky with ribbons of mauve and pearlescent white by the time she was released wearing the loose-fitting shorts and Addison's shirt, and feeling somewhat pain-free. That really was some awesome medicine. A bit shaky, she welcomed the wheelchair then Cora's steadying presence as they headed for the exit. The hospital, with its antiseptic smell, was fairly quiet.

Passing the waiting room Raine stopped so suddenly Cora bumped into her. What snagged her attention—the couple in the room—her in-laws, Roberta and Addison Andrews. Sr. Roberta, a slender, perfectly coiffed gray-blond woman, was pacing the white-tiled floor while her father-in-law, an older version of Addison, sat staring into space.

Thinking it Addison's surgeon, Roberta Andrews turned, gasping in shock at her daughter-in-law's battered condition. However, it didn't stop the venom from spewing. "You witch! You shot my son! You tried to kill him. You should be in jail!"

"I didn't shoot Addison." Getting into an argument with them was the last thing Raine wanted, but she refused to back down from the backstabbing couple ever again. From day one they'd made it abundantly clear she wasn't good enough for their son. Roberta, in particular, made no bones about it, taking every opportunity to get Addison's ear and bad-mouth her. At first, he'd stood up for her but once the alcohol and drugs took control that changed. She'd even bet Roberta planted the worm that she was cheating on her him.

"I don't believe you. You goaded him into another argument and that poor boy only gave you what you deserved. Why he stayed with you putting up with your cheating this long is beyond me." Hysteria turned her voice shrill. People passing stopped to see what the commotion was about. "Why, that poor boy even doubts Katy's his child."

And that snapped the proverbial camel's last straw. Fury raged through Raine so strong she expected her head to explode. Jerking loose from Cora's tugging grasp, she bee-lined to her mother-in-law and oblivious to the onlookers slapped her hard across the face.

"I don't care what you say about me but don't you ever, ever, say another word against Katy. She's as innocent in all of this as I am and as much as I wish it weren't true, your son is her father, but as of now he'll no longer have any contact with her and the same goes for the two of you, you sanctimonious old crone. I've never cheated on your son," she stuck her finger in her mother-in-law's face, "despite the lies you keep feeding him. And I didn't shoot him, either. It's the other way around. He tried to kill me. When he was through nearly beating me to death he tried to shoot me."

Several pairs of spellbound eyes continued watching the two women. Obviously, there was no love lost between them.

"You're lying!" Roberta shouted and Raine thought the word "denial" should be tattooed in great big letters on her forehead. "He'd never do anything like that! You're making this all up and he can't even defend himself." Scorn dripped thick from her voice.

"Yeah, I'm making this up." Raine scoffed. "I did this to myself." She made a sweeping motion with her hand. "Just like I beat myself up the one and only time I came to you for help. No, I'm not making anything up. Your son had the gun. It went off while we were struggling and he shot himself. I'm sure when the police check for prints mine won't be on it, only Addison's. His will be all over it and like it or not, I'm pressing charges." She was fed up with her mother-in-law's poisonous attacks and blaming her for Addison's problems. "And, you're just as nuts as Addison if you believe a woman deserves to be abused. If Ad ever raised a hand to you he'd have come back missing it." She glanced at her father-in-law. He dropped his eyes.

"You're right about that, but no matter, my son being shot is your fault. If you'd been more supportive, not always fighting him, we wouldn't be here tonight."

Incredulousness found its way onto Raine's battered face, "Me? Always fighting him? You really are nuts right along with your drugged-out son!"

"How dare you talk like that to me at a time like this? My son may die and you've the gall to stand there hitting me and blaming him for everything!" Roberta Andrews twisted the handkerchief in her hands.

"Oh, quit being so melodramatic! Addison will come out of surgery just fine. He's too damn mean to die. And I dare say it because you can't run and tell him how disrespectful I've been. Don't worry," Raine looked at her with contempt, "your son will live to torment someone else, but not me. Not anymore. I'm finished with him."

Until that moment she hadn't thought beyond the end of her nose. Whether Addison realized it or not, he'd opened the door to freedom and by God not only was she stepping through it, she was running like hell as far and as fast as she could. Despite her aching body, the knowledge gave her the lift she needed.

"And I don't need to defend myself to you. I don't care what you think, I never have. I put up with you because of Addison, but that's over. And you can tell your son I won't back down ever again."

Her mother-in-law huffed angrily while her father-in-law remained silent. Eyeing the couple, Cora knew exactly who wore the pants in that family. Raine gave her mother-in-law a scathing look that could have singed the hair off her head.

"And I do blame him for everything! And, I blame you for sticking your heads in the sand for years and not getting him help. You're not blind. He needed help long before I ever came along. You knew he had problems but you just made excuses for him, bailed him out then looked the other way. And I did too, but not anymore. And you know," she paused on a sad note, "I really loved him," she paused again, "but I haven't for a long time. Anything I ever felt for him, he killed. I don't deserve to be treated this way and neither does Katy. Addison's too far gone for me to help. I'm done. I don't have it in me anymore. He needs the kind of help neither of us can give him. And honestly, I'm not so sure he wants help." With that parting shot she walked out the door. Beside her, Cora silently cheered. She couldn't have said it any better herself.

CHAPTER SIX

Infuriated, Raine wanted to kick something really hard. She eyed the trash can by the entrance. Better not. It'd only make her more miserable plus damage hospital property. Then, her anger eased and she flashed a wickedly triumphant grin at Cora. "Damn! Telling the old bat off felt great and smacking her even better!"

"Given her rotten attitude, she deserved it." Cora helped Raine into Ethel's jeep. "Ethel parked behind me last night after getting our treats." It was all the explanation needed. It was a 'dition' as Katy put it, that when she stayed with them they had ice cream from her favorite parlor.

An exhausted Raine dozed on the drive but nearing home, she insisted Cora drop her off. "I'll do no such thing. You're not going back to that house! You're coming with me and I won't take no for an answer."

Raine shook her head, "I can't. I need to clean the house up and think of a good explanation for looking this way. I have to protect Katy as much as possible."

"I understand but you're not going back there alone. I'll stay and help you straighten up." At the determined look on Cora's face, Raine relented. A few minutes later, seeing the Lamborghini, Cora's shrill whistle filled the jeep. "I didn't know you bought that beauty. It must have cost a pretty penny."

"We didn't buy it. Addison leased it, said he wanted to ride in style." A giggle slid out of her. "I'm guessing he didn't mean an ambulance, huh?"

"That's cruel." Cora laughed, "Funny, but cruel."

Raine gazed at the surroundings, the lush green of the manicured lawn, the flowerbeds full of colorful, fragrant blooms, the beautiful house that was her prison. In the early morning light it looked so ethereal and serene, quite deceptive given its recent history. No, she amended, feeling a great weight lift off her shoulders. She was no longer a prisoner in her own home. Now she could come and go as she damned well pleased with no threats hanging over her.

Seeing the trashed living room, Cora gasped. In his rage, Addison had turned the room upside down. Anything he'd gotten his hands on had ended up smashed on the floor.

Raine noted it was the china tea set that had bit the dust during their fight. A dark sodden circle was on the carpet and her stomach did a queasy pitch. Peering closer, she was relieved it only water but the mess was even worse than she remembered. Of course, at the time she'd been too busy trying to stay alive to notice the wreckage.

"Don't worry. It's nothing we can't put right," Cora said. "I'll check the other rooms." Fortunately, only the living room and hallway showed signs of their fight. "Everything else looks fine. I'll get started straightening up. First thing is to get the glass cleaned up."

A look of torment that hit right at her heart covered Raine's face that the man who'd sworn to love her had turned on her so viciously, like a rabid dog turns on its loving master.

Cora patted her arm. "Honey, it's hard to take in how a person can totally change, how the person who took a vow to love and protect you, turned on you. Right now, it may not seem like everything will be okay, but it will. In the end, it will all be okay."

"Oh Cora, it's already getting okay. I survived the worst night from hell. From here on out it's a piece of cake. As long as Katy's safe, nothing else matters."

"That's the right outlook," Cora hesitated then asked, "I gather Addison's always had a problem with drugs and alcohol?"

Raine nodded, "I didn't want to admit it at first. For so long you couldn't have asked for a better man, so loving and so much fun. We loved being together, sharing things, and going places. Who knows, maybe he was taking a break from the alcohol and drugs when I met him. The only negative was his folks, and more Roberta than Ad, Sr. Ad may wear the pants in that house but you can bet Roberta tells him which ones and what color." Cora chuckled. "Anyway, I wore the rose-colored glasses until it was too late and he was full-blown gone. It was like one morning he left the house the Addison I'd fallen head-over-heels for and when he came back that evening he'd changed into the monster he is now."

"When you love someone it's hard not to overlook some of their actions and faults. You even make excuses, hoping everything will go back to the way it used to be."

"That's what I did. During those first years everything was great, except where his parents were concerned, especially Roberta. She never liked me, but Addison never paid her any attention. In fact, he took up for me and that really ticked her off. And when I was going to have Katy he was wonderful. He never kept me from working or going any place I wanted. Then he started changing. Little things set him off and his temper got steadily worse. Looking back, I guess I should be thankful he never harmed Katy."

"You'd have killed him," Cora said with certainty.

"Most definitely," Raine's eyes glinted, "but he didn't, at least that I know of, and of course I never left her with him any more than I had to."

A shadow darkened her eyes remembering the one time she'd had no choice but to leave Katy with Addison. Both sisters and Molly had been unavailable, and she'd been a nervous wreck until she got home.

"That was wise," Cora said, eyeing the wet carpet. "At least that's not blood. I'll get started cleaning up in here."

"I'll get the vacuum," Raine said but Cora's firm hand stopped her.

"You leave the clean-up to me. A little straightening and it'll look fine. Take a shower. It'll make you feel a lot better and I'll have a pot of coffee ready when you're done. I don't suppose you could eat something?"

Raine shook her head. "Thank you for being here," she whispered, hugging Cora.

Cora blinked rapidly. "I don't need thanking and enough of this or I'll flood the whole house. Now go get that shower. I'll let Ethel know we're here. Katy-bug will be sleeping, but do you want her to bring her home when she wakes up?"

"Having her home will make me feel a lot better, but have Ethel call first just in case something unexpected crops up."

Nodding in understanding, Cora made the call, "Hey, it's me." She paused, listening. "We're home but the place needs some straightening up. When Katy-bug wakes up bring her home but call first. We should have this place right-as-rain by then." Cora chuckled at her play on words.

Raine smiled, too. Cora being here gave her immeasurable comfort and the idea of a shower sounded heavenly. In the white-tiled shower she adjusted the water to a light, tepid spray. No way could she stand it pounding or as hot as she preferred it. The welts held a low sting when the spray hit them but that she could handle. After what Addison had put her through, there wasn't much she couldn't handle. Sighing blissfully, the water flowed over her, washing away last night's horror.

Slipping on a pale pink robe, she immediately took it right back off, the material was scratchy against her skin. Instead, she opted for a knee-length caftan, its silkiness cool against her burning flesh. Plus, the lilac color positively complimented her purple bruises!

Wiping off the steamed mirror, she grimaced at the reflection staring back at her. Had it been Halloween she'd have scared all the kids to death. She gently smoothed cream on her face and lip balm on her swollen mouth. As for her eyes, there wasn't much she could do about them. Studying Addison's handiwork, she made a firm decision right then. It was time for the next step to freedom. Using the cordless phone on the nightstand she keyed in a set of numbers she knew by heart.

Afterward she headed to help Cora. In the living room, she found everything back in place like nothing had ever happened. She stared at the spot where Addison had laid and thanked God he hadn't bled all over the place. Cora was in the kitchen gazing out the window, a troubled look on her face. Early morning light streamed through the window bathing them in a warm glow. Despite her recent ordeal, peacefulness stole through Raine. This was her favorite time of day. Addison would have left for work taking with him the drama of their existence, Katy would still be asleep, and the quiet morning would be hers. This was the time she pondered her existence and how to deal with her deteriorating situation. Well, thanks to Addison, that horrible situation had resolved itself and today was the beginning of a brand-new start.

Hearing a noise behind her, Cora turned, "You look a little better. Here. Sit down."

"I feel better," Raine eased onto the flower-patterned chair cushion.

Cora set a cup of coffee in front of her. "I think I got all the glass cleaned up but it's a good idea not to let Katy go barefoot in there. That china just had to fall on the one section not carpeted. There might be some shards the vacuum didn't pick up this time. It'll need going over several more times just to be on the safe side."

Raine nodded, "We'll close the doors." She took the first sip, flinching when the hot cup touched her lips, "Mm mm . . . this tastes so good. The coffee at the hospital was passable but this is wonderful. I needed this." Coffee was her version of comfort food. She'd lost count of the number of pots that had seen her through some tough times over the last several months. Maybe she should consider buying stock in a coffee plantation.

Cora studied her over the rim of her cup, trying to decide how best to broach putting an end to an ungodly situation. As far as she was concerned there were only two solutions and both started with D. Hopefully Raine wouldn't get mad and tell her to mind her own business. But it was her business. When Detective Green had knocked on her door in the middle of the night it had become her business. Not for a second could she fathom the vicious beatings and the verbal abuse, and if she didn't speak her piece she might just explode. Taking a fortifying breath, she plunged in with both size seven feet.

"Okay. You may not want it but I'm giving you my opinion, anyway." Raine arched her eyes, which was pretty hard to do given how swollen they were. Always a plain-speaking woman, Cora didn't hold back letting anybody know her mind and this was certainly one of those times. "You've got to get rid of that no-account husband. You got lucky this time, honey. If you stay with him you might not be so lucky the next time. And I'm not saying something you don't already know. We both know there'll be a next time and God forbid, it might be Katy that gets hurt."

Reaching across the table, Raine squeezed her hand. "I promise there won't be a next time. I've already started divorce proceeding." At Cora's surprised look, she explained. "I called my attorney, who also happens to be the husband of my best friend. I figured I'd better get the ball rolling. Gordon's on his way out here right now." She took another sip of coffee.

"Good! That makes me feel a lot better," Cora said, relieved.

"And you're right; I can't go through this again nor put Katy at risk anymore. I should have called Addison's bluff and left for good. I'd already decided to after he left for work, but obviously that didn't happen."

"You should have left sooner," Cora concurred, "but we all know hindsight's always been twenty-twenty." Thank God the girl was using her head now. "And calling your attorney was a smart move, makes me feel better knowing you're thinking ahead of the game. You can't let Addison get the upper hand, not that I think he's got a snowball's chance in hades, but you never know." They heard the soft hum of an arriving car. "That'll be your attorney." She got another cup from the cabinet and filled it. A minute later the doorbell sounded. "You sit. I'll let him in."

Peering through the peephole and seeing the dangerously handsome man, Cora's heart did a triple-summersault that would have qualified her for the Olympics.

Gordon Hanson smiled at the blushing woman who opened the door. "I'm Gordon, a friend of Raine's. She's expecting me." His smile was brilliantly white; the dark cadence of his voice whiskey warm.

"Come in. I'm Cora, her neighbor. She's in the kitchen," Cora said, her heart skipping merrily in her chest.

Gordon Hanson stopped dead in his tracks as absolute shock replaced the smile on his face. "Good God!" he thundered, staring in stunned disbelief. No way was this the same woman who'd been in his office a week ago discussing free-lance contracts. That woman hardly resembled the battered one in front of him now.

She gave him a swollen-lipped smile; it looked more like a grimace. "Quite a sight, aren't I? If it were Halloween I wouldn't need a mask." Her attempt at levity was met by a black scowl. "I know. I know. I look like I've been in a boxing match and lost."

"You better damn well tell me you're pressing charges." It was a demand, not a question. Gordon dropped his lanky frame into a chair and crossed one long denim-clad leg over the other. "Thank you," The smile he gave Cora when she sat the steaming cup in front of him made her heart flutter. This early in the morning Gordon needed coffee by the gallon. With a newborn in the house, he was lucky to get a couple of hours' straight sleep and kept a pot going all the time.

Taking a sip, he breathed a heart-felt sigh of appreciation. "You can't imagine how badly I need this. Since the baby came, sleep's been a rare commodity." He gave Raine an arched look.

"Yes, I'm pressing charges! Addison went too far this time." She said vehemently.

"You think!" Anger slashed across his handsome face. "And what the hell do you mean, this time? This has happened before?" The volume of his voice rose. "For God's sake, why the hell didn't you tell us? We'd have gotten you away from him."

Raine well understood why Molly had fallen hard for Gordon. He had the kind of rugged good looks that made any female between nine and ninety swoon and Cora's rosy cheeks were a testament to that. Tough as nails when it came to defending his clients, for those he cared about inside beat the heart of a great big teddy bear. He loved Molly to distraction, that he was twisted firmly around his new daughter's tiny finger he admitted with unabashed pride. Raine opened her mouth to explain why she hadn't come to them for help but he started talking again.

"On second thought, don't answer that. Of course it's happened before and I imagine each time's gotten worse. There's a pattern. He hits—he's sorry, he hits again then promises it won't happen again. Then some little thing sets him off and he's at it again. It's a vicious cycle in which someone invariably gets hurt." He took another sip of coffee, giving her a knowing look over the rim. "And, if there are any outside influences such as alcohol or drugs, it just makes them more aggressive. They become ten feet tall and bullet-proof." Then he chuckled. "Well, in Addison's case bullet-proof doesn't apply, does it? Sorry." Both chuckled knowing he was no sorrier than they were.

Studying Raine's battered face, Gordon thought her too nice a girl to put up with the likes of Addison Andrews. And that's why he was here very early on a Saturday morning. It had knocked him and Molly for a loop hearing what Addison had done to her. Imagining it was one thing, but seeing it in person was far worse. Thank God, he'd convinced Molly to stay home. Still recovering from childbirth and caring for their new baby, no way did she need to see Raine in this condition. She'd have a temper fit, head for the hospital, and off the S.O.B. Then he'd have to defend her, too.

"You might as well start at the beginning and don't leave anything out," he ordered, taking a legal pad and a pen from his briefcase.

Once again, she re-told what had happened while Gordon made notes in his brand of shorthand only he and Margie, his secretary-cum-sister-in-law, could decipher. Not a pretty story, it was difficult to wrap his head around the fact someone he and Molly were so close to could go through so much hell and they hadn't even known about it. Why hadn't they seen warning signs? Angry with himself, he could only imagine the guilt Molly was feeling.

Over a second pot of coffee they discussed finances and property. From the hiding place beneath the carpet in Katy's bedroom closet Raine retrieved a handwritten list of everything she and Addison owned, both mortgaged and free and clear, as well as what each had brought to the marriage.

"This is good." Some of his other clients could take a lesson from Raine.

"As you can see, I'd started getting my ducks in a row. It was the getting away part that had me stumped."

He shot her a perturbed look as he tucked the documents inside the brief case. "My advice is to take him to the cleaners, get every red cent you can."

"I just want what I had before we married and half of everything we've accumulated together. Don't forget, I own more shares of the company than he does. And I suppose child support for Katy, too, as long as I don't have to deal with him."

"Besides child support, there should also be a trust fund for Katy. If he balks, take the company away from him, or force him to sell it. Once in writing and filed with the court, if he screws up, the law can deal with him."

"Works for me, and that's another thing. I want full custody of Katy. Addison's unstable and I don't trust his folks any further than I can throw them," her voice hardened, "especially after Roberta made horrendous claims about Addison doubting Katy being his."

"The woman's as crazy as her son to even suggest such nonsense." Gordon said.

Just thinking of her mother-in-law's hateful words made Raine spitting mad again. It'd felt damned good smacking Addison's mother.

"I don't think you'll have any problem getting whatever you want. And if Addison's attorney is smart, he'll get him to meet your terms on everything. If not, then we go to court."

"Let's hope he agrees. It scares me to death thinking of him alone with Katy. Although he's never hurt her, there can always be a first time."

Though Gordon wanted to allay her fears, he couldn't. And she should be worried. The Andrews family had plenty of money and connections to fight her. But then again, so did he and he'd do his damnedest to make sure everything worked in her favor. If he didn't, his sweet little wife would kick his ass.

At last they had their legal game plan in order. Before leaving Gordon checked in with Molly. He wore a silly grin on his face when he disconnected. "She said if you need anything, just call her, especially if taking a pot-shot at Addison is involved." Raine laughed. "And she'd loved to keep Katy anytime you need her to." Carefully, he hugged her. "Take it easy and I'll keep in touch and I'll have the paperwork ready ASAP. The sooner it's filed the sooner you get free. In the meantime, stay alert and keep the doors locked," he cautioned, "you never know who might be lurking about."

That was a scary thought. "I'll be careful. Oh! I know Molly; she'll get it in her head to come out but don't let her. If Addison gets out I don't want her or the baby getting caught in the crossfire."

A deadly gleam appeared in his eyes just thinking of Addison harming his woman or his baby. "I'll make sure she keeps her distance. It'll piss her off but it won't be the first time."

Raine watched until he was out of sight, thinking that she'd do better than just keep the doors locked, she'd change the locks and re-code the alarm before she closed her eyes that night. In the back of her mind, however, was the knowledge that if Addison wanted in a locked door wouldn't stop him.

CHAPTER SEVEN

Another sweep of the house ensured all looked normal. She collected Katy's scruffy teddy bear from the living room and hugged it, wishing it were Katy she was cuddling. Then as if by magic the little blond cutie charged through the front door like a mini-tornado, took one look at her mother's face and puckered up.

Katy's reaction galvanized Raine into action. "Oh baby, don't cry." Ignoring her aches, she scooped Katy up, smelling her sweet scent—fresh air, cupcakes, and bubble gum bubble bath. "Mommy's just fine," she crooned. "Really pumpkin, Mommy's okay."

Wiping her eyes with the backs of her hands, Katy thought Mommy looked awful. Her pretty face was black and purple. When she got a boo-boo sometimes it turned purple and boy oh boy, Mommy's face sure had lots of them.

"Did you have a 'dent', Mommy? Where's Daddy?"

Raine eased into a chair. "Daddy had to go out of town." It was the simplest explanation. "And I did fall down. I cried, too, not like you. You never cry when you fall down." Which was oddly true, Katy fell and skinned something quite often but never cried.

Katy bobbed her head in guilty agreement. Mommy didn't know that she used to cry until Daddy told her to suck it up— whatever that meant. Sometimes Daddy was mean. She liked it better when it was just her and Mommy. Gently, she touched one blackened eye before butterfly-kissing the cuts on Raine's mouth. "You always kiss my ouchies better. And Ef'el and me baked cupcakes, too, and I got to lick the bowls. That's the "bestest" part. If you eat a cupcake it'll make you feel lots better, too."

Raine loved her child's logic. "You're right, pumpkin, your kisses already make me feel better and we'll have cupcakes after dinner."

Convinced Mommy really was okay, Katy scampered down. From toddler on she'd been an independent little thing. "Can I watch cartoons, Mommy?" She was already heading for the family room without waiting for an answer.

"I'll get her set up." Cora trailed after Katy while Ethel gave Raine a hand up. They were at the kitchen table sipping coffee and discussing what had happened when Cora joined them.

Ethel was giving her opinion of Addison. "A man like that won't ever change. Oh, he'll act like it but once he's comfortable his true personality comes out again. I thank God every day that my Brad was the decent man he was. God rest his soul."

Cora nodded, "I can't ever imagine Ben raising a hand to me, but if he had, he'd have come back with a stub, and we had some dandy arguments, let me tell you." She wasn't kidding, either. They'd had their share of arguments, shouting matches, slamming doors, the silent treatment, but nothing ever resulted in anything physical. Their love had lasted through thick and thin for forty years then a massive heart attack took him away in an instant, leaving her a widow at fifty-nine. That was three years ago. Now she and Ethel shared the home Ethel and Brad had built early in their marriage. Sadly, Ben and Brad had passed away within months of each other—Brad from pancreatic cancer that took him quickly—Ben from the heart attack.

"Yeah, Brad and I had our moments, too," Ethel smiled in fond remembrance, "but he was a smart man." A twinkle entered her eyes. "He always knew just the right time to let me think I'd won an argument. He always liked the making up part the best!"

Cora laughed in agreement. "Yeah, Ben liked that part of an argument, too. Sometimes I think he'd start one just to have a little make-up session."

Beneath the abrasions and bruises Raine's cheeks flamed hearing the sisters' joke about having make-up sex.

Ethel got to her feet. "Well girls, if everything's under control here I'm heading home. It so happens I've been asked out to dinner tonight." She looked at her sister. "You are staying here tonight, right? I can always cancel and stay, too."

"I'm staying. Raine needs some rest and if Katy needs anything I'll be here to see to it. You go ahead with your plans." Raine started to protest then closed her mouth at the arched-brow look Cora gave her. "Don't argue with me. You know I'm right. You're dead on your feet.

Besides that, if you're here all by yourself you'll hear all sorts of noises and think it's Addison come back to finish what he started." Once Cora's mind was made up there was no sense arguing; an army couldn't change it.

Cora was right about hearing all kinds of strange noises and thinking Addison had somehow managed to get out of his hospital bed and come to finish her off. She rubbed her goose-bumped arms.

"You're right. I might think I'm pretty brave, but right now that's definitely not true."

"Then, it's settled. I had a feeling you'd be staying so I brought you a few things. Let's get them. I just didn't see any sense in lugging them in if you weren't." Out of earshot Ethel said. "Addison really worked her over, didn't he? I could picture him doing a lot of things but never that. And I feel so bad that I didn't see any signs of what was going on."

"Me too," Cora agreed, "but feeling guilty won't help matters. We'll just have to help her from here on out cause you can bet this mess isn't over by a long shot. That Andrews crew will keep right on making her life miserable until someone puts a stop to it. Addison's become the devil's own spawn and as much as

I shouldn't say this, God forgive me, the world would be much better off without him."

"Sure wish that bullet had finished him off, he wouldn't hurt her again. Now you call me if you need me and I'll be here before you can hang up, and when I get home tonight I'll call the hospital. If I'm lucky enough to get someone who isn't up to speed on all that patient privacy mumbo-jumbo, I'll call you."

Over the next few days Cora was a godsend. Raine's battered body protested but she refused to baby herself. She had two feet to stand on and a life to take control of. Both Gordon and the detectives offered to visit her but she declined, wanting to shield Katy as much as possible.

When she arrived at police headquarters, her battered appearance garnered attention from the burly, flat-topped Sergeant manning the desk and the officers in the bullpen. Given the thumb-ups she received, she realized they all knew her story. Nancy Collins beckoned from a corner office. It was painted a cool gray and divided in half giving each their own working space. David Green stood behind a professionally messy desk. On one corner sat a picture of a pretty, dark-haired woman smiling out at him. Judging by the wide gold band on his left hand, the woman in the picture was his wife.

"How are you doing?" He waved her to a chair. Sitting, her audible sigh of relief made him smile. Raine Andrews was one tough cookie. In her shoes, he'd still be clinging to the bed, whining like a baby and demanding Marti wait on him hand and foot. A good patient he did not make.

Raine adjusted the loose-fitting peach-colored sundress so that it fell softly over her knees. Her slim feet were shod in a pair of camel colored sandals with glittering rhinestones adorning the top, her hair hung in a curtain down her back. Today was the first time since the attack she'd put on street clothes. "Considering everything, I could be worse, though I look like I've been in a barroom brawl and came out on the losing end."

David shook his head. "You walked away on your own two feet and without any bullet holes. In my book that definitely makes you the winner." In front of him sat a stack of manila folders. He pulled a set of paper-clipped pages from the top one. "This is your statement. You should read through it before signing."

Quickly skimming it, she signed her name. "It reads like something out of a crime novel instead of real life."

"Unfortunately, it's very real." He made copies then handed them, along with an envelope, to her. "These are yours and there's a set of photos, too. Should you need them, you'll have proof how dangerous he is." David wished he could reassure her it wouldn't happen again but he couldn't promise something he had no control over.

Well, step one had been accomplished. Now for step two. David flicked a glance at his partner leaning against the window sill, then watched as Raine open the envelope. Her face was mirror of emotion as the photos showed how close Addison had come to beating her to death. Her resolve hardened. No way was he getting away with it.

David saw the stiffening of her spine and felt heartened, though adamant about not letting Andrews get away with hurting her, until her name was on the black line he'd had doubts. Now for the next hurdle. Settling back in the chair, it creaked in protest under his weight. Would she still take it? Would she still press charges or had time changed her mind? There was only one way to find out. "Are you still willing to press charges?"

Her outraged look said he was crazy to even ask. Nancy came to his rescue. "Ms. Andrews, it's just that you've had a little time to think things over. Sometimes a spouse changes their mind and decides not to do anything."

"Well I'm not changing my mind!" Raine said vehemently. "You do whatever it takes to make him pay." The detectives exchanged imaginary high-fives. "I'm not dropping anything."

David wanted to kick up his heels. Instead he said. "He's still in the hospital, but we understand he's expected to be released soon. Apparently, the gunshot wound wasn't that bad. He's not under arrest, but we've a guard stationed outside his room just in case he tries slipping out. Once he's released from the hospital we'll bring him here and book him for felony assault and spousal battery." He leveled a steely-eyed look at her. "You do realize there's a good chance he'll make bail?"

Raine nodded. "I just hope it doesn't happen." However, knowing Addison was going to jail from the hospital gave her a modicum of relief. But what if he made bail? Knowing her in-laws, they'd do everything in their power get him out. They were gutsy, that's for sure, even having the audacity to call yesterday. Recognizing the number, she'd let it go to voice-mail then deleted the message without listening to it. They probably wanted to badger her not to press charges against their precious boy. Though he should be held accountable for his actions, they'd do everything to help him get out. She'd do the same thing for Katy but she'd also get her help, not bury her head in the sand and pretend all was perfect.

"There'll be a bail hearing and if the judge grants it we're going to insist he stay at his parents and be monitored twenty-four seven wearing an ankle bracelet. We don't want him skipping town. We also don't want him near you but that'll take a restraining order. If he messes up just once we'll haul him in." David picked up a pen and started threading it through his fingers. "You know you can attend the bail hearing, too." Please say yes, he silently urged. They'd do everything in their power to help keep the wife-beating scumbag locked up, including having the battered wife sitting front and center in the courtroom.

Most definitely she'd be there. She wanted the judge to see firsthand what her husband had done to her. Her chin lifted. "I'll be there. I'm the victim in this mess, not Addison. I want everyone to see what my husband did to me." Anger flashed in her blue eyes.

"No one should be allowed to get away with what he did to me."

"We wish more women felt like you but sometimes the husband can be very persuasive when it comes to getting what he wants. They promise to never do it again. They beg and plead, even cry. Then he brings out the big guns, saying she's breaking up the home; that she needs to think of the kids. Basically, he lays a guilt trip on her until he wears her down. Then once back in the home, he's got full control again and the cycle starts all over. It's rare that it doesn't." Nancy said.

"And," David inserted, "if the wife does threaten to leave again, he tells her to go ahead, she'll never get the kids, that he'll take them away and she'll never see them again. It's the worst kind of coercion used to keep her under his control."

What they were saying hit dead-center-home. "You've probably wondered why I stayed with Addison after he knocked me around but that's exactly what he did. I tried leaving once but was stupid enough to think his parents would help me. Instead, they tipped him off I was there. That's when he threatened that if I ever tried leaving again he'd take Katy and I'd never see her again. And believe me, he would, too. I'm not proud of how much control I gave him but I wasn't losing Katy. But, Addison just kept getting worse so I decided to take my chances again. I'd planned to leave after he left for work Monday morning." Her swollen lips twisted wryly. "Unfortunately, that didn't work out."

Nancy gave her a compassionate look. Her next question was of a very personal nature. It had been on her mind since Saturday night. "This may make you uncomfortable but we need to ask. Has your husband ever forced you against your will to have sex with him?"

Amidst the deep purple contusions, a red flush crawled up Raine's neck to her face. She was the type that when she blushed it showed all over. Right now, she was red from the bottoms of her feet to the top of her blond head. "How did you know?"

A tic attacked the muscle in David's cheek, a sure sign he was angry. "That's usually part of the abuse pattern the wife won't tell us about because she's embarrassed. The husband blames her because he can't get it up and starts hitting. And when he does he forces her against her will. We see it all the time."

He couldn't imagine ever hurting Marti or forcing her to do something against her will. Besides that, if he did he was pretty damn sure he'd wake up missing an important part of his anatomy.

"What about the other night?" Nancy asked, thinking married or no, when a woman said no, it meant no.

Raine shook her head. "At first I don't think it even crossed his mind but when I came to with no clothes on and tied to the bed I thought that was his intentions, but he was trying when the gun went off. Honestly, there hasn't been much intimacy for quite a while. I couldn't stand for him to touch me, and the more he drank the worse it became. I dreaded the evenings he was home because I knew what would happen . . ."

The shrill ring of the telephone interrupted her. Glowering, Green grabbed it, his tone terse. "Henry! I said hold all calls until we were through..." He paused, gnawing on his lower lip with even white teeth. He looked at Raine then looked away. "No. No that's good. Go ahead and patch it through." Steel-gray eyes connected with his partner's as he waited for the call to be put through. Nancy felt his ripple of excited energy, something was up. She knew David well. That tale-tell spark in his eyes, they practically flashed with excitement when a new lead popped.

"This is Green. No. Don't worry about it." The concerned look on his face sent panic rushing through Raine. What was going on? Was Addison out of the hospital already? "Thanks for getting back so soon." This time when he looked at Raine, he wore a big grin and gave her a thumbs-up. "That's the spike I've been waiting on. Hey man, thanks again, I owe you a big one. That was Dale Martin from the lab. He put a rush job running the prints on the gun and the only ones on it are your husband's."

At the relief on Raine's face another burst of anger pounded through him and he swore Addison Andrews would pay for what he'd done. Though positive she hadn't touched the gun, it was wonderful proven right. "I was sure I hadn't touched it but having hard proof makes me feel a lot better."

"Us, too." Green rubbed his hands together with relish. "That's it! We're upping the charges to attempted murder." He watched Nancy nod in agreement. She was just as hell-bent on nailing Andrews' hide to the wall as he was. They'd shared many ideas of various forms of torture to inflict on the scumbag. Nancy favored an-eye-for-an-eye—using a belt on a certain part of his anatomy. He'd cringed at the idea. "Remind me not to let you share your ideas with Marti."

"We didn't doubt what the lab would find but now it's carved in stone. I can't wait to hear his version on how you shot him and left his prints on the gun instead of yours. You can bet it'll be a whopper." David said.

"Yeah, but proof or no, he'll swear up and down I shot him."

"But that won't fly." Grabbing his suit-coat from the back of his chair, he shrugged his broad shoulders into it. "We're going to the hospital to deliver the good news." Adjusting his shoulder-holster, he shot a glance at Raine. "You haven't by any chance tried to see him since the shooting?"

Raine shook her head in the negative, ignoring the twinges it caused. Knowing she'd be driving she'd abstained from any pain medication. Cora had offered but she'd refused, insisting she'd be fine. "Other than in a courtroom, I've no desire to ever see him again. As far as I'm concerned he can rot in hell for the rest of his life." Blackened eyes flashed with fire. "Go arrest him. File as many charges as you can. You don't have to worry about me backing down. I won't do it."

Outside, the morning sun gleamed brightly. Raine started toward her car then turned back. "Do me a favor. Let me know his reaction about my fingerprints not being on the gun."

David nodded. "Ms. Andrews, we can't tell you what to do, but it might still be a good idea to leave for a while, get out of harm's way. We'll keep you posted and if we need you we'll make sure you get back here on the QT. Just think about it, would you?" She nodded solemnly.

David removed his sunglasses from above the visor and put them on. Pulling away from the curb, he glanced in the rear-view mirror to see Raine still standing beside her car, a contemplative look on her face. He certainly hoped she took the suggestion to leave town until this mess was over. His instincts told him, given half a chance, Addison Andrews would make good on his promise to make her pay.

CHAPTER EIGHT

The detectives' concerns weighed heavily on Raine's mind as she headed for Gordon's office. Nothing was carved in stone that Addison would even go to jail. And when served divorce papers, that would not be a pretty sight, he'd get down and dirtier. There was no telling what lengths he'd go to or what shenanigans he'd pull. Leaving seemed the best option.

Parking in front of Gordon's office, she went up the tree-lined sidewalk. A few years ago he'd left the hustle-and-bustle of a burgeoning firm of attorneys to move back to his hometown. It had been a wise decision. He'd married Molly, had a beautiful baby girl, and a steady flow of clients needing help ranging from divorces to wills to felonies. It kept his one-man firm busy. Between them a day hadn't passed that one wasn't checking in to see how she was doing and during that time Gordon worked feverishly until he was satisfied with the agreements.

Before she reached the front door, he was already holding it open. Dressed in his kick-around clothes—washed out jeans, black t-shirt, and scuffed brown cowboy boots, she figured she was his only appointment. His handsome face wore a scowl. "You do know I'd have brought the papers out to you."

"And hello to you, too." She quipped, stepping past him. "Hi Margie, how are you?" She greeted Gordon's assistant/sister-in-law.

Margarita Hanson eyed Raine stoically. "Better than you are but I hear you gave as good as you got." Margie, a pretty brunette in her mid-thirties, was married to Gordon's older brother, Max. In better days she and Addison, Molly and Gordon, as well as Gordon's brothers and their wives had hung out together.

"I tried. I came away quite colorful but he got the bullet." Raine joked back.

"If I'd been in your shoes honey, I'd have put three or four in him."

"Would you believe he actually shot himself?"

"If only he'd done a better job," Margie's mouth turned up in a droll smile. "As long as you're all right that's all that matters. Sooner or later he'll get his due and I'd sure like to be along for the ride when he does. Molly and Becca feel the same way. Just let us at him."

Becca, the wife of Gordon's other brother, Jake, was as much a spitfire as Molly and Margie. Anytime the three could wade into the middle of a fracas they were happy as kittens around the cream bowl. But Gordon wasn't letting them egg his fire-ball wife on. He glared at Margie.

"Just behave yourself and don't get the other two riled up. I'm having a hard enough time keeping Molly settled down. C-section or no, she's ready to whip-up on Addison." Both women chuckled, knowing given half a chance, Molly would try it. Scowling, he ushered Raine into his office. "Just so you know Molly gave me hell for not going to you today. It didn't matter that you insisted otherwise."

Raine laughed. "That'd be Molly. I bet she threatened to bring me those papers herself, too."

"You've got that right. She's one stubborn little girl. Only a few days out from having a baby and she's ready to haul ass out to your place." The pride and love in his voice sent a wave of nostalgia through her leaving a trace of sadness in its wake. She and Addison had been that way once. That is, before the drugs and alcohol stole him away. Then she did a mental check. That time in her life, and that man, were gone. Move on.

Gordon sat behind his desk while Raine settled in a burgundy wing-back facing him. Studying the horrible condition of her face, he vowed she'd get everything she deserved.

"Let's get these signed so Margie can get to the courthouse..." Before he'd finished speaking Raine had signed them and Margie whisked them away. Over coffee she apprised him of her meeting with the detectives, the fingerprint results, the additional charges, and their suggestion to leave town for a while.

"I wholeheartedly agree with them. Matter of fact, Molly and I've had this same discussion. Go. Don't be a sitting duck for Addison and don't tell anyone you're leaving. That way he can't coerce the information out of them and he sure as hell won't get anything out of us." With Molly's hellacious temper, if Addison showed up she'd shoot first and ask questions later.

"I'd already planned on leaving before this happened but obviously I waited a bit too long. If I'd left while Addison was at work maybe this wouldn't have happened."

"Maybe, but you're not a fortune teller to predict what's going on in Addison's head."

"All I know is he'd become worse and I was tired of walking on eggshells and there's not a doubt in my mind it wouldn't be long before he started hurting Katy."

"I just wish you'd confided in us." At his note of chiding she dropped her eyes. "Don't feel guilty. You thought you had no choice. You've been a hostage in your own house even though you've been able to come and go pretty much as you pleased. As long as you didn't make any attempts to leave with Katy you had your freedom." A sudden thought occurred to Gordon that started the fire burning again. He thumped a large fist on the antique desk, startling Raine. "Son of a . . . that's why you canceled several girls' days out with Molly. He knocked you around and you didn't want us knowing."

Raine nodded. "No way could I involve you guys in this mess, especially with Molly being pregnant. Had something happened to her or the baby, I'd have never forgiven myself. One of the hardest things I ever did was pretending everything was hunky-dory at the baby shower but Addison threatened if I opened my mouth I'd regret it."

"Before I'm finished he'll be the one with regrets." There weren't too many people who dared take on Gordon. Not only was he big and lean and fit, he could handle himself in a fight. He'd been a street-wise undercover cop for eight years before deciding to put his law degree to use. The things he'd learned on the streets had stayed with him.

"I've no doubt to what lengths you'll go to making sure we're safe, however, I'm not stupid." She gave him a droll look. "Well maybe I am, but I learn quickly. Leaving's best. If Addison makes bail he'll head straight for the house. He thinks he owns me and the only time he'll let go is when he's finished with me, so leaving's the best answer to a bad situation."

"I agree. And don't waste time, either. Come up with a travel plan and put it into action as quick as possible. The only thing I hate is you and Katy traveling alone. I wish someone was going with you."

"Not happening!" She said emphatically. "There's no way I'm dragging anyone else into this mess!"

He threw his hands up in surrender. "Okay, okay. I get it but that doesn't mean I like it. However, if you're determined to do this alone, just be careful."

"I will and I'll let you know when we leave."

Back home she found Cora fixing Katy a peanut butter and banana sandwich. Funny little kid, she thought, dropping a kiss on her head. What other four-year-old liked peanut butter and bananas smashed together then smeared all sweet and messy on bread. She wasn't complaining, though. It was healthier than a greasy bag of chips and a soda. Filling two glasses with iced tea, she caught Cora's eye and nodded toward the patio.

The light breeze lifted strands of her hair as she updated Cora on her meetings with the detectives and Gordon. Hearing the fingerprint results showed only Addison's on the gun, she gave Raine a high-five. When told that if all went off without a hitch, she'd be free of Addison in about sixty days, she carefully wrapped her in a big hug.

"I'll pray twenty-four-seven for that to happen and I hope he gets his just desserts."

Their backs to the door, neither knew Katy was standing in the doorway. "I want 'ssert, too, Mommy," she said, skipping to Raine and leaning against her legs. Both women exchanged chagrined looks before bursting into laughter. There was nothing like a child to keep you on your toes.

"Tell you what, pumpkin. You can have 'ssert but dinner comes first. How would you like pizza tonight?"

"Yippy!" Katy nodded vigorously. "Can we have the 'roni kind, please Mommy?" Big blue eyes fluttered adorably.

Only four and already using those tactics to get what she wanted. Heaven help her, in a few years she could just see some unsuspecting young man falling under her spell. "You bet!" She tugged gently on one blond pigtail. "Cora, why don't you see if Ethel wants to have pizza and 'ssert' with us tonight? We'll have a party!"

"I'll do it," Cora said, giving Raine a keen once-over, "and you go get comfortable." No matter how subtle, she couldn't hide the grimaces at the material chafing her injured flesh.

Another charge of anger passed over her. "That no account scrub should be locked away forever and the key thrown in the deepest ocean," she muttered. "Come on Katy-bug, let's go call Ethel."

Passing the master-suite, Raine found the door open. This was the first time she'd been near it since the attack. Anything she'd needed Cora had taken care of. Her gaze skimmed over the once calm and soothing pastel colors of the room as images flashed in her head—she was tied to the bed—Addison, his face red and twisted in rage towered over her. She could even recall certain sounds from that night—his harsh breathing, the doubled-up belt cracking and snapping in his hands. Shaking her head, the images disappeared and she found herself staring at the bed. Even if the evilness of Addison was gone, she still wasn't sleeping in that bed. The only good thing from it was Katy. Now she wanted no part of it. She'd burn it before she ever slept in it again.

Wearing a rose-colored caftan, she returned to the kitchen. From the window, she watched Cora pushing Katy on her swing and decided it was a good time to go through Addison's desk. Sitting behind it, she pulled on the center drawer. It wouldn't budge. She tried another, and another. Every drawer was locked up tight. So what was so all important that he'd locked the desk? And where was the key? It wasn't beneath the desk pad or any hiding place she could think of. No problem. Addison himself had taught her a neat little trick. All she need was a bobby pin. Thirty minutes later she was feeling pretty proud of herself for spread out across the desk were several paper files and thumb-drives. Intuition screamed Addison was up to no good. Hopefully the files and thumb-drives contained something useful against him and though she itched to read everything right then, her eyes weren't up to it so she'd wait until they were better.

Once Ethel arrived, they ate in the family room. Normally their meals were taken at the dining table for Addison had been a stickler for this rule but to hell with Addison's rules! They didn't matter anymore and this was much cozier. They could talk while Katy watched her shows. Once engrossed in them, she tuned everything else out.

Raine settled at one end of the overstuffed sofa while Cora sat at the other end.

Ethel claimed the rocker, slowly rocking to and fro. She'd kept her curiosity in check but now was anxious to hear the updates. "So, what's the latest?"

Nibbling the point of her pizza, the tangy tomato sauce stung Raine's lips but it tasted so good it was worth it. Swallowing, she repeated everything she told Cora earlier. Both ladies agreed with the detectives.

"That piece of paper won't stop him but should he try something stupid the police can cart his mama-spoiled-butt back to jail. And you can bet momma's going to hound you. Plus, it'll show him you mean business. If you stay here, you'll need to stand your ground." Ethel said.

That gave Raine the opening she needed. "The detectives share your concerns. They suggested I leave for a while." She looked at the sisters. "Even before this happened I was trying to time it right to leave." Raine balled up her napkin in aggravation. "I know it's necessary but I hate being forced to leave my own home when none of this is my fault. Maybe I should have finished him off. It would've been self-defense, after all!" she exclaimed then shot a glance at Katy. Addison was driving her to say and feel things she'd never have dreamed.

"Don't worry," Cora said, "she's too busy watching that purple dinosaur thingy to pay us any attention. We don't sing and dance, you know. If it were me I'd leave Dodge right now. Let the detectives and your attorney handle things."

"I agree, so we're leaving town for a while." Cora was staring off into space, only half listening, she was mulling over an idea of her own. "I'll get a second cellphone for Gordon and the detectives and keep the old one just for Addison. If he contacts me, I'll have a record of it. I'll set up a new email account, too, and keep the old as well."

Funds weren't a problem, either, for unbeknownst to anyone, save Gordon and Cora, she had a savings account in the six-figure category. At least Addison had never insisted on handling her finances, or known of her investments, or how much money she'd accrued over the years of their marriage. And she wasn't splitting it with him, either!

"Better safe than sorry," Ethel cautioned, "and you can count on Mom and Dad harassing you, and if he gets out, gets drunk, or whatever, you know he'll for darn sure try something. You can just bet your bottom dollar he's already plotting something as we speak. He caused this mess but you can take it to the bank he'll claim it was all your doing."

Apparently, everyone in Phoenix had the same opinion of the Andrews family. Too bad it had taken her so long to figure them out. Suddenly her cellphone rang and for the merest of seconds her heart jumped to her throat. Not recognizing the number, she hesitated before answering. "Hello."

"Ms. Andrews, I hope we're not disturbing you," It was Det. Collins.

"Oh no, you're not." Relief swept through her.

"You wanted to know how our little chat with your husband went. Just like we figured, he "lawyered up" and wouldn't talk until his highfalutin man arrived." She groused. Over speaker-phone, David put in cheerfully, "When we told him his prints were the only ones on the gun I thought he'd stroke-out, but when we told him we were upping the charges to attempted murder he really blew up and started making all kinds of nasty threats against you." Envisioning Addison's face going from red to purple with rage an all-over-body-shiver racked her. "His attorney finally ordered him to shut up but we heard him shouting all the way down the hall when we left. You can bet he'll be earning his money."

"That's what Addison's paying him the big bucks for," Raine quipped.

"You're right about that. So . . . have you given any thought to leaving town for a while?" Nancy asked, holding up crossed fingers to her partner.

Raine looked around for Katy. A touch on her arm had her looking at Cora who mouthed, "Bathroom."

"I have. I'd really like to be here for the bail hearing but leaving's a better idea." Where to go was the sixty-four-thousand-dollar question.

Nancy's crossed fingers became a thumbs-up to her partner. She'd been so worried Raine wouldn't take their suggestion to heart.

"Under the circumstances, it's the wisest decision; and the further away the better and don't tell anyone your plans. Though we're monitoring who comes and goes, that's not to say we know what they're talking about. We haven't wired his room."

"Too bad, there's no telling what you'd hear. I'm a hundred percent certain he'll try something and I wouldn't put it past his folks to cause mischief, either. Anyway, I plan on being gone before next weekend."

"You won't regret your decision," Nancy said then rang off.

"You're really planning on leaving by the end of this next week?" Cora asked. Raine nodded. A determined gleam entered Cora's eyes. "Well, I've made up my mind, too. You and that baby aren't traipsing off by yourselves to God knows where; you just never know what'll happen." Raine started to protest but Cora rolled right on over her. "I'm going and that's final. You might as well accept it," Her tone didn't brook an argument.

"Don't argue with her," Ethel said in mock resignation, though in full agreement with her sister. "Once her mind is made up you can talk until you're blue in the face and it won't do any good. Believe me, I should know. She's the most stubborn, pig-headed person I've ever met."

"Well isn't that the pot calling the kettle black!" Cora harrumphed indignantly. "That stubborn trait runs in the family. I'm not half as stubborn as you are. Remember that trip you and Brad took and you ended up lost in Missouri because you read the road map wrong? You ended up on some godforsaken backwood road out of gas and stubborn as a mule, you wouldn't admit it was your fault. You even made the poor man hoof-it alone to some old farmer's house to beg for a gallon of gasoline to get you to the nearest town. Brad was so upset when you got back home he barely spoke to you for weeks."

Raine loved the sisters' bantering, their love as obvious as the noses on their faces. A curl of wistfulness wafted through her. It was times like these she wished for siblings.

"I remember," Ethel's brown eyes twinkled, "and he never let me near a map again. He really was afraid that old farmer would shoot first and ask questions later." Ethel chuckled remembering her macho, never afraid of anything husband being white as a ghost and sweating bullets when he'd returned with the gas. "But in my defense, I told him I didn't know how to read those stupid maps. I never could but he never believed me. All I can say is thank goodness for the GPS." She chuckled with fond remembrance how irate her late husband had been. Cora was right; Brad was barely civil for weeks after they returned home.

"Okay. If you're dead-set on going, then I'll welcome the company but I don't want to waste time. I want to leave in case Addison makes bail." Raine looked at Cora.

"I can be ready anytime, but before we go you should visit your doctor." Cora scrutinized the patchwork of shades of dark blues, reds, and deep purples.

"You're right. I'd hate going off and then having something happen. I'll make an appointment."

"And I'll make care packages to take with you. Homemade cookies and the likes in case you get the nibbles along the way. By the way, do you have any idea which direction you're planning on heading?" Ethel asked.

Giving Cora a conspiratorial wink, Raine answered. "I'm thinking we should go looking for Brad's farmer. You still have that old road map?" As laughter filled the room, Raine vowed to do a lot more of it in the future.

The decision made, the urgency to leave became all-consuming. She had the check-up, purchased another cellphone and set up a second email address. Explaining her plans to Gordon and the detectives, they all approved. The restraining order was the last thing she did. Not knowing how they worked in other states, she'd cross that bridge should the need arise. And, she knew nothing would stop Addison if he really wanted to get to her.

As for Katy, she used the simplest explanation for leaving—they were taking a vacation. Katy was excited but her question about Daddy coming with them had Raine quickly making up a story why he couldn't go along. "Is Daddy going on 'cation with us?" Katy was snuggled on Raine's lap watching a cartoon. No matter how hurried she was she made sure Katy had this special time.

"No sweetie, Daddy can't. He had to go away. In fact, he left so fast he didn't have a chance to say good-bye to you." Raine hated lying but wanted to curtail further questions about Daddy. "He couldn't even come home when Mommy got hurt."

She couldn't very well tell her Daddy was the one who'd hurt Mommy.

Katy easily accepted her explanation. "Okay, but if you talk to Daddy will you tell him I love him?"

"You bet." Snuggling closer, soon her even breathing said she had drifted off to sleep. Resting her head against Katy's, Raine silently cursed Addison.

Finally, they were packed and ready to go in Cora's SUV. She'd insisted on taking it. "It's big and roomy and it'll be harder for anyone to track us down." Now the extended-size SUV was crammed so full it looked ready to burst at the seams and half the contents belonged to Katy—books, games, toys, even her rocking chair she'd insisted on bringing. And there was one more thing Raine wanted. In Katy's bedroom, she opened the combination bookcase-toy box Addison had specially made. Most people installed safes in their office or bedroom. Not Addison. He figured if anyone broke in they'd never think to look there. In the safe was an envelope containing ten thousand dollars cash. He'd said it was their emergency fund and she considered this an emergency. The cash would tide her over for quite a spell.

Cora and Katy were already buckled in. Ethel had been asked to go but declined, saying she'd stay put and keep an eye out on this end. "Are we ready girls?" She asked brightly as she buckled up. "Are we ready to have fun on our vacation?"

Katy, her mouth stuffed full of homemade chocolate chip cookies, nodded. She hadn't even waited to get on the road before invading the plastic cookie container.

"We're ready if you are!" Cora clapped her hands excitedly for Katy's benefit.

"Then let's hit the road!" She gave one last look at the house that had been her home for the last five years. Scratch that—it hadn't been a home for a very long time. A home was full of love and happiness, not a prison without bars. Looking forward again, not only was she staring at the road but at a new beginning.

CHAPTER NINE

Though joking about Brad's Missouri farmer, it was Cora's interest in the historic Route 66 that decided which direction they'd go. Raine, despite the circumstances, loved stopping whenever the whim hit. After Addison's downhill slide to hell began, there'd been no trips. Most exhilarating was that she had complete control of her life again. Never, ever, she vowed, would another man have that kind of power over her.

The sun was a ball of blazing yellow fire in the mid-afternoon blue sky as they traveled an Interstate that seemed a never-ending black ribbon winding through rolling green hills and valleys. Gazing at the brilliant reds, oranges, and yellows of the fall leaves, she thought to heck with all those modern city sights, she'd take this beauty anytime. A warm feeling stole over her like invisible arms enfolding her protectively.

As the SUV ate up the miles, Raine recalled Ethel's story of getting lost in the Missouri backwoods and an idea started taking seed. For miles, billboards with the faces of the legendary outlaws Jesse and Frank James emblazoned on them had captured her attention, bringing to mind long forgotten tidbits of folklore about the infamous outlaws. Supposedly the James Brothers had used caverns as hideouts when being chased by sheriffs' posses. One story even had the outlaws eluding authorities by fording an underground river in a cave. Whether the timeless tales were true or not, it made the whole outlaw lifestyle sound rough, roguish, and even romantic and the more billboards she passed the more she thought this area was a perfect place to take a break.

Following the billboard directions, she found the exit to the quaint looking mom-and-pop cottage-motel that had drawn her attention. The cottages, pale yellow with white gingerbread trim, boasted a postage stamp size lawn backed up to a fenced-in play yard shaded by huge oak and maple trees. What a great idea! It really was perfect for family vacations. Another feature figured highly into her favoring the location, the garage attached to each cottage. They could park the SUV inside and no one would be the wiser. Please, please let it be okay she prayed, parking in front of the motel office.

A dozing Cora woke up. "What's happening?" Stretching, she smothered a yawn.

"I'm thinking it's time for a break from the road. Cross your fingers this is the place. I'm going to see if a cottage is available to check first. They look great from the outside but you never know."

Cora was ready for a respite from riding too, and liked what she saw. "They're adorable." She slid out, groaning at her stiffness. "You check them out and I'll take care of Katy-bug." Katy had also awakened and the second she spotted the play yard started clamoring to get out. Cora lifted her out. "Come on sweetie-pie. You need to run some of that energy off." Katy's feet barely touched the ground before she took off at dead run, making a bee-line for the gated play yard, her blond curls bouncing about her shoulders. "Wait for me, you little scoundrel!" She might be a tad stiff but she didn't miss a beat as she trotted after Katy.

A loud jangling reminding her of a cowbell greeted Raine when she opened the door. Well that certainly lets you know someone is around. In the glass-top counter she saw raccoon-ringed eyes staring back at her. Even a month later she still sported vivid evidence of Addison's beatings.

Looking around the room, she noted the pictures on the walls and assumed they were either guests or family members.

Sadly, that was something she didn't have—no family and no pictures, not that she knew of anyway.

In one picture an elderly white-haired couple posed in front of the office. Another showed the same couple, but much younger, standing practically in the same spot. Based on the retro signs in the background the place had been part of the Route 66 heyday. Cora would love these, and based on the pictures not much had changed over the years. That it had withstood the ups and down of the economy through those years was amazing.

"Hi. Sorry to keep you waiting." Raine turned. A young woman about her own age possessing a girl-next-door prettiness faced her. Her expressive brown eyes widened at the sight of Raine's face but she didn't say anything.

"I was hoping to rent one of the cottages and wondered if I could see inside one. That is, if you're renting them. They look so adorable and welcoming from the outside."

Callie McGuire steeled herself not to react to the battered woman's appearance and returned her smile while thinking the stranger had a story to tell but she would never hear it. Momma had instilled in all her children to mind their own business. "You never poke your nose into someone else's business unless you want to get poked back."

"They're old and nothing fancy, but we've kept the same homey ambiance grandma and grandpa built. It's what keeps the same families returning year after year." She removed a key ring from the pegboard. "I'll be happy to show you any of the cottages. And you're not being insulting. We do the same thing when we're traveling. There are some pretty scuzzy places that look great outside but inside you find all kinds of vermin. You can never be too picky."

Nine cottages formed a semi-circle with three facing the office. Callie went to the middle one of the trio facing the office and unlocked the door. Stepping inside, Raine was instantly enchanted. It looked just as she'd imagined. The walls were the same light knotty-pine as the office, the combined living room/

kitchen was quite spacious and it had all the modern conveniences. Charming, cozy, and clean—they were staying!

There were two bedrooms, hi-speed Internet, Wi-Fi and cable television in all the rooms. There was also a mini washer-dryer set in the bathroom. It just got better and better.

"All you need are food and clothes." Callie said.

At the back door, she watched Katy swinging in the fenced-in play yard. "This is perfect, that is, if you'll rent it by the week and," she hesitated, "there are three of us."

"I saw your little girl head for the play yard with your mom right behind her."

Raine didn't flicker an eyelash nor bother correcting the assumption, deciding it couldn't hurt to embellish a little bit. "It's a girl's only vacation. Katy's a great little traveler but she needs to run off some energy."

"I know what you mean. My son's about her age and he hates being cooped up. By the way, I'm Callie McGraw, and that's my husband, Dan." She pointed to a tall, broad-shouldered man. "That's him and our little boy, Jack, painting a section of the fence we had to replace." Callie chuckled. "Although, it looks like Jack got more paint on himself than the fence."

"Your little guy looks like he's got mischief written all over him." Raine said.

"Oh, he's full of it, more than you can imagine." There was no mistaking the pride in her voice. "If you're satisfied let's get you registered then you girls can settle in."

"Oh, this will be perfect. The play yard alone would have sold me." Raine said, watching Cora push a laughing Katy.

Registering under Cora's personal information just as they'd been doing since setting out, she paid for the week. She'd hate leaving in the middle of the night owing this nice lady money. Callie McGraw's eyes held unasked questions but Raine ignored them for telling her would mean bringing one more person into the equation.

"We're staying?" Cora asked when Raine returned.

"We are. Go take a look." She edged her out of the way. "It looks like Katy already loves the play yard."

"What gave you that idea?" Cora winked at Katy then went to have a look. Returning, she said, "This is perfect and we've put enough miles behind us it should be okay."

Raine caught her meaning. Addison wouldn't think to look at a place like this and drive right on by. "I've paid for a week. If we decide to stay longer, it's not a problem. It's their slow season, especially since school started." She gave Katy one more push. "Okay, that's it for now, kiddo. You'll have lots of time to play out here. Right now, Mommy needs to get our things and put them away."

"We get to stay here?" Her blue eyes rounded in excitement. "Oh boy!" A sneaker clad foot kicked up a bit of turf trying to stop the swing. Raine's hand on the chain finally stilled it.

"Yes, we do and the sooner we get unpacked and go to the grocery store, the sooner you get to come back out here."

After unloading the SUV, they put off going to the store for a while longer so Katy could play some more. "Just look at her." Cora said. "I think she needed this break more than we did. However, I have to admit it'll be nice staying put for a while. My backside was getting tired of sitting in the car." She patted the rounded portion of her anatomy.

Patting her own backside, Raine grimaced. "I hate to be the bearer of bad news but we need to find a grocery store so both our bottoms are going to suffer a little longer."

"Oh, that's just great!" Cora grumbled good-naturedly.

Raine went to the office for directions to stores. "We have one of those super-discount stores where you can do all your shopping in one stop," Callie told her.

"That works for me. My little girl isn't too keen on leaving the play yard for long."

"There you go, then." Callie watched her new guest walk back across the parking lot. Intuition said the girls-only vacation was a smoke screen and they were really on the run. Well if anybody, especially the man who'd given her the severe beating showed up asking questions, they wouldn't get anything from her. A shudder raced through her imagining what other horrors Raine Andrews had endured. Callie wondered if that was her real name.

Crossing the parking lot, Raine felt Callie's gaze following her and was grateful she hadn't asked about the horrible marks on her face. Directions in hand, they piled back in the SUV and wound their way through the tree-shaded streets until they located the store. And Callie was right; it was the ideal place for all their needs. Back at the cottage they stowed their purchases away and all the while Katy clamored to get back outside to the play yard.

"Be patient a little longer, sweet-pea. As soon as I'm done we'll go out. But you can only play for a little while. We haven't had dinner yet."

Katy's lower lip drooped so low in a pout she could've ridden to town on it. "Fine."

Cora heard the dejected tone. Bless her little heart; all she wants is to play outside. "I've an idea, Katy-bug. If Mommy fixes dinner, I'll come out with you."

Instantly the pout was gone and her cherubic face brightened. Bobbing her head vigorously it set her pigtails to dancing. Raine flashed Cora a grateful look. "That's a great idea."

Katy didn't hesitate. Grabbing's Cora's hand she headed outside; she didn't want Mommy changing her mind.

While dinner was cooking, Raine checked for messages. Ever cautious, she closed the bedroom door for privacy in case Katy came looking for her. She didn't need to know what was going on and so far she'd accepted the continued explanations about Daddy being too busy to join them.

Actually, Katy's Daddy was pacing the length of his eight-by-ten cell ready to commit murder. Every time a clanking iron door slammed shut his vows of revenge increased and right at the top of the list was the bitch. For nearly three weeks he'd been locked inside this stinking jail and that didn't count the two weeks spent in the hospital. Immediately upon release from the hospital those cocky bastard detectives had deposited his ass here.

Feeding his anger was the fact that weeks had passed with no coke or alcohol and now he was battling the constant crawling of jittery nerves beneath his skin. Adding insult to injury, no bail was granted so while he was made to cool his heels the bitch went about her merry way. It was her fault he'd had to punish her and it was her fault he'd been shot. Just thinking about it made the wound throb. She just thought she had the hammer but sooner or later he'd get out—then see who had the hammer. He started to flop down on the bunk then thought better of it, the wound was still painful. Instead, he carefully stretched out, his hands pillowing his head. Closing his eyes, he continued planning his revenge.

While the laptop whirred through its startup procedures she checked both cellphones. There were no messages. She thought of the files and discs tucked away and wondered for about the hundredth time what he'd been up to? Every time she started to look she was interrupted. With Katy occupied now was a good time to find out.

Ten minutes later, she sat back, a stunned expression on her face. Holy cow! There was enough information to get Addison locked away for ten life-times. There was record upon record of drug transactions, money taken in, names, and meeting places. There were shipment times, delivery routes in and out of the country, even drivers' names. And that was just in one file. In another, large sums of money were listed denoting skims from various shield companies. Besides the drugs, Addison had been hiding money from the IRS. Hot damn! With this kind of evidence, she had him by the shortest of short hairs and she would use it to get him to leave her alone. Gordon and the detectives will love this! Once in their hands, Addison might never see the light of day. He might vow to get even but she had the greatest bargaining tools in her possession and there'd be no bargaining unless on her terms. Back in the kitchen she hummed a happy little tune as she set the table.

After dinner, their baths taken and ready for bed, they settled down to watch one of the new cartoon movies they'd bought. Each held a bowl full of mint chocolate chip ice cream. Katy was in heaven—her favorite ice cream and talking animals. What more could a kid want? It was no surprise however, when halfway through the movie she fell asleep. Even Cora kept nodding off, doing the bobbing-dog-on-the-dash act. The last time she woke up it was to find Raine smothering her giggles.

"I'm going to bed before your laughing wakes that baby up and makes you go back and swing some more. It'd serve you right, too!" She grumbled.

"I'm sorry," Raine sputtered over another giggle, "but you looked like one of those bobbing dogs. You know—the one's you see in the back dash when you follow another car." And she bobbed her head up and down imitating one. "I always thought they were funny to watch."

"Ha! Ha! I'm glad I'm so entertaining!" Cora feigned insult. Raine didn't see the smile lighting her face as she left the room. If one of those dashboard decorations made her laugh, then she'd imitate one forever.

Raine tucked a sleeping Katy in then returned to the living room. Now a peaceful silence enveloped the cottage broken only by the soft swooshing sounds of rubber tires against asphalt on the Interstate. Not at all sleepy, she made a cup of tea. It'd been a long time since she'd felt so mellow, so calm and she relished it. Curled on the sofa with her new novel, soon she was swept away from the worries of her own reality.

Fifteen hundred miles away in his jail cell, Addison dozed fitfully. The brutal dreams playing in his sleep would have been Raine's nightmares.

Fifty miles away from the cottages, Jess Harper relaxed in the porch swing enjoying the brisk coolness of the fall night and the leaves rustling on the breeze. A quiet solitude settled over him. What more could a man want? He had a beautiful home, friends he could always count on, and the freedom to come and go as he darned well pleased. He thought of Cooper, of how happy he was married to the love of his life. That's what made Cooper complete. As far as he was concerned he didn't need marriage to complete his happy existence. A woman didn't exist that he wanted as a permanent fixture in his life. All they did was muck up your world.

CHAPTER TEN

As the days passed Raine fell deeper and deeper under the spell of the rolling green hills and autumn splendor. She refused to let her problems concerning Addison taint her new view of life. Plus, she now had the means to deal with him. When told what she'd found, Gordon wanted it ASAP. "This is your guaranteed key to freedom and whatever you want."

After enjoying several days of idleness, Raine suggested touring the caves Jesse James used as a hideout. At first Katy balked, crossing her arms stubbornly over her chest. "I don't want to go!" It wasn't the first time she'd bulled up, refusing to go with them, preferring to play on the swings and slide.

"You mean you don't want to wear your cowboy hat? Or go exploring the caves? There's no telling what you might see. And we can have ice cream after the trip through the cave." There you go, bribing your child. But she'd learned a long time ago how to win the battle. As long as ice cream and mac-and-cheese existed she had it made.

The mention of ice cream put the winning point in Raine's column. Katy's blue eyes took on a speculating gleam. "Ice cream! I get ice cream, too? Okay! Let me get my cowboy hat!" She dashed to the bedroom re-emerging with a pink felt hat perched precariously on her head, the tight chin tie keeping it in place. "Okay. I'm ready to go 'sploring' Mommy." Raine rolled her eyes while Cora chuckled.

The road leading to the park was as twisty and windy as a confused snake. No wonder it'd been a great hiding place, she mused, looking at the dense woods on either side of the road. A body could easily get lost in them. She imaged what it must have looked like in the outlaw days—nothing but wilderness, the rolling river, and a few roughhewn cabins sparsely scattered about.

As they waited in line for the next tour, people eyed Raine with open curiosity; she just smiled at them. Their guide, a young woman, perhaps twenty, dressed in a khaki-colored uniform, was thoroughly versed in the history of the caverns and their most infamous occupants, Jesse and Frank James. Leading the way, she soon had everyone enthralled in the stories about the caverns where Jesse James and his band of outlaws had outwitted sheriffs' posses by hiding in them and eventually swimming to freedom in the nearby Meramec River.

Totally fascinated, Katy listened in awe. She knew who Jesse James was from watching him riding a horse and shooting a gun in old movies. "Are they still here?" She asked in wide-eyed wonder, her gaze sliding from the replica of the outlaw's campsite, around the shadowy cavernous rock walls as though she expected them to suddenly appear out of the darkness. Several amused chuckles echoed in the cavern.

The young woman shook her head. "No, they're not here anymore. They left a long time ago." Raine sent her a grateful smile, appreciating she hadn't said the outlaws were long dead and ruining Katy's avid enjoyment.

Afterward, the promised ice cream in hand, they hiked one of the nature trails meandering throughout the park. Later they enjoyed a late afternoon picnic while in the background the river roared softly as it headed downstream. Nibbling on a chip, Raine studied her precocious child. Fascinated with the tour, Katy had asked questions and made her own observations.

"I still didn't see any grapes and I'd have eaten some, too." She meant the stalactites, or rock formations created from water dripping for years and years molding rock into what resembled clusters of grapes. Pride swelled inside her. She had such a smart little girl.

Nearing the end of their week at the cottage Cora suggested doing some exploring. Even Katy, who earlier declared she was never leaving the play yard, was up for it.

"There are roadmaps in the office," Raine said, pulling on a light jacket against the slight chill in the air. "I'll get one."

Callie was working at the computer when she entered. "Hey. How's it going?"

"Just fine," Raine replied, picking up a map from the holder. "We want to go exploring so I figured I'd better get a map."

"Good idea. Here." Callie took the map and spread it on the countertop, indicating where they were. "You're here." She marked the spot with a yellow Hi-Liter from a cup of pens on the counter. "From our location, it's pretty easy finding your way back from any direction. If you keep heading east on the Interstate you'll eventually reach St. Louis. Otherwise, just follow the map. If you get turned around just stop and ask directions. You'll find ninety-nine percent of us Missourians would love to help in any way we can."

Obviously, Callie hadn't heard about Brad's farmer. She also detected Callie was referring to more than directions. She was still curious about the injuries to her face but good manners kept her from asking. Though weeks since Addison had beaten the daylights out of her, she was still black and blue and sore. Shadows turned her blue eyes darker than storm-tossed seas thinking of the vivid nightmares she wrestled with every night. Thoughts of that night, and Addison, were never far from her mind.

"Callie, thank you," Raine said, squeezing her hand before leaving. Callie surmised she was being thanked for not prying.

In the SUV, Raine said. "How about we take the country roads and see where we end up. We have the map. Surely, we can manage our way back here. And who knows, we might even run across Brad's old farmer."

Chuckling, Cora pointed to a squiggly line. "Let's go that way."

"That way, it is! Same road-rules apply, girls, if we see anything interesting, we stop."

"You know," Cora said awhile later, gazing at the passing scenery, "I really like it here. Everyone's so warm and friendly. And the country's so pretty. It'd be so beautiful all covered in snow."

A vision of a snow-covered wonderland filled Raine's head. And a white Christmas—that would be totally awesome. An idea started forming. Nothing was settled concerning Addison so why not remain here through the holidays? She'd see what Cora thought about it.

The road, blacktopped and emitting the sharp tang of freshly laid asphalt, was a breath-holder of hair-pin turns with hardly any shoulder. Heaven forbid they would meet another vehicle, she'd for sure slide right off into the steep ditch and it wouldn't surprise her if it had started as a cow-path cleared by earlier settlers. She pictured wagon loads of families rolling their way to the nearest town for supplies or church on Sunday. Later they'd make their way back home in the gathering dusk, ever-conscious of wayward outlaws and marauding Indians. And without a doubt, Indians had made these hills their home long before any settlers came along.

The road led to a river that had to be crossed if they were to continue. The only problem was the rust-stained iron skeleton of a bridge. Goose-bumps peppered her body and her hands turned clammy. Was she having a panic attack? Get a grip! It's only a bridge and not the first one you've ever crossed. Yeah right! Only this one looked like its warranty had run out years ago. Creeping onto the one-lane contraption, she had a white-knuckled grip on the steering wheel. It was foolish that the old bridge scared her. Obviously, other people crossed it every day. Even now someone was waiting at the other end.

"Oh . . . my, this is scary," Cora stared wide-eyed at the green-tinted waters flowing several feet below them. One thing was for darn sure, if they plunged off it she wouldn't worry about drowning, she'd die of fright before she ever hit bottom.

Along the riverbank, a picnic area was dotted with tables and barbecue pits. Two weathered looking shanties sported all manner of advertisements from float trips, to boat rentals, to soda ads. The place was busy though, she noted, taking in the number of vehicles. Maybe they did have something here. It just might be fun taking a float trip some time—when it was warmer, that is.

Raine darted a sideways glance then focused her eyes back to the narrow strip of road between the sides of the bridge.

Excited, Katy craned her neck to see the river. "Let's go 'fimming,' Mommy! There's a ribber! And we can go fishing, too! Please Mommy, pretty please."

"It's too cold to go swimming now, Katy-bug, but when it gets warmer I promise we'll go." Glancing in the rear-view mirror, she wasn't surprised to see the lower-lip-droop.

"But those people are 'fimming," she pouted. "They don't 'fink it's too cold."

"That's because they're used to the cool water, baby, and we're not. But I promise, as soon as it gets warm I'll take you swimming. How does that sound?"

Ever the bargainer, Katy asked. "Do I get one of those floaty-ring things?"

Raine laughed, her daughter would make a terrific attorney someday. "Yes, you can get one of those floaty-ring things."

"Okay." Seeing the dimpled smile, a rush of love flooded over Raine. As long as Katy was happy she could handle anything.

Reaching the end of the bridge, she heaved a huge sigh of relief. Give her a shoulderless road over a rickety bridge anytime. Waving to the patiently waiting driver, she mouthed "thank you."

Eventually they came to the city limits of a small town, the picturesque welcome sign read: "Green Glade, Population 2,121." The lamp-post lined streets held an old-world ambiance with their stately old homes nestled under centuries-old trees amid lawns still lush and green. Friendly waves from folks puttering in their yards or relaxing on wide, wrap-around verandas had her waving back and wishing she could join them. They came upon an ornate old stone courthouse centered on the town-square. At least a hundred years old, she could only imagine the history it had seen.

The street ran down a steep hill that had Raine riding the brake, her stomach doing cartwheels and Katy squealing, "Wheee . . .! It's a roller coaster! Let's do it again, Mommy!" And so they did. They hadn't planned on stopping but they spotted a fast-food restaurant, and Katy suddenly had to use the potty.

Raine gave Cora a knowing look. "Then I guess we'd better find you a potty." Their entrance attracted curious looks that turned to deeper scrutiny. They weren't being rude so Raine just smiled back. After using the facilities, Katy announced she was starving and just had to have a burger. Raine gave Cora another, I-told-you-so look.

Everyone returned to their conversations save for one woman who kept glancing in their direction. Raine saw the curiosity but also something else, compassion. "You know," she looked at Cora, "something tells me this might be a good place to stay. It's got such a safe, cozy feel." Scanning the town-square, she noted the police station on one corner. Across from it was the bank. Only a crazy person would rob a bank with the police right next door. Rob the bank. Go to jail. Go to court. No collecting two hundred dollars. Actually, it was a pretty nifty set-up.

"It's out of the way, too, if you know what I mean," Cora pointed out.

Let's take a really long vacation." Raine suggested. "Let's find a place, maybe something outside of town, though." Not wanting to be easy pickings.

"Can I have a f'ing-set?" Katy chimed in, waving at one of the strangers. It was the same staring woman.

Watching the trio, Inez McCullin felt the inexplicable need to get more acquainted. Maybe it was the battered, golden-haired woman that drew her, or her God-given makeup to help people and this young woman had help-needed written all over her. She also had a story to go with it and before too much longer she'd pry it out of her.

"Hon, I'll be right back," Inez said to the man beside her. Hank McCullin shook his head at his wife, knowing curiosity over the newcomers was killing her.

Reaching them, Inez addressed Raine. "What a precious doll-baby you have." Katy beamed at the compliment. Inez smiled at Cora. "You must be so proud having such a little cutie-pie for a granddaughter."

Cora gave Raine a furtive look. It was fine if people assumed they were mother and daughter, figuring the fewer who knew the real truth the better to keep Addison off their trail.

"I can't tell you how proud I am of both my girls." Cora never batted an eyelash. After all, she did consider them her girls, and she was proud of them.

"I'm Inez McCullin," the attractive, silver-haired woman dressed in blue jeans, low-heeled black boots and a sweater of sage green said. "You all must be new to the area. I know just about everybody and their dog in these parts and I don't recall ever seeing you before."

Unease rolled through Raine. "We're just doing a little exploring. We stopped for gas and the clerk said we should check out the area." The white lie had her blushing. It was partly true. They were exploring, they had stopped for gas, only no one ever mentioned the little town. Suddenly an idea flashed like a light bulb switched on. A slight nod from Cora said they were on the same train of thought. Hopefully it wouldn't derail. Tucking a strand of hair behind her ear, Raine took the bull by the horns.

"Actually, we're looking for a place to stay for a while. I was in an accident and I'm not as up to par as I thought." Eyeing Katy, she motioned to another table some distance away. "I didn't want my little girl hearing us. You know what they say about little pitchers having big ears."

"Yes, I do." Inez agreed. "I've got six grandbabies about your little one's age and the things that come out of their mouths sends my kids into fits. I keep telling them they should be more careful. And I raised four kids so believe me," she speared Raine with a keen stare, "I know when someone's pulling my leg, telling one whopper of a lie. Now young lady, what's your real story? There may be some frost up-top but I'm sharp as a tack and those marks didn't come from any car wreck." Her tone dared Raine to deny it.

"How'd you know?" Caught in a lie, Raine was mortified.

"Easy. My girl looked just like you and to keep her daddy and me from knowing what was going on she concocted some cock-and-bull story about being in a wreck, said those pesky airbags caused her to look like she'd been in some kind of battle." Inez made a face. "I guess in a way she was, and by the looks of you, the same kind. I hope you gave him as good as you got."

"Depends on how you look at it. He got shot." It was out before she could stop her wayward tongue. Well hell! Might as well call the news stations and broadcast her story worldwide. However, instinct said to trust this stranger and the next thing the whole sordid story came spilling out like water from a faucet.

Inez let out a shrill whistle that had several heads turning in their direction. "Sorry. It was out before I couldn't stop it."

"Don't worry, and I didn't shoot him. The idiot shot himself. So, what did your daughter do in her situation?" Raine asked.

Amusement lit up Inez's face. "Simple. She divorced him. I'd have done more than that but Cory, that's my girl, just divorced him. Anyway, it was either divorce or one of them was going to get killed. But don't think he just walked away. No sir . . . ree! That man tormented my girl for months until one night she finally had her belly full of his shenanigans. She met him at the door with a loaded shotgun. He got the message all right, when she shot the hat off his head." Inez chuckled with pride. "Her daddy taught her to shoot like that, her sister and brothers, too. Anyway, she warned him if he came around bothering her anymore the next round was going further south than his head, she was done warning him and he knew what to expect. Bless her heart, that girls got a lot of me in her. Just to make a believer out of him she put a round in the porch between his legs. He took

YOU'LL COME TO ME

off like his pants were on fire and she hasn't seen hide-nor-hair of him since. Shoot, it was worth repairing the hole in the porch just to get rid of him."

Raine laughed at the picture Inez painted of the incident. "Your daughter sounds like a very strong woman. I'd like to meet her some time."

"She is a strong woman, and if you stick around these parts long enough I'm sure you'll meet her. She's a deputy with the sheriff's office. Cory Dugan's her name." There was no mistaking the pride in Inez's voice. "And, it seems you two have something in common already—ornery men. Sounds like that husband of yours was well-deserving of the dose of medicine he got. Too bad it didn't finish him off." Inez McCullin reminded her of Cora, she didn't hold back her opinions, either.

As for Inez, the minute the trio walked in and seen Raine's injuries she'd known where they'd come from. They'd come from a very brutal and very angry man. She'd never understand why a man got off beating on a woman, no matter what the circumstances. In her book, he was nothing but a low-life slug. She also imagined there were more than just the visible injuries, too. Her heart was hurting, too, but it wasn't broken because a man who loved you never raised a hand to you. Her gaze swung to the little girl. No doubt the S.O.B. had used her as leverage for no woman worth her salt stayed with a man like that. And she figured there was a boatload of guilt for not leaving sooner but she shouldn't feel guilty for doing what she thought best. Now she needed help and was getting it.

"Are you really looking for a place to light?" Raine nodded. "Then I know just the place." And all she had to do was convince that wickedly handsome but irascible devil, Jess Harper, of it. It wouldn't be easy but she knew just the right way to handle the man. Trick him! Back him into a corner! "It'll take a little coaxing of the old boy. He's the loner type, a bit stand-offish, if you get my drift. Cantankerous, too, but he's got a heart of gold, especially where kids are concerned. Even lets out his cabins to the county children's home as a sort of youth camp."

Raine pictured some smelly, crusty old buzzard, a beard down to his knees, living in some stinky hovel in the woods. Probably didn't bathe except for Saturdays. Okay, Raine, you've been watching too many old westerns. Though she appreciated Inez's help, she had a feeling the crusty old man definitely wouldn't want three females intruding in his hermit world.

"I appreciate your help but I can't accept it. We don't want to be someplace we'll be intruding on."

"You won't be intruding," Inez informed her quickly, maybe a little too quickly.

"I also don't want to bring any trouble down on anyone that helps us. I don't know if my husband's looking for me but it's a very good possibility and he's not beyond going after anyone helping me and that could include you and your friend."

"Don't you worry about us; we're a tough and hearty bunch around these parts. You just let me handle everything. And you won't be intruding. It'll do him good having some company around that rambling old place. There's plenty of room for all of you and the cabins are set far enough apart you won't be in each other's backyards." Raine opened her mouth then closed it, knowing she'd be wasting her breathe for Inez was already keying in a number on her cellphone. "You just sit tight while I talk to Jess; tell him what we're doing." More like he'd be telling her where to go. Oh well, she thought, heading outside. This call needed privacy.

Returning to the table, she found Katy playing in the enclosed playground while Cora sipped on a cup of coffee and kept a watchful eye on her. She pushed a second cup toward Raine. "So?"

"Ms. McCullin wants to help and knows the perfect place for us. Apparently, some old geezer owns a bunch of cabins and she's calling him to see if he'll let us have one. They're supposed to be back in the woods off the beaten path." She took a sip of coffee. It tasted pretty good for fast-food coffee.

"I know we had the same idea but are you sure we can trust her?" Cora sounded unsure.

"I do. We're total strangers, too, but she's willingly extended a hand to help us. I think we should accept it." Reaching across the table, she squeezed Cora's hand.

"I appreciate your concern. You've been with me all the way since this whole mess started. If you're not comfortable doing this then we'll forget it."

"Oh, stop it!" Cora sniffed. "Okay. If you think she's all right, then so do I. And if that old geezer will rent us one of his cabins then we ought to stay." A horrid thought had her shuddering. "Oh Lord, I hope the place is habitable. I can just see pigs and chickens running all over the place!"

"Stop it! You've been watching too many old Ma and Pa Kettle movies. Ms. McCullin wouldn't recommend them if they weren't livable. I just hope the old geezer's not so cranky he scares Katy." Raine's preconceived ideas of Jess Harper couldn't have been further off the mark, as she was soon to learn. "And being off any main roads will be safer, too." If Addison knew she'd left he might have his minions looking for her. "I know its wishful thinking but why couldn't he disappear forever and leave us alone."

"Fat chance that'll happen! You can take it to the bank he'll get down and dirty before he's through. No way will Addison let you go without a fight."

"You're right, and changing our route will buy us some time should someone be following us." Glancing out the plate-glass window she saw Inez McCullin talking, pacing, and waving her hands agitatedly. A let-down feeling settled over her. "Ms. McCullin doesn't look happy. He must be refusing to let us stay."

"Could be," Cora was watching, too. "It's amazing a complete stranger who doesn't know us from Adam wants to help us."

"She saw right through that accident story. Told me her daughter used the same one to cover up what was happening with her husband."

While waiting, Raine related Inez's story about her daughter and her now ex-husband. When she reached the part about shooting into the porch between his legs, Cora laughed with relish.

"Good for her! I don't even know the girl and I already like her. Apparently, it takes a bullet to make thick-headed men listen."

They were still laughing when Inez McCullin returned. "Everything's all set. Jess Harper's happy to put you girls up for a spell." Well, happy wasn't exactly the way she'd describe his reaction but he'd get over being mad as soon as he got a glimpse of Raine Andrews. Despite the deep bruises and purple-ringed eyes she was a looker and what man could resist that river of waist-length blond hair. "Just whistle when you're ready and I'll lead you out to the Harper place."

Raine hesitated. "Before we go, how much is he asking to rent the cabin?"

Money was no object, plus she'd done several editing jobs since leaving Phoenix. She had a good reputation and that meant staying on top of her game and keeping her name active. Also, working helped take her mind off her problems. Some nights after Katy and Cora went to bed she'd edit for hours until her eyes turned bleary with fatigue. Then she'd crawl into bed and pray the nightmares stayed away. There were too many nights she woke up heart pounding in sweat-soaked panic, sure that Addison had found them.

"Four hundred a month, that includes utilities. This time of year the cabins sit empty so the extra will be a little bonus for 'ole' Jess."

Raine's mouth dropped open and her battered eyes widened with shock. Surely Inez was mistaken. Cora strangled on her coffee. Gasping, she asked. "Are they livable? Is there a roof? For that price are you sure they aren't falling down around his ears?"

"Don't you worry; you'll love the place so much you'll never want to leave. And once you get to know Jess Harper you'll find he's not so cantankerous."

A moment of trepidation filled Inez. Should Raine's husband find her here there'd be fireworks for sure. She'd hate for Jess to get hurt. On the other hand, her new friends needed help, and besides that, it was going to be such fun watching Jess handle the three females, especially the pretty but battered young mother.

CHAPTER ELEVEN

Jess glared at the cellphone clutched so tightly in his hand it was a wonder it didn't shatter. Why hadn't he ignored the call the second he saw her name on the caller ID? Dammit! That sly old dog had out-maneuvered him, announcing slick-as-you-please a complete stranger, a woman, was renting one of his cabins. In dire need of a place to stay, she'd volunteered his place for her to recuperate from the horrible beating her husband had given her and they'd be out in a bit. He tried telling her he wanted no part of her mercy mission, but it had gone in one ear and out the other. When Inez was on a roll, you might as well forget it. A concrete wall listened better than she did.

Everyone was right about her—when Inez set her mind to something you could forget about changing it. She reminded him of a dog digging for the buried bone; she kept digging until it was in her teeth. Lean fingers raked through crisp blue-black hair leaving it in messy layers. At the moment, he wasn't sure who he was more aggravated at—himself for letting her back him into a corner—or Inez for picking up another stray and forcing it on him. Frustrated, he heaved a resigned sigh. Out-maneuvered and no choice in the matter, he'd better make sure a cabin was ready. However, when he got Inez alone he was tearing into her like a buzz-saw running through soft wood.

Shoving the phone in his pocket he stomped up the hill toward the cabins, the crisp breeze rifling through the short layers of his hair cooled his temper. At the top, he paused to admire his handiwork. Rehabbing the four old cabins dating to the eighteen-hundreds had painstakingly, and lovingly, taken many months to complete and they looked damned fine even if he said so himself. For a time, he'd thought of razing them but in the end didn't have the heart.

However, bringing the rag-tag cabins back to life hadn't been easy, especially with no clue where to start, but help and stories from the old-timers in the neighborhood helped his vision come to life. Though keeping the cabins as original as possible, they had all the modern-day, creature comforts including cable television, WI-FI, and the latest in appliances.

Once done refurbishing, he'd set about implementing the next step in his plan. That's when Inez had charged into his life at the county commissioners meeting where he'd been presenting his idea of using the cabins and property as a summer camp for kids from the county youth home. Without Inez on his side he'd never have gained approval so he guessed he could put up with her for a little while. And anyway, how much trouble could one middle age woman cause?

As he readied the cabin, Jess pondered Inez's sketchy information. In a nutshell, the woman's husband had beaten the living daylights out of her one too many times and she'd finally gotten the gumption to leave him. Intuition said there was more to the story but Inez had cleverly sidestepped his questions. However, she did say the woman wasn't exactly on the run but there was a pretty good possibility he might hunt for her.

He'd never understand a man raising a hand to a woman. To his way of thinking the scumbag deserved the same kind of retribution and he'd be quite happy going toe-to-toe with him. If he found her here he just might get the opportunity to put a few knots on the man's head. Jess caught himself flexing his fists. Okay, calm down, you're getting as bad as Inez ready to fight everybody's battles. He didn't want, or need, that kind of trouble. His quiet country life with no one to be responsible for was great and he was quite happy not having a clinging female demanding permanent ties. He wanted nothing emotional cluttering up his life. He wasn't bitter about having been down that road once, a long time ago, but he was definitely not making the trip again.

Despite his aggravation, he admitted one thing was for certain, you couldn't have anyone better in your corner than Inez. It wasn't her fault God had given her such a big heart. If someone was in trouble, Inez was the first one to step up to the plate. He figured the saints were watching over this woman when they brought her in contact with Inez.

Forty-five minutes later he was at the woodpile, rhythmically swinging an axe splitting firewood. Hearing cars, he looked up to see Inez's powder blue pickup and a darker blue SUV.

Laying the axe aside, he snagged the blue plaid wash-worn flannel shirt he'd discarded when he started splitting wood and shrugged his broad shoulders into it as he headed toward them.

Unaware of how hot and sexy he looked, the breeze ruffling his blue-black hair, his long-legged stride easily ate up the distance, his tanned, damp chest gleaming under the sun's rays before he covered it up.

But, Raine was thoroughly aware as her senses went spiraling crazily like a spinning top while heat flooded places that hadn't been hot in a long time. Watching this most attractive man striding toward them, she decided he wasn't Jess Harper, the crusty old hermit.

"My, oh my, but he sure is purty," Cora drawled causing Raine to roll her eyes. "Well, he is!"

"Careful there or you'll be drooling down your chin," Raine teased.

"Just wipe the drool from yours, little missy!" Cora shot back; thinking surely this couldn't be the crusty old geezer Inez McCullin had described. Then it dawned on her—Inez never actually said Jess Harper was crusty, or old, or a geezer. Oh brother, that woman had a devious mind and she was coming to like her more and more.

As for Inez, she watched Jess heading their way, his heavy scowl a good indication he was not a happy camper. Any second she expected steam to shoot out his ears. For sure she'd pay hell later.

"What the hell!" Jess muttered, for getting out of the driver's seat of the SUV wasn't an older woman, but a younger one. And lord, she had the longest corn-colored hair he'd ever seen. The golden tresses framed her softly rounded face, most of which was obscured by large sunglasses. It hung sleek and shiny clear to her waist, a waist that flared into womanly rounded hips covered in clinging denim. A surge of heat sizzled through him like sputtering oil in a frying pan, heating him up where he didn't want to be heated. Instantly there was a distinct stirring. Great! One glimpse of a pretty face and you get all hot and bothered! Now wasn't the time and there'd be no way to hide it. He watched her walk to the back of the SUV and reach inside emerging with a little girl. Even from a distance there was no mistaking the grimace when she settled her on her hip. Looking at the little girl, Jess's eyes softened. A cutie-pie, about four-years-old, she favored the young woman immensely, obviously mother and daughter. Then the front passenger door opened and an older woman alighted. Ah . . . his tension eased, this must be the woman Inez had befriended. But where did the other two fit in? It didn't take long to find out.

As the four, Inez, the hot blond carrying the little girl, and the older woman drew nearer, he saw the brutal evidence of abuse on the younger woman's face, or at least what the sunglasses didn't hide. His stomach lurched sickeningly. Some man had used his fists on this petite and pretty woman? Now he was downright pissed off at everybody—Inez for misleading him and the unknown scumbag for beating his wife. Dammit! Inez would get an earful when he got her alone. That sneaky woman had purposely led him to believe it was an older woman who needed the cabin.

"Jess, meet your new tenants," Inez flashed him a bright smile but there was no mistaking his confused displeasure or the surprise on Raine's face.

Yep! He was definitely furious. Well, Inez reasoned, it was his fault for assuming an older woman needed the cabin. Still, a twinge of guilt nagged at her conscience for not coming clean with him. "This is Raine, Cora, and this little sweetie-pie," she patted Katy's arm, "is Katy. This is Jess Harper, a really nice guy, and he owns the place."

Katy's angelic smile just melted Jess's heart. Kids were his Achilles heel. Returning her smile, he acknowledged Cora, but when he looked at Raine again he was shocked. She'd pushed the sunglasses atop her head revealing her battered face and eyes that were darkly ringed like a raccoon. His anger returned as he stared. He knew it was rude, but didn't give a damn. No way in hell did he need this kind of trouble! He wanted to ignore the smooth hand with the pearly pink polished nails extended toward him but good manners kept him from doing it. When his fingers closed round hers his attitude immediately mellowed and his attention focused entirely on her—for a moment.

As for Raine, she wasn't sure which curled faster—her hair or her toes when he gripped her hand. Inez had purposely given the wrong impression of the man. That woman was proving mighty sneaky. Jess Harper was more than she had expected—far more. Not that she was looking for a firecracker-hot man, or any man. Addison had done quite a number on her in that department. Still, she could look her fill, just not touch. Surely, that couldn't hurt?

"Ms . . ." The whiskey-timbered voice held a caressing tingle but the heart-stopping smile he'd bestowed on Katy was gone, replaced by a forbidding scowl but there was no denying the undercurrents of attraction flowing between them, and given the ruddiness beneath the tan of his chiseled face, he felt them, too.

"Andrews," she completed huskily, her hand growing steamy in his grip. Actually, she was so steamy-hot she needed a fan to cool herself down. Forget the fan! She needed an icy shower. "Raine Andrews," she added.

The huskiness in her voice sent another sensation of heat racing through Jess, setting his pulse to racing harder and his hormones kicking in, which was stupid since he'd just laid eyes on her. However, if he didn't get himself under control he'd be embarrassing himself and that was not happening. And he'd changed his mind. He wanted them gone. His eyes took on an insolent gleam. Maybe acting a lecher would send her high-tailing it out of there.

But, Raine caught on quickly and decided two could play the conceited jerk's game. Whatever he dished out, she could, too. She wasn't about to cow-tow to another man. As the saying goes—she'd been there, done that. And that sly Inez! She'd purposely planted the old-codger misconception in her head! Raine shot her an accusing look. Grinning, Inez shrugged.

Turning blue eyes on Jess, the man most definitely wasn't the rickety old hermit she'd envisioned. Instead he was much younger and built like one of the solid oaks shading his front yard, tall and strong, able to bend but never break. Jess Harper was every romance writer's inspiration—Tall, Dark, and Handsome. Yes indeed, he'd make any heroine lust after him. She certainly was! Another wash of heat tickled the secret parts of her body. It surprised, and pleased her, for she'd had no feelings of desire in a very long time. Well the gorgeous hunk had certainly perked up something she'd thought dead forever. No way was she leaving.

"We appreciate your hospitality." He didn't respond, just stared harder as though trying to read something written in very small letters on her forehead. Okay . . . now he was really starting to tick her off but she masked her irritation returning his stare with a smile. And the antagonizing glare still didn't change. Obviously, Inez hadn't told him the whole truth. Fine! On second thought, he could keep his precious cabin! She refused to beg! Back to the cottage it was!

Hitching Katy higher, Raine grimaced. She'd be so glad when completely healed. Unfortunately, according to the doctor, that would be a long time.

Seeing the grimace, his face became a thundercloud. He turned killing eyes on Inez. It was a good thing those nasty looks he was shooting her weren't bullets or she'd be dead, Raine thought, yet she felt no fear of him.

"I want a word with you. Alone." His tone was clipped. Ignoring the sparks of battle in Inez's narrowed eyes; he turned on a dime striding toward the sprawling cabin and leaving her to follow. Inez gave Raine a perplexed look and then followed after him.

Though they couldn't hear the heated exchange, it was quite obvious Jess Harper didn't appreciate being fooled. Raine couldn't tell who was the angriest, but considering the rigid lines of his body and scowling face, he might be the winner. Then again, Inez reminded her of an agitated chicken flapping her wings and pacing back and forth. Every once in a while she'd get in his face, a move he didn't like one bit. It didn't look good. She nodded at Cora to get back in the SUV.

Jess towered over Inez, his large hands planted firmly on his hips. "I. Don't. Want. Them. Here!" He gritted, bluntly enunciating each word to get his point across.

"And. Just. Why. Not?" Inez jerked her head back and forth, enunciating each word back at him. "They need a place to stay; you have plenty of empty cabins. They've been driving for weeks and that little one needs some space to run and play."

"Then they can damn well turn around and go back where they came from. According to the tags I believe that's someplace in Arizona. If they hurry they might even make it before the first snow falls." Jess shot back belligerently. Inez tried to interrupt but he rolled over her. "You deliberately led me to believe an older woman needed a place. I don't need some sweet young thing cluttering up my space. She won't be here more than ten minutes before she's finding some stupid excuse to bother me."

"I did no such thing!" She harrumphed, sticking a stern finger in his face nearly clipping his nose. "You just assumed it, so don't blame me. What's the old saying—when you ass-ume something it makes an ass of you and me? Well right now you're the ass, not me." He wanted to shove the finger she was shaking at him out of his face. "You should be ashamed of yourself!"

Now she was poking that evil finger in his chest. "You've only just met her! How can you make a stupid assumption like that? Your problem is you're already attracted to that sweet young thing and you'll be the one who can't stay away from her." A gnarly growling came out of him.

"Have you taken a real good look at her?" She demanded, wanting to kick the living daylights out of him. "She's still sporting the handiwork of a husband who beat the tar out of her. And let me tell you, it's not a pretty story and I'm sure there's a heck of a lot more to it than what I managed to get out of her. Trust me, if it'd been me I'd have shot him dead and dumped the sucker in the deepest pond around. But again, it's not my place to tell you anything. If she wants you to know, she'll tell you. That is, if you'll quit being a stubborn jackass and let them stay." Jess opened his mouth but Inez wasn't through. "And what does age have to do with anything? So she's young, probably a beauty when she's not all black and blue. But does that make her need our help any less? I don't think so!" The slamming of a door made Inez whirl around to find them back in the SUV. "Hey! Wait a minute!" She yelled, sprinting back across the yard at the same time yelling at Jess, "Get yourself down here!" Darn it! This was not going at all the way she'd planned.

Jess obeyed the barking command, his temper rising higher as he went. He wasn't used to taking orders and it rankled him.

"It's okay, Ms. McCullin," Raine said when a breathless Inez reached them. "We don't stay where we're not wanted, and obviously Mr. Harper doesn't want us here." Reproach flashed from purple-ringed eyes. "We'll find someplace else."

"Now you wait just a minute!" Inez ordered but Raine wasn't waiting another second. Hurriedly, as if the devil, or Addison, were chasing her, she started the engine just as Jess reached them. He laid a staying hand on the door.

"Wait a minute. Just wait a minute. If you really want to stay then fine, the cabin's yours. I'd already prepared it so you might as well stay." He sounded as gracious as a cat with its tail caught under a rocking chair runner and it got her dander up.

"Thanks for the gracious offer, Mr. Harper, but no thanks. We're not welcome so we'll go." She sounded just as snarky and had the satisfaction of seeing his face turn ruddy at her dig.

Foot on the brake, she put the SUV in reverse then gave a parting shot. "And you're nothing but a crabby old hermit!"

"Young lady, don't you dare go anywhere! Don't move another muscle!" Raine wasn't sure why she obeyed but she put the SUV back in Park and listened with pure enjoyment as Inez lit into him.

"Now look what you've done, you pig-headed idiot!" And that's why she'd obeyed, and snickered. "You've offended these nice ladies all because you don't want any trouble. Well hells-bells, everybody has troubles of some kind and if we don't help each other then I don't know what this world's coming to. Now you mind your manners! Tell her you're sorry!" Inez huffed, hands on her hips.

Cora, thoroughly enjoying the show, laughed heartily. Inez's maneuvering skills were spot-on; she had them right where she wanted them. Having picked up on the instant snap of attraction between them, it was plain as the nose on her face she'd get her way.

Studying Jess through the windshield, Cora thought it too bad things were such a mess with Raine right now for instincts said he could be the right one and she always went with her first instincts. They hadn't been wrong yet.

Furious, he thought his head would explode. What this 'old hermit' wanted was kick them the hell off his property. And it really burned him that Inez was right about his attraction to the pretty blond but he sure as hell wasn't admitting it or she'd be shoving him down the marriage aisle before sunset.

"And you get out of there," Inez pointed that stern finger at Raine. Cora chuckled, earning herself another killer glare even as Raine obeyed Inez's command. The breeze lifted strands of her hair as she stood face-to-face with Mr. Cranky-Pants, for that's what she'd nick-named him. His expression a mixture of held-in-check anger and exasperation, his eyes burned with something else, flaming desire. Her insides glowed warm and tingly with sensations she hadn't felt in a long time. "Now the two of you get together. Let's get this deal done. I don't have all day!" Inez snapped out the order.

Sheesh! Inez should have been a general, Raine thought; having no idea her thoughts ran parallel to Jess's. Behind the protection of the sunglasses she detected he didn't like being ordered about, either. A wave of satisfaction swept through her, her lips twitched. Good!

Jess caught the smirk. She's laughing at him! Brown eyes narrowing, they trailed rakishly down her body.

Seeing it, for a nanosecond she had the overwhelming urge to knock that smirking grin off his good-looking face, then she mentally head-slapped herself. "Quit acting like an idiot."

Reading her mind, he grinned broader, daring her to do it. Fed up with his attitude she slid her sunglasses up to meet the irascible man eye-to-eye. "Okay. We'll take it."

The devilment in her eyes increased his irritation. She was thoroughly enjoying his being put on the spot! "Just remember, I won't tolerate any trouble and I don't want to be bothered. I like my space and I intend to keep it that way!"

"Not a problem, Mr. Harper, you won't even know we're around. I'll get my check book and give you the rent right now." She stepped toward the SUV then turned back, her blue eyes flashing another challenge. "That is, if you trust me enough to take a check, me being a stranger and all."

Jess accepted the challenge. "Since Inez trusts you, I'll trust her instincts. I'll take your check but perhaps you should see the cabin first. You might change your mind; decide you'd rather not stay after all." He lobbed his own challenge out, hoping to keep her from staying.

"That's okay. I'm sure it'll be just fine. We'll take it sight unseen." No way was she backing down in this battle of wills. That cabin was theirs come-hell-or-high-water and she didn't care if it only had two walls and a leaky roof. As much as he didn't want them there, the more she was determined to stay.

"Good. Good." Inez relished the battle of wills between Jess and the pretty, petite blond. Her gray eyes twinkled mischievously. Oh yes! Her matchmaking skills were still in top working order. The second she'd learned they were looking for a place to stay she'd thought of Jess. It was going to be fun watching them go toe-to-toe with each other. "I'm glad you two "finally came to an agreement." It earned her a glare from Jess and another smirk from Raine.

The scowl remained as he watched her walk back to the SUV. Stubborn woman, he thought while enjoying the enticing sway of her jean-clad hips. He glanced at Inez to see her grinning. Though she remained silent, her knowing look said she knew where his mind was.

"You might as well drive up to the cabin," he called out. "Go through the gate and stop at the first one." Following the direction he pointed, she saw the electronic gate blocking the entrance. Looking further up, she looked for the cabin but the colorful foliage hid it.

"Well, that was certainly interesting," Cora remarked. "Are you sure we should stay here? Mr. Harper doesn't seem too happy about us being here. He's not very receptive to having his space invaded by a bunch of females."

Raine burst out laughing. "Yeah, I know. I love it."

"You are a devil!" Cora said. "But I think we should stay, especially since it's off the beaten path."

"That's a huge plus," she glanced in the rear-view mirror, returning Katy's sweet smile. "If-you-know-who's looking for us, he won't look here. The opinion is I'm too snooty for the country, or so I've been told." Addison was so wrong. "And as far as Mr. Harper's attitude, Inez is the true culprit, rearranging some facts, or should I say, leading him to believe it was you, not me, needing a place to stay, so I really can't blame him for being upset. After all, she let us think he was some smelly old man." She backed out of the drive. "And," sarcasm laced her voice, "in case you missed it with all you're cackling, it's not a bunch of females but one in particular he doesn't want. Me. That's what put the burr under his saddle." Then she laughed again. "He sure isn't a happy camper, is he? Though I can't imagine why the age would make a difference."

"Who are you kidding? That woman knew exactly what she was doing, pretty young woman—handsome young man—a great recipe for romance. She's got a conniving heart all right and you struck a chord in her. She wanted to help and knew exactly how to get her way. Once we were here he couldn't refuse. He tried squirming out of it but she had him hooked and reeled him in like a big ole catfish. There was no way he could disagree with her scheme."

"Oh God, you're right," she laughed again. "It was sheer enjoyment watching her work him. Jess Harper was ready to explode but he never lost his temper," she observed, "and I never once thought he'd turn violent." Jess Harper had been put on the spot, and despite Inez's machinations, had stayed in complete control. She didn't know him from Adam but he had her respect on that level.

"It's reassuring you don't think all men are like A . . ." Cora stopped just in the nick of time from saying Addison's name.

"Oh Cora, I know all men aren't like him. There are more good men in the world than bad. I just had the bad luck to find one that kept his spots covered until the ring was on my finger. I was all starry-eyed in love and blind to all the signs. Now I'm just not sure that I'll ever trust myself again to know if or when the right man comes along."

Anger kindled inside Cora. Raine's self-confidence had taken a beating right along with the rest of her. "Need I remind you things could've turned out a whole lot worse? Stop blaming yourself! It's not your fault! He hid his dirty deeds and nasty little habits for a long time. Count your blessings you came out alive."

"Oh, believe me, I do. But as far as men, I'm not sure I'll ever want to take a chance on another one." This wasn't the first time she'd voiced her doubts. They crept into every conversation involving Addison. Raine was too hard on herself for not seeing the signs early on and by the time she had, it was way too late. Every time she poured her heart out Cora wanted to mete out her own form of justice. Cora also harbored guilt for not picking up on the girl's troubles she'd hidden so well. Now all she could do was listen. As for trusting her judgment—that was something Raine had to work through on her own.

Pulling through the electronic gate, they stopped at the first cabin and it was love at first sight. Nestled beneath a canopy of colorful maple trees, it was right out of one of those old western movies she loved. The only thing missing—a horse tethered to the rail. In her estimation, there was nothing better than a good John Wayne western. Fate had surely brought her here.

Jess and Inez stood on the porch of the cabin. Mad and not speaking, their eyes threw daggers at each other. From the tinted interior Raine drank her fill of the handsome man. My, oh my, but he was gorgeous enough to eat! Her heart fluttered in agreement. Then she gave herself another mental slap. Stop it! Stop it, you idiot! You don't need his kind of trouble and he certainly made no bones how he feels about you.

In the cabin, Katy instantly started roaming around, her sighs of appreciation resonating from each room. Hearing her, Jess smiled and Raine added another point in his favor—he had a fondness for children.

Katy wasn't the only one impressed. The second Raine stepped inside she knew she was home. The living room and kitchen were combined and a floor to ceiling stone fireplace took up the entire wall at one end of the room. All it needed was a cheery fire blazing in it and she'd never want to leave. Aged hardwood floors were covered with earth-toned braided rugs and arranged in front of the fireplace were a rocking chair, a sofa, and a recliner. Running her hand over the brown leather sofa, she found it buttery soft.

Flinty-eyed, Jess trailed Raine's movements. When her fingers skimmed over the soft leather of the sofa a tingling skimmed through him wondering how it would feel to have her touching him that way, her caresses feather-light on his body.

He jerked as though stabbed by a live wire. Jesus! Get a grip before you embarrass yourself!

There were three fully furnished bedrooms and the most beautiful quilts she'd ever seen topped the beds. Given their intricate designs, she figured them handmade. The rooms had flat-screen televisions, DVD players, and off each was a small but well-equipped bath. And she already had plans for the third bedroom. Since Katy slept with her, it'd make a perfect office. All it needed was a desk and chair and she'd be set.

"Mommy! Mommy! A f'ing set. Can I f'ing? Please Mommy, please, please!" Before she could utter a word, Katy was dragging her out the door to the swing-set. "Push me, Mommy. Push me really high."

Cora nudged her aside. "Go finish your business. I'll handle Katy-bug."

Watching Katy, Jess smiled again but it disappeared when Raine moved toward him. The man's cranky attitude rubbed her the wrong way so much that she deliberately walked a very slow gait toward him. Cora and Inez watched, loving the snap of abrasiveness between them and shared a conspiratorial grin.

Jess swore a wooly worm could have won a foot race against her. And she was doing it on purpose! The woman pushed him to the edge and she hadn't even moved in yet! When he spoke it was to the point of rude. "Well, do you still want the place? Or wouldn't you rather be in the city, not in the sticks and off the beaten path. You know, something more suitable to what you're used to." For his peace of mind he hoped it was too far off the beaten path; if Raine Andrews stayed his world would never be the same again.

Her chin shot up and her eyes glittered as she snapped. "What I'm used to? Mr. Harper, you're jumping to conclusions. You've no idea what I'm used to! Actually, this lovely cabin will suit us just fine. We'll take it."

Animosity hung so thick a chainsaw couldn't have cut it, yet in spite of everything, waves of attraction washed through him as he gazed at the cascading blond hair shimmering in ripples down her back. He was sorely tempted to thread his fingers through it to see if it felt as silky soft as it looked but good common sense stopped him. Snippy as she was, she might bite him. Abruptly, he stepped inside the cabin, leaving her to follow.

The man was so infuriating she couldn't help it; she stuck her tongue out and crossed her eyes at the broad back he presented her. And that childish action broke Cora's self-control. She burst out laughing. "Ms. McCullin, I've got to hand it to you. You were a pro at reading those two. They're knockings sparks off each other and they've only been together half-an-hour. I wonder how long before there's a squabble."

"It's Inez, and I believe they're in the middle of one right now. That girl's got a lot of spunk left in her even after what's she's been through. I'm betting she'll be making him start losing sleep tonight."

Inside the cabin the male object of their conversation sat astraddle a kitchen chair, his muscled arms across the back. Still standing, Raine tested him. "How much a month did you have in mind?"

"Four hundred, utilities included." Jess replied; half-wishing he'd doubled the price to keep her from staying.

It was the same amount Inez had quoted. Jess Harper seemed a man of his word. "That sounds fair enough." Heaven knew it was cheap enough. She eased into the chair across from him, took out her checkbook and quickly calculating the months, wrote out the check. When he took it their fingers touched and sparks flew.

Jess ignored them. No way would she know how crazy she was driving his libido! Now if that certain part of his anatomy a little further south would behave, he could get through the next little while with no one the wiser. Not bothering to look at the check, he folded it in half with still tingling fingers and tucked it in his shirt pocket.

Raine bit her lip to keep from smirking. She'd give her right arm to see his face when he realized he was stuck with them until spring. Had he looked at the check right then he'd have kicked them off the property without a second thought. Planning to pay by the month, his cranky-pants attitude irked her so much she decided to pay through March and Mr. Cranky-Pants Harper could deal with it. But more important, when the holidays arrived they'd be settled in and able to enjoy them. Maybe they would have their white Christmas after all.

The holidays...for the first time in a very long time she looked forward to celebrating them. Gazing at the picture window she envisioned a beautiful tree aglow with twinkling lights and shining ornaments and beneath it wrapped gifts. With a fire blazing and the holiday scents permeating the air it would be perfect.

Obviously not getting rid of them, Jess gave up the battle and took a key ring from his pocket. "These are the cabin keys and this is the remote to the gate. You'll need it to get in and out."

"You don't believe in taking chances, do you?" The added security was great but nothing was infallible if someone was determined to get in.

"I learned a long time ago to be aware of the surroundings and what's going on. The gate and fence are to keep people from trespassing. Most of the time it works, but once in a while someone tests it"

Suspecting brown eyes met narrowed blue eyes. "Do you have any enemies trying to get in?"

"No. How about you? Any enemies I should know about?" He challenged. Would she answer honestly?

Raine hesitated. Should she mention Addison? No. Let sleeping dogs stay locked up. She looked him straight in the eye. "Not a one."

She's lying! It was in her eyes. She had a deadly enemy—her husband. Jess opened his mouth to call her out but Inez chose that moment to appear announcing she had to get home to make cookies for the grandkids. Jess glowered but followed her and Raine outside.

Raine hugged Inez. "Thank you for everything. We must have been destined to meet you today."

"No thanks needed. I was glad to help. Now you'd better head back for your things if you're planning on coming back here tonight. Where are you staying, anyway?" Raine gave the location and what the cottages looked like. "I know the place. We pass it going to Branson. I've always thought it a neat little place. This time of year the tourists slack off but in the summer they look full. And being so close to the state park and the Jesse James Hideout makes it a natural for families to want to stay there."

Jess also knew the place. It was at least fifty miles as the crow flies. Following an Interstate was one thing, taking the back roads another. Admiration filled him and though he couldn't explain it, he was glad she wasn't traveling alone.

Hearing a sniff, Raine turned, catching Katy's intentions. "Katy Andrews, don't you dare wipe your nose on your coat!" The combination of brisk temperatures and the exertion of swinging caused the little button nose to run. She pulled a tissue out of her pocket.

"It's `not, Mommy," Katy said while trying to wiggle out of her hold. From baby on, she'd hated having her nose wiped. No matter, as soon as she was done Katy ran her nose down the sleeve of her coat, anyway.

"I know what it is." Embarrassed heat flushed her cheeks. There were times she wanted to Velcro shut her free-speaking daughter's mouth, this being one of them.

Jess tried not to laugh but a chuckle slipped out anyway. It earned him a glare from a pair of striking blue eyes and the shock to his system was like a bolt of lightning, it went all through him. Better tread carefully, my man, or you'll find yourself ensnared in her silken web. And from the bright spots on her cheeks she felt the connection, too. Another tingle raced up his spine. This woman was trouble with a capital T and on that thought he abruptly stalked away.

Inez glowered at his rudeness then followed behind him. Glee filled her, anyway. It was going to be totally awesome watching Jess Harper dance to Raine Andrews' tune. Oh, he'd walk barefoot through a nest of fire ants before admitting to already being smitten, but she knew better.

Inez wasn't the only one thinking the man ruder than a prickly desert cactus. Raine was of the same opinion but as she watched his retreating back it was comforting knowing Mr. Cranky-Pants would be close by. However, not being a helpless female, she wasn't running to him for anything.

Chapter Twelve

Raine swore she was standing center stage of good fortune, surrounded by guardian angels in Cora and Inez McCullin. She had her precious Katy, a cozy out of the way place to live, toss in Addison being in jail—life was good. And, a little voice chimed in, don't forget Jess Harper. Okay, life was getting better and better.

However, a new problem surfaced while returning to the cottages. Discussing how much fun it was going to be decorating the cabin and putting up a Christmas tree, Katy went from loudly singing "Jingle Bells" to eventual silence. In the rear-view mirror Raine saw her fighting tears but her quivering bottom lip gave her away.

"Hey, baby girl, what's wrong? Don't you feel good?" Katy was never sick. Was she coming down with something?

Katy puckered up. "No. I'm sad cause Santa won't find me in 'dem' woods and I really, really want that dollhouse in the toy book." A heart-wrenching sob tore from her and tears rolled in twin salty trails down her cheeks.

Thinking fast, Raine had a solution. "I've already thought about that, pumpkin. Tomorrow we'll write Santa a letter telling him where you are and that you really want that dollhouse more than anything else in the world. He's still at the North Pole so he'll have plenty of time to get your letter and make your dollhouse. How does that sound?"

Katy liked Mommy's idea. Mommy could fix everything. She had the bestest Mommy in the whole wide world. "Are you sure he can find me in all 'dem' woods and not get lost?"

"Katy-bug, I guarantee Santa will find you. And Santa doesn't get lost," she said with authority. "His reindeer have built-in radar so no little bit of woods will keep him from finding you. Plus, you've been a very, very good girl this year. Of course he'll bring you your dollhouse, cross my heart," she said then did it.

Relief brought on a watery smile. If Mommy crossed her heart then it was true. "Okay, then I want to stay in 'dem' woods. I like all the pretty w'eaves and I really like the f'ing set," then her cheeks turned a rosy pink, "and I really like Mr. Jess."

Astonishment filled her. Oh Lord, Katy had just discovered the opposite sex and heaven forbid, her first crush had to be on the man who'd made no bones about being left alone. Well, given Katy's crush he could toss that idea right out the window.

"Then it's settled. We'll live in the pretty cabin with the swing-set." Raine was filled with glee imagining Mr. Cranky-Pants Harper dealing with the monster crush Katy had on him.

Happy again, Katy started singing "Rudolph the Red Nose Reindeer" while Raine damned Addison to hell for the upheaval in her life. It was his fault she'd been uprooted from everything safe and familiar. She hoped he would stay locked up forever.

They were nearing the cottages when Katy became silent again. Peering in the rear-view mirror, though she appeared deep in thought, Raine knew that look; her precocious child was cooking something up. Whatever it was, she'd find out in due time.

But Katy wasn't cooking up anything. She was thinking about Daddy. She hoped he didn't come for Christmas.

Packing and checking out didn't take long; then they headed back to the cabin. Stopping for dinner, it was long past dark when they pulled through the gate. The later it'd become the more concerned Jess became that something had happened. Then he heard a car. On the monitor before him he watched the SUV drive through the gate and as relief swamped him he became aggravated that he'd been worried about them. Hadn't they been traveling on their own for a while?

Admit it buddy, a little voice chided, that hot little blond has got your shorts in a wad. Jess tipped an imaginary hat to her. She'd certainly pulled a fast one on him. When he'd finally looked at the check his eyes had nearly popped out of his head seeing she'd paid six months in advanced. One crafty little gal, she'd definitely one-upped him. Now he was stuck with them longer than he wanted so he'd just have to suck it up. For damn sure he was none too happy being forced into this situation so maybe it was just as well she'd paid in advanced. This way they could stay out of each other's hair. Yeah, right, the little voice scoffed, that's just one more stupid idea you've had since she arrived on the property.

In the following days Jess got his wish, not that it made him happy, either. He caught glimpses of Raine coming and going but she never came near him. And that aggravated him, too. Being left alone had been his idea but he'd changed his mind. Now he wanted to get to know the pretty blond in every way possible and he planned to do something about it.

As for Raine, the quiet solitude proved a soothing balm to her tormented mind. On long walks through the brisk fresh air she pondered the months of abuse that ended with Addison's shooting. Never once in her whole life had she ever imagined finding herself in that kind of situation. Perhaps if she'd left sooner she might have escaped that last horrible night. But then Addison wouldn't be locked up. Fate had dealt this hand so she'd play it, using the time to heal, regroup, and plan for the future. She couldn't continue the nomadic existence forever but the idea of returning to Phoenix sounded awful. There had to be some-place to start anew. A little voice said this was it.

A few days later she and Cora were sitting at the picnic table enjoying the warmth of the fall sunshine and she shared her feelings. "I can't explain it but this place makes me feel safe and not so worried about you-know-who. Of course, that might be because he's still locked up."

"Could be," Cora, swiped at a pesky gnat flitting around her face, "but being here's doing you a world of good." Cora credited part of the medicine to that lanky, handsome man they were renting from. She might deny it but Raine was highly attracted to him, maybe even falling for him. And Jess Harper might say he wanted to be left alone but the man always had an excuse to show up.

Watching Katy, she seemed happy as a kitten with a ball of yarn. "She's settled in, too."

Raine nodded. "Once convinced Santa would find her she's been just fine and it's been a while since she asked about Addison."

Katy was running around the yard catching leaves that were floating down from the trees. "Can we make a turkey picture, Mommy," referring to making pictures of turkeys using the outline of her hand as the body and the red and oranges leaves for feathers. Several of her masterpieces hung on their refrigerator. Inez had one, and of course, so did Mr. Jess. And a few days ago Katy had discovered every little girl's favorite pastime—making mud pies and that's when Raine found herself in a muddy-pie-pickle.

Katy had been making her pies when her blue eyes suddenly lit up and scooping dirt in a tin pie-pan, announced. "I made Mr. Jess a pie, Mommy. See? I call it choc'lit mud pie. He'll love it." Intent on her mission, Katy dashed down the stone path.

"Wait! Katy-bug, that's not the kind of pie you eat. Mr. Jess won't like it." Then again, the cranky man deserved to eat a bit of dirt for his snarky attitude. In the weeks they'd been there he was always friendly to Katy and Cora, with her—not so much. "On second thought," she muttered under her breath, or so she thought, "Mr. Cranky-Pants deserves to eat a little dirt."

Jess had been replacing a rotten board on the fence when he heard his name being called, "Mr. Jess! Mr. Jess!" Hooking the hammer over the top board, he watched Katy barrel down the hill toward him, but it was Raine trailing after her that he couldn't tear his eyes away from. She wore jeans that molded to her thighs like a second skin and a burgundy sweat-shirt. Nothing he hadn't seen on other women but on her it was totally sexy. Her hair caught the sun's rays turning it into a mass of spun gold. Battered face and all, she was sexy as hell and that familiar curl of desire came to life inside him. It happened every time he caught a glimpse of her which meant he was pretty much smoking hot all the time. Frustration put a dark scowl on his face when he locked eyes with her.

Mistaking the scowl for annoyance, it fueled her ire. Now she really wanted Mr. Cranky-Pants to eat the dirt pie. She'd planned on saving his ornery hide, but now? Not so much.

Katy eagerly held out the tin pie-pan. "Mr. Jess, I made a pie for you. You can eat it now if you want."

Swallowing hard, Jess eyed the pan of dirt, his stomach going queasy. Should he be grateful that a lot had bounced out in her headlong rush down the hill? Help! How in the hell was he to refuse the dirt pie and not hurt the little cutie's feelings? He'd tasted dirt before. It was gritty and mealy nasty stuff. Pasting a smile of gratitude on his face, he hunkered down to her level. "Why thank you, Katy. I've never had a mud pie before."

"You have to eat it, Mr. Jess. I made it just for you." She smiled adoringly at him.

Drawing closer, Raine watched him eyeing the dirt pie with the grimmest expression. She could have spared him but that fierce scowl came to mind again.

"Yes, Mr. Jess, she made it especially for you." Raine tongued her cheek to keep from laughing but a sarcastic little snicker slid out, anyway.

Hearing it, he caught on real quick. She was enjoying his predicament. He'd even bet she'd instigated the whole dirt-pie-eating and figured a bit of retribution was called for.

"Tell you what, Katy-bug. I just had lunch so I'm not hungry right now but I'll have some later and Mommy can have some, too." He looked up at Raine with feigned innocence.

And that's when another Velcro moment occurred. "That's okay Mr. Jess, Mommy doesn't eat dirt but she said you should. I heard her. She said Mr. Cranky-Pants should eat dirt."

Raine flushed guiltily as the wheels of the gigantic bus Katy had tossed her under rolled over her. No self-defending words came out. Instead, she looked like the proverbial deer in the headlights, wide-eyed and frozen in place.

The calculating gleam in his dark his eyes didn't scare her. It intrigued her, made her heart skitter wildly in her breast as rising to his full six-foot-four height, Jess slowly closed the distance between them. Frozen in place, she couldn't have run if a herd of buffalo stampeded directly at her. Excitement rippled up her spine when he stopped in front of her.

"Is that so?" His voice was a low drawl. "So, Mommy thinks I'm cranky and should eat dirt, huh?" Retribution hung heavy on every word, sending a tingle through her. He wondered how far down the blush staining her cheeks traveled and wanted to find out.

Katy opened her mouth but Raine jumped in ahead of her, not wanting the bus backing over her. "Mommy was just teasing, sweetie. We don't really want Mr. Jess to eat dirt." Some-day she'd learn to keep her wayward mouth shut when Katy was around. Her guilty gaze dropped to the tips of his work-worn cowboy boots before looking up at him. She had a piece offering in mind. "Maybe we can bake a real pie for Mr. Jess?"

And Jess did an imaginary fist-pump. Score one for him! "Sounds great to me," he answered quickly, gloating that he'd bested her. "I like apple pie—with lots of sugar and cinnamon."

"Okay, Mr. Jess, we'll bake you an apple pie." Katy bestowed a love-struck smile on him making Raine roll her eyes. She sure had it bad for him. So have you, spoke the little voice in her head, the heat coursing through her signaled it was time to get out of Dodge.

"Thanks squirt, I'll be waiting on my pie." He tugged her pig-tail but his gaze was fastened on Raine's mouth. "My mouth's watering just thinking about it." He'd bet she'd taste sweeter than any apple pie.

Blushing at the hidden innuendo, she grabbed Katy's hand. "We'd better let Mr. Jess get back to work."

All the way up the hill she felt his eyes on her. Darn him! He'd neatly turned the tables on her and because of her stinker-daughter's big mouth she had to bake him a pie, and she'd been doing so well avoiding the prickly man, which was nearly impossible considering he was always outside or stopping by to see if they needed anything. For a man who wanted left alone he seemed to be at their door a lot.

Mr. Cranky-Pants may have been a prickly thorn in her side but the monster in her life remained locked up. According to Gordon, Addison was impatiently stewing in jail and one irate S.O.B. Gleaning details of the latest jailhouse meeting, she could have scripted every word. Addison had already blown one gasket when served divorce papers. This meeting had been about the property disbursement and custody terms. His fury was bound-less and his rants and threats had been recorded by Gordon.

"I may not be able to use it in court but God forbid some-thing happen to you, we'll have the threats straight from the horse's mouth." Then he played the tape. Hearing Addison's voice made the hair on her neck stand straight up.

"I'm not signing a damned thing! I'll see the bitch dead before I split anything with her.

You tell her she'd better be looking over her shoulder all the time! You tell her no matter where she goes I will hunt her down and make her wish she were dead."

Gordon's angry growl filled the air. "Watch it, Addison; you're in no position to make threats!"

"You watch it!" Addison snarled back and she imagined the hate gushing from his eyes like black oil from a geyser, his burly fists clenching and unclenching. "I never did like you, you bastard!"

As for Gordon, she picked up on his goading Addison to taking a swing at him, wanting a reason to pound him into the ground. But then Gordon changed tactics. To get Addison to see things his way, with casual deliberation he mentioned certain shady dealings and how delighted she'd be testifying against him.

Addison finally relented, albeit with more threats. "You do realize one of these days I'm getting out of here and when I do you and that crazy bitch better watch out! I'm coming after both of you and if anyone gets in my way it'll be too damned bad."

"Good God, Addison!" His attorney roared in the background. "We're trying to get you out of here! Keep making stupid threats like that and the judge will damn sure throw away the key with you on this side of the bars. Control yourself!"

"Are you threatening my family?" Gordon's feral growl rose higher and higher as he shouted. "Because if so; I'm the wrong one to mess with. You think you've got problems now, you get anywhere near my family and the tax payers won't have to worry about paying your room and board. You got that!"

"Yeah, yeah, you just tell that bitch this isn't over by a long shot!" A fist pounding the metal table echoed round the room.

"You're wrong, Addison. It is over. And if you were a smart man you'd plead out, accept your punishment and move on." Contempt laced every word.

Enraged, Addison stood his ground. "Move on? The bitch shot me! She should be the one in this stinking hell-hole!"

"The evidence shows otherwise so why not save everybody a lot of trouble and do the right thing?" Then Gordon changed back to the nonchalant route. "You do know Raine's against any plea-bargain. She'd rather air all your dirty laundry and see you rot in hell where you belong."

"You don't have any evidence on me. I handle that gun all the time."

"And there's your admission of guilt, counselor. Raine's prints weren't on the gun." She heard the gloating in Gordon's voice.

"You go to hell and take that bitch with you!" Addison roared.

Oh, I'm sure I'll go to hell, but I'll see you there, too, that's a promise you can take to the bank. "Oh," he snapped his fingers, "speaking of bank, money, I'm sure the IRS could be enticed into an investigation. With the right tip, there's no telling what all they'd find."

Raine imagined the thunderous look on Addison's face knowing exactly what Gordon was referring to. She heard the rustle of papers then the fierce scratching of the pen as Addison angrily scribbled his name on them.

To Addison's attorney she heard Gordon say, "You'd be wise to get shot of this scum-bag before he drags you down with him." But it was Gordon's parting words to Addison that stayed with her long into the night. "Just tell me one thing, Addison. What happened to turn you the way you are? You had a beautiful wife who loved you until you started batting her around. There's a sweet little girl who's going to hate you when she grows up for what you've done. I hope to hell the drugs and alcohol were worth destroying your family. I hope it was worth going to jail for."

CHAPTER THIRTEEN

A frosty crispness clung to the evening shadows as the girls put the finishing touches to Katy's Halloween costume. From the get-go she'd insisted on being a scarecrow just like the one in Ms. Inez's garden and thanks to some treasured finds at local thrift stores she looked one hundred percent scarecrow. Even Mr. Cranky-Pants got in on the act supplying straw to stuff her with. She looked so darned cute, Raine snapped picture after picture of her. They were headed to Inez's to go trick-or-treating with her grandkids. Not knowing the safest places in the area, she'd asked Inez where to take Katy and had been invited to go with them.

Katy hopped impatiently from one foot to the other. "Come on, Mommy! We've got to trick Mr. Jess! I bet he's got candy for me." She darted off at a dead run down the path, in her wake was a trail of straw. Raine followed her runaway scarecrow down the path, calling for her to wait for her. Before Raine was halfway down the path Katy was knocking on Jess's back door.

In his office, Jess was concentrating on the details of the newest security system he was designing when it finally dawned on him someone was knocking at the back door. At a crucial point, he damned the interruption. Who the hell . . . Never mind, he sighed irritably, the only people around were the trio of females up the hill. He didn't want the intrusion but the persistent person wasn't going away.

Scowling, he strode to the back door. Jerking it open he saw Raine hurrying down the path and opened his mouth to chew her out when a child's voice trilled out. "Trick-or-treat!"

His mouth snapped shut but the mesmerizing vision coming toward him, silken hair flowing behind her like spun gold, held him spellbound. An intense hunger filled him that had nothing to do with food. Reluctantly, he dropped his gaze to the miniature scarecrow sporting painted freckles, straw-hat and red wig. And he laughed. The kid was so darned adorable!

"I didn't know scarecrows ate candy." He teased.

Giggling with an unabashed coyness, she said, "Mr. Jess, it's me, Katy!"

Tilting his head, he pretended to critically survey her. "Well, I'll be darned! I didn't recognize you. Gosh! You make a really awesome scarecrow. If I were you I'd be careful. Someone might think you're the real McCoy and put you in their garden." He teased and was rewarded with another giggle. Suddenly her words sank in and his stomach dipped like a chip. Hell! It was Halloween! She was here for candy! An awful thought struck him—did he even have any?

"Oh man! I'm not sure I have any candy. I don't usually get trick-or-treaters out here." At her crestfallen look he shifted into high gear. Think man, before she starts crying. Did he have a couple of chocolate bars left in his stash? "Let me see what I can find. If I have a trick-or-treating scarecrow then I guess I'd better keep that scarecrow happy."

"Katy, Mr. Jess probably doesn't get many trick-or-treaters out here," Raine panted, out of breath, ribs aching as she arrived at her daughter's side. Even from a distance she'd seen the panic on his face and guessed why. "He probably doesn't have any candy."

Katy gave her a "well duh" look like she hadn't a lick of sense. "Oh yes he does, Mommy, he was just going to see."

"She's right. I was. Come on in." Holding the door open, she stepped past and her sweet scent teased his senses, stirring heat through him, tempting him to nibble on her.

Raine, struggling with her own wayward attraction, wanting to latch on to that sexy mouth and drown in his taste. Needing a distraction, she looked around his home. Tastefully and comfortably furnished, totally masculine, definitely a man's home. Being a large man, it was a given he'd have the king-size sofa, recliner and easy chairs in tones of brown and cream. Braided rugs adorned the pine floors. Though secretly pleased finding no female touch, she wondered if he had a girlfriend. Surely a man this attractive had one or two dangling on a string. The idea left a bad taste in her mouth then she reminded herself it was no business of hers if he had a hundred girlfriends. Besides, he was single and she wasn't. Don't go traveling a road going nowhere, even if you wanted it to. Still married, she had no business entertaining ideas like that—but when she was free. . .The firm closing of a cabinet door snapped her to attention. "Good!" She heard him mutter. So, he had been worried about not having any candy. Jess might be grouchy and cranky-pants with her, but not Katy.

"There you go, little Miss Scarecrow." He dropped two candy bars into the goody bag. Astounded, Raine recognized the familiar yellow packaging. Who'd have thought Cranky-Pants Harper liked the same candy bar she did, or had a sweet tooth for that matter.

"What do you say, Katy?" Raine prompted.

"Thank you, Mr. Jess." She blushed prettily.

"You're very welcome." He saw Raine mouth the words "thank you." Up close, he noted the bloody whites of her eyes were clearing up. So were the deep bruises that had covered a good deal of her face when she'd first arrived. His stomach did a sudden swan-dive thinking of the vicious beating she'd endured and the urge to kiss her injuries better was overpowering. His gaze swept over her. She was a knockout all right, and soft and curvy in all the right places. A man would find heaven in her arms . . . then he drew up short, clamping down the yearning. Those kinds of thoughts led to nothing but trouble, especially since he'd changed his mind about getting close to her.

Raine quickly dropped her eyes from the mixture of emotions cluttering his face. Oh yes, she was attracted to him but did he want her as much as she wanted him . . . and that brought her wayward thoughts to a screeching halt. No way was she getting involved with Jess Harper; it would only end in heartbreak. It was time to go.

"Come on, Katy. We're supposed to meet Miss Inez so you can go trick-or-treating. You don't want to be late, do you?" Katy shook her head vigorously, sending bits of straw scattering all over the hardwood floor. Great, Raine sighed, another thing to prolong leaving. "Sorry. If you'll get me a broom, I'll sweep it up."

"No." Just being in the same room was playing hell with his mind, and his body. He needed her gone before he did something stupid, like take her in his arms and kiss her, knowing that if he did he wouldn't stop. "Don't worry about it. I'll clean it up. You better get going before all the candy's gone."

That pushed Katy's alarm button and she started tugging Raine out the door. "Mommy, come on! I don't want the candy to run out!" A quick glance back showed Jess in the doorway, a brooding expression on his face.

The evening was lots of fun and if there was a Halloween Heaven, then Katy was in it. By the time they reached the last house they could have stocked their own candy store. Exhausted and full of sweets, Katy conked out two seconds after being strapped into the car-seat.

The delicious aroma of coffee drew Raine with invisible fingers from the bedroom where she'd tucked Katy in. Bless the woman so much like herself. Cora seemed to know just when it was needed.

"I'd say that was some quick thinking of Mr. Harper. I'm guessing he gave her his stash." Cora handed her a cup.

"I'm thinking you're right." She blew on the steaming coffee before taking a sip. "Mm . . . Mm. This is wonderful. Whoever discovered coffee should be put up for sainthood. Anyway, I'll pick him up some the next time we go to the store."

"You ought to take him some of yours." They didn't fool her for a second. The attraction was thicker than heavy cream and she was of the opinion they needed a big shove in the same direction—towards each other—and she would be happy to do it. From that first abrasive encounter a month ago they walked a wide berth yet they always seemed drawn like magnets to each other.

"Maybe I don't want to share my candy with him!" Raine said tartly, even as excitement rolled through her at the prospect of seeing him.

"You be nice! He gave up his candy so as not to disappoint Katy. Take him some!"

"Okay, fine!" Her chin jutted out as she caved ungraciously. "I'll take him some tomorrow. Heaven knows, with that crush Katy's got on him she'd have been devastated. She thinks he can walk on water!"

"Then go. Take it to him now. He's probably having chocolate withdrawal even as we speak." There was a determined gleam in her eye.

Raine threw her hands up and flounced to the cabinet. "Okay, okay, you win." She gave Cora the evil eye. "And don't think I don't know what you're up to, either. But it's not happening."

Not right now, anyway, she added silently, pulling on her coat and firmly shutting the door on Cora's smug grin. Above her the twinkling stars shimmered like diamonds on a bed of black velvet, a glowing harvest moon lit the way. Her insides went jittery thinking of seeing Jess again. Thankfully, Addison hadn't killed the capacity to feel attraction to another man. In fact, she'd even doubted being able to bear a man's touch on her body. Apparently, she didn't have to worry about that because Jess Harper made her fantasize constantly what it would feel like to have him touching her, making love to her.

Fantasies were wonderful but not for her, not now anyway. She kicked a tuft of grass. The timing sucked. She had to get rid of Addison before ever contemplating another man in her life.

It wouldn't be fair to him, or to her, for that matter. Yet knowing she could entertain thoughts of meeting someone else lifted her spirits. A tiny seed of hope started to sprout inside her. Maybe, while waiting for her divorce to become final, she'd find a way to get past Jess's don't-bother-me-wall. The idea, and the challenge, put a determined gleam in her eye.

Frustrated and chocolate-deprived, Jess was rummaging through cabinets in search of any kind of chocolate to soothe his craving. Giving squirt his last two candy bars had wiped out his supply. Now he was so bad off he was seriously contemplating downing the chocolate syrup straight from the bottle. The slamming of the cabinet door coincided with a knock at the back door. Not hearing a vehicle, it had to be either Raine or Cora. What the hell did they want? He was cranky and craving chocolate almost as much as he craved a taste of that gorgeous little blond. Despite telling her he didn't want to be bothered, he kept changing his mind.

In the porch light yellow hair shimmered. Hallelujah! It was his tormentor and his desire launched into a full-blown flame. Not a blind man, he'd seen the heated looks she gave him. She was attracted to him all right, and this was an opportunity he wasn't about to pass up. Then he froze. On second thought, being near her would lead to nothing but trouble, though married, she was temptation and trouble with a capital T and he could easily succumb.

Better make up your mind, buddy boy, a voice echoed, because right now that little filly twisting your shorts is at the stable door. He could ignore her but that wouldn't work either, she could see him through the window. Heaving a pitiful sigh, he opened the door and every argument vanished. A smile curved his sensual lips and with one whiff of her perfume he was in big time trouble. Then common sense kicked him. This was not the time to get involved. Siding with common sense, he had to get rid of her even if it meant making her mad. Running her cute little behind back up the hill would be his savior!

"I thought I said I didn't want to be bothered!" He snapped.

Wonderful! The man had more moods than women had shoes and right now he wore his cranky-pants mood. She was sorely tempted to take her candy and go home. Shaking her head, soft strands of her hair swayed against her cheek and that most innocent move sent a branding rush of desire racing through him. He wanted to wrap his fingers in the flowing tresses, draw her head down and taste her mouth. Then he gave a start. Stay focused, dammit!

"I didn't come to bother you. I came to thank you for giving Katy your candy. So . . ." she unzipped her jacket and reached inside. "Here." She handed him the unopened package of candy bars.

"Oh . . . there is a God." And his cranky attitude changed on a dime. He grabbed the candy from her outstretched hand. "How did you know?" Though trying hard to keep his cranky-pants on, it wasn't working, especially when now he wanted to take hers off. Great! A pretty face, a great body; toss in his favorite candy bar and she had him hooked. The woman certainly knew how to kick a guy's best laid intentions out from under him.

"Actually, the credit belongs to Cora. She figured you gave Katy all you had."

"She was right. No way was I disappointing Katy if I could help it." His strong fingers tore the wrapper and heat skimmed through her tempting her to devour every sexy inch of him from his dark tousled head down the muscled length of him. She bet his feet were as sexy as the rest of him, too. Maybe someday she'd get the chance to find out. Never had she considered herself a foot girl but a foot led to a leg to a muscled thigh to a firmly curved. . . . Did he wear tidy-whiteys or boxers? Maybe she could help him off with . . . Then she did a mental slap! Stop it! You're not helping him off with anything! You'll only get into more trouble, trouble you don't need! However, it was wonderful knowing she could think that way and not be filled with revulsion.

"I thought I'd put some away and forgotten about them. I always pick up a couple of packages every time I go to the store. I guess I haven't shopped in a while." Still half-fantasizing, Raine forced herself to focus. "I was getting pretty desperate, ready to hit the chocolate syrup then the bittersweet coca next. Unfortunately, my craving for chocolate gets pretty wicked at times." He had another craving, a sinfully wicked one and it was standing in front of him.

And she wasn't immune, either. That rosy blush staining her cheeks had nothing to do with the cold. Was she craving him, too? Most definitely! And just the thought of giving into it nearly undid him. He was a normal healthy male with a normal healthy male appetite and heaven help him, Raine Andrews was one gorgeous woman he wanted to feast on.

But first he needed his chocolate fix. Handing her a chocolate bar, their fingers touched, and tingled. Unwrapping the bar, the intoxicating aroma of chocolate wafted out. Taking a bite, he growled with satisfaction. And the sexy sound, more enticing than the chocolate, wove a strand of heat low inside her, tempting her to nibble on him. Instead she took a bite of her bar, savoring the sweet confection.

"Mm . . . Mm . . ." A delicious sigh accompanied the pink tip of her tongue moistened her lips.

Beneath hooded eyes Jess watched the enticingly innocent actions. The woman was torturing him! Did she have any idea how much she turned him on? But more than that would she enjoy him . . . Okay! That's it! The mind-blowing images had his pulses triple-timing. To hell with not getting involved! He never walked away from trouble, or a challenge, and the woman standing before him was both. Somehow, someway, he'd get her into his bed but he was still of the 'love-em-and-leave-em' frame of mind; come March he'd damn sure have her out of his system.

Raine opened her eyes to find him devouring her with heavy-eyed intensity, as though he could eat her alive. A hot flush seeped all through before reaching her cheeks. "If chocolate does that for you I wonder what else would." He didn't utter the words but they were in his eyes and her body responded even more to the forbidden invitation. Heat swirled in an out-of-control whirlpool in the very center of her. The forcefulness of it astounded her, especially after Addison's brutality. She'd even wondered if she would ever want anything to do with a man.

Well she didn't have to wonder anymore! Now all she had to do was reach out, draw his head down and taste his mouth. It would be a kiss that was sure to drag her under then breathe life back into her. How heavenly to have those strong hands holding her, caressing her, giving her pleasure. And of one thing she was certain—the man couldn't give off those heated looks and not feel something. Then realty jolted through her with a mighty crash. She couldn't, make that wouldn't, act on her attraction. Legally she was still married and as such would remain faithful to her marriage vows. And when she was ready for a relationship it would be with a man she could build a future with. Was Jess that man? Only time would tell so until free she'd keep a safe distance. Knowing one of them had to be strong enough to break the silken threads ensnaring them, she stepped up to the plate.

"Your home's beautiful. In fact, the whole place is like living in a western wonderland. Even the cabins could be straight out of the old west. I can't imagine what they looked like when you purchased the place."

Jess caught on quick. Safe talk would lead them away from very combustible territory. For the time being he'd follow along. "Rough's an understatement," the whiskey-timber of his voice was an imaginary caress spreading fire through her. "They were so bad I almost razed them but I couldn't do it. According to old documents I found in the attic they were built in the mid-eighteen-hundreds. Originally there were seven cabins, not counting this one, but a fire burned one to the ground and father-time took two more." He tossed the wadded candy wrapper into the trash can. "The place used to belong to a large family and so the story goes as each child married the father offered a cabin if the couple would stay and help work the land. At least seven kids stayed on." He poured two glasses of chilled white wine.

Chardonnay and chocolate—a heady combination. She started when their fingers touched, "I gather later descendants wanted no part of the place and it was left to seed." He took a sip, meeting her blue eyes over the rim.

"How long have you lived here?" she asked.

"You mean Inez hasn't told you everything there is to know about me? She must be getting old." Then he grimaced in mock horror. "Oh God, don't tell her I said that. She has ways of paying a person back."

A thin eyebrow lifted. "Was that what she was doing when she sprung us on you? Paying you back? She meant well even if she did sort of mislead you about me."

"Sort of mislead?" Jess grunted. "Yeah, that's Inez for you. When she sets her mind to something there's no stopping her. She becomes an out-of-control steamroller. Get in her way and you're a goner. But she's a good-hearted woman and a good friend to have in your corner. I'm just surprised she hasn't told you all about the place."

Raine shook her head. "We haven't seen much of her. I think she's giving us time to settle in. I'm sure given time she'll fill us in on everybody and their dog in the county." It hadn't taken Raine long to figure Inez out.

"I was on leave and had business in St. Louis. When it was finished, I started driving around and stumbled across this place. It was for sale. I called an agent. He met me and we walked the property. Despite its abandoned state, I loved it and I'd have roots to come home to when I retired so I made an offer. Unfortunately, somebody beat me to it." Using the poker, he re-positioned a log. It crackled and popped in the peaceful coziness of the room. "I was disappointed, figured that was the end of it until a couple of months later when the agent called to tell me the contract had fallen through and the property was available if I still wanted it. I only had a couple of months left until retirement. That was three years ago."

In the firelight, he was all sensual shadows and edgy planes. The man really did fit the tall, dark, and handsome role. Single now, she wondered if he'd ever been married.

"Have you ever been married?" The words popped out of her mouth quicker than popcorn could pop. Just because she'd been thinking it didn't mean she'd meant to ask. He was probably thinking her nosy as Inez and set to football-punt her back up the hill. So okay, had he ever been married? She watched the play of emotions on his face, wondering if it a painful memory he didn't want to discuss?

That wasn't it at all. He was thinking of what it'd be like making love to her for hours on end. "Once," he stared steadily into eyes he could drown in, "years and years ago. Rae was a nice girl but we learned early on we weren't meant to stay together. The last I heard she was remarried with a passel of kids. I hope she's happy." He turned back to the fire.

Jealousy, aimed at his ex-wife, hit her hard. No one should be married to him but her! And the idea rocked her. What the heck was wrong with her? But she knew. From day one she'd started falling in love with him. Closing her eyes, she drifted into fantasy land, imagining what it would be like to be loved forever by this man, to be his wife, his best friend, his lover.

Would it be heady? Oh yes! Intense? Mind blowing! Tender and sweet? The answer was in the languid weakness invading her limbs as though he were already plying her with caresses.

The man was igniting long forgotten fires inside of her. With Addison, all she'd felt was revulsion crawling over her skin when he touched her.

The classic beauty, the soft, Mona Lisa half-smile, stole his breath away. Was he the reason for it? Giving into temptation, he covered her mouth with his and his body responded with crackling sparks that rivaled those in the fireplace. His lips moved on hers and he felt her shuddering response. He deepened their kiss, holding her lips as if committing them to memory. He caught her soft moan of pleasure.

Returning his kiss with an unfamiliar intensity, her senses swirled as her fantasy came to life. With a low growl Jess hauled onto his lap, his mouth still clinging to hers, his heart thundering against her hers, her firm breasts pressing against his chest. Finding the hem of her sweater he skimmed the warm flesh beneath in search of a lace covered breast. Using only the tips of his fingers he tenderly caressed her through the lace.

Shivering need cascaded through her. It had been so long since she'd been touched so tenderly. His caresses sent darts of pleasure low inside her. His touch, his kisses felt so right she fully admitted falling in love with him. And just as abruptly the knowledge acted like a slap of icy water snapping her to her senses. If they didn't stop now there'd be no turning back. They had to stop for as long as she was married she would continue honoring her vows. She wouldn't break them, no matter how she felt about him. It might not be how she wanted it, but it was how it had to be.

"No! This isn't right." She cried, pushing away and scrambling to her feet.

Despite wanting to go on kissing and touching her, he didn't. Never let it be said Jess Harper forced a woman to do anything against her will, but his brow furrowed. Was she uncomfortable with what just happened? Was she embarrassed at her own response? His hands were firm but gentle as he drew her comfortingly back against him. "Don't feel bad about what just happened. We were only kissing."

Though longing to stay in his arms she shrugged his hands off. When she spoke again her tone was icy-cold. "And it was a mistake, one I can't afford to make. I can't get involved with you, Jess. I'm still married and I won't dishonor my vows with you or any man."

Anger and jealousy raced through him at the idea of her with another man, even her husband. "We weren't doing anything wrong so you're not dishonoring anything. All we did was kiss. We connected on a mutual feeling and there's nothing to be guilty about. It wasn't like we were naked, rolling all over the floor." And that's exactly what he wanted do with this woman. He wanted to love, and be in love with her. And the thought rocked him to the core.

Eyes downcast, she didn't see the stunned expression on his face. She was too busy trying to shake the vision of them naked, entwined from head to toe making love in front of the fireplace from her head. Didn't he realize this was for his own good, as well as hers?

"I know that. And yes all we did was kiss; but it could have gone a lot further and that can't happen." She snagged her jacket off the chair. "I need to go home and we both need to forget this ever happened." Her voice hardened. "Need I remind you of what you said when we moved in here, that you don't want any trouble? We're done here."

The doorknob was in her grasp when his grip whipped her around. "You can forget what I said back then, and we're not forgetting this. This wasn't a mistake and you shouldn't feel guilty over a few kisses between a man and a woman extremely attracted to each other. If you still loved your husband I might understand, but you don't. Not after what he did to you..." he trailed off, his expression turning incredulous that she could still love her husband. She wouldn't be the first woman to love a man who beat the hell out of her. Demanding eyes stared long and hard into hers, waiting for her to deny it.

Unknowingly, he'd just tossed her a life-line and she grabbed it with both hands. She stared stonily back at him, watching the anger replace desire.

Every muscle hardened to chiseled stone and his jaw clenched so tight he thought it'd never open again. Damn her! Damn her to hell! Just when he was ready to come to her and be damned his rule of not getting involved with a married woman, she stomps all over him. Furious, he wanted to shake her until her teeth rattled.

"We are going to finish what we started here, lady." Anger throbbed in his voice. "Not now, but someday there'll be a reckoning, and you'll come to me and I won't care if you still love that sick bastard you call a husband. I want your body, not your heart. And believe me sweetheart; when I set my mind to it getting it won't be any trouble at all." Before she could stop him his mouth crashed down on hers, this time branding her clear to her soul. With a desperate cry she wrenched free, rushing head-long out the door and up the path toward her cabin as if the hounds of hell were chasing her.

Jess watched until the darkness swallowed her up, his body afire, aching even as his heart screamed he'd acted a jerk. Be damned his heart! "One of these days," he vowed aloud, "one of these days when she had no more excuses she was going to be his. Body and soul she was going to be his, but also in heart. His temper had gotten the better of him and he'd lashed out but he still meant what he said. It was up to her to come to him. Then he'd apologize. Until then, he'd do whatever it took to leave her alone.

In the silent cabin Raine poured a cup of coffee and wandered to the fireplace. Staring into the glowing red embers, she pondered her strong response to Jess's lovemaking. One minute they'd been having a sane conversation and the next locked so tight together a piece of paper couldn't have fit between them. She fingered her kiss-swollen lips. Just the memory of his searing kisses, the heated caresses, increased the yearning even more and threatened her self-control. She hated misleading him about still loving Addison but the crazy ruse worked. Iron-willed she might be, but how long could she hold out against the all-consuming need for the man, when she'd fallen in love with him. All it would take was one weak chink and she'd tumble like a rockslide down a Tennessee mountain. But that wasn't happening and she shored up her resolve. Until her divorce was final she'd run as fast as she could in the opposite direction every time the prickly man came within sight.

Sure you will, chimed the jeering voice in her head. Who are you kidding? You talk the talk but can you walk the walk? Damn right she could! Jess Harper had met his match and when the timing was right she'd set him straight on several things!

His pride had taken a nasty blow and he'd hit back. She might deserve his anger but she'd be damned if he was getting her body without her heart. It'd be a cold day in hell before that happened. Come to him? By the time she was finished with Mr. Cranky-Pants Harper he wouldn't know if he was coming or going! A confidant smile spread across her face. She wanted more than just a casual fling with the man, she wanted forever and she was getting what she wanted.

On that solemn vow, she went to bed.

Chapter Fourteen

Fluffy snowflakes peppered the ground coating it white as they stowed away the groceries for Thanksgiving Dinner. It looked like they had enough food to feed the county and still have leftovers. The weeks had flown by quickly, Halloween had disappeared about as fast as the trick-or-treat candy and tomorrow was Thanksgiving. Soon it would be Christmas. Raine was glad the time had flown. Now only four days remained until she had her freedom then she was going to pin back that infuriating man's ears and he'd be the one running to her! Just thinking of his stupid remark sent her blood pressure soaring.

She eyed the twenty-pound turkey on the counter. "Think we went a little overboard?"

"What gave you that idea?" Cora was unloading a grocery bag. "How about inviting Inez and her family to dinner? Heaven knows there's plenty of food, and we do owe her our deepest thanks for directing us here. Without her who knows where we'd be right now."

"That's a great idea." For sure, if not for Inez they wouldn't be living yards from the orneriest man she'd ever met. Almost a month had past and he still gave her fits because he believed she still loved Addison. If he only knew!

"And I think we should invite Jess, too," Cora added innocently; well aware of the emotional war waging between them since Halloween. She could guess what transpired that night and in her opinion both were acting like idiots.

"I doubt he'll want to join us." Raine shot her a discouraging frown. The last thing she wanted was to look at that insufferable man across the table. Ever since Halloween she was never sure which Jess Harper she was dealing with—the one who kissed her senseless or the downright rude cranky-pants one.

It was those rude times he'd see her, shake his head in disgust and stomp off muttering under his breath that she wanted to brain him. And it didn't make any difference where it happened, either. They'd literally bumped into each other in the grocery store. Turning to apologize, he saw who it was, scorched her with a scathing glare and huffed off leaving his cart full of groceries in the middle of the aisle. Later she'd seen him unloading bags of groceries from that big black truck of his. Obviously, he'd shopped someplace else.

Then there were the times he'd be oh-so-sweet, catching her off-guard and kissing her passionately before she had a chance to say no. Those were the times she'd reconsider telling him the truth then he'd make her mad all over again, so she kept her mouth shut.

"Oh, he'll come," Cora said confidently. "There's not a man alive who could turn down a home-cooked meal."

"Then you've just met your first one. There's no way he'll come for Thanksgiving dinner. Haven't you noticed he's avoiding us like the plague?"

"Not us, just you. And not all the time, I might add, or was that lip-lock you two were in the other day a new type of avoidance?" Cora smirked. "I've seen quite a bit of him and he hasn't kissed me that way. Shoot! Just about every time I'm outside he makes time to visit, always asking if we need anything. Oh! And he really enjoyed that apple pie you made him."

The rat! The low-down dirty rat! Now she wished she'd put something extra in that pie besides the sugar and cinnamon. Still, a warm glow filled her that he'd liked her homemade apple pie.

"Fine! Invite him! But don't blame me if he's a no-show." Head in the refrigerator, she missed the bound-and-determined look on Cora's face.

"He'll come, all right." Come hell, high-water, or ten feet of snow, tomorrow that man will be sitting at that table. Looking out the window at the falling flakes, Cora thought the ten feet of snow a good possibility. She called Inez but the invitation was declined, Inez explaining it was a family tradition that all the females, young and not so young, spent the weekend shopping while the men watched football.

"Let's go shopping tomorrow, too." Raine suggested upon hearing Inez's plans.

"Fine with me," Cora said, dialing Jess's number.

Raine half-hoped he'd say no. Maybe he had dinner plans with a girlfriend, given how often he left in the early evening and didn't return until late at night. Not that she was spying on him. But the idea of Jess on a date, holding another woman in his arms, kissing her, making love to her, set her temper to flaring. It was she he should be holding, kissing, making love to, and as soon as she was free she'd get the man's proper attention, even if she had to hit him over the head with her brand new cast-iron skillet! Infuriating as he could be, she still wanted him.

The fireplace blazing, chores done and the snow coming down, Jess thought it a good time to kick back and watch an old western movie. Then his phone rang. It was the cabin's line. Was it the pesky little blond calling to apologize? Nope! Not the pesky little blond. It was Cora with an invitation to Thanksgiving Dinner. Would he like to join them? Oh, yes indeed. Home-cooked meal aside, he wasn't about to pass up a chance to be near that exasperating woman.

Hanging up, Cora smiled smugly. "See, I told you he'd come. Said he'd love to join us. He's such a nice man."

It didn't take a rocket scientist to figure out he'd accepted and the 'nice man' part was up for debate. Crossing her eyes at Cora, she set about making Katy a cup of hot chocolate.

Jess settled back in the recliner. Spending the special day with Raine sounded wonderful, plus it was time to take the bull by the horns and make her admit she couldn't love a man who beat her. Somehow it just didn't fit into what he knew of her situation, but then again, he'd witnessed a lot of crazy things in his life. No matter, he was determined to get answers.

After a light dinner of grilled cheese and tomato soup, they spent the rest of the evening prepping for the next day. They baked cornbread and biscuits for the stuffing, chopped onions, celery, and baked the pumpkin and chocolate cream pies. From scraps of left over dough they made pie-crust strips sprinkled with cinnamon and sugar. They were lightly browned and crusty when they sat down to enjoy them. Later with Katy and Cora in bed, Raine stepped outside. Gazing down at Jess's cabin; she decided to tell him the truth.

The next afternoon she was basting the turkey when he knocked on the door, and her heart started dancing with giddy anticipation even as she looked at Cora and nodded toward the door. "You invited him, you let him."

"Go let him in. It's cold out there." Cora scolded, grinning when Raine stuck her tongue out at her.

Taking a deep breath to quell the butterflies in her stomach, she opened the door. And stared. Snowflakes dusted his Sherpa-lined coat and clung to his hair. She'd have sworn something flared in his brown eyes, then it was gone.

"Happy Thanksgiving, Jess." She said.

And, he ignored her. However, he didn't miss the yearning she wasn't quick enough to hide. Good! She still wanted him just as badly as he wanted her. Now he was glad he'd stuck by his decision to have dinner with them. , A couple of times he'd waffled.

"Happy Thanksgiving, Jess." Cora welcomed him with a bright smile.

He kissed Cora's cheek. "Thanks for inviting me."

His back to her, Raine crossed her eyes and mimed a, "And a Happy Thanksgiving to you, too, Raine." She shut the door with a firm hand.

Her miffed reflection in the oval mirror on the wall told him she was in a snit because he'd ignored her. Served her right, being upset went both ways. He'd had his share of bad moments over these last weeks, but upon waking this morning decided it was time to call a truce. Thinking long and hard, he could see his testy attitude wasn't helping matters. Besides that, he'd decided he wanted more than memories of stolen kisses to keep him company. It was time to play nice.

Jess carried a bottle of white wine and the chocolate soda that Katy loved. He handed them to Cora. "It sure does smell good in here." And, sniffed appreciatively then moved closer to Raine, his warmth wrapping round her like rays of sunshine. "And you look nice," he leaned in, "smell good, too, like vanilla and cinnamon, makes me want to nibble on you." He growled, his voice whiskey-rough, just loud enough for her alone. A whisper of breath tickled against her ear. "Happy Thanksgiving," and he kissed her cheek, too.

Darn that man! He moved quicker than an F5 tornado and was smoother than a calm lake at midnight. His actions put flags of red pleasure blossoming in her cheeks. Careful or you'll be drowning in that lake. Right now, he's being nice, but when will it change?

"Hi, Mr. Jess!" Katy scrambled over the back of the sofa to fling herself into his arms. "You wan'na watch the parade wif' me?"

"Hi Katy-bug," he used the endearment Raine and Cora called her, pressing his lips to her silky blond hair. "I'd love to watch the parade if Mommy and Cora don't need my help." Like he'd been doing it for years, he settled her on his hip.

Serious sapphire eyes met warm brown ones. "They don't. They told me to stay out of the kitchen 'cause I might get burned. That means they don't want you in there, either. You might get burned, too."

Who could argue with the child's logic? Out of the corner of his eye he saw Raine listening. "Is she right? You don't need any help?" His gaze lingered on her mouth.

Shaking her head, the fire burning in his eyes turned her warm. "You might get burnt."

Desire darkening his eyes, barely audible was his, "Too late."

Catching his meaning, she blushed. Cora bit her cheek but a snicker slipped out, anyway. Who did those two think they were fooling? They had it bad for each other.

Jess held Katy on his lap as though he'd been doing it forever. She kept him entertained with a running monologue on all the cartoon characters. He wanted more moments like this, her on his lap, fireplace aglow and Raine at his side forever. This needed some serious thought.

Katy thought it'd be fun to float in the sky and some day she was going to do it. Impressed at her young intelligence, Jess didn't doubt the little daredevil for a minute. He had a feeling most of the credit belonged to Raine. He'd never seen a more nurturing, patient mother than she was. And what kind of father would throw away this child's love?

Stirring the bubbling gravy, Raine thought Jess and Katy made a beautiful picture and a lump of emotion thickened in her throat. She thought of Addison's actions, of what he'd tossed away like trash and decided again to tell Jess the truth. As if picking up on Mommy's thoughts, Katy asked Jess if he had any little kids.

He shook his head solemnly. "No. I don't have any kids at all. I haven't got to be a dad yet."

She became studiously quiet but when she spoke again it wasn't what any of them expected. "I have a daddy, Mr. Jess, but he had to go away so he couldn't come on 'cation with us." Both women shared a perplexed looked and stopped to listen. "I'm glad he couldn't come 'cause Daddy's mean. Sometimes he makes Mommy cry. I like it when Mommy doesn't cry 'cause she has pretty blue eyes just like me and they get all red when she cries. Daddy couldn't even come home when Mommy fell down and got hurt real bad and couldn't open her eyes."

Jess remained silent but his assessing eyes met Raine's over the top of Katy's head. Katy, unaware of the angry currents flowing through him, was on a roll and everything bottled up inside her little mind tumbled out as her mother stood listening helplessly.

"Daddy yelled at me and made me cry, too then he made me promise not to tell Mommy."

"I'm sorry he made you cry, sweetheart," Jess said gently, though fury pounded inside him that she'd been carrying the burden of these experiences on her tiny shoulders by a drugged-out excuse for a father. He wanted to ask what Addison had done, but tamped down the urge to prompt her. It was better she explain in her own good time.

Raine moved closer. All kinds of horrible thoughts flashed through her mind. What had Addison done to make Katy cry, then swear her to secrecy? If he'd laid a hand on her, God wouldn't be able to help him. She'd catch the next plane back to Phoenix and shoot him—on purpose and right between the eyes. Her hands clenched into white-knuckled fists.

"Mommy had to go to the doctor and Daddy said I could stay with him. I really wanted to go with her, but I was 'fraid the doctor would give me a shot. We were playing outside and Daddy was pushing me on my swing then he said he had to go do something but would be right back, but he didn't. He was gone a really long time, and I had to go potty really bad. He was in the bathroom, too," Katy looked at her mother, "you know Mommy, the one in your old room, the one you used to sleep in before you started sleeping with me?" Raine nodded, feeling Jess's eyes boring into her but she refused to look at him. "I 'prised' Daddy and the powder he was playing in went everywhere. Daddy yelled at me and I didn't do anything wrong. Daddy was playing in your powder, Mommy, not me." Her bottom lip quivered and tears filled her eyes. "Then he told me he was sorry and said not to tell you. Daddy said you'd be mad at him." Tears rolled down her cheeks. "I thought you'd be mad at me, too."

Raine scooped Katy up from Jess's arms. "Shush, baby." A soothing hand smoothed up and down her back. "Katy-bug, I'm not mad. I'm just sorry Daddy made you cry." She cuddled Katy closer. "It's all right, baby girl. I promise, you didn't do anything wrong. Daddy did. You were being a good girl doing what he told you. Daddy was wrong, not you, but from now on if you have anything, even a secret that makes you feel bad, you tell me. Okay?"

"Okay," Katy wiped her eyes on her sleeve.

Cora quickly produced a tissue just before she wiped her runny nose on the same sleeve.

"Here, sweet-pea, use this instead of your sleeve." Thoroughly ready to tear into Addison herself, Cora thought it time to lighten the mood. Any second she expected both Raine and Jess to explode, taking the roof off the cabin. "I don't know about the rest of you but I'm starving. I think we should eat."

Fire burned Jess's belly and his appetite had disappeared but following Cora's lead, he hid his angry emotions from Katy. "I'm starving, too! That turkey sure does smell good and I can't wait to have some pumpkin pie and chocolate pie! How about you, Katy-bug? Do you like pumpkin and chocolate pie?"

She gave him a water giggle. "I love them. And I'm hungry, too."

"Give us a couple minutes to finishing setting the table." Raine said, wiping the remaining tears off Katy's cheeks then kissing them. "Do you know how much I love you, pumpkin?"

"This much." She spread her small arms out as wide as they would go.

"Oh! Much more than that! I love you as big as the whole wide world." Raine snuggled closer.

"And I love you big as the wide world, Mommy." She felt better, too. She didn't like keeping secrets from Mommy. She crawled back on Jess's lap and Raine saw his strong arm encircle her protectively.

Outwardly happy, inward Jess seethed as a thousand questions pounded in his head and only one person could provide the answers. He skewered her back with an angry glare, the truce idea forgotten. Never would he understand how she could still love a man who beat her, snorted coke in the same house as his child, and then blamed her for it blowing away.

They gathered round the dinner table laden with the golden, brown turkey and all the trimmings. Katy was back to her chatter-box self. Raine, however, was furious that Addison dared expose her to his addiction. How stupid was he to bring cocaine into their house? What if she'd thought it powdered sugar and ingested it? Her baby could have died. Clearly, he hadn't cared about Katy's safety. Drugs and alcohol controlled his life and this just proved it. He'd rather expose his daughter to harm than kick his habits.

And why hadn't she known? She wasn't oblivious to what went on inside her home. But she knew the answer—Addison was an expert at hiding things. Again, she berated herself for not having been stronger, for not standing up to him. But should-haves were like chasing raindrops, once they hit the ground they were gone. One thing was for damn sure, come trial time she'd be there front and center. That reminded her; Gordon needed this information as additional evidence.

After dinner Jess offered to help cleanup but they wouldn't hear of it so he took Katy to build her first snowman. It meant a lot that she'd opened up to him. The ground was covered in several inches of thick fluffy snow and it clung to the cedar trees' branches as though someone had sprayed them with whipped cream. Raine watched out the kitchen window as they worked diligently rolling snowballs to form the body. Katy resembled a little pink creampuff in her snowsuit, her face barely visible from the fur-edged hood.

Just as Jess hefted one rounded snowball onto another, her mischievous laughter rang out and she blasted him square in the face with a snowball. Raine's astonishment matched the surprise on his face then he was laughing, his teeth flashing white, as he chased her around the yard. Katy's high-pitched laughter echoed on the cold air. When she sprawled face down in the snow he immediately righted her, dusting the clinging snow off her. Instinctively, she knew Jess would make an excellent father. A wistful fantasy flitted through her head wishing to be his children's mother. Sadly, it was only a pipe-dream.

They used tree branches for the snowman's arms and chunks of burned wood as eyes and buttons and Raine supplied a carrot for its nose. "He needs a pipe, hat, and scarf. Come on Katy-bug, I've got just the thing." Clasping her mitten-covered hand, they went down the hill to his cabin. Finding what he was looking for, they retraced their steps. Jess made a mental note to clear the stone path off. And ever in the back of his mind lingered Katy's earlier revelations.

"It's 'the bestest' snowman ever," she declared when they were finished and insisted Raine take pictures of her and Jess posing with the snowman. Afterward, they enjoyed steaming cups of hot chocolate. Katy, hers cooled with milk and whipped cream, finished first and announced she wanted to watch a movie.

"Thank you for helping me, Mr. Jess." She stood on tiptoes to kiss his cheek.

"You're very welcome, sweetheart. I had fun, too, and we'll have to build more."

Covering her with a quilt, Raine knew Katy would be asleep before the movie ended. Re-joining them, Raine was barely in her seat before Jess opened his mouth.

"Your husband's a real piece of work. He needs a real good wake-up call and I'd sure as hell like to give it to him."

She started to tell him Addison was soon to be her ex-husband but something held her back.

"You've no idea." Cora interjected. "That whole family's a real piece of work. Why at the hos . . ." She broke off when Raine kicked her beneath the table. "Snobby as all get out, too." She finished lamely, puzzled that Raine didn't want him knowing the details of what had happened to her, especially given Katy had revealed so much already. Taking the hint, she took the conversation to the humorous side of the situation. "You've got to admit, aside from Katy catching him doing the dirty deed, it's kind of funny."

"Yeah, I can picture him getting ready to get a nose full of coke—Katy pops in—and he blows it all over the place." Raine gave a derisive little chuckle.

"That baby was so relieved to finally unload her secret. It was dirty, him making her promise not to tell you. I know one thing; I'd loved to get my hands on him. I'd teach him a lesson he wouldn't soon forget." Cora's eyes glinted with anger.

"We all share that sentiment. What worries me is there could be more she's holding back. I've got to make sure that's the only time he's done something bad in her presence." She was still kicking herself for not seeing what was right under her nose. God! Sometimes I wish that bullet had killed him. She thought she'd been thinking it until she heard a loud, "What!" and saw the shocked expression on Jess's face.

"What bullet? Who got shot? Explain!" he demanded.

Hell no! She was in no mood to explain anything to anyone. "I'm not explaining anything." She'd been thinking and it just slipped out. "Besides, Katy might overhear us." Which was a lame excuse when a quick glance showed she'd already drifted off to sleep.

"Get your coat!" He scraped his chair back to tower over her.

"I'm not going anywhere." She gritted mutinously.

"Oh, yes you are. When guns and bullets are involved I want to know what the hell is going on. Now get your coat." He ordered again, this time through clenched teeth.

She wanted to argue, tell him it was none of his damn business. But it was. He was only thinking of their safety. Feeling like a kid in trouble she went to get her coat.

Face stormy, he watched her stalk away before turning to Cora. "What the hell all happened to her? I know she was knocked around by her husband but I'm realizing there's a hell of a lot more than just the bare-bones facts she's told me." In fact, he was damn certain something very horrific had happened at the hands of her husband, something involving guns.

Fire burned in his gut that she could still care for the scumbag. Well, come hell or high water, it was time he got the story out of her.

"Get her to tell you all that's gone on, then I'll be happy to discuss it with you. And just so you know; it's going to take a lot more than a few kisses and sweet-talk to get her to do what you want." She gave him a pointed look.

Jess flushed ruddy red. Damn! The woman didn't mince words. At least he was saved from responding by Raine's mutinous return, still scowling, plainly not wanting to go. Well, that was too damned bad. Things were going on, had gone on, that he needed to know about. Pronto! He practically shoved her out the door while Raine shot a pleading look at Cora, who only shrugged her shoulders, knowing it was time they talked.

Taking the lane fronting the cabins, for a time they walked in hostile silence. The newly fallen snow lay brilliantly white against the golden glow of the early evening sun. Here and there red-headed cardinals, blue jays, and other birds she couldn't name gathered beneath the snow-tipped evergreens. So beautiful, yet Addison's intrusion cast a pall over it. Would she ever be totally free of him? Jess expected explanations, especially after that remark about the shooting. But she didn't want to rehash those awful moments with him, especially on this day. She was just grateful to be alive, to celebrate with the people she cared about, and that included him. Somehow, he'd stolen into her heart in too short a time and she really couldn't let him be there, at least not until she was free. Unfortunately, her heart hadn't cooperated from the get-go; she'd lost it to him at first sight.

Their footsteps crunching through the unbroken snow echoed in the cold air. The quiet peacefulness should have soothed the acid raging in Jess but it didn't. Instead it grew thicker. Veering off, he headed deeper into the woods. In the distance was a fenced corral attached to a red and white painted stable. Approaching it, he put two fingers between his lips and gave a shrill whistle. Immediately two horses—one a sleek midnight black, the other a burnished chestnut, emerged. Their smooth coats gleamed in the fading sunlight. Both horses waited eagerly at the corral, nickering softly at his soothing voice.

"How are my girls, today? Did you think I'd forgotten you?" They nickered again as if answering. From his pocket, Jess withdrew a bag of sugar cubes he carried for them. Anxious for the sweet treat, their velvety-smooth noses poked between the wooden slats, their lips flaring back in a wide grin. Jess fed each a cube then dropped some of the small white squares into Raine's hand.

"They're beautiful, Jess." She and Katy periodically brought them sugar cubes and had become friends with the gentle ladies. The nibbling of their big velvety lips tickled the palm of her hand. She gently stroked each horse's head and spoke softly to them.

"These ladies are spoiled worse than babies." It was the first time he'd spoken since ushering her out of the cabin and it irritated her. He was the one who'd insisted they talk.

As though reading her mind he looked at her expectantly, one dark brow arched so high it disappeared in his hairline. "You're the one who wanted to talk," she glared at him, "so talk!" Rubbing her hands on her jeans, she turned her back and stared into the surrounding woods.

"No," he drawled, "you're the one who mentioned someone getting shot, that someone being your husband. In my book that means I deserve an explanation, especially since you're living on my property. If you'll recall, I said I wanted no trouble and if he finds you here it will definitely mean trouble. I have to prepare to keep you safe."

Raine turned her head, staring into his angry eyes. "There's nothing to prepare for. Addison's in jail awaiting trial." Then she turned away again.

Her dismissal aggravated him. No way in hell was she ignoring him. Wrapping a hand around her arm he roughly spun her to face him. "Lis . . ."

Not prepared for the hand that grabbed her arm, for an instant she reeled back in time and with a sharp cry threw her arms up to protect her face then mortified, quickly dropped them. Oh my God! This wasn't Addison. This was Jess and no matter what, he'd never hit her.

Shocked to the core, his face turned gray as he let go; speechless, he stared at her frightened pallor. Had she really thought he'd strike her? The very idea fueled not only his temper and made him sick, it cut a wide swath of hurt deep inside him.

"Good God woman! I'm not going to hit you." He raked a hand through his hair. "Dammit, Raine, I've never harmed a woman and I'm not about to start now and I damn well refuse to be lumped in the same category as your husband." Oh yes, there was a hell of a lot more to her story and the defensive reaction was proof, and he was going to find out and he didn't care how mad she got. However, he stepped back giving her some space. "Obviously, he's a real piece of work but no man goes on trial just for roughing up his wife. So, tell me what he's being tried for."

The hurt impacting his dark eyes tore at her heart more than his anger. She hadn't meant to react that way. It was a reflex action; one Addison could take all the credit for. How many times had she thrown an arm up to protect her face from his vicious slaps? There were too many to count. And Jess was wrong. She didn't lump him in the same mold as Addison. Jess was a good man, a kind man, a man who would never hurt her.

"I'm sorry. I reacted out of instinct. I know you would never hit me. I may not have known you very long but that's one thing I'm sure of." She started to touch his arm but dropped her hand when he stared at it as though it were a snake about to strike. She flinched at his rejection.

Seeing it, satisfaction coursed through him. He was being churlish in not accepting her sincere apology but her defensive reaction left him raw and insulted. When he spoke, his tone was hard as nails, his eyes frosty and forbidding.

"I don't want your damned apology. Let me repeat myself. Just tell me what he did to wind up being shot and in jail.

You're living here, that means I have a right to know what I'm dealing with in order to protect you!"

The rebuffed apology acted as a slap in the face making her angry and fed up with his attitude. So, he wanted to know all the sordid details? Well, fine! Blue eyes glittering, she spat. "You want to know what happened, what was so god-awful bad? I'll tell you! My husband tried to kill me. He was in a mad rage, had a gun, and was going to shoot me. We struggled, it went off and he shot himself instead." As if happening right then, once again she saw Addison pointing the gun at her. "He even told the police I shot him but when they tested the gun for fingerprints the only ones on it were his. That's why he's in jail. He couldn't beat me to death, so he was going to finish the job by shooting me."

She refused to tell him of being stripped naked, tied down and whipped unmercifully. That feeling of being totally helpless, under someone's sadistic control, haunted her constantly. No one knew that a night rarely passed without nightmares plaguing her sleep. Visions of Addison, a belt in one hand, a gun in the other, would jerk her into sweat-laden, heart-pounding reality.

"What makes you so sure he's still in jail? You're obviously on the run from him. Scared spit-less, I'd say, and no way of knowing just how far behind you he is."

"Oh, that's where you're wrong, Mr. Harper." She said sarcastically. "I know everything because I have people keeping me informed. Addison was arrested as soon as the fingerprints came back and no bail was granted. And for what it's worth there's a restraining order against him. I have separate phones, one for him and one for everyone else. So far, he's made no attempts and it's been almost three months. Obviously, I'm doing everything in my power to keep all of us safe. All. Of. Us." Each word was emphasized with a sharp stab of her finger in his chest. "I don't need your protection. You can shove it where the sun doesn't shine!" His jaws clenched in angry reaction but he didn't say a word. "And just so you know, I'll do anything to protect my daughter from her father. Including another gunfight if that's what it takes. But you don't have to worry about any trouble. We'll be long gone from here by then."

Despite what she said, something nagged him raw and he didn't stand back on asking, either. "Tell me something. If things were so bad between you two, why did you stay with him all this time, put up with him beating you? If you'll do anything to keep Katy safe, then why didn't you leave the bastard sooner? Or do you love that sick son-of-a bitch so much you'll put him before your child and go back to him?" The questions had been slamming around inside his head. How could she feel anything but hatred for the bastard? He wasn't trying to be judgmental but it came out that way.

And Raine took it that way. "Why? Why didn't I leave sooner?" How dare he sit in judgment of her! "I'll tell you why!" An ache of guilt so strong struck her, nearly doubling her over. Didn't he know she lived with recriminations every day for not leaving sooner? Still, she defended herself. "Because he threatened that if I ever left him again he'd hunt me down, take Katy away, and I'd never see her again. I tried leaving once. It didn't work." Scorn filled her voice. "It's so easy for someone who's never been in my shoes to question why I didn't leave sooner. And I know that sounds lame but that's just how it is. Don't you think I feel guilty? Especially after finding out he snorted coke while she was with him." Her voice shook with anger. "Had I realized it I'd have left before that last night turned so violent. Protecting Katy is my priority and Addison's threats don't scare me anymore. Love him or no, if I have to go back and have another showdown with him I will, but I'll have my baby and he'll never get to her. As for you . . ." Suddenly out of steam and emotionally battered, she had to get away from him. Without another word, she struck off at a fast clip.

Jess remained motionless, conflicted in everything she kept saying about her husband. Then he went after her. This time when he gripped her arm she made no defensive moves. Instead, she found herself locked tight against his chest. She wanted to resist even as her traitorous arms stole round his waist. She didn't want to fight anymore. She laid her head against his chest. She wasn't the needy type but she needed his strength, his faith, his safeness. She wanted everything with him, could love him forever, if only he would let her.

He still puzzled the contradictions that weren't meshing. There was more than what she was telling but for now he'd have to be satisfied. Gently putting her away, he gazed into the wet blue pools of her eyes then lowered his head. The moment his lips touched hers he was lost. He loved this woman so much he never wanted to let her go.

It was like a sledgehammer slammed into his chest. Holy hell! He really was in love with her! What happened to his love-and-leave-them motto? Yet hadn't he been thinking in terms of the future? Hell, he hadn't even dated her and he was so sappy in love he wanted to kick up his heels and howl at the moon yet in the next second feeling like a semi-tractor free-falling off a mountain—the crash-landing could be deadly. Space! He needed space. He had some serious thinking do. After years of protecting his bachelorhood this was the last thing he expected.

With the direction his emotions were headed he'd be marching down the aisle before dark. It was insane to pursue a woman nearly half his age, and with a kid to-boot. And a husband that was sure to hunt her down, a husband, that despite his evilness, she professed to still love. It was re-con time! Abruptly, he jerked away.

Raine opened her mouth to confess at the same time Jess jerked away. Something had suddenly changed him and his rejection spoke volumes, his shuttered looked confirmed her suspicions—she had too much baggage to take on. Flirt and tease? That he could do. Have a casual affair? Absolutely! But a relationship that came with baggage? No way. And she'd been foolish to entertain the fantasy. Numb, she walked away swallowing back a sob and praying the physical ache in her heart didn't knock her to her knees. He'd cut and run and she hadn't even told him everything, nor showed him the photos of how badly Addison had beaten her. Falling for Jess had been stupid, the lesson tough, but from here on out she was staying as far away from the man as possible.

Returning home, for the next hour Jess shoveled snow while analyzing his feelings, and the whole time wanting to race to her and spill his heart out. His sudden coolness coming on the heels of their kiss had to hurt. No doubt she believed him disgusted learning what had gone on. He was disgusted, but more outraged that she could still love the bastard. But something else ate at his soul. He'd fallen in love with a married woman. And that wasn't right. But maybe it wasn't love but pure old lust. Yeah, right, the irritating voice in his head jeered.

The physical work didn't help. He still yearned go to her, to love her, claim not just her body but her heart, too, and it ripped him apart that she still loved the man she was also hell-bent on keeping behind bars. And that was a piece of the puzzle that didn't mesh.

Had Jess been thinking clearer he'd have realized she was lying. Instead, he vowed to do his damnedest to stay away, no matter what methods it took. Banking the fire, he slammed out of the house. She might not be in the same building but she was on the same property and he needed more space to think. Pulling onto the snow-covered road, Jess had no clue where he was going, only that he had to put distance between them before he did something really stupid. Like tell her he'd fallen in love with her.

Chapter Fifteen

Thanks to a nightmare-plagued night in which Addison chased her round the cabin brandishing his belt and a gun, Raine awoke edgy and exhausted but refused to let it ruin their Black Friday outing. After all, nightmares were only bad dreams, nothing that could hurt her, right?

Despite her downcast mood, she put up a happy front for Katy but Cora saw right through it. The girl had been in a funk since yesterday. Napping, she'd awakened to find Raine curled up in the recliner staring forlornly into the blazing fire and quickly surmised the talk had not had a pleasant ending. When the angry man had practically forced her out of the cabin, she'd felt sorry for her. She'd looked like a prisoner being led to the gallows.

Pulling into the crowded parking lot, it appeared Black Friday was the busiest shopping day of the year no matter where you were. The mall was a veritable Christmas lover's feast of brightly colored lights and decorations. Christmas Carols filled the air and the enticing scents of roasting nuts and the sweet aroma of hot chocolate teased their senses.

Spotting Santa Claus shot Katy straight to heaven and she insisted on telling him what she wanted for Christmas. "You know I've been good. And don't forget, he has to find me in 'dem' woods. I don't live in my old house so he has to know where to find me. You said he'd find me, Mommy."

"I did. And remember, we sent him your letter." It dismayed her that Katy still worried Santa wouldn't find her. "And I guarantee you he knows you live in that pretty cabin in the woods." But they stood in line behind several children. When it was Katy's turn, she didn't waste a second climbing on the jolly fat man's lap. Eyes sparkling with Christmas fairy-dust, she started chattering. Standing aside, Raine heard the conversation between Katy and Santa. "I wrote you a letter. Mommy helped me. We mailed it to you at the North Pole. Did you get it yet?" she asked but didn't give him a chance to answer. "I hope you'll bring the dollhouse I saw in the toy book and the baby doll that cries like a real baby and a baby-buggy I can push her in."

With a barely discernible look from Santa, Raine nodded, assuring him all was under control. Santa told Katy he'd indeed received her letter and put her wishes on his list. Lastly, he cautioned her to continue being a good girl. Happily satisfied, she scampered off his lap, a red-and-white-striped candy cane clutched in her hand. She fairly floated on air the rest of the afternoon.

At one point they separated, setting a time to meet in the food court. Katy liked the idea for she wanted to buy presents for Mommy and Cora. It didn't go unnoticed that she didn't mention buying anything for her father. The less her absentee father was mentioned the better off she was.

Window-shopping, Raine's thoughts were on Jess. The man was so . . . suddenly her attention was drawn to an oil painting displayed in the window of a small art gallery. The artist had painted the scene of a lone rider making his way through a wintry, snow-covered wilderness to a lamp-lit cabin nestled in a stand of pines. The painting reminded her so much of Jess, a solitary man answering to no one other than himself and the elements of the universe. Before she could talk herself out of it she was inside buying it. She'd give it to him for Christmas and if the stubborn man didn't want it he could use it for kindling.

Stowing the carefully wrapped painting in the SUV, Raine checked her watch to find it was time to meet up with the other two. They were already at a table and Katy was happily munching on chicken nuggets and fries. Sliding into the seat beside her she dropped a kiss on her head.

"So, what did you buy?" She asked, eyeing several bags on the spare chair.

"I got Ms. Inez a fluffy pink scarf and I got Mr. Jess a checker game and a puzzle 'cause he likes to play checkers and when it snows real hard and he can't go outside he likes to put puzzles together. Maybe he'll play checkers with me, and let me help put the puzzle together."

Apparently Katy knew more about Jess than she did. "That was very smart of you to listen to what Mr. Jess liked and I'm sure he'll play checkers with you and work on the puzzle."

"Too bad somebody else doesn't listen." Cora muttered under her breath. Hearing it, Raine subtly, and childishly, stuck her tongue out at her then said she wanted a hot chocolate.

Cora grinned, shaking her head.

Just as Raine set the cups of hot chocolate on the table, the old cellphone in her left pocket vibrated to life. Instantly the hair on her neck prickled. Only one person would call that number and she refused to let him ruin their fun. The voicemail got it instead. Seeing Cora's curiosity, she mouthed "later." But as they continued shopping she couldn't help thinking about the message on the cellphone.

With the time change, darkness fell earlier making it seem later than it actually was. Leaning back in his chair, Jess rubbed at the tension gripping his neck, hating to admit being worried they weren't home yet. Then as if by magic the SUV appeared on the monitor. Finally, he could relax knowing his girls were safely tucked in for the night. Then he grimaced. Since when had he come to think of them as his girls? No matter. They were and as the twilight had turned to darkness he'd become increasingly concerned about them. This morning he'd watched them drive away, grateful for more breathing space from Raine. The cabin might be several yards away but ever since the explosive talk yesterday she'd been too damn close for comfort. Last night he'd driven from one end of the county to the other looking for answers to his problem, returning well past midnight but it hadn't done any good. He was still twisted in knots.

While Raine tucked Katy into bed, Cora fetched the bags and put on a pot of coffee. "The only thing left is that big package." She called from the spare bedroom.

"It's a painting I saw on display in the art gallery. It reminded me of Jess and I couldn't resist. I got to talking with the owner of the gallery and he told me that it and all the other paintings in his gallery are done by local artists."

"I know the place you're talking about. I saw the same painting flash by me as Katy raced past the window. He'll love it." She gave Raine a sharp-eyed look that could have pinned a dinosaur to a corkboard. "So, when are you going to listen to the message? You know who left it."

"I just wanted to make sure Katy's asleep. I don't want her hearing anything. In her little world, everyone is supposed to be nice." Tiptoeing to the door, she peeked inside. Katy was on her side, her pink teddy bear clutched in her arm. Motioning to Cora, they headed to the third bedroom but not before getting coffee. Setting the phone in the middle of the desk she put it on speaker-phone then heard evil speaking.

"Happy Thanksgiving . . . bitch." The snarling familiar voice instantly raised every hair follicle on her body. A long pregnant pause followed before he launched his attack. "You do know no matter how many times you divorce me you'll always be my wife. Remember our vows, dearest—till death do us part. When I catch up with you, and make no mistake I will, you'll wish you'd died that night and that's a promise, not a threat. You should know me by now. You know I never make idle threats. Just remember—you belong to me until death do us part. Damn! Sorry to cut this short but don't worry, I'll be in touch again. And kiss my Katy for me. Tell her Daddy loves her and he'll get her real soon. You too, bitch!" Then silence.

Pushing the save button, an icy chill raced through her. These weren't idle threats. They were deadly promises. Addison

was coming after her, hunting her down like an animal to
kill her.

Cora gnawed her lip. "That's bad, real bad. You've got to call
Gordon right away. He has to know Addison's finally stirring
the pot contacting you." She snapped her fingers. "Check your
emails. You know he won't stop with just phone calls. He's out of
control. Nothing's going to stop him from getting to you. Even
behind bars he's gutsy enough to reach out and touch you, to
intimidate you. And let's face it, that restraining order's no more
going to keep him away from you than it would a buzzard after
road kill. It's probably worthless here, anyway."

Everything Cora said was true, point in fact—look how far
he'd made her run. Wearily, she shoved a swath of hair over her
shoulder. "You're right. First though, I need more coffee."

While the laptop booted up she refilled their cups. There was
no message icon. "He may not have access to a computer." And
Cora was right about alerting Gordon. Addison just couldn't
stand losing so he was determined to make everyone miserable.
"I'll call Gordon about the message and see if he's heard anything from Addison's attorney. I'm still torn. Part of me wants to
do a plea bargain and not air our dirty laundry in public, while
the other part wants to have a showdown. No person should
beat a woman, or anyone, nearly to death and not be made to
pay for it."

"I'm still trying to understand how he could become so
violent and we not know it." Cora said.

"Addison's a pro at hiding his habits and still maintaining a
normal façade." She gazed into the flickering flames dancing in
the fireplace. "You know, Cora, I can't remember the last time
I even told him I loved him. I think he started killing my feelings for him with the first slap and each time he hit me a little
more died. And you know we hadn't shared a bed for quite
some time." Turning from the fire, there was a haunted look on
her face.

"You'd told me, but then Katy mentioned it when telling
us about Addison's little fit when she caught him snorting up."

Dread churned the acid in her stomach. Raine was about to confide something she wasn't sure she wanted to hear after all and from the grim look on her face she guessed what was coming even before she opened her mouth.

"One Saturday night back in the summer, Addison had a poker game with his friends. That wasn't unusual. They all got together and played poker once a month at someone's house. Usually the wives went along and we'd do our thing while the guys played cards. Not one of them knew how bad he treated me and I couldn't say anything. I didn't dare. You can't imagine what it was like pretending nothing was wrong when what I really wanted was to scream the truth."

Coffee in hand, she eased into the rocker. Her throat suddenly dry as sawdust, she took a sip before continuing. "Katy had a bug that particular Saturday night so I told him to go without me and he had no problem with that. I honestly believe he was relieved not to have me along. And he sure wasn't staying home. By then his playtime came first no matter what. Me? I was glad to have a few hours without him in the house. Anyway, when he got home that night I was already in bed. When he came to bed I pretended to be asleep hoping he'd leave me alone but he didn't. I told him to leave me alone, that he was drunk and to go to sleep. I rolled over with my back to him. The next thing I know I'm on my back, he's choking me and everything's going black as he's ripping my gown off telling me what he's going to . . ." her voice became a tortured whisper, unable to say the vile words Addison had spoken. A shudder of revulsion passed through her reliving the awful thing he'd done to her.

Grim-faced, Cora knew what Raine couldn't bring herself to say. "You don't have to say it. I can imagine, honey."

"Anyway, by the time I came round he'd done what he wanted then left again. He could have killed me and Katy would have been there alone. I should've left then, especially when he didn't show back up until three days later then he acted like everything was honky-dory and not one remorseful bone in his body. He didn't bother telling me where he'd been and I didn't ask. By the time he came back I'd moved in with Katy."

Disgust welled that the man who'd pledged to love her violated her against her will. Cora's hands tightened around her coffee mug—wishing it were Addison's throat. She'd see how he liked being choked to death. And castration was too good for him. Thinking back, she recalled Raine wearing scarves around her neck during that time and thought it part of her fashionable style. Instead, she'd been hiding the marks around her throat. Perhaps if she or Ethel had been more observant this whole mess could have been prevented. They'd have quite a conversation when they talked next.

Seeing Cora's guilty expression, Raine hastened to reassure her. "Don't feel bad. There was nothing you or anyone else could have done. It was my problem, my dirty little secret, one I had

to handle on my own. But after that I knew there could come a time he might kill me, but I also knew I had to be careful. The urge to run was overwhelming but I needed the timing to be right. Unfortunately, everything nearly blew up in my face."

Cora looked at her questioningly. What on earth could possibly be any worse than what she'd just learned? "What do you mean?"

"Remember when Katy was telling about Addison yelling at her for surprising him when he was snorting coke and she said I had been at the doctor?" Cora nodded over a sip of her coffee. "Well," Raine hesitated then took a deep breath. "I went to the doctor because I thought I'd gotten pregnant from the night Addison forced himself on me, not that he knew why I went. Anyway, weeks earlier he'd found my stash of birth control pills and in a fit of rage flushed them down the commode. Not that we'd been intimate very much but there was a bit of a gap between when he threw them away and when I got more but during that time was when . . . anyway, I was late with my period and scared to death I was pregnant. You can't imagine how many bargains I made with God not to let it be so. As much as I wanted more children I didn't want them with Addison, and not that way. A baby should be made out of love, not force."

"God must have heard you. Obviously, you weren't pregnant." Abortion was something Raine wouldn't consider. There was so much secret pain she carried, never letting anyone know what was happening.

"No, and I thank God every day I wasn't. The doctor attributed my being late to stress. If he only knew! Anyway, he prescribed nerve pills but I never took them. I needed all of my wits to handle Addison." She twisted a strand of hair over and over. It was a habit she always did when upset. "Anyway, Addison left me alone once I moved into Katy's room. It wasn't until the party that he started in again and you know the rest from there." Cora nodded. This was a lot to take in. "I wish with all my heart things could have been different with him. In the beginning, I really did think I loved him or I wouldn't have married him. Now I'm wondering if I was just swept off my feet with all the attention he paid me. He was so handsome, so caring and kind, so confidant and sure of himself. Maybe I should have been able to see behind the mask to the real person hiding there."

"Uh-uh." Cora shook her salt-and-pepper head. "You loved Addison, and he loved you, but he came to love the drugs and alcohol more. You once came first, but you had been replaced. You have to look at it that way and if nothing else good came from your marriage, the hell you've been through, you were blessed with Katy."

Raine nodded. "She's the best thing that ever happened to me, even if Addison is her father."

"That's one special little girl and we'll make darn sure she stays safe." Cora swallowed the last of her coffee, rinsed her cup, and set it in the drainer. "As far as Addison's concerned, he's behind bars for the time being and can't touch you and in a few more days you'll be free of him and life gets even better. Now I don't know about you but all that shopping wore me out. I'm taking a shower and crawling under the covers with one of my new paperbacks. One thing's for sure, I don't have to worry about caffeine keeping me awake. It never has and I don't suppose it ever will."

"Me either. I could drink a gallon of it right before bed and still drop right off to sleep in five minutes. And your book idea sounds great. First thought, I'll let Gordon know Addison's up to no good. Maybe he'll have some good news for me." On a sudden impulse, she hugged the older woman. "Thank you for going through all this with me. I don't know what I'd do without you. I can't tell you how much you mean to me."

Emotion constricted Cora's throat. "I love you too, honey, and I don't need thanking. Now go make your call."

Gordon answered on the first ring. She'd actually been expecting Molly. "I hope I'm not interrupting anything."

"Not a thing. The football games are in half-time and my teams are losing so you can interrupt me all you want. Molly and the baby are having a little snooze so I have plenty of time to chat. So, what's happening in snowy Missouri? How was Thanksgiving?" He propped his feet on the coffee table, crossing them at the ankles.

"Thanksgiving was wonderful, and all is quiet, or it was until today. Addison decided to stir the pot. He called this afternoon."

"You didn't answer it, did you?" He snapped out, sitting straighter.

"No. I let it go to voicemail. Want to hear it?" She asked.

"Hell yes, I want to hear it." Holding the new cellphone over the speaker of the old one, she played the message. "He's trying to spook you," Gordon was fired up when she came back on the line. Even through the cellphone his anger was audible. "He's crazy angry. The divorce will be final Monday and there's not a damned thing he can do about it. Is this the first time he's called?"

Excitement washed through Raine that in mere hours she'd have her freedom from Addison! "It's the first time and though I've been expecting it, I was caught a little off-guard."

"I can imagine. He's allowed phone calls but none to you, he knows better. However, Addison doesn't play by the rules and nothing's going to deter him." He let the words sink in then pushed the point home. "You do realize that, don't you? Whenever he gets out he's coming after you and we both know there's only one way you'll be safe—him dead."

"I know but I'm hoping he will be locked up for years to come. Part of me hopes he'll plea bargain and everything will be over while the other part wants a showdown with him."

"I'd prefer the showdown and it might come to that. As of this morning he wasn't dealing but now that he's pulled this, and however veiled the threat is; it's there. Plus, with what's in those files you sent me we have the hammer. I don't care if it is the holiday weekend I'm calling his attorney. He'll get an earful on what his client's been up to. Maybe he'll talk some sense into Addison. Otherwise, trial's in two weeks. You know I've been pushing hard for a speedy trial date."

"I'll be there anytime you need me." Despite Addison's threatening message and Jess's cranky attitude, she was light-hearted. "Oh gosh, what a wonderful Christmas it would be to have this mess behind me." Maybe there really is a Santa Claus after all.

"I'll be in touch as soon as I know Addison's decision. In the meantime, enjoy the rest of your weekend and look forward to being a free woman come Monday morning."

Raine wandered to the kitchen window and saw the faint glow of lights at Jess's. Sadly, she understood why he'd turned colder than a buffeting Arctic wind toward her. What man in his right mind wanted the baggage she carried? If he'd cared for her it wouldn't make a difference. Her chin lifted. She'd be damned if Jess Harper would get her down when everything was looking up!

The next morning they decided that if they had Christmas presents then they needed a Christmas tree to put them under. The church they'd started attending had a tree lot operated by a Boy Scout troop, so they headed there. An hour later Raine was certain they'd checked out every tree in the tent-covered lot before finding one Katy deemed perfect. After two scouts' fathers secured the tree on top of the SUV, both women stared in dismay, not sure how they'd get it down.

"Oh boy, it sure is big. Getting that sucker off ought to be fun," Cora said dryly.

Raine's mouth twisted, "Fun wasn't the word I was thinking of."

They decided to unload the tree first then go back out for decorations. "Let's not forget a tree-stand," Raine said which prompted a cacophony of questions from Katy ending with her explaining in detail what a tree stand was. Katy still wore a puzzled look on her face. "Maybe you'll understand when you see it." Raine added.

Jess was sweeping leaves off the front porches of the cabins. Earlier, Kevin Forsythe, director of the county social services office had called asking for a special favor. Several children remained without homes for Christmas and he hoped Jess would open his cabins to them.

"You've got it, my friend." When it came to those kids he'd bend over backwards for them. "You knew I couldn't say no. I'll always do whatever I can for them." And he would, because a long time ago he'd been one of them and sworn someday he'd do his best to help less fortunate kids like he'd been.

The now familiar sound of the SUV had him looking up to see it returning with a big tree tied to the top. Leaning on his broom, he watched them try to wrestle it down. The tree seemed to be winning the battle. Jess figured he'd better go help or the poor thing might lose all its branches. Propping the wide-brush broom against the cabin, he cut through the yard.

Concentrating on their task, neither of the women knew he was around until he said, "Here, let me do it or the poor thing won't have any branches left to put decorations on." Edging them out of the way he effortlessly lifted it off of the SUV. The sinewy muscles beneath his blue flannel shirt flexed and a warm tingling skimmed through Raine as she fantasized gliding her hands up and down that solid body and running her fingers through

the crisp curls on his chest. Would they be soft and springy . . .
Katy's exuberant clapping jerked her back to reality.

Jess leaned the tree against the cabin. Dusting his hands
off, fleetingly, his eyes met hers. In them was a look he couldn't
fathom.

"That's our Christmas tree, Mr. Jess." Katy snagged his attention. She stroked the green branches lovingly.

"I think that's the prettiest Christmas tree I've ever seen,
Katy-bug. Did you pick it out?" She was rosy-cheeked adorable.

"I did, and we got it from a boy scout, too. Now we have to
get 'rations for it. And Mommy says it needs a stand." Her blue
eyes adoring, she asked, "What's a stand?

Cora snickered and Raine rolled her eyes. Obviously, the
little stinker thought Jess smarter than she was.

"It's what makes the tree stand up straight and not fall over,"
he explained simply. "Tell you what, Katy-bug, when you get
back with your tree-stand let me know and I'll come help you
put it up."

"Okay, Mr. Jess." Katy agreed at the same time Raine said,
"You don't have to do that. We don't want to impose. I'm sure
you have other things to do besides put up Christmas trees."

"I know I don't have to but I want to. Besides, I think I'll be
doing the tree a favor if I put it in the stand. You girls might have
it hanging upside down from the ceiling before you're through,"
he teased which instigated another burst of giggles from Katy at
the idea of the tree hang from the ceiling.

Suddenly the giggling stopped. "Mommy! Potty!" And she
dashed inside, shutting the door with a resounding slam. The
three adults winced.

In the ensuing silence, Raine looked at him, wanting to tell
him the truth about Addison and how she really felt about him,
but she'd wait, make sure everything was still a go, for knowing
Addison he was liable to throw a monkey wrench in the divorce.
But come Monday, sure of her freedom, she was storming Jess
Harper's defenses and setting him straight about a lot of things,
mainly that he was her man and he could handle her baggage!

The insanely stubborn man had feelings for her and he was going to admit it!

While Raine's mind meandered through minefields, Jess told Cora about the kids. "I thought I'd better warn you the other three cabins will be occupied starting the weekend before Christmas with some kids from the county home."

"That's wonderful, Jess," Cora nudged Raine's shoulder to get her attention.

"Oh. Yes. Wonderful. Is there anything we can do to help?" Having lived in foster care she could empathize with the kids.

Well . . . since she asked. "As a matter of fact, there is." Moving closer, the scent of her perfume wafted around him. It was something flowery along with the underlying scent of baby powder and sugar cookies. Did they actually put that in bottles and sell it? His gaze slipped to the ripe fullness of her mouth. Undeniable heat shimmered between them like hot lava and if he didn't stop staring at her he was going to have to kiss her. Then what would she do? Kiss him back? Or tell him she was still in love with her husband even though he'd beaten the pulp out of her? That last thought killed his desire. She wasn't free and by her own admission still loved her husband. It was possible she'd go back and give their marriage another try after he was released from jail. After all he'd seen and done in his forty-plus years, nothing would surprise him.

Focusing on Cora, he ignored Raine. "All the kids are boys except for one little girl. I don't want you feeling obligated but I was hoping she could stay with you. She's only five and I've a feeling she'd have more fun bunking with Katy then a bunch of rowdy boys."

"I think we can handle one more little girl, don't you?" Raine said, annoyed at his evasive countenance with her.

"Oh, most definitely she'll stay with us. Katy-bug will love having another little girl to pal around with." A scheming light suddenly lit up Cora's eyes. It was time these two had a moment alone. "I'd better check on Katy." She was inside, the door shut, before she'd finished speaking.

Raine glared after her, wise to the conniving woman's mission—giving them a chance to talk. It was a waste of time. The man was all friendly smiles with Cora and Katy but toward her he was iceberg cold. At their forced togetherness, Jess felt bound to look at her and immediately felt the pull to her beckoning mouth. Powerless, he leaned closer, a moth to her flame, drawing nearer and nearer all the while knowing she could burn him badly. Despite it, a powerful surge of desire rushed through him, the need to touch her was all-consuming. But he shoved the fiery yearning away, drawing back in the nick of time. If she was going back to her husband, no way was he jumping from the frying pan into the fire.

Again, Raine wanted to confess misleading him, and she would—in two days—when she had her freedom. Staring at him, the light bulb of remembrance flashed on. Come to think of it, she'd never actually said she was still in love with Addison. Well, hopefully her misleading him wouldn't come back to bite her before she could make things right with him. As for the stubborn man, she was positive he felt more than just lust for her and she'd prove it once she blasted through the wall around his heart. Then a horrible thought zinged through her head—what if he had just been playing her with his kisses and innuendos? Soon she'd have her answer. And that scared her, too. Talk about being tied up in knots of confusion. She might never get them undone!

Focusing on the matter at hand, she said. "It's wonderful what you're doing. If I could, I'd take in every child who needed a home."

And he plunged, like diving from the highest cliff, deeper in love with her. This was the kind of woman he wanted to share his world and his dreams soared skyward only to crash and burn in the pits of hell remembering she was still married, still in love with her husband. Dammit! The woman had him so screwy he might never think straight again, so, like flipping a light switch, he flipped his emotions off. If he didn't want to get hurt any worse he had to keep his distance, be strictly landlord and nothing more. Married, he couldn't be in love with her and that sentiment hardened his resolve, and his heart.

"I better get back to work. The kids will be here in three weeks and I want to make sure everything's ready."

"Let us know if you want some help..." Raine trailed off, staring at the rigid back walking away from her. Damn him! Damn him and his frosty attitude! She wanted to knock him to his knees and find out what had turned him cold again. Between his moody attitude and her own whirling emotions, she was going crazy. Just get a grip and ignore Mr. Cranky-Pants. They had decorations to get!

By late evening the tree was up and glowing with lights, tinsel, and shiny Christmas ornaments and surrounded by presents. True to his word, Jess put the tree in the stand in front of the picture window. Katy deemed it the boo'tilest tree she ever saw.

Chapter Sixteen

Sunday found Raine antsy, unable to concentrate on anything. Even during church services she'd squirmed like an impatient three-year-old earning a 'sit-there-and-be-still' glare from Cora. Afterward, to kill more time they went shopping, ate lunch and dinner out, and took in a movie. Finally, it was Monday morning and Raine lay wide awake even before the neighbor's rooster started crowing. It was D-day. Divorce Day. Hallelujah! Impending freedom never felt so good. Raine wondered if she should be sad her marriage was over. Nope! How could she be sorry ending something that had become a hellish nightmare? She thought of Jess. As a precautionary measure, she wanted the green light before going to him. A glance at the bedside clock said she'd better wait to call Gordon. Even if they were her best friends, they wouldn't appreciate being woken up this early, especially with the baby.

In the stillness, she reflected on the past five years. She couldn't regret the early years of her marriage. They'd been good and those were the memories she'd share with Katy. Turning on her side, she tucked a hand beneath her cheek, watching the soft rise and fall of her chest. "Oh sweetie," she whispered, "life's only going to get better for us." Katy deserved an emotionally stable life and it was her responsibility to provide it. Starting today!

Too impatient to lay there another moment she padded to the shower. Afterward, surveying her face in the mirror, she noted the deepest of the bruises were mere shadows of color now. However, her ribs were still tender, especially if she moved wrong. As for her kidneys, no longer feeling any discomfort, she assumed they were okay. Overall, she considered herself lucky. Things could have turned out a lot worse.

Katy woke while she was combing her damp hair. "I'm hungry, Mommy."

"How about pancakes and bacon," she scooped her from the covers, ignoring the twinges in her ribs and headed for the kitchen.

Cora came out just as she was lining crisp bacon strips atop a paper towel covered plate. "Mm . . . Mm. I love the smell of bacon frying."

"Mommy's making pancakes and she's making me itty-bitty ones. You and Mommy get big ones cause you're grown-ups. When I grow up I can have big ones, too." Katy leaned against Cora's legs.

Picking her up, she kissed a rosy cheek, loving Katy as if she were her own grandbaby. "Let's set the table while Mommy finishes up with the pancakes."

After breakfast, she took Katy outside while Raine checked for messages. Wanting more ammunition, Raine wanted Addison to contact her again. Unfortunately, he hadn't. Still too early to call Gordon, she headed outside to join the fun. Under an overcast sky boasting heavy banks of dark clouds, they took turns pushing Katy on the swing-set and playing in the snow with her. Her peals of laughter drifted up to where Jess was fixing a board on the porch at the next cabin. Katy's laughter made him smile. The kid was a cutie-pie and the spitting image of that gorgeous momma of hers. Then he scowled and pounded the board harder—which loosened another.

A while later he heard Cora say she was ready for a break and he totally agreed. He was ready for a break in more ways than one. Despite vowing to keep his distance he was constantly tempted to seek out the thorn in his side only to remind himself that she was off-limits, still married, still in love with her husband. Pulling out his phone, he keyed numbers. He'd see if Cooper and Belle wanted to meet for dinner again.

Raine was aware of his presence and wanted to talk to him. Oh, be truthful, that aggravating little voice chided, talking's not what you've got in mind and her cheeks warmed. Yes, she wanted more. She wanted a relationship with him, one that would lead to a future together. Just the idea of another relationship should scare her to death, especially after Addison, but Jess was definitely not Addison.

It ended up that Gordon called first. Jubilant and teasing, he'd figured she'd have been on the phone to him before daylight. "I woke up about five a.m. my time and thought about calling, but figured you wouldn't appreciate the baby waking up at that hour."

"Thanks for the concern but the little stinker was demanding a snack right about then. So, I just came from the courthouse. Do you want the good news or the good news?"

Her heart thumped excitedly. "I'll take both—the good news, and the good news."

"First off, you are officially no longer Mrs. Addison Paul Andrews. The judge signed off on the decree this morning."

"Yes!" She did an air-fist pump. "I've been so afraid Addison would do something to throw a monkey wrench into the works." Suddenly she was laughing and crying at the same time. Using the sleeve of her sweater, she scrubbed her eyes. Great! She was picking up Katy's habit. "So, what's the other good news?"

"Addison agreed to the plea bargain. Per his attorney, he decided it was in his best interests to accept the deal." There was no mistaking the gloat in Gordon's voice when he added, "Especially since I informed him Addison had played his 'I'm stupid card.'

The relief was so intense she plopped down on the bed totally zoning out. "Hey! Raine! Say something!" Gordon's alarmed voice was loud through the phone.

"I'm here. I'm here. I'm just shocked that he agreed." Tears trickled down her face.

"You bet it's over. Now you can come home whenever you want. Don't be in any hurry, though. Enjoy the holidays and if I need you, I'll let you know."

"You did it, Gordon. Thank you. Bless you."

"Don't thank me, sweetheart. You did it all on your own. If you hadn't stuck to your guns, no pun intended, it wouldn't be over now. Now go celebrate."

The second Raine stepped into the room Cora saw the red-rimmed eyes. "You're not divorced," she said flatly. Then Raine's face lit up bright as sunshine.

"Oh, yes I am!" Giving a loud whoop, Cora jumped up and they danced and giggled happily around the room. "Everything's over including the case against Addison. Apparently, he had a change of heart and accepted the plea bargain"

"This calls for a celebration!" Cora declared exuberantly. "We're going out to dinner and it's my treat." Worried something would go wrong, she'd prayed every day that her girls would be all right. Then a sad realization struck her that they didn't need her anymore and she'd go back to Phoenix. The idea didn't sit well but today was a time for celebrating. She'd worry about leaving tomorrow.

"Gordon said the same thing and that's exactly what I'm going to do. If there are any loose ends, he'll let me know." Loose ends, she mused for a moment. Was Jess a loose end? Would he even care if she went back to Phoenix? And why did returning there sound depressing? She knew the answer. Phoenix wasn't home anymore, home was here now. And in that moment, she decided she wasn't going anywhere. Instead, she was digging her heels in and Jess Harper would have to run her off his property with a bulldozer because she wasn't leaving.

Cora's next statement surprised her. "You know, I'm thinking of staying on here for a while. I've grown rather fond of this place and the people we've come to know. I'll miss Ethel but it's time she had her home back, and we can always fly back and forth. When we leave here I think I'll find an apartment."

Watching Cora making a fresh pot of coffee, for now coffee was their celebration drink, an idea was quickly taking shape. If Jess ran her off she'd need a place to live. "You know, there's still about four months left on our lease. How about toward the end we start looking for a house around here? We can all live together. I don't want to go back to Phoenix either so I'll have Gordon list the house with a realty company."

Cora's face lit up. "Let's do it!"

"Then it's settled. We . . ." she broke as the new cell phone rang. Caller ID showed the mall's toy store. Answering, she was told the dollhouse had arrived. Raine told the clerk barring any bad weather she'd be in tomorrow to pick it.

"That was the toy shop," she whispered, not wanting a certain little girl with big ears to hear, "Katy's dollhouse came in. Weather permitting, I'll get it tomorrow."

"I'll keep squirt with me," Cora whispered back, "we'll bake some cookies."

"Mm . . . homemade cookies, I loved the one's Ethel made for our trip. Katy deemed them the 'bestest' she ever ate. And she should know. She ate enough of them," Raine said wryly.

"I know what you mean. I went to get the last one but the little stinker beat me to it— scarfed it down and then laughed at me."

As they talked, Raine kept wandering to the window. She was anxious to tell Jess her news and Cora couldn't blame her. She only hoped the girl didn't end up getting her heart broken a second time. For some reason, Jess was playing dangerous games. Though sparks had flown between them from day one; ever since Thanksgiving he'd turned pricklier than a Christmas cactus and her bright-eyed idea of leaving them alone on Saturday had bombed royally. She got Raine's not-breaking-the-wedding-vow bit, they were sacred to her, too, and the guilt would taint any possible relationship with Jess. But enough was enough. It was high-time to take the proverbial bull by the horns and get them together.

"Okay! That's it! Its time you two cleared the air of whatever's ailing you." Raine remained silent, knowing when Cora had an opinion she was going to voice it. "Look, I understand you had to be free of Addison; no matter you've really been free from him heart and soul for a long time. Now you are legally free and it's time you and that hard-headed man get together." She took Raine's coat off the rack and put it in her hands. "Go!"

Hesitant, yet excited, she tucked a strand of hair behind her ear. "Okay. Maybe you're right."

"There's no 'maybe' about it. I know I am."

"Okay. I'll go. But if he tosses me out on my fanny it's on your head! He gets cranky when I get near."

Cora's laughter followed her out the door into the crispy air. Breathing deeply, she literally felt the start of a brand-new life. It was her spring emerging out of the winter of her dead marriage. Giddy with the knowledge, she did a little skip-and-jig on each stone down the path. But when she knocked on the door there was no answer. He's probably cowering behind the curtains, she snickered. Next, she headed through the crisp crunching snow to the barn. He wasn't there either, but the shiny black truck was so he had to be around somewhere. Then she had a hunch and headed for the stable. At the doors, she heard his soft murmurings as he talked to the horses. Each whickered as though trying to uphold their end of the conversation. Entering the dimness, the earthy scent of hay, horses, and leather greeted her.

Sensing her presence, his yearning shifted into overdrive. Never had another woman affected him on such an emotional level. Every time he looked at her or thought of her, he either wanted to make love to her or shake some sense into her. And keeping his distance was increasingly difficult, especially when he wanted more than just a few hours in a bed with her. He wanted forever. But she didn't. On Halloween she'd made two things abundantly clear—she wouldn't break her marriage vows—and she was still in love with her husband. He got the not-breaking-her-vows but not the idea she could still love the low-life scum who'd treated her so badly. And what kind of sick puppy did that make her? Angry, he wanted to shake her until her teeth rattled, until she got it through her head it was him she should love. So why the hell was she here now? When she drew closer he noted her eyes were red from crying. Were the tears for her husband? "What's wrong?"

His acid-sharp tone alerted her that she wasn't exactly welcome. Adjusting to the dimness, she took a moment to drink in the sight of him, so vibrant and totally alpha male. She wanted him to hold her as she confessed her love for him. Actually, she wanted to do more than that, but apparently he was wearing his cranky-pants.

Shaking her head, her hair swayed in a mass of spun gold. "Nothing's wrong. I needed some fresh air and found myself up here." Her eyes crinkling, she teased, "I didn't mean to intrude on your conversation with the girls. It sounded like they're try-ing to talk to you."

A trace of a smile appeared on his lips and she recalled the feel of them on hers. "I'm probably glad they can't. There's no telling what they're saying." Then he fell silent.

As the silence thickened she looked at the darkening sky visible through the open doors. "It looks like we're in for another round of snow," she said then gave an imaginary head-smote. You're so pathetic! You've got this gorgeous man alone in a stable, you're ready to tell him you're free, that you love him, and all you can talk about is snow? But his coolness put her off. Was it because he believed her lie about Addison? If not, then what was bothering him?

"Yeah, the last I heard the storm's predicted to hit sometime late tomorrow night." The whiskey-roughness of his voice sent shivers sliding through her. Laying aside the currying brush he used to groom the horses' manes and tails, Jess stepped in front of her, tracing the path left by her tears with a thumb. Not even conscious of his intentions, he drew her into his arms and low-ered his mouth to hers. And the lushness, the sweet heady taste of her, sent every bit of common sense flying out the door.

Sighing deliciously, she burrowed closer. Through the thickness of her coat his heart thundered like a herd of horses as wave after wave of heat throbbed so hot and strong she ached to be become a part of him forever. Hurriedly, she undid the buttons of her coat, not caring that it landed on the straw-sprinkled floor. Feeling him warm and hard against her was all that mattered. Her arms encircled his neck as her mouth moved feverishly against his. She had waited so long for this.

Jess didn't care that his intentions went up in flames at the first touch of her lips. His need was so great that all he wanted was to touch her, to hold her and make her his. It was all he thought of at night alone in that big bed of his. His questing hands slid beneath her sweater finding the warmth of her smooth back. He hissed a sigh of pure desire deep into her mouth. Soft moans filled the stable as his tutored, work-roughened hands caressed her. She wanted this man to love her, not just with his body, oh yes she wanted that, too, but also with his heart. And if he'd let her, she'd love him forever. She would show him heart, soul, and her body, just how much she loved him. As far as she was concerned Jess was the only man she wanted in her life. She undid his belt and the snap of his jeans.

Totally immersed in the plethora of decadent sensations he was drowning in, suddenly loud warning bells clanged in his head when her hands became busy at his waist. His head cleared just enough to get a grasp on his out-of-control desire. Roughly, he shoved her away before she could touch him. If she did, there'd be no turning back and for both their sakes this couldn't happen. He didn't want guilt afterwards and he wanted more than just a casual fling. There were plenty of women for that. His face hardened into a cold mask. You're a big delusional fool, Jess Harper. Get it through your thick skull you'll never have anything with her because she's still married, still in love with that slime-ball. You forgot Rule Number One—no married women. Get rid of her! Get her out of your head and out of your heart before you fall any deeper into hell.

Adrift in the glorious feelings he brought to life in her, Raine had no clue the direction of his thoughts nor was she prepared when he jerked her arms from his neck and shoved her roughly away. His rejection was like a shotgun blast to the heart, splintering it into a million pieces. Flummoxed, she stared into the stormy depths of his. What the hell was wrong with him? One minute he's all over me and the next treating me like I have leprosy.

"Why? Why did you stop? You want me and I want you."

Surly, he went on the attack, "I stopped, sweetheart, because you're playing games with me and I won't have it." He re-fastened his jeans and belt. "If you want to play your head games go find somebody else. Just don't mess with me. I'm better at any game you could ever play." He tapped her cheek smartly. "Just be glad I stopped because I could have had you down on the floor before you knew it and you wouldn't have had a chance to stop me. Now get the hell out of here!" He yelled, roughly shoving her out the door and tossing her coat after her.

Stunned, she barely got out, "You don't understand . . .," before the doors slammed in her face and the lock bolt slid shut. "The man's a flipping idiot!" she fumed, "Has he totally lost his marbles? Why did he suddenly turn meaner than a junkyard dog? Well so much for telling him I'm free and don't care a fig for Addison. Obviously, he doesn't give a tinker's damn. Well, I don't either! To hell with him! Playing games, my foot! He's the player and as far as she was concerned he could just play the touchy-feely games with someone else. No! Scratch that!" The idea made her want to punch the unknown woman. Instead, she kicked the stable doors. Pain shot through her foot. Ouch! Ouch! Ouch! Dammit! Now he was provoking even her violent tendencies. If he hadn't locked the doors she'd march right back in there, grab him by the scruff and shake some sense into him. No, on second thought, leave him be, in the mood he's in he's liable to kick me off the place. Shaking her head in disgust she flounced-limped back to the cabin.

From the loft, Jess watched her limp back through the woods and rubbed his face wearily. The situation was getting out of hand. He should just refund the rent money and send her packing, but that idea didn't sit well, either. And given how hard she'd kicked the door, the crazy woman was liable to file an injury claim against him. Finally losing sight of her he climbed down and took a different path back to the house.

CHAPTER SEVENTEEN

Hearing footsteps on the porch, an impatient Cora yanked the door open and started peppering Raine with questions. "Well? What'd he say when you told him? Do we need to change our plans so you two can go celebrate?"

At least Cora was a constant, never beating around the bush. Tossing her coat on the hook, Raine shook her head. "Nope! Our plans are still on. I didn't tell him. He's wearing his cranky-pants and not so nice so I didn't tell him. I'll wait till he isn't so grouchy." And she sarcastically wondered when that would be—in her lifetime, maybe?

"What put a burr under his saddle?" Cora eyed Raine shrewdly. "What's the real story? Come on, out with it!" Arms folded beneath her breasts, her foot tapped impatiently. These two were really ticking her off. She had a good matchmaking track record and they were not going to ruin it!

Raine poured a cup of coffee. "Beats me, I tried telling him but he went all crazy on me. Accused me of playing games then told me in no uncertain terms to get lost. You're not going to believe this but he even shoved me out of the stable. He was so scared I'd come back in he bolted the doors. So no, I didn't tell him my divorce is final. As a matter of fact, I don't care if I ever tell him. Men are such stupid idiots!" Once again she wanted to kick something, or someone. A wicked gleam appeared in her eyes as Jess Harper's gorgeous backside came to mind.

Cora chuckled, "Oh brother! The battle of wills continues. Who will be the stronger of the two? Why you, of course. No woman will ever argue that point with you and we all know that sometimes they think with the southern half of their bodies." Raine laughed. She could always count on Cora to see the humor in a situation. "Just leave him be and mark my words, he'll come round." Raine looked doubtful. "He's fallen for you and fighting it. And you've got to admit things sparked up pretty fast between you two. Now he's feeling the pressure but everything will work out. You'll see I'm right." Cora took a sip before continuing, "Did you know I was nineteen when I met Ben? Bet you didn't know we eloped after only knowing each other for three weeks, either?"

Raine's eyes widened, "No way, you're kidding, right?" Actually, she could picture a very young Cora getting into the car with young Ben Grey and driving off into the future. And she could see herself doing the same thing with Jess, once she crashed through that wall surrounding him.

"I kid you not. We went around with friends but never went on any real date until the night we eloped. I was nineteen and he was twenty-one. We didn't need any long courtship. Our feelings were based on more than raging hormones or short-term attraction. There was much, much more so we found a justice of the peace and plunged headlong into marriage. We were married for forty years before that heart attack took him and never regretted a minute, either."

Cora's wistful longing for the love of her life was evident.

"You miss him, don't you?"

"There's not a day goes by that I don't think of him." She patted Raine's arm. "Jess will come round. He'll wake up and see what an idiot he's being."

Raine gave her a rueful look. "I guess I'm partly to blame for his attitude, too." At Cora's questioning look she made her confession.. . . "So, I guess I'd feel the same way if he led me to believe he was still in love with his ex-wife."

Cora stared, dismayed. "I'm thinking your plan backfired and it's come back to bite you in the backside. No wonder he's so upset. It's killing him that you could actually still love a man who was so cruel to you. He's got feelings for you all right and it's got him all twisted up. Just give him a little space. Trust me. Everything has a way of working out." Cora squeezed her shoulder. "Now, it's time to celebrate. Dinner's still my treat. Let's try that restaurant Inez recommended. We'll get all gussied up and have a night out on the town."

Leave it to Cora to make her feel better. Everyone should be blessed to have a Cora in their life. She wrapped her in a tight hug. "Whatever would I do without you?"

"You'd do just fine." Cora hugged her back. "Now let's get all prettied up."

Katy took her bath without a fuss. "I like going out to eat, Mommy."

"I know you do, and you always act like a little lady. Tonight's one of those times. We're going someplace new so we have to use our manners."

"I know, Mommy. No loud talking, no crying, and sit real pretty." She smiled, her tiny white teeth sparkling. "Daddy always calls me his little lady." Katy grew pensive. "Mommy, how come Daddy doesn't call me?"

The unexpected question caught Raine off-guard. "I don't know, baby. Maybe he's someplace where he can't make any calls. He hasn't called me, either." Save for the threatening voicemail. "You know he would if he could."

But Katy's next words surprised her, and explained why she hadn't asked about Daddy for a while. "Yeah, but Mommy, I'm glad he hasn't. Daddy hasn't been very nice in a long time. He's really grouchy. I hope he's nicer when I see him again. I wish he was nice like Mr. Jess."

So Katy had been aware of the changes in Addison. And comparing him to Jess was like comparing heaven to hell—Jess being heaven. Jess would protect those he cared about with his life. Hadn't he done just that by serving his country for so many years? If Jess had your back, you never had to worry.

"Maybe he will be. Maybe Daddy's someplace thinking real hard about how grouchy he's been." Yeah right. The only thing Addison's thinking about is where his next hit of coke is coming from.

"Mommy, can we stay on 'cation?' I don't like my old home anymore. I like it here, and I like Mr. Jess. And Santa will find me here, too."

"Don't worry about anything, Katy-bug," she squeezed warm water over her to rinse the bubbles off, "we're staying here for a long time. And I promise, cross my heart, Santa knows exactly where you are. Okay pumpkin; out you get. Would you like to wear your new red dress?"

Katy nodded, holding her arms up to be lifted out of the tub. Raine wrapped a thick fluffy towel around her slick little body and carried her to the bedroom. Later, standing beneath the hot spray, Katy's words replayed in her head. Katy was torn—part of her missed Addison while the other part was glad he wasn't around. As for Jess, she'd loved him from that very first day. Just like you, a little voice said. Annoyed, she flipped on the cold water tap.

The second they stepped inside the restaurant they were delighted. The ambiance— flickering candles, dancing shadows on the cherry-wood walls, and soft music—a nineteen-thirtyish gangster-feel had Raine expecting zoot-suited gangsters carrying tommy guns to materialize. A tuxedoed maître d' led them to a white linen-covered table. Passing a couple of business-suited men sitting at the highly sheened mahogany bar, they smiled appreciatively. Her lips tilted in a half-smile of acknowledgement as the gentle sway of her hips led the clinging black dress like the maestro leading an orchestra, every movement set to a mesmerizing beat. The admiring looks bolstered her very battered ego. Eat your heart out, Jess Harper!

After giving their drink order Raine looked around. "This is wonderful. It reminds me of the nineteen-thirties. I bet if they could talk these walls could tell some stories..." Suddenly prickling sensations had the hair on her neck standing at attention. What had set off that internal alarm? Scanning the room, her gaze landed with a resounding crash. Stricken to the heart, she stared in abject misery at Jess and the beautiful woman with him. Now she knew why he'd tossed her out of the stable. He had someone else.

Seeing Raine's stricken expression, Cora looked in the same direction and started steaming seeing Jess in the company of another woman. For two-cents she'd march over and box his ears until they fell off.

The oddest sensation came over Jess as he took a sip of his drink. Glancing around, shock crashed through him when his eyes collided with a stricken Raine's. Good God! This couldn't be happening! Momentarily he panicked, then quickly recovered, plastering an insolent smirk on his face to send her a message. Still holding her gaze, he deliberately reached across the table to clasp the woman's hand in his. This ought to get his point across.

For a second, he looked stunned to see her but Raine got the message loud and clear with a jolting revelation—he preferred this woman over her! The death throes hurt so bad she thought she'd die right then and for a panicky moment she actually felt physically ill. Then the fury started. How dare he kiss her so passionately then turn to another woman! He'd been playing her! First Addison, now Jess. She really was a loser with men. Blinking furiously through her tears, she turned away.

Cora watched the battle for composure. It was the deep cleansing breath and desolate sigh of resigned acceptance that signaled the conquering. Then she glanced at Jess, caught his eyes and gave him a look that should have knocked him out of his chair. "How about we go someplace else to celebrate?" She suggested

"I'm all for it." Raine whispered.

"What are you doing?" Isabella Michaels, otherwise known as Belle, hissed, her green eyes flashing. "Look how upset she is. She thinks you're on a date with me! You let go of my hand this second, you jackass, and quit tormenting that girl or you'll be sorry! You're either trying to make her jealous or shove her away. I don't know which but I won't be a party to your shenanigans! Look at her!"

"Technically speaking, I am on a date with you." Jess grinned sardonically, but it didn't quite reach his eyes.

"Stop it!" She smacked his hand. "You know what I mean. I know she's the woman you're crazy about because Cooper told me so."

"Damn him," Jess swore. "Cooper's got a great big mouth," he said sarcastically.

"That's what husbands and wives do, you ass! They tell each other everything, and if you weren't so stupid and thick-headed you might find that out for yourself."

One thing about Belle—she told you how it was—whether you wanted to hear it or not. "Well I don't have any intention of finding out, smarty-pants. And, I'm not stupid, or an ass, either." He glared. Sometimes she could really be irritating. Belle was his best friend, too, but there were times he really wanted to choke her. Now being one of them.

"That's still up for debate!" She tossed her head.

Leaning back, he crossed his arms defensively. "You women are all alike. Once you get a guy's ring on your finger you think all men should make that trip down the aisle. Well I've been down it and back with no intentions of doing it again. That would be stupid." He took a big slug of his scotch then gasped as it burned all the way down. His eyes watered against the burn. "Of course, I wouldn't mind being married to her for a night or two." He said, knowing it would get a rise out of her. Sure enough, sparks shot from her glittery green eyes.

"Watch it buddy boy, or I'll march right over there and tell her how you really feel about her." Her evil-eyed look made him cringe. She might've said it in jest but it didn't fool him, it was no idle threat. "It's a good thing Cooper's on duty or he'd be in the thick of your little game. You know—the one where you're trying to make another woman so jealous she wants to get into a catfight over you." She teased smugly.

Jess gritted his teeth. "Damn! Cooper really does have a big mouth. What else has he told you?" he demanded, a get-even gleam in his eyes. Cooper Michaels just didn't know when to keep his mouth shut. There were a few things he hoped his old buddy really had kept mum about. Besides, he hadn't played those kinds of cat-and-mouse games in years. Those game-playing days were in the past. Now he was a one-woman-at-a-time man.

Grinning, Belle patted his hand. "Never mind, I'll keep your sordid little secrets." But there was a hint of shadow in her earnest green eyes. "Just a word of advice Jess; if you love her, tell her. And it doesn't make any difference how long you've known her. Don't be playing stupid games. Don't let her get away. Life's too short for that."

Belle's sincere advice came straight from the heart. She'd met tragedy up close and personal having lost her first husband when he was killed in the line of duty. Answering a domestic dispute call, Michael Parks had been shot dead before he had a chance to draw his gun. His killer was sent to prison but the drama continued when he was mistakenly released. Hell-bent on revenge, he had a score to settle. The officer he blamed for his incarceration was no longer alive so he went for the next best thing—killing that officer's wife—Belle. He'd badly injured her, putting her in intensive care. When the attack happened, it was his friend Cooper that Belle had been dating. Now they were married. Jess considered Belle a strong woman to fall in love with another man who wore a law enforcement badge—Cooper being a sheriff's deputy. And Belle was right about life being too short to let Raine get away.

"You've made your point. After everything you've been through and were fortunate enough to find happiness twice in one lifetime I think I can take a page out of your book. It's time for me to get on the stick and try to figure things out with her no matter how complicated they are."

At her questioning look, he explained about Raine still being in love with her husband. Belle shook her head emphatically. "No way, no sane woman loves a man who beats her."

"She told me so!" He protested.

"So what, I'm sure you spouted a lot crazy nonsense to her, too. Now it's time for honesty, on both your parts."

Maybe Belle was right on both points. "You're right. I guess now's as good a time as any to tell her I was only playing her." He started to get up but stopped short. His timing sucked, they were already walking to the door. "Well hell," he muttered, sitting again.

"Serves you right; you lunk-head!" He glared at her. "There goes your chance to start making amends and I must say, by all the admiring looks she's attracting from the guys at the bar, it won't be long before someone snaps her up. Age is catching up old boy. You're definitely not quick on your feet tonight." She grinned cheekily and was rewarded with a warning lift of a dark brow. Ignoring it, she rubbed her hands together and taunted. "I can't wait to fill Cory in."

"Belle!" His tone was threatening. Having Belle after him was bad enough, put her and Cory together and he'd never get any peace.

"Okay, pokey," she relented, "I'll take pity on you." She laid her napkin on the table. "Now I should be heading home."

After paying the check he walked her to her vehicle. "A word of advice, Jess, if you don't want to lose that lady you better figure something out."

"Thanks for caring." He nodded, kissing her cheek.

Driving home Jess mulled Belle's advice. Somehow, he had to fix what he'd messed up and prove he was the man worthy of her love. One thing was for sure, after tonight his work was cut out for him. Now he had hurdles to jump—a husband she supposedly still had feelings for, and convincing her that Belle was only a friend. He just hoped this silly stunt didn't come back to bite him in the ass.

As for Raine, seeing Jess with that woman put her on an emotional roller-coaster that hauled her into a sleep plagued with nightmares involving Addison, Jess, and that sultry, dark-haired woman. While Addison whipped her unmercifully, Jess and the woman jeered. "You shouldn't have played games with him." More than once she awoke sweat-drenched and sobbing. After the last time she refused to shut her eyes again. Easing from bed so as not to wake Katy, she padded to the kitchen, put on a pot of coffee and decided to work. Maybe it would take her mind off the mess her life was in. Four hours and two pots later she stretched her aching muscles and scratched her head as if to wake up her flagging brain. Keeping focused, she'd worked through three short stories. She thought a shower might rejuvenate her, however, the reflection staring back remained washed out and haggard, the dark circles gracing her eyes looked like she'd been punched again. Thank goodness for concealer.

Over breakfast, they listened to the weatherman's prediction that the snow wouldn't arrive until late evening. There was plenty of time to drive in, get the dollhouse and be back before it set in. Yawning, she took another sip of coffee. Maybe she'd catch a little cat nap later and hopefully the oh-so-real nightmares would stay away.

While dressing, she thought of Jess and the woman and admitted they made a striking couple with that raven black hair and the woman's porcelain complexion was a perfect foil for the thick cascade of curls. If he preferred that woman over her then fine, she didn't care anymore. It was plain he'd just been playing games, that getting her in to bed his ultimate goal, and like a fool she'd almost fallen into his trap. As far as she was concerned from here on out he could give all his attention to the dark-haired woman. But the idea sent her heart crashing to her toes.

"While you're taking care of business Katy and I will make some cookies," Cora called from the living room, interrupting her grim musings.

"I wish I didn't have to go. I'd much rather be baking cookies," she called back for Katy's benefit.

"We'll save you some, Mommy," Katy promised. Secretly, she couldn't wait to eat the cookie dough. That was "the bestest" ever part of making cookies!

Suddenly she swore she heard the rich timber of Jess's voice then decided it was someone on television. Then she heard it again. Great! Just great! He was the last person she wanted to see. And what was he doing up here, anyway? They needed absolutely nothing from him! Rent was paid through March. She had no desire to set eyes on the man. Irritation raked through her. How dare he show up after being with that . . . woman and so obviously enjoying her company! She wanted to run him off and wished she had a cattle prod to do it. Contradicting her head, her heart skipped merrily in her chest. "Don't you get excited, you idiot," she scolded her heart. "After the way he's acted you'd better not, I repeat, better not get all soft and gooey at the sight of him." But in the war between her head and her heart, her heart won out.

If she was going to get to the mall and back before the snow set in, she'd better quit stalling. Why hadn't she left a few minutes sooner, she'd have missed him. Pulling on her coat, she walked into the living room. The scent of him—subtle spice and fresh, crisp air wafted over her. For the rest of her life those two scents would always trigger images of him.

Though conversing with Cora, Jess was attuned for any sound of Raine. After last night's idiotic behavior he had to start fixing things between them. Seeing her, his mouth went dry as a parched desert, his world tilted crazily before righting itself. Ignoring him, she dropped a kiss on Katy's head. Mesmerized, he couldn't tear his eyes away from the way the dark denim of her blue jeans molded to her trim thighs and backside as she leaned over the couch. A sharp stirring of desire warmed him.

"You be careful," Cora said, "Take your time, but watch the weather. Weather forecasters are sometimes fooled by Mother Nature. She looked at Jess. There was a determined gleam in his eyes and it wasn't for her. She figured after last night's fiasco he was here to do some fancy foot-kissing. Seeing him with that other woman had knocked Raine for such a loop she was ready to pull up stakes. And just where did that woman fit into the scheme of things, anyway? He hadn't stayed with her last night. He'd arrived home shortly after they had. Yes indeed, something was very rotten in Jess Harper's world. She sort of felt sorry for him, knowing his work was cut out for him, but not too sorry. Smitten and fighting it, it turned him into a moron. Hopefully he wouldn't wait too long to tell Raine how he felt. Things were turning dire. Upon leaving the restaurant she'd started talking of going back to Phoenix instead of staying here. However, she planned to do everything in her power to stall her. Inez would help, too. She was of the same mind that the two mule-headed people were perfect for each other. As soon as they walked out the door she'd call Inez.

"I will," Raine answered at the same time Jess demanded, "Where are you going?"

Her furrowed frown matched his furrowed frown. Didn't the man know how to ask a question without it sounding like a military command? Besides, it wasn't any of his business where she went so she ignored him.

Bristling, he repeated. "Where are you going?"

And again, it wasn't any of his business. As far as she was concerned he could jump in the nearest icy river and take that . . . woman with him. "That's none of your business."

A warning brow shot up. "Let's get something straight. As long as you live on my property it is my business." On top of that she was his woman and she could put that in her pipe and smoke it, too!

"Well that can be remedied!" Venom spewed from her glittering eyes.

Oh brother, Cora grimaced, seeing the fire glittering in Raine's eyes. She wouldn't have been surprised if the sparks didn't singe the hair right off Jess's gorgeous head. And he was no better, getting angry because she wouldn't give him the time of day. What had he expected? But she noted something different about him—gone was the self-protective shield. Had he finally seen the light? Again, what about the woman from last night? It was time the two hard-headed people got together. Plus, knowing Raine didn't want Katy finding out about her present, she could kill two birds with one large boulder.

"Okay you two, out the door. Get going. Time's a wasting." And she shoved them out and slammed it.

Scowling, Raine thought Cora had been taking lessons from Jess on giving people the bum's rush. She was almost as good as the teacher himself!

"What the hell was that about? What suddenly put a bee in her bonnet?" he demanded.

Groaning in exasperation, she jerked on brown leather gloves. "Not that it's still any of your business, but I'm going to the mall. The dollhouse Katy asked Santa for arrived and I'm headed to get it. She's really worried Santa won't find his way out here in the woods." Making a gesture that encompassed the whole snow-covered area. "Now I've got to go. I want to be back before it starts snowing." Stepping around him, she unlocked the SUV.

Watching her, Jess glowered. If she thought she was going alone with a snowstorm headed their way, she was crazier than a bed-bug at a mattress convention. "I'm going with you," he said, quickly confiscating the keys before she realized his intentions then opened the door to the cabin and tossed them to Cora. "I'm driving her into town." He said while ignoring Raine's, "but I don't want you to go with me."

Cora caught the keys in midair. "Good. I'll feel much better knowing she's not out there alone, especially if the weather turns bad." She grinned seeing Raine mouthing traitor, traitor, at her over and over then gave Jess a warning look. "You just be careful."

"Don't worry. I'll take good care of her." He glanced at Raine. The glare she shot him sent one dark brow arching as if asking innocently "What did I do wrong?" He expected an argument but she surprised him by clamping her mouth shut. Still, there was no mistaking the mutiny in her eyes. She was definitely ticked and he knew the reasons why—last night with Belle, the scene in the stable, and not being in control today. Well she could be mad. If the weather turned bad he didn't want her out alone. She wasn't used to driving in the deep snow predicted so she would just have to suck it up and put up with his company. As for Belle, he'd explain about her later.

Hot with anger, she didn't need a coat to keep warm and she was sorely tempted to knock that arrogant grin off his handsome face. She didn't want his company. As far as she was concerned he could go drive his girlfriend around.

"I'm perfectly capable of driving to the city and back without your help." She jerked her arm, trying to loosen it from the hand hooked around it as he escorted her down the shoveled path.

"I'm sure you are but you might as well give in graciously! You're not going to win. I'm driving you and that's that. Look hard-head," he stopped suddenly, his eyes steely hard, "I either drive you or you don't go. Take it or leave it."

It was like waving a red flag in front of a charging bull. Who the hell did he think he was giving her ultimatums, especially after last night? Furious, she shoved him so hard he almost lost his footing. For a second his grip loosened and she jerked free, whirling on him.

"You don't tell me what to do, buster! You have no say in anything I do! I'm just your tenant!" She stomped her foot childishly. "Go drive your girlfriend around! She might want your company! I. Do. Not!" Each word was enunciated with a hard poked in his chest.

Hallelujah! Not only was she madder than hell, she was jealous, too. And Lord, but she was so damned hot when she was mad he was tempted to kiss her. Instead, he started to confess everything then clamped his mouth shut deciding to let her stew a while longer; see just how jealous she really became. And did this jealousy mean she didn't love her husband after all?

"Never mind her," he said dismissively, "she was yesterday; this is today." She opened her mouth but he cut her off. "I'm not arguing with you. You know the deal on the table. Either I go with you or you don't go at all." Fascinated, he watched her puff up like an outraged bull frog ready to explode. Heaving a weary sigh, Jess prepared for battle, knowing she wasn't going to agree. He was right.

"I'm damn well going and you can't stop me!" She gritted through clenched teeth.

Dark eyes glittered at the challenge. "Don't kid yourself. I can and I will. I'll keep you from getting through the gate. In case you've forgotten, I have complete control of its opening and closing. I can reset the remote code and you'd never be able to leave except on foot." What should have been a simple matter was getting out of hand. She opened her mouth to argue but he cut her off. "Look. Just humor me. Calm down and think about it. These roads can be a bitch when it snows and I should know. You slide off in a ditch and you could be stuck for hours before anyone comes along. Last winter I spent nearly four hours in a drift before anyone came by." He really hadn't but she didn't need to know that, and a little white lie wouldn't hurt if it got her to agree with him.

Though she'd die before admitting it, he made sense. She really didn't want to be stuck off alone for God knows how long if she ended up in a ditch. "Fine! You drive." She snapped and flounced the rest of the way down the stone path.

Behind her he heaved a huge sigh of relief that she'd finally seen his point. Round one was his. Ten more to go, he thought ruefully.

CHAPTER EIGHTEEN

Anger radiated from her as he unlocked the passenger door and waited for her to get in. He wanted to laugh at her but knew it would only make her madder. Wisely, he choked it back and shut the door. All-righty then, this should be a fun morning, he thought as he rounded the hood.

Settling in the plush seat, the new vehicle scent wafted around her. The truck was big and roomy with a hard-shell top on the back. That would be good to put Katy's present in to keep it dry. Okay. Maybe taking his truck would prove useful after all. Jess turned the key and immediately loud music blasted from the speakers.

"Sorry." He turned the volume down.

Well, that was something else in his favor—he liked country music, and he liked it loud when by himself, so did she. Not that it mattered since this was the only time she'd ride in it.

"Nice truck," she commented, keeping her tone neutral. "It still has that showroom-floor smell."

"It's fairly new. I got it just before you moved in. It was time. I kept the old one for emergencies and working around the place. The old one's more than served its purpose." A man-and-his-truck affection filled his voice. Looking both ways, he pulled onto the blacktopped road. There were still icy patches scattered here and there from their last snowfall and skidding on one of those patches was not in his plan. As the old saying goes, he'd been there, done that. He certainly did not want to crash with this passenger.

Raine observed his strong, capable hands controlling the large truck with practiced competence. She might itch to kick him to kingdom come but she felt safe with him behind the wheel. She could trust him with her life, but not her feelings, not after last night. But that didn't stop her fantasizing having those hands touching her all over and the wanton images heated her so thoroughly she unbuttoned her coat. Cheeks burning, she averted her face. Glancing over, Jess caught the red creeping into her face and wondered what had caused it.

The silence remained thick until she spotted a trio of deer at the far edge of a field. "Oh . . . look!" she exclaimed, her aggravation momentarily forgotten. "Katy would love them."

"She'd want one for a pet," he laughed.

"You're probably right. She already wants a baby cow, as she calls it." Her throaty chuckle stirred a curl of longing within him that had him shifting in the seat and his own face reddening.

They entered the tiny village of Vail. Loving legends of old towns, Raine figured this one was fairly steeped to the waist in it. Even its name had her wondering who, or what, it had been named after—an early settler, the town in Colorado? She'd have to find the library and brush up on the local lore. On one side of the road sat the dilapidated remnants of the town's former hotel. She bet it had been quite grand back in the day and her fertile imagination conjured up all sorts of ghostly people passing through its ornate doors. Presidents, public figures, even famous stage actors in all their glittery finery catching the attention of the local residents. And there'd have been out-laws, riverboat gamblers, maybe even mobsters. Off the beaten path, it would have made an excellent outlaw haven. Then the truck slid on an icy patch and reality returned in the form of the rundown building. What a shame it had fallen into such disrepair and left to ghosts. She sighed heavily, knowing she'd take the ghost of Jess with her when she left.

The melancholy sound drew his attention. Her pensive reflection had him wondering why she looked sad. Was she thinking of yesterday? He was. His shabby treatment at the stables and then of last night was constantly in his head. "Something wrong?"

"No, just thinking of ghosts." She nodded at the vacant buildings they were passing, "Of letting go." Her cryptic words sent an icy chill through him, making him consider his feelings for her. He didn't want to let them go. If he did she'd forever haunt him.

When they eased into another sharp curve Raine was positive a cranky rattlesnake cut the path for this road, given its winding, twisting curves. As though reading her mind, he said. "Sometimes I wonder what it was like back in the days when this was probably nothing more than a rutted path. It must have been pretty rough going. Can you imagine riding a horse all the time or driving a wagon, or stage-coaches running through here carrying passengers, even payrolls, to the miners working in the lead mines."

"Lead mines?" Raine looked at him, her curiosity piqued.

He looked at her, noting she looked tired, as though she'd spent a sleepless night. Was he the reason for it? She sure as hell was the reason for his.

"Mining's been a mainstay for folks around here for years. It was a dirty job and in the past life expectancy was pretty short given how dangerous the mining conditions were. I've heard tales about more than one cave-in burying miners alive. I guess the methods have improved but no matter how it shakes, it's still mining—it comes out of the earth in one way or another."

At an intersection, they stopped in front of a rustic log cabin. Three stories high, it sprawled in ragamuffin grace across a snow-covered lawn. This morning plumes of smoke curled into the overcast sky from two chimneys and lights cast a cheery yellow glow behind lace curtains hanging in the paned windows. Several snowmen stood in various areas of the yard and two little boys bundled up against the cold were rolling in the snow. Even from inside the truck their shrieks of laughter could be heard. How wonderful it would be to raise a family in a sprawling old home like that with Jess.

The idea set her pulse racing as though she'd run the Boston Marathon and won. Then, a picture of him with the dark-haired woman flashed before her eyes and the fantasy crashed and burned. She was surprised he didn't hear the explosion. Silly girl, you're not the kind of woman he prefers. Give it up; accept you have no place in his life. Another woman stands with him behind that wall and three people don't fit. Facing that reality made her decision to leave easier.

Attuned to her moods, something had just changed. Was it last night? He'd seen her reaction—betrayal, hurt, jealousy, then anger. The jealousy really got him. If she was still in love with her husband, why be jealous? And this chilly politeness was getting to him, too. He'd rather she tear into him than be coldly quiet. When he'd insisted on driving her, he'd expected her to fuss at him every mile of the trip. And, what would he have done if she'd called his bluff? Followed along behind her, that's what he'd have done.

He marveled at his own change of heart. His vow to steer clear of her had lasted about as long as ice in hell. At first physical attraction had drawn him, then his heart had gotten involved and his no-ties motto bit the dust when the pesky little blond sitting beside him stormed his defenses, ruining all his best laid plans. But he'd done something stupid he had to fix. Sometimes he was his own worst enemy, he thought wryly.

Then his mind turned to another enemy—her husband. Maybe Belle was right. Maybe Raine was blowing smoke. Hadn't he asked himself a thousand times how she could kiss him with so much passion if she loved another man? A sharp stab of anger ripped through him. Dammit! If she was jealous then she had to care for him. If not, she needed to hightail it back to her husband. But the seeds of doubt Belle had planted said she didn't want her husband, especially after last night's reaction to Belle. This possibility strengthened his determination to do whatever it took to make Raine his. This was a high-stakes game and he had no intention of losing, even if he had to play dirty and use whatever tactics it took. This game was his. Glancing at her left hand, his jaw clenched. The enemy's gold wedding band was still on it. No way! There was no way in hell she could still be in love with the S.O.B. Taking a cleansing breath, he decided it was time to turn on the charm and get back in her good graces.

Making a pretense of looking at something on his side of the road, Raine saw the half-smile on his face. He's thinking about the pretty brunette, she thought grumpily. Just then he looked her way and winked. Her eyes narrowed suspiciously; certain he was up to no good again. He was up to no good; she could feel it in the marrow of her bones.

Gazing out the windshield, she noted flurries speckling it. As long as it stayed light they could pick up Katy's present and be back before the heavier snow set in. As long as Katy had that dollhouse on Christmas morning nothing else mattered. Not Jess, not her feelings for him, nothing. She sighed heavily.

Lost in thought, the betrayal on her face from last night remained in his head making him feel like a cheater. But he wasn't and it was time to concentrate on winning over the love of his life. Happy in his decision, he relaxed—for about ten seconds then a new seed of doubt sprouted and once again he was tensing up. If he succeeded would he be her rebound? That idea made him ill. Great! Just great! The woman had him so twisted up if he wasn't careful he'd be selling the farm and renting a room from Cooper and Belle. That idea made Jess shudder, not in revulsion, but in fear—of Belle. The woman was a force to be reckoned with. No doubt she'd be after her pound of flesh for last night.

Okay he decided, until she was free there'd be no more hot kisses and no more tantalizing caresses that left him yearning for more. Unbidden, the scene at the stable flashed through his mind. She'd been in his arms before he'd realized it and he'd shot straight to heaven but then reality broke through and he'd had to act fast. Despite his all-consuming need, he had to get her out. As far as he was concerned, if and when she came to him again, there would be no guilty shackles attached. If and when she was divorced from her husband, he'd be willing take all she offered; however no way in hell would he be a stand-in for that low-life wife-beater. No way was he a rebound for any woman, especially the one sitting beside him. He rather she be gone!

Glancing at her again, images of her hair fanned out in all its golden glory on his pillow made him shift again. This new resolve was already getting slipperier than a greased eel. Damn! Thank God for the length of his coat. That was all he needed—to have his hormones raging out of control. Clamping down on his wayward desire, a trace of humor surfaced; if he touched her she might bite him.

What were the odds they'd end up in the same restaurant, at the same time, and on the same night? And lord-a-mighty! That black dress had set his pulse racing. It'd clung in all the right places, hinting of the delicious curves beneath. A quick glance around the room had confirmed what Belle had astutely pointed out—he wasn't the only male admiring the alluring beauty of Raine Andrews.

Overwhelming possessiveness shot through him. She was his woman and she was coming to him on his terms, she just didn't realize it yet. And he was going to turn the charm on so high that soon he'd be charming those jeans off of her lovely body. He smiled when the southern part of his body throbbed in agreement.

Raine watched his sexy mouth tilt in a smile again. Nice to know someone's happy, she groused before taking herself to task, just enjoy the few hours together and stick to safe subjects like the kids and Christmas. "How did you come up with the idea of using your home for the camp for kids?"

At least she's not freezing me out anymore, he thought. "It was easy. I grew up in the system. I know first-hand what it's like not to have anyone or anything. The rest of the year you can slide through but the holidays are the pits when there's nothing special about them." He glanced at her then back at the highway. "It's especially hard for the older kids. The younger ones are the first to get placed but the older you get, well, there aren't many families willing to take on older children. I suspect folks figure they've already picked up bad habits and don't want to deal with them, especially if there are other children already in the home, leastways that was always my take on it."

A lump lodged in her throat. Jess had been one of those older kids no one wanted? She'd just assumed he'd come from a loving home with brothers and sisters. It proved you should never assume anything. Uncannily his experiences mirrored hers. She also understood for she'd had her share of foster homes.

"If you're lucky you get a family that's willing to go through the whole rigamarole of adoption. Sometimes it takes years before it's finally through the system. Then there are the foster families who'll take in a whole passel of kids and treat them like second-rate citizens just for the money." Slowing, he exited to the mall parking lot and found a parking space close to entrance.

"What about you?" She made no attempt to get out of the warm cab. She'd learned more about Jess in the last fifteen minutes than she had in the last eight weeks.

"No adoption." He shook his head. "A few foster families, some good, some not so good. I probably gave them my fair share of fits. I stayed around the last one for about a month, until I turned sixteen," that young, wet behind the ears kid seemed a long time ago, "then one night I got what few belongings I had together and the money I'd been saving from a part-time job and split in the middle of the night. I guess you could say I've pretty much been on my own since that night."

It was said so matter-of-factly, as though an ordinary part of life. Her heart ached for that long gone little boy trapped in the system. "Where did you go when you left? What did you do?"

"I knocked around here and there then fell in with a group of pretty unsavory kids. We crashed wherever we could find a place to stay, did a few questionable things to put food in our bellies, change in our pockets, petty stuff." He made a scoffing sound. "Then they did something really stupid. They robbed a gas station one night and got caught, and even though I wasn't part of it I still got my ass arrested and hauled off to jail." This was a subject he usually kept locked firmly away yet here he was telling her details about himself that only Cooper, Belle, and Cory knew. He stared out the windshield at the big fluffy flakes hitting it. When had the flurries changed to bigger flakes?

"What happened after you were arrested? Surely the police cleared you, let you go when they found out you didn't rob the station?" Her blue eyes stared intently at him. Not for a second did she believe him capable of any crime.

"Eventually they did but they kept me locked up overnight. It was quite a wake-up call and the best thing that could have happened. It scared the hell out of me all right, made me realize I wanted more than to knock about life like I'd been doing for a year. Fortunately, when the police reviewed the surveillance tapes, there wasn't a sign of me anywhere so they couldn't charge me with anything."

Raine continued studying him, unable to picture him robbing a gas station, or doing anything illegal, for that matter, but she wanted to hear him say again that he'd been innocent. "So, you really had nothing to do with the robbery?"

Meeting her steady gaze head-on, the silence thickened in the truck as he held her eyes. "What do you think?" The challenge was thrown out like a gauntlet. He wanted, no, needed to hear her say she believed in his innocence.

The honesty in her vivid blue eyes took his breath away. "I don't believe you were involved. I don't believe you'd ever do anything against the law."

His pent-up breath hissed out. "Good, because I wasn't anywhere near that gas station. While those idiots were hanging out getting into mischief I'd found a job slinging burgers. I was working when they robbed the station and didn't have a clue what they'd done until later. It took a couple of days for the police to track the guys to our hang-out then they bided their time watching us come and go. When they made their move they arrested everyone, including me." Jess recalled with great clarity how much he'd protested his innocence at the top of his lungs but the cops hadn't believed him. In their eyes he'd been judged guilty simply by association.

"That was too close a call for me. I talked my boss into letting me live above the café and never saw that crew again. Of course, they ended up behind bars. I stayed there until just after my eighteenth birthday then one day I found myself standing in front of a recruiting office staring at a poster for the Marines. One minute I'm outside and the next I'm in joining up. I finished high school, got my engineering degree, and the rest is history. The Marines became my life. Now I have a good retirement, my own business, and I'd saved practically all my pay since I lived on base most of the time, except for the short I was married. And when I retired I had the property to come home to."

He didn't have to say it for her to know he was very proud of his accomplishments. And she was proud of him, too, wanted to tell him so but having no place in his life, didn't. He had the dark-haired beauty to praise him.

The myriad of emotions flitting across her face were like butterflies fluttering over a field of wildflowers. Was she thinking of her own parents and how fortunate to have them? And why hadn't she turned to them for help? Or was she thinking about her incarcerated scumbag of a husband? He had no idea how far off base he was.

"You know about my lack of family. What about you? Why aren't your folks helping you through this mess with your husband?" Since they weren't divorced he refused to say ex-husband.

Shadows turned her blue eyes even darker. This subject had molded her ideals for being a good mother. There was the slightest hesitation before she answered. "I . . . don't know who my folks are, or where they live, or if they're even alive. They left me on the steps of a church. Like you, I grew up in foster care and as soon as I could, I hit the road. Even though I didn't have any bad experiences, I needed to prove to myself that I could make it on my own."

Learning she hadn't come from a loving family and that her experiences mirrored his own surprised him. He understood about making it on your own. Being his own man had been the driving force that had him enlisting in the Marines. The service had made him grow up, made a man out of him. And though he'd had some close calls, he'd survived and never once regretted his decision. He'd joined up a wet behind the ears kid and left it a man. The day he'd stepped out of that jail cell he'd vowed to make something of his life, to make a difference and he accomplished that with his years of service, his education, his security designs, and his camp for kids.

"No clue at all who they are?" He asked.

Raine shook her head. "I know I was left there along with one little suitcase filled with a few articles of baby clothes, a rag doll, and a birth certificate with the name Raine Elizabeth Danvers on it. The hospital where I was born was listed on it but nothing else. Actually, the birth certificate looks like a copy someone made up. I'm not even sure if it's real, for that matter." There was a pained look in her eyes. "The nuns figured I was about two days old. A night watchman making rounds found me." Raine gave half a laugh, "I guess you'd say I was born that day. That's the date I use for my birthday, anyway."

Jess ached to comfort her. He couldn't ever fathom abandoning his child. "Did you ever check hospitals' birth records around the time you were born?"

"I did, but the place had been turned into medical offices. No records remained from when it was a hospital. Even after Addison and I got together, we tried. We went to other hospitals in the area but no one could tell us where the records were. I even went to the county courthouse but that didn't help, either. Eventually I just gave up, told myself it was for the best. I figured if they didn't want me then I didn't want them."

"Maybe they had good reasons for leaving you at the church. Maybe they couldn't take care of themselves, let alone you."

"Possibly, but that's something I'll never know." And that was enough about her since he had that other woman. She turned the subject back on him. "I assume you don't know why you ended up in foster care, either?"

"Oh, I know." As whenever he thought of it, his heart turned sad. "My folks were killed in a car crash. I was with them but I survived. I was four, an only child with no relatives to take me in. I was literally left all alone."

"I'm so sorry, Jess." Impulsively, she touched his arm. They both had survived the hard knocks life had given them.

"Don't be sorry for me, Raine. It's not something I'd have ever dreamed of happening but I survived it just fine. It made me tougher." He sounded tough, too.

There was no arguing about that, she thought, shaking her head. "I'm not sorry for you, the man you've become. I'm sorry for that little boy who had his whole world ripped to pieces. I can't imagine Katy going through something like that." Growing up in the foster system had instilled the greatest need to give her own child a stable, nurturing environment and she was doing just that despite Addison.

Something occurred to him, something so sickening his stomach curled painfully. Given the condition she'd been in when he'd first met her, she'd been in one hellacious fight for her life. So why still love the man? There was definitely more to her story and one of these days he'd get it out of her.

Feeling the intensity of his stare, she looked at him and saw the brooding look on his face. Obviously, something was seriously eating at him. She opened her mouth to inquire then thought better of it. He's thinking of his girlfriend and comparing us and no way could she ever compete with her. Quit thinking those torturing thoughts or you'll never get through today without totally breaking down.

Meeting her blue-eyed gaze, Jess saw the exact moment she shut down. Had she been reading his mind? Unconsciously, he shook his head. Raine misinterpreted that he preferred the other woman to her and her heart wilted. Opening the door, she slid into the blowing flurries. He didn't see the tears she quickly blinked away.

Chapter Nineteen

She spied the mall directory in the "T" where the branches of the mall split off. Reaching it, she scanned the list of stores then set off down a wing of the festively decorated mall, not waiting for him. "Friday, I was all over this place and got completely turned around. It's this way."

His booted footsteps echoed, letting her know he was close behind her. Then he was even with her. "You're not losing me that easily."

"I should be so lucky." She muttered then heard his deep-throated chuckle. Blushing, she refused to look at him. Drat the man! He had the hearing of an elephant. She'd better work harder at keeping her smart-ass comments to herself.

Jess shortened his long strides to keep pace with hers. She might have indulged in pleasant conversation coming in but she was still in a snit and his ego inflated like a gigantic balloon in the Macy's parade knowing she was jealous. Again, why the jealousy if she were still in love with her husband? Well now . . . he just might have to do something else to shake her up, make her even more jealous.

"There's the toy store." Her voice broke into his plotting mind.

"I'd have never figured that out." He said, allowing her to enter it ahead of him.

It didn't take him long to get caught up in the magic of the toy store. It had been years since he'd been inside one. This store was huge, boasting every kind of toy imaginable. Shelves displayed animated toys just begging to be played with, and boxes and boxes of games and puzzles were stacked ceiling high, and glory be, there was even an area replicating a miniature zoo with kid-sized stuffed giraffes, zebras, monkeys, and gorillas big enough to handle toddlers crawling all over them. Jess chuckled at two very determined little boys around the age of two looking ready to come to pudgy-fisted blows over a black and white striped zebra. One mother grabbed her child directing him to a giraffe while the other partnered her little scrapper with a gorilla.

Another area had a miniature farm with wagons painted glossy greens and reds and hooked up to the tractors. Holy smokes! This was kid heaven. Shoot, who was he fooling? He was no kid but he was already mesmerized. Passing another display, he became ensnared by rows and rows of musical Christmas toys beckoning "press my tummy and I sing." Unable to resist, by the time they reached the end of the aisle everyone within a twenty-foot radius was being serenaded by a dozen different quirky songs. The deep timber of his laughter rang out as he started singing along with some of them.

Quickening her step, Raine tried getting away from him. It didn't help. He just quickened his pace. "You know, I could spend all day in here getting all those singing toys going." He said innocently, aware of her attempt to ditch him.

"Then it's a good thing you're not. I've a feeling the manager would throw you out and bar you forever." She said.

A boyish grin lit up his face almost making her forget to be mad at him. When he grinned like that—carefree and young at heart, not that he was old by any means, she pegged him forty or so—she went weak in the knees. If only there was some way to make him forget that woman. This needed some serious studying, especially if she stayed, but leaving was probably better.

Had he known she contemplated leaving, he'd have told her the truth right then that Belle was a friend he'd used to make her jealous and he'd have abandoned all his crazy notions. Instead, his mind buzzed with all kinds of ideas.

"Nah, I'd end up buying a ton of them to make up for the aggravation. Any kid would love to have one of them." She caught another glimpse of the little boy inside the man and it occurred to her he probably hadn't had many toys, so let the little boy inside the grown man enjoy himself. The smile she gave him was bright as a ray of sunshine lighting the inky blackness of a cave.

"You're right about that. Katy's got a bunch of them. She must have one for every holiday you can think of. For Easter, she has this quaking duck and a bunny that sings and dances and hops around. Gosh, I can't even think of all of them right now. But you've given me an idea. She doesn't have anything for this year. I'll get her one."

"Let me do it," he requested, giving her an appealing look.

She gave him a blue-eyed evil look. "Okay. But if you buy the most obnoxious one I'll have to kill you!"

"Would I do that?" He feigned mocked innocence but looked as if she'd promised him the world.

"Don't play innocent with me, big boy. I know you're going to do it! Now go find your toy while I take care of the dollhouse."

Jess rubbed his hands together. "Good! Great! I already know which one I'm getting her. I'll get it and meet up with you." He turned away then turned back. "Raine?" Questioning sapphire eyes met warm brown eyes. "Thank you." A smile tilted the soft fullness of her lips and he recalled how they'd felt against his. She nodded and a rush of emotion thickening in her throat. Despite last night's devastation, he'd just put another hash mark in the plus column.

The pick-up clerk was just bringing the large dollhouse box from the stock room when Jess re-joined her carrying a large shopping bag emblazoned with the store's logo. She tried peeking inside but masses of red tissue paper kept her from it.

He held the bag away from her. "Un-huh! No peeking. I told the clerk to wrap it in extra paper, that momma would be nosy and try peeking in the bag."

"Fine!" She huffed.

Jess easily hefted the dollhouse box on his broad shoulder. "I'll take these out to the truck and be right back. While we're here I might as well do some shopping. I don't come here very often." At the mall entrance he suggested, "Why don't you wait here," and half-expected her to protest but she didn't. From the swirling pools of blowing snow, it appeared the wind had kicked up during the short time they'd been inside but nothing to worry about, he decided.

Watching him through the window, she wondered if he was shopping for the dark-haired woman and a stab of jealousy cut through her. And who knows, maybe he's got a whole stash of girlfriends. Oh, stop it! Quit making yourself more miserable. Besides, it's none of your business who he buys presents for, who he takes to dinner, or who he shares a bed with. Red-hot ire rose thick and intense inside her at all three ideas, especially the latter. But then she was now free to do as she pleased and see who she wanted. So there, Jess Harper! Put that in your damn pipe and smoke it!

He was whistling a jaunty little tune and his cheeks were ruddy from the cold, his wind-mussed dark hair glistening with melting snowflakes. He couldn't miss the sparks of fire in her eyes. They'd appeared the second he mentioned shopping and he had a pretty good hunch where her train of thought was leading—straight to last night and Belle. The idea of shopping for Belle was so hilarious he chuckled. If he bought Belle anything it'd be a spiked dog collar.

Catching her by surprise, he linked his arm through hers. "I'm thinking some high-octane caffeine's needed for this shopping expedition. Come on, let's get some and get started."

After perusing several shops, Jess found the lingerie boutique and started browsing through the tantalizing fluff while enjoying the fragrances spritzed through the air ducts.

A mutinous Raine stood silent, the little green-eyed monster on her shoulder tapping its green-tipped fingers angrily and swinging a green leg agitatedly. It nearly punched him in his aristocratic nose when he held up the sexiest black nightgown she'd ever seen. Her face was just too honest to hide her emotions and he was thoroughly enjoying himself at her expense.

Feigning innocence, he said. "I kind like this little number. What do you think?"

"Pretty, but obviously not made for sleeping." She tried sounding nonchalant when she really itched to rip the filmy material to shreds. She didn't have to ask who it was for—the dark haired woman would look hot and sultry in the wispy confection.

Glee filled Jess. He should be ashamed for baiting her but he was having too much fun. "Isn't that the whole idea? Talk about mood setting. I won't sleep a wink tonight for picturing a certain woman wearing it. This enticing little number is tops in my book and I have to say I'm getting pretty enticed by it already. No doubt about it, I need this."

Seething, she snapped her jaws together so tight she thought they'd never open again. For two cents she'd kick him, and the woman, into the next world.

Aware of the temper she was in, he added more fuel. Humming softly, he sniffed a couple of perfume samples on a glass display before selecting one. Next, he made his way to the matching bra and panty set display and making his selections, added them to his pile. Picturing her wearing them sent a curl of heat wafting through him.

As for Raine, her fuse was growing shorter than the wick on a stick of dynamite. The gown was bad enough then add in the perfume that smelled like sweet heaven and those scanty sets, it was enough to make her do him physical harm. Like punching the hell out of him!

Jess left her stewing in the middle of the racks while he chatted up the pretty sales clerk who happened to be checking out more than just his purchases. Raine watched the young woman openly flirting and she couldn't blame her. Jess was a very handsome man and not the pasty, soft-handed kind of handsome but the rugged, outdoorsy type. The clerk batted her eyes at Jess and jealousy stabbed her again. She'd better quit ogling him or so help me . . . her fists clenched wanting to punch the sales clerk and then Jess. Then she scolded herself. For someone who'd had the holy hell beaten out of them several times she was becoming pretty volatile herself. But he was making her crazy, making her feel things she never had before. Or, she amended, dared to without suffering the consequences.

Her obvious jealousy inflated his ego even more. She assumed he was buying the gown and the other gifts for Belle. Since the woman had his emotions flying all over the place like an out of control rollercoaster, she deserved some payback and he wasn't confessing he was buying the gifts for her. And man, she was smoking hot when she was mad! It was all he could do to keep from grabbing her and kissing the stuffing out of her. Instead, he enjoyed himself in a different way—at her expense. Feeling proud, he mentally slapped himself on the back.

When he'd entered the shop he'd only done it to let his imagination run wild with images of Raine wearing some of the sexiest little scraps of clothing he'd ever seen but her reaction had spurred him on. It was turning out to be quite fun, and it was shaking her up, knocking her off balance.

Glancing at her, he winked. Gritting her teeth, she pasted on a smile all the while chewing nails. So help me God if he winks at me one more time I'll flatten him. Then she took herself to task. Just get through the day without being an idiot. After that she got in a better frame of mind though every now and then the green-eyed monster goaded her to smack him, especially when images of the dark-haired woman wearing the black nightgown, and Jess removing it, flashed through her head. Then she'd get angry all over again. Actually, she was enraged that he had the audacity to buy that stuff in her presences intending to give it to another woman. Unconsciously, her fist doubled up then forced herself to calm down vowing to pretend everything was just hunky-dory even if it killed her.

Leaving the shop they strolled along until Raine paused in front of a jeweler's. The dreamiest look came over her face seeing the style of ring she'd always dreamed of having.

Elegant and tasteful, its antique filigree band was white gold, the center setting a heart-shaped diamond surrounded by sapphires. This ring was completely opposite the one Addison had given her. Why he'd bothered asking her preference she had no clue. He'd considered the one she wanted too old-fashioned, not flashy enough. Instead, he'd bought a gaudy ring with a giant rock that screamed, "Look! At! Me!" Flashy and gaudy weren't her style. It had just been another of Addison's controlling decisions that should have been an early warning of what was to come. However, her spirits lifted remembering that he no longer controlled her. As for the gaudy and very expensive ring, it was locked in a safe deposit box until she sold it.

Watching her studying the ring while absently fingering the one still on her left hand, Jess wondered when she'd remove it then he quashed the thought. Stupid man! If she's still wearing it, obviously she's not divorced and going back to the guy. So why remove it. His stomach slithered with tension. The woman was doing her share of keeping him off balance, too. Leaving her behind, he walked on.

Jess's sudden brooding baffled Raine. Was he wishing for the company of the dark-haired woman? Dejected, she lingered longer before catching up with him. Even then it was a long time before either spoke. While she was thinking of ways to get rid of the dark-haired woman, he was thinking of ways to get rid of Addison.

Jess finally got his perspective back in place and announced he was starving.

"Are you sure we shouldn't be heading back? I wouldn't want us to get caught out in a snowstorm," she asked.

"Not to worry," he steered her into one of the sit-down restaurants, "there's plenty of time. It wasn't bad when I went to the truck. We're fine and I promise to deliver you safe and sound at home." A hostess, menus in hand, seated them in a cozy corner of the restaurant then a waiter arrived bearing a pot of coffee and two waters.

Raine ordered the French Onion Soup and ham and cheese croissant. "It's the double cheeseburger and large fries for me. This shopping's worked up my appetite." Jess said.

I'd like to help him work off that appetite, the thought popped right up turning her cheeks a pretty crimson color. Oh, Lord, she'd better get a grip on her runaway thoughts! Down, girl, down. Remember all that sexy lingerie? He sure didn't buy them for you! The truth hurt and put a damper on her wayward hormones.

"I need to wash my hands," she said abruptly.

"I'll go when you get back." Sipping his coffee, he enjoyed the enticing view she presented walking away, particularly the way her rounded hips swayed tantalizingly with each shifting step she took in those jeans that fit in all the right places, places he'd love to explore and become very familiar with. As a matter of fact, he was bound and determined to get to know every single solitary inch of her. Before he was through, she'd be eating out of his hand. Well, maybe not eating out of it but willing to take it for life, first though he had to get rid of her husband. Suddenly he knew there was something else to add to his little stockpile of gifts. He couldn't get the way her eyes had feasted on the wedding ring out of his head. If that was the ring she longed for then he was getting it for her. One of these days he'd surprise her and ask her to be his wife.

Wife. The word played in his head. Since his divorce all those years ago, he'd never thought of remarrying. He wasn't against marriage, it was great for others. But, he thought wryly, it just goes to show how a man's thinking can change direction in a matter of seconds. His had veered off the chosen path the second he'd answered Inez's phone call.

Raine was barely seated before he was on his feet. At first she sat calmly sipping her coffee and watching people but as time passed and he was a no-show, she started getting peeved. How dirty could the man's hands be? It didn't take that long to wash ten hands. Intuition said he'd left the restaurant, that he was buying something he didn't want her seeing. Fine! Let him keep his damned secrets! She wouldn't give him the satisfaction of asking either, even if it killed her.

Hesitating in the doorway, Jess watched her and if the glower on her face was anything to go by then she was pretty ticked at him for leaving her sitting so long. Again, he thought she was smoking hot when in a temper!

Raine watched him walk to the table, appreciating his masculine grace. Every female eye in the room watched him, too. And he was grinning like the happy cat that ate the canary—feathers and all. It was all she could do not to hang this cat by his tail.

Glaring, she said. "Your hands must have been very dirty." Even to her ears she sounded snarky.

Getting comfortable, he sipped his coffee to keep from laughing. Not wise—he strangled on it. "A bit," he rasped out. Yep! She was upset. God forbid Belle walk in right then. Raine would deck her, then him. Then he'd have to do a lot of foot-kissing to get back in both their good graces. Her curiosity was piqued but too stubborn and full of pride, she wouldn't ask. And he wasn't enlightening her, either.

Over the rim of his cup he took in the soft curve of her peaches and cream cheeks. Her eyes were a shade of blue that reminded him of the ring in his pocket and the sapphire stones and her eyes were a perfect match. He looked at her hands.

Though small with slender fingers, they were strong and capable hands, hands capable of giving comfort and love as well as stirring a man to passion. Instantly, he veered away from that direction.

"This tastes mighty good," he set the cup back on the saucer. "You know, I can work outside all day long; not feel a bit tired but put me in a mall and it's a totally different story. I feel like

I've put in a seventy-two-hour day and it's barely been a couple of hours. I don't know how you women do it."

Despite her annoyance, she laughed seeing his pained expression. "It has to be a trait passed down from Eve. I doubt if Adam would have been crazy about shopping, either." Being jocular was better than brooding, she decided.

While they waited, they talked more about the kids and Christmas and the things that still needed to be done before their arrival. When the waiter set Jess's plate in front of him the pile of piping-hot, golden brown fries looked so mouth-watering she couldn't resist snatching one off his plate. In the blink of an eye, her hand shot across the table then her pearly white teeth bit into it. "Um," she closed her eyes, savoring the salty crispness. Her blissful expression said it tasted just as good as it looked. A strong fantasy crossed his mind sending a fiery shaft of desire shooting through him and he was grateful the tablecloth hid the evidence of his marauding thoughts. He better quit thinking like that or he'd never be able to leave the restaurant. Swallowing past the thickness of desire in his throat, he picked up his burger and took a bite. Big mistake! How was he going to choke the burger past the lump blocking his throat?

The strange expression on his face puzzled her but she'd be darned if she'd ask what caused it. Was he thinking of the other woman and wishing she was here instead? Well that was just too bad! He insisted on tagging along so he's stuck with me until we get home. If not for making a scene, she'd have given him swift kick in the shin. Then she took herself to task for about the tenth time. You're just getting rid of one man and this one's made it plain you're not for him. Get over it! And the band of tension around her head eased.

While they ate, she spoke of Katy and how excited she was having another little girl to play with. "That's about all she talks about and she made me promise she'd get to see Santa, too. I even had to pinkie-swear."

Whether Raine knew it, her face lit up whenever she talked about Katy. No one had to convince him how much she loved her, or that she would fight to the death to protect her. Someday Katy would know just how lucky she was to have Raine as her mother. His children would be lucky to have her for a mother, too. The thought nearly knocked him out of his chair. Stop it! Quit fantasizing, big boy. Treading amongst those thoughts was like walking through a minefield, they could explode at any time and the aftermath would be devastating. Yet the image of her full and round with his child stirred the fire in him and once again he was glad for the table-cloth. And that image cued him it was time to call a halt to this day. Ring or no, he needed breathing space.

Raine, thinking the exact same thoughts about Jess, that he'd make one great dad for Katy and their children, drew up short. Fool, get it through your head there will be no other children, at least not with Jess. A bereft sadness filled her like she'd suffered a profound loss.

"Are there any other stores you want to go to before we head back home?" He signaled the waiter for their check.

"No," her voice was flat, "I've had enough for today." Jess frowned, detecting she meant more than the shopping.

Reaching the entrance, he was surprised to find a crowd milling around the plate-glass windows and looking outside with concern. Was there was some kind of altercation going on? But nearing the windows he saw everyone's cause for alarm. There was nothing to see save for thick, furiously blowing sheets of snow.

"Damn!" He swore at the snow coming down thick and swirling helter-skelter in the strong gusts of wind. The snowstorm forecasted to arrive late evening had apparently caught everyone, including the weathermen, by surprise. There were several inches of the white stuff covering the ground, quite a different scene from when he'd stored the gifts in the truck earlier. So much for getting home before the snowstorm hit. Snowstorm, my ass, this is a blizzard.

Staring in amazement, Raine wondered how so much snow could have fallen in such a short amount of time. Now she was extremely glad he'd driven her.

"Are you ready to make a run for it?" She nodded. "Then let's go."

Opening the door, the force of the wind nearly ripped it from his grip but he braced against it until she was clear then sheltered her from the blowing, stinging snow. She burrowed closer to him as they fought their way to the truck. What had seemed like a close parking spot earlier now seemed a mile away. Getting her inside, Jess fought the wind's resistance to the driver's side. Huge flakes swirled inside the cab before he shut the door. Blowing on his cold hands, he started the truck, turned the heater full blast and cranked the volume on the radio to hear the weather bulletins and the traffic reports. He wanted the interior warm through and through before starting out and he wanted to know the road conditions on their route. No doubt they'd be slick and hazardous as hell.

The weatherman reported the snowstorm expected later that evening was already bearing down on them, and according to the National Weather Service it was just the beginning of a very strong system and to expect blizzard conditions, winds in excess of fifty miles per hour with gusts up to eighty in some sections of the listening area. He went on to say the expected accumulation for areas in the city was from eight to twelve inches, with heavier accumulation expected in the counties located south of St. Louis, and all law enforcement agencies wanted anyone not needing to get out in the inclement weather to stay home. Road crews were spreading salt and cinders, but the storm hit so quickly it was a race against the elements.

From the sounds of it the brunt of the storm was heading in the same direction they were. Annoyance racked him that he hadn't paid better attention to the weather instead of getting sidetracked by his present company. His face was grim. "I should have kept a better eye on the weather. I just didn't believe it'd get this bad this fast. I should've known better, though. Remember?

This is the "Show Me" state. The sun can shine one minute and the next it's storming to beat the band or in this case, snowing like hell."

Raine shook her head. "No one's to blame except Mother Nature. And we all know you don't mess with her."

"That's for damned sure." He grunted. "Well, let's head that way. And don't worry," he gave her a reassuring look that turned her insides warm as honey, "I have it on good authority this truck will do great on snow. It's four-wheel drive so we shouldn't have any problems getting stuck."

"I'm not worried." Her confidant words stayed with him as he eased through the blowing snow to the highway. Traffic was crawling along at a sedate pace and he hoped it remained slow-going the rest of the way home. One erratic driver could send things spinning out of control.

Though keenly aware of the hazardous conditions, Raine wasn't worried. She had the utmost confidence and knew he'd do his best to keep them safe. Not wanting to break his concentration, she remained silent, staring out the window for anything that might be familiar. Honestly, she had no clue where they were. Now she was extremely grateful he'd insisted on driving her to the city.

The muscles in his neck and shoulders bunched and screamed at the tension gripping them. It had been over two hours since leaving the mall and save for a few comments about the road conditions, conversation remained at a minimum as they listened to the weather updates.

They were a couple of miles from their exit and Jess was beginning to feel the tension lessen when a red compact car flew up on his bumper then cut around him. "Damn idiot!" He swore, keeping a tight grip on the wheel. "People like him cause accidents!" No sooner had the words left his lips then it happened. One second the speeding car was in its' own lane then it braked suddenly and cut sharply into Jess's lane, clipping the truck's front fender with a metallic thud. One second they were traveling straight down the highway and the next they were spinning round and round, careening out of control. He fought to control the big machine, but it was a losing battle under the hazardous conditions. Jess realized their situation required immediate nonstandard response on his part. There was only one choice—turn the truck toward the guardrail and hope it held or they'd be crashing into the rock bluff.

"Hold tight!" He yelled.

Instinctively knowing what he was attempting to do, Raine grabbed the handgrip above the door and fervently hoped it worked. Over and over she prayed. "Please, please let us make it."

Jess did everything in his power to keep the truck from breaking the guardrail but it was impossible. The grating, tearing sounds of metal roared inside the truck as it tore through the metal guardrail, down the steep embankment and slammed face first into the rock face of the bluff.

Raine closed her eyes against the horror of the rock bluff coming at her. She heard the explosion of the impact before darkness took her under.

The last thing Jess felt was the sharp pain exploding in his head as he smashed into the windshield from the force of the impact.

CHAPTER TWENTY

A throbbing in her head brought Raine back to groggy consciousness and knowing something had happened, but she couldn't remember. In her head a dozen jack-hammers pounded on her skull. She clamped her eyes shut against the stomach-roiling pain then they snapped opened. Where on earth was she and why was she lying in a pile of cotton balls? And why were they wet? What had Addison done to her now?

Then the muzzy layers cleared and memory returned. They'd crashed and it wasn't cotton balls but thick snow spilling through the shattered windshield. What about Jess? She looked in his direction to find him slumped against the driver's door. Out cold, his face was the color of putty. Panic galvanized her into action. He needed help! For all she knew he could be dead.

Struggling with the door handle, it finally opened and she staggered and fell to her hands and knees in the snow. Tears streamed as wave after wave of sickness washed over her. No! Jess needed help. No way was she tossing her cookies while he could be dead. The awful thought spurred her into action again. She made it to one sodden knee when voices penetrated and several pairs of hands carefully lifted her out of the snow.

"Come on. Easy does it. We'll get you up the embankment to the ambulances." The man behind the voice nodded toward the top of the embankment but she ignored them, more concern for Jess and getting to him. He could be badly hurt.

"Let. Me. Go!" Fighting the hands, she collapsed back down in the snow. Have to get up! Have to get to Jess! Don't they understand? Through gasping breaths she tried to get her idea across to him. "Have . . . to . . . get . . . help . . . Jess . . ."

"Its' okay, miss, the other crew's taking care of him." Relief swamped her when his words finally penetrated.

It was toasty warm in the ambulance and she shivered against the change in temperature causing spasms of pain to radiate through her back and side. Doing an exam, an EMT ran a hand over her ribs and Raine hissed out a groan. "I've got a feeling you may have some fractured ribs."

She wasn't concerned about herself, she was concerned about Jess. "How's Jess?" She asked.

"Okay, Miss. We're sending you to the hospital." Looking at her, he said. "As for your friend, they haven't brought him up yet."

"Then I'm staying." She said stubbornly. "I'm not budging until I know he's all right."

"If you refuse to go we can't make you." He answered.

"I'm not refusing, we're just not moving until I know he's all right." The mutinous expression on her face said it was useless to argue.

"Okay, but you should lie down. In the meantime, I'll go see what's going on." Climbing out of the ambulance he shut the doors with a firm slam. Damn stubborn woman, he thought but smiled. He had one safe and sound at home just as stubborn. If that was him lying unconscious she'd be pitching a fit, too.

Raine didn't lie down. Wrapping her coat about her, she stepped into the blowing snow, catching sight of the other crew of paramedics assisting a banged-up Jess. They were headed toward the other ambulance until a desperate Jess spied her. Shaking off the hands assisting him he switched direction and albeit a little unsteady, headed toward her.

Screaming his name, she rushed to him and he caught her, crushing her to him, never wanting to let her go. Raine didn't care that pain ripped through her ribs. She didn't care that snow was coming down in thick sheets. She'd thought he could have died. Nothing else mattered.

Jess claimed her mouth in a kiss born of desperate fear that quickly changed to passion. Beneath his demanding mouth her lips parted and she kissed him back just as hungrily. He drank deeply as hard shivers of reaction attacked him and he clung even tighter. At last he lifted his mouth only to bury his face in her neck, breathing in the cold air and the sweet scent that was only hers.

His voice was ragged with pain. "Are you all right? You're not hurt?"

"I'm fine." His grip around her was killing her but knowing he was alive made the pain worthwhile.

Recalling his first conscious moments after the seconds it took to remember what happened, he'd looked over only to find an empty seat where she should have been and the gaping hole in the jagged windshield. Terror unlike anything he'd ever known had ripped through him. Frantic, he'd fought the hands helping him.

"She's not here! Where is she?" He yelled over and over. "Dear God! Did she go through the windshield? Please tell me she wasn't thrown through the windshield! Tell me she's not dead!"

Quickly, the paramedics had assured him. "Take it easy. She's doing fine."

Those moments thinking he'd lost her had driven him insane with grief. Once again, his arms tightened like bands of steel around her. "I thought you were dead! Dear God, I thought you were dead." His voice was gruff. He'd been so scared.

"I'm fine. Really, I am. But I thought you were dead, too. You were out cold when I came to." Her voice was tremulous as she leaned back to look into his eyes and cupped his face in her hands. It was time to tell him how she felt. She could have lost him and he'd never have known. "I . . . Jess . . . I . . ." She started then was interrupted.

"Let's get you two to the hospital and make sure you're all right." The paramedic gave Jess a scrutinizing look said. "You took a nasty blow; should probably have a CAT scan since you were out for a while. You have anything else not feeling quite right?"

"My shoulder; it's killing me." Flexing it, he groaned. The EMT gently poked and prodded, eliciting more groans.

While Jess was occupied with the paramedic, Raine regrouped. In her panic that they could have died she'd almost spilled her heart out to him. Thank God, the paramedic's interrupting them had stopped her. Now wasn't the time to be confessing her love for him, not in front of total strangers, anyway. Later, when alone, she'd tell him the truth about everything and hopefully the dark-haired woman meant nothing to him.

If she hadn't been so worried about Jess she'd have noticed the television reporters filming their touching reunion. The accident had drawn several stations and their cameramen filmed scenes of the accident, showing Jess's twisted, mangled pickup crushed against the rock bluff while bundled up reporters interviewed witnesses.

One man shook his head in disbelief. "I sure don't know how he managed to keep from plowing into any other vehicles. He just kept spinning round and round and then he was crashing through the guardrail, down the embankment and straight for the bluff."

Another driver added his opinion, "It was his quick thinking that probably saved lives. It's a miracle, all right. Somebody was watching over us today, that's for darn sure. Those two must have guardian angels watching out for them."

Raine wouldn't know until much later that they'd been taped, or that the snowstorm attacking the Midwest would end up on national news that very night. Nor did she realize it would send the hounds of hell chasing her.

Upon reaching the hospital they were separated, Raine to one triage room, Jess to another. X-rays and a CT scan were taken. The radiologist reading the films of her ribs wore a puzzled frown. Besides the new fractures, there appeared to be older ones not completely healed, not from this accident, and he wondered how she'd acquired them. While Raine was being wheeled back to her room, the tech pointed them out to the attending physician.

"These aren't from this accident. They're older. I'm thinking she's had another accident before this one."

"Sure looks like it, Hank, and I'm about to find out."

Raine was resting when Dr. Cash, the ER physician on duty, stepped through the door. Tall, blond-haired, Raine guessed him forty-five or so and quite handsome when he wasn't sporting a frown. In his hands were x-rays films, obviously hers. He got quickly to the point.

"Ms. Andrews, these are x-rays of your ribs. You've got some fractures from this accident but the radiologist noticed older ones not quite healed yet. Can you explain how you got them? Were you in another accident prior to this one?"

She should have known the x-rays would detect the old injuries. For a moment, she contemplated not telling him then decided honesty was the better policy. "No. My husband caused those injuries several months ago..." She trailed off when his face turned livid.

In two steps he was at the door again. "I'm contacting hospital police to have your husband arrested."

Panic raced through her. Good Lord! He thought Jess was her husband. She had to stop him before he made a terrible mistake and had Jess arrested. Sliding off the examining table, she grabbed his arm before he got any further.

"No. Wait! Mr. Harper's not my husband. He's my landlord. He didn't do anything to me. He was concerned the snowstorm would hit before I made it back so he drove me into the city to pick up my daughter's Christmas present. And he was right, but he's not responsible for any of my injuries." Other than her battered heart, she could have added. "Right now, my husband's behind bars in Arizona. In a nutshell, he went completely crazy. Besides nearly beating me to death he tried to shoot me."

Dr. Cash made an angry growling sound. "Instead, he shot himself. It's a long, ugly story but I ended up here after being advised to get out of Arizona for a while."

It relieved him knowing the man down the hall wasn't responsible for hurting this woman, and judging by the way he kept demanding to see her, his feelings went way beyond being her landlord.

"Let's get you back up there where you can rest more comfortably. I have a few more questions." He helped her back on the bed then leaned against the counter. "Is there any chance you followed up with a doctor since you arrived here?" Raine shook her head. "Then it's high time you did. I imagine there were other injuries besides the rib fractures."

"Some kidney bruising and for a while I'd pass blood but that hasn't happened for a few weeks."

"Show me exactly where the pain was." She did and he gently prodded the area. Her sharp intake of breath was a good indication his hunch was right, the injured kidneys weren't healed as much as she'd thought.

"Let's do some tests to see what's going on. I don't believe they're as healed as you think and those babies are nothing to mess around with. You may have two of them but let's keep both healthy; play on the safe side and have them checked them out."

The tests done, she was allowed to get dressed. A nurse offered to help but she refused. "I think I can manage, but thank you."

"The Dr. will see you as soon as he has the results. It shouldn't be long. He put a rush on them."

Dressing ended up being a painful challenge and a couple of times she reconsidered and started to call the nurse then changed her mind telling herself to suck it up. She was only in a little bit of pain—her arms weren't broken. She was in the middle of pulling on her boots when the door opened and Dr. Cash stepped in. Pain lanced through her and she couldn't suppress the groan.

"You should've let the nurse help you." He waited patiently until she caught her breath then gave her hand up on the bed. "I hate to be the bearer of bad news but those kidneys aren't healed and I imagine the jarring has aggravated them. I've written a couple of prescriptions to help with the healing and the pain." He saw her frown. "Take them. There's no sense in torturing yourself."

She tucked the scripts into her purse. "I'll get them filled as soon as I can."

"Here." He handed her two bottles. "These will tide you over for a few days. Once the roads are clear get those prescriptions filled."

Raine nodded but was more concerned about Jess. "How's Mr. Harper doing?"

Removing his glasses, he grinned at her. "If the hell he's giving my nurses is anything to go by then I'd say he's doing pretty good."

Not surprising. Jess was a man used to being in control. "I've only know him a few months but one thing I've learned is that he's independent, used to marching to the beat of his own drum, and hates anyone giving him orders." She laughed. "I bet he's getting pretty obnoxious about now and demanding to go home."

"Actually, he's demanding to see you and if that doesn't happen pretty soon he's going to start 'yelling the roof down'—his words, not mine."

A warm glow filled her. "Then I guess I'd better see if I can calm him down." Was Jess worried about her as the injured passenger in his truck or did his feelings go deeper? After that all-consuming kiss, it'd damn well better be the latter. In her bemused state she thought she heard the doctor mutter "good luck" as he walked beside her.

Sure enough, the object of their discussion was indeed giving a nurse hell. Raine heard him before she ever reached his room. Jess's head was pounding something fierce, a kettle drum would've sounded quieter and it felt like as hot poker was lodged in his shoulder. He hoped like hell nothing was broken, he had things to do before the kids arrived. And adding to his grumpiness—the chirpy nurse wouldn't leave him the hell alone. If he wanted something for the pain he'd damn well ask for it.

"I don't need that damn stuff. Give it to someone who does." There was no mistaking the snarl in his voice. Even fifty feet away Raine heard his cranky grousing. Jess gave the nurse the evil eye, thinking if she smiled she'd be down-right pretty but right now her fit-for-battle gray eyes were staring him down harder than any enemies had ever done. It was down to a battle of wills and he was determined to win.

The nurse, dressed in blue scrubs with a panda bear pattern, was about his age, and just as determined. For the last fifteen minutes she'd been after him to take the painkiller still sitting in the disposable cup on the tray.

"Look, it's okay for even a former jarhead to take something to take the edge off the pain." She held out the cup with the pills in it. There was a determined gleam in her gray eyes. "I can always give you a shot, you know. You can drop them britches and I'll gladly shoot you where the sun don't shine!" She threatened cheerfully.

Jess gave her a scathing look. "I don't think so. You'd enjoy it too much." Another time he'd have laughed with her. The service was inclined to stick a needle in that particular region of the body. But an axe was attacking his skull and nothing was funny. On top of that they wouldn't tell him how Raine was doing.

"You bet I would," she came right back, her sassy eyes sparkling with challenge.

"How the hell did you know I was a jarhead, anyway?" He demanded, curiosity getting the better of him. Maybe he should take the pills and start feeling better. "You've never set eyes on me before." With that crusty, hard-edged, take-no-guff-attitude, Jess thought she'd make a great drill sergeant.

"No, but I've got eyes, twenty-twenty vision, too. I can spot a Marine Semper Fi tattoo a mile away. Just like that one right there on your upper arm. You've had it quite a few years; it's got that worn look. You know, lots of sun, lots of wind and rain, which means you put a lot of years into the Corp." She watched his brow lift in surprise and she smiled. And he'd been right—she was pretty when she wasn't being "Ms. Bossy Nurse." "I've been military all my life. First my dad, then me, and I married a career Marine to-boot. In fact, I met my husband while stationed at Camp Lejeune. After we both retired we found this pretty area and put down roots here."

This place just seemed to draw people in and never let them go. "I did the same thing," he said, warming to her with the common bond they shared. He moved his head, it throbbed. Why didn't he just take the pills? "I came for a visit, liked the area and found some property. When I retired, I started working on the place making it livable. It'd been neglected and so overgrown, I found things I didn't even know I owned."

"I can well imagine," she laughed, finding pleasure in talking to a comrade. "Fortunately for us our house was move-in ready. I can't say the same for the rest of it. Bill, that's my husband, cleared brush, graded the drive over and over, and hauled so much rock for the first few years we could've started a quarry. I finally convinced him to pave it. It sure has made a difference when the snow starts flying. Like now. When I get off," she looked at him pointedly, "which is when I'm done with you, mister, he'll have the driveway all nice and cleaned off and a hot drink waiting." She stuck the cup out at him one more time. "Now quit being stubborn and take these. They'll make that jackhammer pounding in your head calm down to a dull nail-gun."

Dr. Cash walked in and immediately sided with her. "She's right, you know. If you'd taken them when she first gave them to you, that headache would be next to nothing." In his hand were the films of Jess's shoulder and head. "The good news is your shoulder's only sprained. The bad news is the pain is just the same. And you'll have that headache for a while but the scan was clean."

That was good news; he had too many things to do before the kids arrived to be laid up with anything worse than a bum arm. "I can live with that and since nothing's broken or bent, you can discharge me. As soon as Ms. Andrews is released we'll head for home. How is she?" Ever since they'd been separated he'd asked over and over how she was but all he'd gotten was the runaround. "We're doing some tests; x-rays, that sort of thing." She hadn't seemed too injured when she'd kissed him at the accident scene. Even in the ambulance she'd seemed only a bit banged up. Still, she could have had internal injuries and panic welled up so strong he thought it would suffocate him. What would he do if he lost her?

A sound at the door interrupted his runaway train of thought. Seeing her standing there robbed him of speech but his profound relief was a loud audible sigh. The first things he noticed were her ashen face and the arm cradled against her right side.

"What's wrong with your arm?" He demanded. The thought of her being hurt made him ill.

Raine made light of it. "It's not my arm, it's my ribs. They must have taken a hit when we crashed. They're a little tender." Tender my foot. They hurt every time she moved or breathed. Easing onto the plastic chair, she thought it best not to mention her kidneys, he seemed worried enough already.

Dr. Cash gave her an appraising look. Instincts said Ms. Andrews had feelings for this man, too. As for the ex-husband, he shared the same opinion as the radiologist—do away with the S.O.B. He scribbled on the chart. "I'm releasing both of you," he pointed the pen at Jess, "but you're waiting until these pain pills kick in." Jess started to protest. "If you argue I won't release you." He threatened sternly.

Raine hid a smile. Jess was being a very bad patient and the doctor was having none of it. In this battle of wills, Jess would come out the loser so she came to his rescue.

"He won't argue, Dr. Cash, he'll take them," she promised, while daring Jess to disagree. The lines around his mouth attested to his thundering pain. "While they're taking effect

I'll call Cora to come get us." That should appease him. "It'll take her a while to get here and that'll give the medication time to kick in."

"Fine! I'll take them," he grumped, "but I hate dragging Cora and Katy out in this mess. I wish there was someone else to call." He considered Cooper but he'd be pulling duty with the storm.

"Me, too, but there isn't. Cora will be extremely careful. She won't take any chances with Katy."

As for Cora, she was listening to the news reports and pacing the floor, her low-heeled boots wearing a path in it as she went from window to window hoping for any sign of them. So far, the only sounds were the howling winds and the blowing snow pinging off the window panes. At first, she hadn't been too concerned but as the time passed and the snowstorm worsened, she'd become worried. Something was wrong; she could feel it. Just then she caught the tail-end of a report about an accident at the same time the phone rang. Relief flowed through her seeing Jess's name on the caller ID. "Jess," was all she got out before he cut her off. Hearing the strain in his voice, her panic returned. Something was wrong.

"Cora, we'll fill you in on everything later but right now we need you come get us. We're at the hospital."

"The hospital!" It came out shrill. "Oh my God, are you two all right?"

Jess rushed to reassure her. "We're fine, a little banged up but otherwise we're both fine. Cora, we hate dragging you and Katy out in this mess but we need you to come pick us up."

"Never mind that, I'll bundle Katy up real good and be on the way in a jiffy. And don't worry. I'll be real careful."

"I know you will. Just take it slow and easy. We don't need you getting into an accident, too." Raine waved to get his attention. She put two fingers to her lips and mouthed Katy. "Cora, give Katy a kiss for Raine and tell her she loves her," then he added, "do the same for me, too." His request turned Raine's eyes misty. "Remember, the roads are a mess. I'm sure the plows haven't made it out there yet so just go slow. When you're ready, here are the directions to the hospital."

"I'm ready," she wrote them down, "and don't worry about us, we'll be just fine." She hoped she sounded more confident than she felt.

Hanging up, Cora took a minute to gather her thoughts. She'd never driven in a storm of this magnitude but she was no sniveling female and no little bit of snow was going to stop her!

However, going out in this mess called for safety measures so the first thing she did was start the SUV to get it good and warm. She made thermoses of hot chocolate and coffee and put together a bag of snacks. If they got stuck along the way they'd have something hot to drink and something to eat. She stacked several blankets in the seat next to Katy's car-seat in case they needed to wrap up in them. Looking around the cabin she reviewed a mental check-list. Better turn the crock-pot off, there was no telling how long the trip might take and she'd hate to burn the cabin down. Ready and armed with the directions, she locked the door behind her then secured Katy and her pink teddy bear snuggly in the car-seat. She'd already explained that Mr. Jess's truck had an ouchie.

As Cora tediously made her way to the hospital, two state highway patrolmen, Officers David Carson and Seamus O'Rourke, arrived to see if Jess was up to giving them a statement. They found him and Raine in the ER waiting room sipping hot coffee. Jess started to get up but they waved him back down.

Both officers appeared to be about his age, both a bit over six-feet, hair cut short, one was red-headed, the other black-haired with traces of gray peppering through it. They were lean and well-muscled and he pitied anyone stupid enough to take either man on.

"From what witnesses say, it looks like you did everything you could to keep your truck under control after that car hit you. That was some spur-of-the-moment thinking, turning into the bluff like that. If you hadn't, who knows how many more might be injured, or dead. And you two can count your blessings, too, since the airbags didn't go off. From the looks of the truck you're both lucky to escape with minor injuries."

The dark-haired officer's face twisted in a sorrowful grimace. "However, I've got a feeling your truck's history. It's been towed to Wertman's Garage."

"I know the place. I'm not worried about the truck. There's insurance to cover it. Just as long as no one was hurt that's all that matters." He looked from one patrolman to the other. "Any chance anyone saw the fool that hit me?"

Redheaded Officer O'Rourke grinned broadly. "As a matter of fact, someone did even better than that. The fool idiot stopped for fast food on the other side of town. Lucky for us a witness followed him and waited until a unit showed up. Despite having the eye-witnesses, the guy swore he didn't do it but he couldn't explain the black paint on his dented red fender, or the smashed tail light. He was pretty cocky at first but we had him dead-to-rights. He's been charged with leaving the scene of an accident with injuries. What we can't figure out is how that little tin can of his didn't go end-over-end." Officer O'Rourke closed his note pad and stood up. "I think we've all we need for now. If not, I've got your contact information." Looking outside, he grimaced at the thick snow still coming down. "I've a feeling this is going to be one long night. The latest reports say the storm's stalled over us for the next eight to ten hours. Well, you folks take care getting the rest of the way home."

Jess shook hands with the two men. "I don't envy you your jobs. I've got friends with the sheriff's department. Times like this make me glad I have a profession I can do from home. Thanks for letting me know where my truck's at. Be careful out there."

Cora and Katy came through the double-glass doors as the two officers walked out. "Mommy! Mommy!" Katy squealed excitedly then stopped short, her face scrunching up as two big fat tears rolled down her face. Although she still didn't fully grasp the situation, she knew Mommy had been hurt again.

Raine quickly picked her up and Katy wrapped her arms around her neck in a stranglehold. "Did you fall down again, Mommy?"

"No," Raine rushed to assure her, "Mommy didn't fall down. We had an accident in Mr. Jess's truck."

Watching Raine comfort Katy was such a beautiful picture that he longed to be a part of it. Then reality reminded him that wasn't possible and for the first time in many hours he came to his senses. Scared spit-less thinking her dead, he'd been desperate to know she was all right and once in his arms, he'd had to kiss her, feel her breathing life into him that he'd completely forgotten one little fact, she was still married.

His gaze dropped to her left hand. The gold band gleaming in the florescent light confirmed that what he wanted didn't matter, not so long as it remained on her finger and it turned him icier than the blowing winds outsides.

Over their protests, he commandeered the keys. "God forbid, but if there's another accident I'm going to be behind the wheel." His mean-eyed look dared them to argue. Both women shut up.

Crawling through the darkness and thick blowing snow, Raine kept watch on Jess. He'd taken quite a blow to the head, enough to render him unconscious. He seemed to be doing okay, even if he was cranky. Obviously, something was eating him that had nothing to do with the accident. Her thoughts turned to the heated kisses they'd shared after the accident, their panicked reactions each thinking the other might be dead. Surely it meant he loved her. It had seemed so then but given his icy countenance now, she wasn't so sure.

It took three painstaking hours of hard concentration to make the treacherous drive, made even more so due to the increasing winds and drifting snow. More than once the SUV was blown by the wind. Reaching the cabin, all three adults heaved an audible sigh of relief while Katy wanted to drive around some more. "Please, Mr. Jess. Can we ride some more in the snow? That was fun."

"No way are we driving any more in this mess, sweet-pea. It's not fit for man, or beast, or little girls, no matter how pretty they are." Katy bestowed a guileless smile on him at the compliment.

"You're having some dinner with us," Cora informed him. To Raine she said, "Go put something comfortable on. Take a couple of those pain pills, too. I'd imagine there are a few places that could use some relief." Raine wondered how she'd known about the re-injury to her kidneys. There'd been no time to discuss what the doctor had said. The woman was just too astute but she was glad she hadn't mentioned them in front of Jess. She started for the bedroom. While you're at it bring a couple for Jess. "He looks terrible and I think he's got a shiner coming to that right eye." Cora called to her.

Backtracking, she stood over him. His eyes were closed and strain dug deep grooves around his mouth. He looked exhausted and in pain and sure enough his right eye was turning the prettiest shade of purple.

"You look like you've gone ten rounds with a compact car." She teased. The urge to kiss away the pain etched on his gray face overwhelming. A lump thickened in her throat recalling those first frantic moments believing him dead.

"My head feels like it, that's for sure." Opening one eye, he squinted at her and another burst of anger shot through him. She had no right looking at him that way, or kissing him so passionately after the accident when her heart belonged to her husband. Suddenly he was desperate to get away from her before he said something he'd regret. Surging to his feet, he grabbed his coat off the back of the kitchen chair.

"I'll take a rain check on dinner. All I want is to lie down." It was the truth. A sledge-hammer pounded in his head and his stomach was wave-slapping queasy. It was good enough reason to put some distance between them.

Raine shook her head in puzzlement then turned away. When she turned back her face was as blank and cold as his. Two could play this game. "Then take some stew and rolls with you for later."

The look he gave her was devoid of any emotion, so was his tone when he spoke. "Get some rest." He brushed a hand over Katy's hair. "Sleep tight, Katy-bug." He accepted the bag with stew and rolls, and stepped out into the blowing blizzard feeling her questioning stare drilling a hole in his back.

Staring at the closed door, Raine wondered what had put an ice-burg in Jess Harper's saddle. Men! Go figure. One minute they're so glad to see you they're kissing the stuffing out of you and the next they act like you've got the plague. And did that dark-haired woman have anything to do with this current mood? Thinking of the woman with Jess set her heart to aching worse than her ribs.

Chapter Twenty-One

As Raine soaked her aching body in a tub of hot frothy bubbles, over a thousand miles and a snow blizzard separating them, Addison lounged on his bunk, sipping on a steaming cup of coffee and munching on an ice cream cone while watching the evening news on the flat screen television in his cell. As a matter of fact he'd paid, or rather dear old dad had, to have several televisions installed throughout the jail. Of course, it'd been done anonymously as a donation.

The reporter on the screen was bundled up, battling high winds and snow, and prattling on about the blizzard attacking the Midwest and the resulting accidents. The current footage showed an accident that had happened on some snow-covered Interstate and the reporter was interviewing several witnesses.

"If that man hadn't done what he did there's no telling how many people could have been hurt, maybe even killed. And it's a wonder those two weren't killed."

A cameraman panned the surrounding area and what Addison saw commanded his full attention and made the blood boil through his veins. He increased the volume. He couldn't believe his eyes—or his luck for there in another man's arms stood his wife. Make that ex-wife. As of yesterday, they were no longer married but as far as he was concerned she'd always be his wife. Till death do them part, they'd vowed in front of God and the minister. And that's exactly how it was going to stay.

So that's where the conniving bitch had scurried off to all those weeks ago, he thought with a sneer. No wonder she couldn't be found, she was hiding from him. It'd seemed as though she'd disappeared into thin air. Well surprise, surprise. She'd just been royally busted. And thanks to the media it wouldn't take much to track her down. She might have succeeded in getting him locked up but the joke was on her. She'd counted on him being locked away for years and years. Wrong! Wrong! Wrong! Lady Luck was performing her magic and he'd be walking free a hell of a lot sooner than he'd agreed to in his plea bargain. But that was his little secret and when he was released he was going to tear up her cozy little love nest.

It was time to set the wheels of his plan in motion and revenge was going to taste oh so sweet. Tossing the cone in the trash, he called to the guard on duty. "Sonny?"

"Yeah man, what cha' need?" A tall, skinny man with a blond flat-top appeared in the doorway, munching on an ice cream cone, too.

"I need your phone."

"Sure thing," he extracted it from his uniform shirt pocket, handed it to Addison and walked away.

Addison always used the cellphone from whoever was on duty. Though traceable, it couldn't be proved he'd made the calls. A couple of minutes later he was deep in conversation with his father getting the telephone number of the private investigator he used. His next call was to Robert Ford, Private Investigator. Addison explained in precise detail everything he wanted pertaining to his ex-wife.

"I want everything, location, pictures, and anything you come across even if you think it's irrelevant. I want you to stick like glue to her. Find out what her habits are, who she sees, where she shops, where she gets her pedicures. Just make sure she doesn't realize she's being tailed."

While listening, Robert Ford berated himself for not letting the voicemail pick up the message. Not recognizing the number, he'd answered it and now had agreed to work for the demented man. The guy was twisted; there was no two ways about it. He held his ex-wife solely responsible for all his problems and ultimate downfall, and was hell-bent on making her pay. The wife had been right to flee the crazy man and divorce him. Unfortunately, fate was working against her and he'd found her. Now he wanted her head delivered to him on a silver platter.

A brief pang of guilt rippled through him. Had he not needed the money so direly he'd have refused but he owed some dangerous people lots of money and preferred keeping both kneecaps intact. Ignoring his conscious, he wrote down the information Addison gave him.

"I've made the first part easy for you. All you have to do now is catch a plane to St. Louis, rent a car and get directions to where that accident happened. Do whatever it takes to track her down and get whatever you can then report back to me. And don't worry about your fee and expenses. Just contact my dad. He's expecting your call. He's handling the finances right now."

"Right," Ford agreed with trepidation. "I'll be in touch as soon as I have something. Don't get upset if it takes a while."

Addison grunted, "Don't worry. I'm not going anywhere for a while." Then he flipped the phone closed. The evilness on his handsome face made him look entirely like the devil as he hissed. "Oh, you little bitch, you're going to pay for putting me here. By the time I'm finished you'll wish you'd died in that wreck."

Another surge of excitement raced through him as he fondled the vial of white powder in his pocket. There was something to celebrate and he had just the thing. Thanks to the many people in his back pocket he could do anything he wanted, get anything he wanted, except his freedom and that was in the works.

A smirk touched his mouth. What were they thinking locking him up in some po-dunk jail? Even he was honest enough to admit that rightfully, he should have been sent to one of the state prisons for what he'd done but his plea concession had included being able to serve his sentence elsewhere. Told their intentions, he'd thought his attorneys were whistling in the dark. And learning Raine's attorney, that bastard Gordon Hanson, had agreed, albeit with vehement protests, you could have knocked him over with a feather.

They should've known better, he thought smugly, everyone had a price and once behind bars it hadn't taken long to slick up the country-bumpkin jailers. A promised job to be a guard at one of the sites was all it took, and the sheriff was none the wiser. He was proud of his ability to lure people into his spidery web of deceit then use them to further his ambitions. But the investigator made him leery. He'd immediately picked up on his qualms so once his usefulness was over he'd just have to disappear. He could ill afford anyone knowing he'd had anything to do with what was going to happen to Raine. The guy's demise was a minor detail he'd work out later. If nothing else there was bound to be a river to dump a body in.

Stretching out on the bunk, he continued thinking. If his plan worked, the bitch would be out of the way and he and Katy would be embarking on a new life, in a new country, with new identities. Nothing could stop him! He had the ways and the means—even in this place, to get anything he wanted including the little bottle of white powder in his pocket. Yes indeed! Tonight was turning out to be his lucky night. He was getting to do one of the things he enjoyed immensely and the icing on the cake was seeing his beautiful ex-wife on television. Too bad that crash hadn't done the job for him, but now he'd have the satisfaction of doing it himself. Patience was all he needed. He'd bide his time, use it wisely perfecting his plan to catch his unsuspecting wife totally by surprise then she'd get her comeuppance.

Not once in the four days following the accident did Jess venture outside. Between his aching head and throbbing shoulder, he hated moving. The least movement made his head feel like it would shatter into a million pieces. His shoulder remained snuggly in its sling, especially after he'd made the mistake of going without the pain meds and sling, only to find he could barely move it the next day, so he'd consigned himself to staying flat on his back with the remote and pain medication close by. And thanks to concerned neighbors, anything needing doing was taken care of.

Seeing the news, they'd all come to check on him as soon as he'd turned on the lights. He had good neighbors and appreciated their care and concern. Numerous times in the past two years he'd come to their aid, now they were returning the favor . . . "That's what neighbors do, son," his neighbor across the road stalwartly informed him around the toothpick he worried between his lips.

Cooper had been in the middle of working another accident in the southern part of the county when he'd learned of the crash. The minute he was free he'd called. "I hear you tried bluffing your way through an accident."

"Ha! Ha! Very funny, unfortunately the bluff won but give me a couple of days and I'll be good as new, and no, don't you and Belle come out here. I have everything I need." He should have saved his breath; they'd showed up bearing care packages the next morning.

And Cora traipsed through the snowdrifts to check on him. After that first trip she shoveled a path and brought Katy along. And bless her heart, she'd even made sure he had a double stash of chocolate bars. And thanks to Cora, he was able to keep tabs on Raine.

"Like you, she's taking it easy. Those ribs have been through the mill over the last few months, but she's stubborn, she'll tough it out, though I threatened to padlock her in her bedroom if she didn't do as I said," Cora chuckled, remembering Raine's mutinous glare. "She reminds me of someone else just as hard-headed," and gave him a pointed look, "and in case that knock on the head addled your brain, I'm talking about you." Childishly, he'd stuck his tongue out at her. And that was something Raine had done a lot of, too.

Flexing his shoulder, it only hurt a little this morning and the jackhammer inside his head had eased to a dull thud. Cabin fever was setting in and feeling better, he was desperate to get out. Plus, he had a list of things a mile long that needed doing. Topping it was checking out his truck to see how totally toasted it was and while there he'd get Katy's dollhouse. Then he'd see what Raine wanted to do with it.

Laid up, he'd done a lot of thinking about their situation. He tried convincing himself that fear made him kiss her after the accident. But that wasn't true. Fool-hardy, he'd tumbled hard, in over his head in love with her. Now the million-dollar question was what to do about it.

Until Raine, he'd always vowed to never, ever, get involved with another man's wife and that vow wasn't making the situation any easier. Hell! Nothing about them was easy and just because he owned up to loving her didn't alter the facts. Plain and simple she was married; still in love with her husband. There was no room for him. That fact was seared painfully into his heart with a red-hot poker. Wanting her like no other woman, he dreamed of her, yearned, and burned for her. He wanted her in his bed, but more than that he wanted to build a life with her as his wife, the mother of his children, sharing the good times and the bad. That's what he selfishly wanted but it would never come true and every time he looked at that gold band on her left hand it slammed home the hopelessness. He'd never make her choose between them. Finally, Jess made the only decision he could live with. From here on out the only contact would be strictly as landlord and tenant. Surely, he could do that until she left?

Shrugging on the fleece-lined coat, his shoulder pinged but it wasn't too bad. Outside, he breathed the crisp fresh air. Exhaling, it seemed all the heaviness inside blew away and his head and heart were at peace that he'd made the right decision. At least that's what he had to keep telling himself.

Hearing a car, Raine glanced out the window in time to see Jess drive slowly down the snowy driveway in his old truck. Alone for the first time since the accident, the cozy silence of the cabin was wonderful. Cora, the huddler, had taken Katy and gone to visit Inez. All of them were suffering cabin fever but wisely she'd opted to stay home.

Pouring a cup of coffee, she settled in the recliner, her thoughts on Jess. The man had her twisted in so many knots he confused her with his many moods. Like his actions after he finally made it out of the truck after the crash, instead of climbing into the ambulance he'd made a beeline straight for her, kissing her like it was the last one they'd ever share on this earth. So . . . was it only a frightened reaction that caused him to kiss her that way? No, it wasn't. There'd been more in his eyes than mere concern, but just before leaving the hospital he'd turned stone-faced and remote then he'd rushed from the cabin like his pants were on fire. It'd have served him right if he'd slipped and slid all the way down the hill on his gorgeous backside. It might have knocked some sense into him; obviously, his brain had taken a vacation.

Aggravated that her feelings ran up and down like a yoyo on a string, she got up and briskly mixed up cornbread batter, taking her frustrations out on it and wondering how much more she could take from him.

It was late afternoon before Jess returned from town. Not quite up to par yet, he was worn out and the jack-hammer in his head had picked up the pace. As soon as he got inside he'd take something for it. The news wasn't good about his truck. The insurance company had totaled it out. It was sad, like losing an old friend. In the short time he'd had it he'd come to love that truck as much as he did the old one. There's just a special bond a man makes with his truck. Parking inside the barn, he slowly trudged up the path to Raine's cabin. Frowning, he wondered when he'd started thinking of it as hers. Reaching it, he saw the SUV gone. Was anyone home? He knocked and waited, figuring he'd have to come back later to see what she wanted done with the dollhouse. Right now, he needed a couple of pain pills and a lie-down.

Raine was attempting a bit of work when she thought she heard a knock at the door. Before today she hadn't even picked up a pencil. Approaching the door, she saw a large shadowy figure and instantly the hair on her neck rose. Addison! The blood drained from her body leaving her weak. Had he somehow escaped and tracked her down? Then she got control of herself. Don't be ridiculous. Addison's locked up tight behind iron bars. If he was loose Gordon would have called, especially since he'd seen her on the news and called to check on her.

Tip-toeing closer, relief washed over her in buckets seeing the familiar broad shoulders and handsome face. It definitely wasn't Addison. The alarm long gone, giddiness gave her a head rush. Jeez! Get a grip. You're not some love-struck teenager with a crush on the star quarterback. Still, she smoothed her hair, pinched her cheeks then looked down at her red socks. Those snowmen gracing each toe were certainly attention getting. Oh well, if he wouldn't look her in the face maybe he'd like her snazzy socks. She opened the door.

Jess was about to leave when the door opened and there she stood gazing at him with those intense blue eyes and so damned gorgeous with that peaches and cream complexion and shining cascade of blond hair. A feral look entered his dark eyes as hungering need started burning inside of him. His gaze swept over her from the top of her gleaming golden hair to the tips of her snowman covered toes. Seeing her festive footwear, his lips twitched in a grin. She couldn't possibly know how sexy she looked in those well-worn jeans, faded and soft after so many washings. A red sweatshirt, a colorful picture of Santa Claus on it, met her thighs midway. And she looked so damned young he got a reality check. She looked like a dewy-fresh teenager and all his nearly forty-one years dumped down his throat at one time. He'd been out of his mind to even think of pursuing a long-term relationship with her. Seeing her like this bolstered his resolve to keep away from her. He was too old for her. Or maybe she was too young for him. After all, he preferred women nearer his age and knowing the score—no ties, no commitments, when it was over it was over.

Taking a step back, he reminded himself that, most importantly, any woman he took out had to be single—he'd always prided himself on that rule and for a while he'd ignored it.

Years ago he'd made a promise that no matter how strong the attraction, he was staying away from married women. Getting entangled with one had been a sure-fire way to send his military career down the tubes. It happened all too often. They couldn't restrain themselves until either the woman or man was free and eventually the spouse found out and trouble started. He'd wanted no part of it then, and definitely not now. His lips thinned as he zeroed in on the ring still on her finger. Thank God he'd come to his senses before crossing that line and spent the rest of his years living with self-loathing. A man had to have self-respect if he wanted it from others.

The war of emotions on his face baffled her. For a moment, she'd have sworn he was happy to see her, but now? Not so much. Now he looked grouchy and unapproachable as an old bear disturbed during his hibernation, and a grouchy old bear with a black eye at that. Fine! She could be just as snarky even as she yearned to throw herself in his arms. However, she refrained. If she touched him he was liable to hip-toss her into a snow bank.

"Did you need something?" Her features remained neutral, her voice haughty. One dainty brow lifted inquiringly. Leaning against the door, she crossed her arms beneath her breasts, stretching the material across them.

"I didn't think anyone was home." He was trying not to stare at her chest.

"Well, that's what you get for thinking, isn't it?" she said waspishly.

Irritated, he hit out, "Yeah, I guess so. That's why I try to think before I act, do something stupid and end up regretting it. Anyway, what do you want to do with Katy's dollhouse? I picked it up when I went to check out the truck." His tone was colder than the snow on the ground. Her jaw visibly clenched. Good! If he pissed her off enough, it might keep her away from him.

So, the blooming idiot put her in the 'something stupid' category. Who did he think he was, riding up here on his high horse? She wasn't some dark-headed bimbo to fall down at his sexy feet. Not hardly. He could take his attitudes, and the bimbo, and jump off a bridge and she knew just the one. She'd been doing just fine before this contrary man—she'd do just fine without him. That conviction set her back ram-rod straight. Her flashing eyes brimmed with new determination. She saw him shiver but she'd be damned if she'd invite him in. He could freeze to the snow covered ground first.

"I'll keep it here. We'll work on it after Katy goes to bed." She looked around but didn't see the large box. "Where is it?"

"In the truck, I left it there until I talked to you."

"I'll bring it up here. I've imposed enough as it is."

Anger washed through him that she coldly shut him out. His blood pressure rose as the pounding in his head increased. Damn it to hell, what did she expect from him? He took a calming breath. "Look, leave it with me just in case the little minx gets nosy. I can put it together for you. Besides, those ribs must be pretty sore. I've had a few cracked ones and I remember how bad it hurt just to breathe let alone do anything physical." He just couldn't stop his blathering mouth and he wanted to yank the offer back.

The offer ticked her off even more. There was no second-guessing him and she let him know it. "Just who the hell do you think you are?" She lit into him. "You change attitudes so fast I can hardly keep up with you! First you seem glad to see me then the next minute you're scowling like some cranky old bear. Now you're offering to put a dollhouse together!" God! She wanted to shake him, or knock that gigantic chip off his shoulder. Actually, doing both sounded pretty damn good. "Well don't do me any favors!" She yelled loud enough to cause an avalanche. "I'll carry it up here myself! I don't want your help!" The door slammed shut but less than thirty seconds later it opened again and she marched out wearing coat and boots. Ignoring him, she headed down the hill at a brisk pace to the barn.

Jess clenched his fists to keep from slamming them into the wall in frustration. This woman was driving him nuts! Why couldn't she just graciously accept the offer? The answer was clear—she was as stubborn and full of pride as he was. They were like two peas in a pod.

Raine skidded down the path, nearly losing her footage several times. Stubborn woman, he'd bet the farm her ribs were killing her, served her right for being so hard-headed. He opened his mouth to tell her so then snapped it shut, knowing it'd only provoke her to go faster. She was mad and that was a good thing. It'd be easier to keep her at arm's length until they left. Three more months, he sighed, three more months of cold showers and long frustrating nights with little sleep. Somehow he'd get through it come hell or high water and if it meant using Belle again, he'd do it. Belle could exact her revenge later.

He thought of the jeweler's box on top of the dresser. Talk about thoughtless mistakes; that had to be the worst one he'd ever made. But it could easily be rectified. The next trip into the city he'd return the rings and get his money back. Stupidly, he'd also bought a wedding band for himself. Still, the thought of returning them didn't make the pain any less. He trailed behind her at a much slower pace.

By the time Jess reached the barn she'd wrestled the box out of the bed of the truck. "I'll get it up the hill, even if it means dragging it through the snow," she vowed doggedly.

Aggravated, Jess shook his head. It pounded harder. The hard-headed woman would drive him to drink before he was rid of her. Yet admiration filled him. Stubborn and gutsy, she'd carry the box herself before asking him for help. And if those grooves etched deep around her mouth were anything to go by, she was hurting something fierce.

"Give me the damn thing before you hurt yourself even worse!" he snapped, yanking it from her arms and ignoring her breathless protests. He really didn't want to pack it all the way up the hill but knowing her, for spite she'd tell him to take it there. The pounding in his head grew harder by the second and he was positive it was more tension than the knock he'd received. At the open doorway, he demanded over his shoulder. "Are you sure you want it up at your house?"

Hidden in the shadowy darkness of the barn, Raine leaned against the pickup's tailgate, massaging her lower back and berating herself for biting the hand offering help.

She was being stubborn, she conceded while eyeing the large box hefted on his shoulder then his face. It was white beneath his tan. Now she felt petty for being so childish. After all, he'd been injured in the accident, too.

"Fine," she relented and he turned away, grinning triumphantly, not daring to turn around lest she see it and change her mind. This round was his. Better make the best of it. He took a couple of steps. "Keep it at your place but I'm helping put it together." He hesitated, mid-stride before continuing toward his house.

The hesitation spoke volumes and a big fissure split her heart wide open. He didn't want her—he wanted the beautiful brunette. Had he turned around right then he'd have seen the devastation on her face. But he didn't and she quickly blanked it, refusing to give him the satisfaction of knowing he hurt her. Loving Jess, she realized, was as dangerous to her health as Addison was. Addison had tried breaking her body. Jess had the power to inflict the worst kind of damage—tearing her heart to pieces. Maybe it was time to consider leaving sooner than March. After Christmas, they'd head back to Phoenix. Staying near him no longer seemed a good idea and with Addison behind bars it was safe to return.

The sound of the door slamming echoed up to her and it felt as though it'd slammed on her heart. Tears burned her eyes as she trudged back up the stone path. She had some serious thinking to do.

From the window Jess watched her wipe at her eyes on the sleeve of her coat. She wasn't the only one who felt like crying. His heart screamed to go tell her everything was a ruse but his head wouldn't let him, and the battle was killing him. Leaving the window, he put the dollhouse in his office. Had he been fully on his mark instead of preoccupied, he'd have checked the surveillance screens. As it was he missed the lone figure hastily

retreating into the snowy woods behind the barn. Returning to
the living room, he stoked the banked embers in the fireplace,
adding a couple of pieces of wood to it. Grabbing a bottle of beer
from the fridge, he dropped into the recliner and stared into the
yellow flames, soon lost in thoughts of what to do. There were no
easy answers.

Neither was aware of the man hiding near the barn or that
he'd taken pictures of them. Ignoring his misgivings, Robert
Ford had wasted no time. Once the St. Louis airport re-opened
after the blizzard he'd caught the first available flight out of
Phoenix. On arrival he'd rented a four-wheel drive jeep, bought
a map and set out for the town mentioned in the news reports.
Once there, he'd found a hotel to settle in and began search-
ing for Andrews' ex-wife. Under the pretext of an interview, he
sought Jess, not Raine. A few well-placed questions had produced excellent results. People, he'd learned early in his career,
always liked to talk, especially about heroic incidents involving
one of their own. With the help of those unsuspecting souls, it
hadn't taken long to narrow his search to the Harper place.

Watching the big man head toward the larger cabin, he'd
hoped the Andrews woman would follow but she hadn't.
Instead, she'd headed up the path to another cabin. Disappointed
he hadn't gotten anything useful right off the bat, for the time
being he was calling it quits. He wasn't prepared to spend hours
on end in the frigid temperature. Wet, cold, and hungry, he was
going back to the hotel for a while. Later, after dark, and better
prepared, he'd return and watch some more.

He slipped stealthily through the woods to the jeep hidden
further up the road. All he needed was for some local yokel to
spot the unfamiliar vehicle and get suspicious. That would bring
the cops calling and he sure as hell didn't need that trouble. He'd
hate to explain he was sneaking around trespassing on the big
man's property to get dirt on Andrews' wife. Plus, the guy looked
big enough to mop the floor with him and not even breathe
hard. Extreme caution was called for. This was definitely not the

easiest job he'd ever done but that rich snake Andrews was paying him tons of money to do it.

That evening Cora studied a withdrawn Raine as she sat at the table coloring with Katy. The girl looked sad, like she'd lost her best friend. Something or someone, probably that handsome scoundrel, was the cause and she really wanted to give him a piece of her mind.

Conscious of Cora's concern, any second Raine expected the grilling to begin, but it didn't. After dinner she'd tell Cora of her decision. After all, she played a big part in them.

When Katy was asleep she told Cora, "Jess has the dollhouse. He's keeping it so she won't see it but I'll help put it together."

"That's a good idea," Cora agreed before saying, "now tell me what's bothering you. Something's going on."

"There is. I think we should return to Phoenix after the holidays are over." Staring into the flames burning in the fireplace, she didn't see Cora's frown.

"But I thought we were here until the end of March. You've paid Jess through until then and after that we were going to find a permanent place around here," Cora protested.

Raine shrugged her shoulders evasively. "I know but things have changed and I'm thinking we're better off going home." Keeping her face averted, she daren't look at Cora. If she did, everything bottled up inside would come tumbling out. "With Addison in jail, there's nothing to keep us here."

"Did you and Jess have a disagreement?" Cora flat out asked.

Leave it to Cora to figure it out on the first try. "No . . ." she hedged, "I wouldn't exactly call it a disagreement."

"Then what would you call it to cause this complete change of heart?" Cora wasn't sure who she wanted to shake more—Raine or Jess. Darn! She couldn't do either since they were both banged up from the accident.

"I just think it's for the best if we let Jess have his cabin back. Like I said, Addison's safely locked up. There's no need to run and hide anymore." Even to her ears the excuses sounded lame.

And Cora wasn't having any of it. "Are you turning chicken? Are you letting him run you off?" The question brought Raine up short, her eyes full of guilt. From her reaction that's exactly what she'd been planning. "Raine Andrews, I never thought I'd see you turn tail and run from him. Fight, yes. But run? Never! And you can fool yourself, but not me, not one bit. I know how you feel about the man. You love him."

Raine threw her hands up in surrender. "All right, yes I do. But it's not me, it's him. Granted, at first we made it clear neither one of us wanted to get involved. I didn't because I was still married. Not because I still loved Addison. That died a long time ago. It was because I respected my marriage vows. I know that sounds hokey but that's just me. I let Addison take away a big portion of me by staying and putting up with everything he did to me. The one thing I refuse to let him take away is that."

"Have you told Jess you're divorced?" Cora asked.

She shook her head, "I tried but he's built this wall around himself and won't let me in. I know he wants me . . . well you know," and she actually blushed, "but I want more than that. I don't want just an affair. I want it all with him, the ring, the white picket fence, lots of babies."

"But honey men can be so darned hard-headed, pig-headed, whatever you want to call them. Sometimes you've got to hit them over the head to get their attention." She sat down in the rocking chair. "Oh, I don't mean literally, although I've known a few that deserved a good smack up-side the head. I've an idea. Why don't you mosey down there, tell him you want to work on the dollhouse tonight? It'll get your foot in the door." A bright twinkle of devilment sparkled in her eyes. "I'm thinking it's time for round one in this boxing match and my money's on you." Cora knew what she'd use to knock that hot hunk of a man upside the head with. Women had so many hidden weapons to knock even the largest man off his feet.

"You like stirring the pot, don't you?" Blushing, Raine knew exactly what Cora had in mind. "If I go down there he might just chase me off with a shotgun! And don't forget, he's got a girlfriend. "

"Girlfriend, schmirl-friend, she doesn't mean a thing. And he won't run you off, not if he's the smart man I think he is. Besides, you've got the same means, same weapons, to get the drop on him as she does. You just have to storm the enemy camp, take him by surprise, take him your prisoner. Shoot, I bet he'll even tie the bindings himself. There's no way you or anyone else is going to convince me he's not in love with you."

"Yeah, well if he is he's got a funny way of showing it but okay, I'll do things your way but if you hear me screeching for dear life you'd better be holding that door open for me."

"Trust me. That man will be eating right out of the palm of your hand before the evening is over, especially when you tell him you're divorced." Cora gave a dreamy sigh. "I just love happy endings."

"You're a dyed-in-the-wool romantic." She teased, light-hearted for the first time in days. Maybe Cora had the right idea that it was high-time she made him listen to her. Then if she didn't get the right response she'd know leaving was the right decision.

"That I am," Cora said, "always have been, always will be. I believe in happy endings, honey. The road may be full of pot holes, but it's worth it when you reach the end. Now you go pay that stubborn hunk a visit. And don't hurry back," she ordered, a gleam in her eye. "Take as long as you want. Katy and I will be just fine. Go on," she urged when Raine hesitated.

Chapter Twenty-Two

Anticipation and misgivings left her breathless as above her the inky-black sky was dotted with twinkling stars cheering her on in her tearing-the-wall-down mission. What she needed was a magic laser gun to blast that protective wall to smithereens and make him admit it was she, and not the other woman, he loved.

As for the intended target, the weirdest feelings had driven him to the bank of security cameras checking for anything amiss. The knocking on the back door interrupted his concentration. Intuitively, he knew who it was. Pinching the bridge of nose, his eyes landed on the dollhouse box. Feelings raw and ragged, he wasn't in the mood, but obviously he had no choice.

Wearily, he got to his feet, the chair creaking in relief. He supposed he could ignore her then maybe she'd go away but the repeated knocking negated that idea. "Damn!" He muttered, stomping from the room. Why couldn't she leave him in peace? Still fussing, he flicked the curtain back. Sure enough, there stood the tormentor of both his mind and his body. Oh be truthful! She's been tormenting your soul from the second you laid eyes on her.

Through the square-paned glass his face appeared, the scowl on it seemed a permanent fixture and a sure sign she was as welcome as a case of itchy chickenpox, but she refused to let it put her off. Jerking the door open, he demanded tersely. "What do you want?" The porch light created a halo around her golden hair and he itched to thread his fingers through the silken tresses while his body tightened in response to the desire gliding through him.

Wonderful, he's in his Mr. Cranky-Pants mood; better keep a grip on her temper. "I thought we'd work on Katy's dollhouse but if it's inconvenient I'll come back another time." He'd better not be busy, she fumed, her gaze roaming from the top of his finger-tousled dark head to the tips of his polished black boots. She itched to run her fingers through the softness of his hair. Instead, she clasped them together. If she touched him he might bite her.

With perverted satisfaction Raine hoped she was the cause for his crankiness. He deserved to be as knotted up as a twisted piece of thread.

"Now?" He snapped.

"You have other plans?" She swore if he had a date with that woman she'd punch him in the nose. She swept past him, the sudden change from freezing cold to welcoming heat flushed her cheeks a rosy red. At least the room was welcoming, which was more than her reluctant host; his reception dripped icicles.

The door shut with a decisive snap. Leaning against it, one staggering thought hit him—she belonged here, belonged with him. His scowl grew fiercer.

"This feels great," she said, holding her hands to the warmth. "It's really cold out tonight."

Jess hadn't moved but his eyes followed her every movement. His back teeth ground together. Couldn't she see he was in no mood for idle chit-chat, or putting a dollhouse together? Why couldn't she just go back home? And he meant Phoenix!

The hostility nettled her. Damn the man! Her shoulders stiffened as though preparing for battle. The movement thrust her breasts out, ensnaring his rapt appreciation. A slow burn started that had nothing to do with his temper. He wanted to slide his hands over her silken . . .

"So, where's the dollhouse?" She asked, and the vision vanished like a magician's rabbit. Seriously! She really meant to work on the dollhouse? The scowl never left his face.

"In my office, I wasn't planning to work on it tonight but since you traipsed down here I don't want it said I'm not an agreeable landlord."

As he stomped off, she snorted. Agreeable ha! You're about as agreeable as a crabby old hermit with his private island invaded by a gaggle of obnoxious tourists. Despite his prickly attitude however, a wave of yearning swept over her. The man oozed sex appeal with a capital S and a capital A and he'd be oh, so good to touch, to run her fingers... Stop that! Touch him now and you'll get frostbite. His shifting moods mystified her. How would he react learning she was free and it was him, not Addison that she loved? And what of the dark-haired woman, what were his feelings for her? In a tumbling rush, doubts returned. Maybe coming here was a mistake after all.

Had she and Cora read him all wrong and all he wanted was a little flirtatious, no-strings-attached fun? Images of him with the other woman flashed in her and despair washed through her. The handwriting was on the wall, all right. Coming here was a big mistake. It was time to move on before he hurt her any worse, for Jess could hurt her in a way even Addison couldn't. Addison had inflicted physical pain. Jess could wield a deep, heart-breaking hurt she might never recover from.

"Yep!" the exasperated little green monster on her shoulder said in a voice sounding a lot like Cora, "that's exactly what you should do. Turn-tail, be a coward, run away, let her have him, but if you want him stand your ground, you're green-eyed jealous otherwise why else would I be here?" Laughing hysterically, the imaginary little monster jabbed his pointy boot in her. She brushed at her shoulder as if to knock him off. But the voice was right, it was pure old-fashioned green-eyed jealousy eating her alive.

In his office, Jess reined in his raging desire while glaring at the dollhouse box. There had to be a way to make her leave, unfortunately nothing came to mind. Dollhouse in hand, he returned to the living room. She'd removed her coat and heat smoldered again seeing the way her jeans molded to her hips, showing their feminine roundness. Her sweater, a rich shade of hunter green with a scooped neck emphasized the fullness of her breasts. Around her neck a delicate gold chain with a locket lay nestled in the creamy cleavage. A sharp ache stabbed through him imagining their creamy softness beneath his lips. Right then he slammed the door on the yearning. Remember, you're too old for her, you're not going to be her rebound, and most importantly you don't mess around with married women and she's not going to be the first.

Eyeing the locket again, an ugly thought occurred to him. Did it hold a picture of her husband? Flinty eyes zeroed in on her left hand. Oh yes, she was definitely still married, her wedding band was firmly in place. The heat died an instant death, as though he'd plunged head first into a freezing pool of water. He couldn't handle this. There had to be a way to get rid of her.

"Ready?" His tone abrupt, his stare was calculating. The eerie tang of sharpness alarmed her but it was the cold look in his eyes that set her teeth on edge. She nodded warily.

The look stayed on his face for most of the next two hours as they worked side-by-side until the dollhouse was completely put together. Their stilted conversation, what little there was, centered round the dollhouse. Every now and then she'd catch him staring at her as though assessing her like a wild animal after its prey.

"Katy will be ecstatic Christmas morning. She's still worried Santa won't find her here in the woods..." she turned to find him staring at her in that odd way again. A sharp ripple of desire, and fear, shimmied through her.

Renewed passion flared in Jess, driving him to desperation mode. He had to get rid of her or he'd be making love to her, married or not. Then an idea flashed in his head, one he prayed he could pull off and it not backfire. He was about to execute the most devastating mission he'd ever been on. Not giving himself a chance to back out, he closed the distance between them.

Entranced, Raine watched him come closer then she was in his arms, his mouth fierce on hers as he drank deeply.

A delicious rippling slid under her skin and she responded with an abandoned long forgotten. His kisses created intoxicating, delicious sensations weaving through her. Pressing closer, she twined her arms around his neck, opening her mouth to his demanding tongue, while snug against her was proof of his desire. Her soft moans filled the room.

A moan slipped from him. He couldn't take much more or he'd be making love to her instead of running her out the door. It was do-or-die time while he was still coherent enough to execute his plan. Aflame for her, craving her like a thirsty man in a desert craves water, his heart was dying because he was about to destroy her in the worst possible way.

"Oh baby," he rasped, nipping at her lips, "I know you want this as bad as I do. I've tried fighting it but I can't, not anymore." One hand forayed under her sweater, finding the curve of a lace-covered breast. The other cupped her bottom, bringing her closer. Raine shivered deliciously. The soft movement aroused him even more. His feigned—no damn it, he wasn't faking—a groan of desire melded with hers. Get it over with! Get it over with! His heart and body screamed in agony, unable to take anymore. "I know you want it. You've been hot after me since the day you got here." His mouth never leaving hers, Jess eased her down on the sofa while working at the fastening of her jeans. His hands trembled. Please, please, he prayed desperately, help me get through this.

She was drowning in the most delicious sensations and he was right, she wanted him in all the ways a woman wants a man. Arching into the hard strength of him, the timing was right to tell him she was free. She opened her mouth but his next words knocked her into the next world.

"You're so hot," his breath caressed her neck, his tongue leaving a wet trail to her ear, "no wonder your husband went crazy. I would too, if you gave other men the sultry turn-on, come-on looks you've been giving me. You give them a little taste, a little tease. You've been giving me signals for weeks that you want me in your bed. Admit it sweetheart, you want me filling you, giving

you what you crave and what your husband can't give you." Even
as he reveled in the scent of her perfume, the silken texture of
her skin, he was dying inside uttering the cruel, hateful words.

Shock ripped the air from her lungs as his words sank in.
Stiff as a board, heart-wrenching sobs welled and burst from
deep within. Now she was desperate to escape him, frantically
shoving and bucking until he rolled off her then she was scrambling up on legs that threatened to fail her. Furious, she jerked
her clothes straight as his words blared over and over in her
head. How dare he blame her for Addison's behavior! Tempting
any man, my foot! Right now she was sorely tempted to plant
her foot so far up his backside he'd need surgery to get it out!

The devastation ravaging her face was almost more than Jess
could bear. He'd hurt her with the untrue things he spouted, had
done it out of necessity, but that didn't mean he didn't want to
get down on his knees and beg forgiveness. He wanted to confess
it a cruel ploy to make her stay away from him, but he didn't.

Fury stained Raine's ashen face and her bloodless lips twisted
with scorn. White-faced, she swayed on her feet and for a
moment Jess thought she'd collapse. He stepped toward her but a
shaking hand warded him off.

"No! Stay the hell away from me," She hissed raggedly. The
blue eyes he loved so much brimmed with contempt. She put
the sofa between them. "How . . . how could you blame me for
Addison's behavior? You don't know anything at all about me if
that's what you believe. I knew you could be hard and arrogant,
but never mean and cruel. You have no idea what you're talking about. No idea at all. But there's one thing you won't have
to worry about from here on out. I won't ever bother you again.
As far as I'm concerned you no longer exist. God! I can't even
stand the sight of you! Go play your games with that woman
from the other night! She's your type, not me!" Grabbing her
coat, her blue eyes glittered like diamond chips. "I hate you Jess
Harper! I'll never forgive you for this!" The door slammed hard
behind her.

"Rai . . ." The slamming door splintered his heart into a million jagged pieces even as he told himself he'd done the right thing. You don't need that kind of complication in your life. But love was a complication and my God, he'd just smashed their worlds to smithereens and her parting words would haunt him for the rest of his life.

Tears streamed as she raced through the darkness as though the devil himself was hounds of hell were chasing her. She fell on the slippery ground but the pain was nothing compared to the jagged spears ripping through her heart, she might never recover. Reaching the cabin she stopped, dragging in deep breaths of icy cold air, but didn't go inside, not with the mess she was. Brushing snow off one corner of the picnic table, it dawned that in her mad rush to get away from him she hadn't put on her coat. Slipping it on, she sat down, ignoring the wetness of the table. She wiped the tears but they continued to flow in steady streams. She'd been so sure he cared for her but she'd been dead wrong. Instead, he thought her free and easy and even held her responsible for Addison's vicious attacks; that she deserved everything he'd done to her. That blow struck so deep she wasn't sure she'd ever recover. But he wouldn't have to worry about her presence much longer. They were leaving very, very soon. If Christmas wasn't so close she'd pack up and leave tonight but she wouldn't do that to Katy. No way she was up-ending that baby's world right now.

A derisive laugh echoed in the night. Cora sure called this one wrong. Jess had been the one to do the hitting and the club he'd used had knocked her senseless. That the one weapon he'd picked to beat her heart to pieces with was the reason she'd never forgive him—he'd taken Addison's side. Sitting there, burning anger began replacing anguish. Jess Harper could think what-ever he wanted. She didn't care anymore, that dark-haired bimbo was more than welcome to him. Why she'd thought he'd be dif-ferent was beyond her. Addison should have been a lesson well-learned but instead she taken a chance and lost again. Her fists clenched. She would never forgive him, not that he'd even care.

Tears of anger changed to tears of deep sadness for what might have been. The thickness in her throat threatened to choke her as a sob escaped and everything came crashing down on her, the years of putting up with Addison's brutal beatings, the brutal way Jess had just treated her, it was too much for her mind to contain. Gut-wrenching sobs racked her and wrapping her arms about her, she rocked back and forth as it all tumbled out.

For a long time she cried her heart out but finally the firestorm wound down and though emotionally exhausted, she was at peace with her decision. Gazing at the stars twinkling in the clear night sky, she read their message—it was time to leave, time to follow them home. And it was time to go inside. With a last look, she whispered a final goodbye to Jess and slipped quietly inside. The closing of the door was also the closing of her heart to him.

From the window, Jess watched her race up the path. When she slipped and fell it took every ounce of restraint not to rush out and pick her up, to confess he hadn't meant any of the rubbish he'd spouted. But he didn't. Instead, he hardened his heart and stayed right where he was. When she was at last out of sight he turned from the window, shut off all the lights and sat staring into the flames, replaying the scene over and over. He'd had to do it, he kept telling himself. He'd had no choice. He'd done it for both of them.

"Bingo," Robert Ford said, wispy white vapor forming a cloud in his face. He just snapped several shots of the couple inside the big guy's place. "Andrews was right about his exwife—she indeed has herself a new man." He sipped from the extra-large Styrofoam cup of coffee.

His hunch was paying off in spades. Better prepared against the frigid Missouri temperatures, he'd set out to do some nighttime surveillance. Per the woman working the fast-food drivethru, this had been the snowiest, coldest winter in more than twenty years.

Wonderful! Just where he wanted to be—freezing his ass off in some backwoods hick town but the trip after dark was proving fruitful. Using the zoom lens, he'd aced some great shots of the action in the guy's house. Things were cooking pretty hot until Andrews' ex-wife suddenly ran out. Probably teased the poor guy unmercifully then when he started going for it she'd put the skids on. Andrews, he hated conceding, knew her pretty well.

The action obviously over for the night, Robert Ford crept back through the woods to the jeep. Reaching it, he heaved a huge sigh of relief. Lighting a cigarette, he drew deeply, holding the smoke in his lungs before releasing it in a gray curling stream. With this job he'd better stock up on the smokes. Until now, he hadn't realized he was nervous. He was heading straight for the motel lounge and a couple of stiff scotches.

Cora was awake, wanting to know how Jess had taken Raine's news but peeking out she caught the glint of tears on her face. Instinctively, she started out but Raine was already shutting her bedroom door so she crawled back in her bed, punched her pillow for a more comfortable position and thought the man at the bottom of the hill needed a real swift kick in the pants.

The next morning she found an exhausted looking Raine at the kitchen table nursing a cup of coffee. The girl looked as though she hadn't slept a wink. Cora could empathize, she'd laid awake into the early morning hours, wondering what had reduced Raine to tears.

"Morning." She said, pouring a cup of coffee.

Raine smiled wanly. "Hi."

They sat in silence then Raine sighed heavily, "I've made a firm decision, Cora. The day after Christmas we're heading back to Phoenix. I'd go now except for Katy. She's already worried to death Santa won't find her here. Uprooting her right now would only upset her more." Raine looked at Cora with red-rimmed eyes, the bruises beneath them deep shades of purple. "It's the best thing for me and Katy, there's nothing to keep me here anymore."

Cora nodded unhappily. "Whatever you think's best, you know I'll back you." For Raine to be in this funk and leaving the day after Christmas; whatever had transpired between her and Jess had ended in disaster. Sipping her coffee, she knew something had to be done quickly to get those two hard-headed people together. It was time to call Inez for help.

CHAPTER TWENTY-THREE

From that night on Raine avoided Jess like he was a leper. Whenever outside, she refused to look for him and when in the kitchen, closed the curtains to keep from looking toward his place. The only problem was Katy. Adoring the man, every chance she got she dashed off to see him. Thankfully, knowing her turmoil but not the reason behind it, Cora would go after her.

However, a frustrated Cora was also making her opinion known about the whole rotten situation—she thought Raine was giving up without fighting harder. But there was nothing left to fight for when he'd blasted her clear out of the saddle with a giant canon. He'd done the irreparable, ultimate wrong—he believed she'd driven Addison to do the monstrous things he'd done. She'd never forgive him.

If Raine was in hell, then so was Jess. But he'd achieved his goal. By championing her husband, by blaming her for their problems, his mission was a success—no matter that he'd destroyed her in the process. Filled with regret, there wasn't a minute he didn't wish to turn back the clock and confess none of it true. But the damage was done and she'd never forgive him. As the old adage went—there was no use crying over spilt milk. He loved her, wanted her, but he'd never change his mind as long as she wore that gold band on her hand. He'd never pursue another man's wife, so he too, went out of his way to avoid her.

Christmas was less than two weeks away when Gordon requested she come back to take care of some paperwork. The last time they'd spoken was after the accident. They'd seen her and called immediately. After finding out Raine was only a little banged up, Molly had launched into her twenty-question grill about the gorgeous hunk she'd been in a lip-lock with. Side-stepping Molly's grilling, she'd explained the man was her land-lord, to which Molly had smugly commented, "I never kissed my landlord that way."

"I've got some paperwork I'd like filed right away. I don't trust Addison. If he thought he could still pull a fast one over on you he wouldn't hesitate. I can over-night them but I thought if possible, you could fly back to Phoenix to sign them."

"You're right about him messing things up. I'll check the airlines for the next available flight out and call you back."

Disconnecting, she frowned. There was a slight problem. Just where was the airport? And how did she get there? The idea of asking Jess popped into her head but just as quickly popped out. She'd rather walk barefoot on a bed of hot coals than ask him for anything. Nope! They had GPS; they'd get there on their own.

Cora wasn't worried, either. "I don't know where it is but we'll find it. And don't worry about Katy; she'll be just fine here with me. We'll be so busy baking and shopping she won't even have time to miss you."

"I don't know what I'd do without you." Raine hugged her tightly, aware of Cora's presence in the doorway the traumatic night she'd returned from Jess's.

"Honey, you'd do just fine with or without me." Cora returned the hug. "Now get along and find a flight."

Unfortunately, the last flight for Phoenix had already departed but there was a seat available early tomorrow morning. She booked it then called Gordon back with the flight informa-tion. Later, before going to bed, she removed the gold band from her left hand. Oddly enough, it hadn't occurred to her to remove it until then. After all, it'd been on her finger for five long years. Fingering it, several emotions warred within her—sadness, a sense of loss, but most of all, intense relief. She dropped it in the jewelry box and closed the lid.

The next morning they were out in the crisp morning darkness headed to the airport long before Jess was even up. She didn't know his restless nights were filled with tormenting dreams of her. She hadn't let him know her plans. Given the way he'd treated her, why should she? That he thought she deserved everything Addison had done was poured in concrete and engraved in great big letters. However, she did tell Cora to go to him should she need help with anything.

"Just don't tell him where I am. It's none of his damn business," she said vehemently.

Cora was stumped trying to figure out what he'd done to affect her this way. She wasn't sleeping and had no appetite. The girl was thin enough already, she didn't need to lose any more weight. Men! Some of them needed a real good wakeup call—like dangling them over alligator invested waters until they came to their senses.

Though early, not yet five a.m., the airport garage was busy with people arriving and departing but they found a space on the fourth-level parking. In addition to everyday travel, the terminal was teaming with holiday travelers. Raine considered herself lucky to get a flight at the last minute. Checked in and boarding pass in hand, she hugged Cora and kissed Katy. "Be good and help Cora make lots of cookies while Mommy's gone. And you better save some for me, too." She planted little butterfly kisses between Katy's neck and chin.

Katy giggled, "We will, Mommy. I love you."

"I love you, too, baby-girl. Now go with Cora." She handed her off into Cora's arms. "I'll call you later on."

Cora noticed the ringless left hand. So, it'd finally dawned on her to take her wedding ring off. Good for her! It was a sure sign she was moving forward and she wondered what part Jess might play in the moving forward. As it stood now it looked like none.

"Do what you have to do and don't worry about us. We'll be fine. Come on, Katy-bug, we're going out to breakfast while

Mommy catches her plane." As their elevator door closed Raine felt suddenly alone and more disturbingly there was a tingling sensation on the back of her neck. Glancing around, she didn't recognize anyone. Shrugging it off, she studied the departure board, unaware Addison's trench-coat-wearing private investigator caused the warning prickles.

Robert Ford was feeling pretty pleased with himself. Since the night he'd snapped those pictures of her and the Harper guy he'd taken to watching her at all hours of the day and night. The decision to be back out before sunrise had proven a wise one. He'd watched the trio climb into the SUV and Andrews' wife had been carrying a suitcase. So far his hunches were paying off. He'd figured there were only three reasons why anyone left a warm bed so early on such a cold morning—work, someone was sick, or someone had a plane to catch—hence the suitcase. He'd followed them from the cabin right to the parking garage. Now he was near enough to touch her and the flowery scent of her perfume teased his senses. He admired her sweet, blond good looks and when she'd smiled at the little girl it was like a ray of sunshine burst forth making his conscience kick in again. She didn't deserve what her ex-husband had planned for her and if he were any man at all he'd chuck the whole thing and tell her right then and there that he'd found her. But he couldn't so he checked the overhead departure board, noting the flight to Phoenix. Well. Well. Well. She's headed home but the kid and the old lady are staying behind which means she's coming back. Glancing at his wrist-watch, he had plenty of time to buy a ticket. Hopefully there was an empty seat.

His luck held. A last-minute cancellation enabled him to get on the same flight. Shadowing her every step was starting out easy. Just as their flight was called he finished paying for his coffee and got in line. Once boarded, he caught sight of her several rows further back. Perfect. He'd be off the plane first and waiting to follow her.

Despite another sleepless night Raine couldn't doze. The situation between her and Jess weighed heavily on her mind.

Knowing his true feelings should make leaving easier, but it didn't, and that was okay, she'd live through the heartbreak. "You sure know how to pick men," she thought dourly as the landing gear dropped into place with a solid thump. Addison had beaten the holy hell out of her physically and Jess had done a hatchet job on her heart.

She rented a car and was zipping out of the airport in no time. Behind her another rental followed at a discreet distance. Reaching Gordon's office, she didn't see his car so she went for coffee at the bakery across the street. Studying the quiet thoroughfare, she noted nothing had changed while she'd been gone. Beside the bakery was a salon offering mani-pedis while getting your hair done. Festive Christmas lights glowed in the storefront window of the bakery. The second she stepped inside the most heavenly aromas made her mouth water.

Robert Ford pulled into a side alley with a view of the bakery and sat back to watch. Forty-five minutes later she crossed the street to a one-story hacienda-style building that looked more like a residence than an office.

Walking up the sidewalk, another round of prickly sensations raised the hair on the back of Raine's neck. Glancing in both directions, she saw nothing suspicious. "You're just being silly," she muttered. Only Cora and Gordon knew she'd been coming here. So why was she having these feelings?

Watching from his vantage point, Robert Ford made a quick search of the address on his laptop. Andrews' ex-wife was visiting an attorney, Gordon M. Hanson, Esquire. This tidbit would be something Andrews would want to know about. After she disappeared inside, he left his hiding place and crossed to the bakery. Hungry, he bought a large black coffee and a cheese-filled Danish. Up early, no sleep on the plane, he needed the caffeine and sugary refreshment. Pocketing the receipt, on the job, this was coming out of Andrews' expense account.

As soon as Raine stepped through the door Gordon greeted her with a warm hug. "Gosh, it's good to see you." Standing back, he scrutinized her. "You sure look a heck of a lot better than the last time I saw you. Molly's going to be sorry she missed you. She took squirt to visit her folks for a couple of days."

"Darn! And I was hoping to see them. I bet the baby's growing like a little weed."

"That she is." Gordon grinned proudly, reaching for his wallet. It was loaded with baby pictures. "I'd have emailed you pictures but I didn't want to chance someone stumbling across them. Where Addison's concerned, you can never be too careful. You never know who might be hacking in." He was referring to any minions willing to do Addison's bidding.

"Margie's on vacation," he nodded at the empty desk, "so I'm holding down the fort on my own. Molly offered, but I suffered one of those all-over-body shivers and reminded her of the mess she made of things the last time she helped out." Just remembering the chaos left behind in her wake had them both laughing. "I wasn't sure if Margie was going to clean Molly's clock, or just quit."

Gordon settled behind his desk. Raine took a wingback. Studying her, he noted the bruised shadows beneath her eyes and exhaustion lines bracketing her mouth. Gut instinct screamed they had nothing to do with Addison but something else. If not connected to Addison then something was going on in Missouri. Still, she looked a lot better than the last time he'd seen her. The physical marks from Addison's beatings had faded away, but what of the mental ones? And that led him to the newest wrinkle in the Addison Andrews saga. According to the call he'd received early this morning, changes, and not for the better, were in the air. According to Detective Green, talk around the courthouse was that Addison would be breathing fresh air instead of jailhouse fumes in the very near future. If true, she needed to be on her guard. He just hated being the bearer of bad news.

On top of his desk sat a manila folder. "These are the documents. The first is the custody agreement, the other the property disbursement. You might want to review them in case you want to make changes before they're filed. I have to ask one last time—are you sure you don't want to make him sell the construction company?"

Raine shook her head. "I'm sure. As long as I own shares, I've got leverage. That precious company means everything to him and if he wants to keep it, he's going to do it on my terms." She quickly scanned the pages while Gordon got them coffee. "Thanks." Grateful, she took a sip of the strong black brew. "I need all the caffeine I can get. I've been going since two this morning and the coffee they served on the plane was so weak you could see the bottom of the cup. These are fine. Hopefully, aside from retaining those shares, this is the last thing I ever have to do concerning Addison."

Gordon slid the documents back in the folder, hating to burst her happy bubble but she had to know Addison's attorney had finagled a reduced sentence and he'd be out in a few short months. "Don't count on it. There may be a new wrinkle."

His grim countenance set her teeth on edge. "What's that supposed to mean? What's Addison done now?"

"Detective Green called me early this morning. Rumor is Addison's getting out on a reduced sentence." He hated what Addison kept doing to her. If only there was some way to get rid of him for good short of killing him. Then again . . .

Raine surged to her feet. "What idiot judge would cut his time short? Doesn't he understand what Addison's capable of? Just read the damn file and see the pictures and he'd know. And I didn't agree to a plea bargain just to have his sentence reduced further. If I'd thought for one second this could happen I'd have never done it. He should be locked away forever." She took a calming breath. "So, when's this supposed to happen? And shouldn't I have a say? After all, I'm the victim, the one he was hell-bent on beating to death. I'm the one he was trying to shoot when the idiot shot himself." She paused, her voice thick with irony. "It's the same old story, isn't it? The victim gets the short end of the stick while the guilty get taken care of."

"So it would seem." He had to agree, justice was siding with Addison. "Green said approximately four months. I'll be talking to Addison's attorney to find out if it's really true or just a rumor."

"Come on, Gordon." Agitated, she paced the length of the room, rubbing her arms briskly as if warding off a chill. "This isn't a rumor. Whether I like it, whether it's fair or not, in a few months he'll be walking scot-free." So be it. If she couldn't stop Addison's early release, then she wanted to know the second he stepped foot out of jail. "Obviously, there's nothing we can do to stop it and though the Feds have the information on the thumb drive, those investigations take time. Just do me a favor. I don't care if it's the middle of the night, call me. There are more people involved in this than just me and Katy that I have to look out for."

"Don't worry, I'll keep you posted. And Raine, if you were contemplating returning I think you'd better stay away. See how all this plays out. You don't want to give Addison the opportunity to creep up on you. We all know him. He's slick when it comes to getting his way and that includes playing the good-boy role in pulling the wool over the judge's eyes."

This new development certainly put a kink in her plans. Once free, Addison would hound her to death. As for remaining at the cabin, that was out of the question, too. So fine, they'd move on as far away from Jess as she'd run from Addison. She was becoming an expert at starting over and getting away from Jess was imperative or her heart would never mend.

"Don't worry. I'm staying as far away from Addison as possible." She stood up. "I guess if I'm not coming back for a while I need to get on the stick and take care of a few things." She hugged him. "I'm glad I've got you and Molly on my team." She draped her coat over one arm. "Now I'd better get going. I still need to check into the hotel and let Cora know I made it okay. She wanted me to stay with Ethel but I didn't think it a good idea just in case Addison somehow figured out Cora and Ethel helped me. There's no telling what he might do to them."

"I wouldn't put anything past him and you need to be on your toes while you're here."

"I will. I'm only here for a day or two. I don't want to be away from Katy for very long."

Gordon laughed, "I understand completely. I have a hard time just leaving the house since the munchkin was born." He hugged her. "Pass that on to Katy. We miss our little sweetie."

"You do the same for Molly and the baby. I'm sorry I missed them." The constriction in her throat made it difficult to swallow.

"I will. If I didn't have meetings the next two evenings, I'd treat you to dinner. Take care and try not to let this news get you down." Opening the door, he looked up and down the street before stepping aside for her to pass.

"I'll try and if there's anything I can do to get the judge to change his mind, I'll do it." She still had a trump card even Gordon didn't know about. She'd found another USB drive hidden in Katy's scruffy pink teddy bear with more incriminating evidence on it and she'd use it to full advantage, especially since it contained proof that Addison was indeed a big-time cocaine supplier. Able to move freely across the borders with no questions asked had definitely allowed him to do business with no worries. She didn't know beans about the drug business but the astronomical figures on the second drive were proof his business must be very profitable. An involuntary shiver raced through her, she wanted no part of his dirty drug money. It would only lead to more trouble.

Putting off checking into the hotel, Raine drove out to her former home. There were demons that had to be laid to rest, plus the drive would give her a chance to think about the new quandary Addison's possible early release caused. Like it or not, she'd have to re-think her plans and it angered her that Addison still controlled her life.

Pulling into the driveway, a jittery trepidation filled her. Any second she expected Addison to jump out from behind a bush. Parking in front of the house, she gazed at her surroundings. Everything had changed. Katy's swing-set, always in motion, now stood abandoned. The flowerbeds, once teaming with brightly colored blooms contained only spindly brown stems.

Addison had insisted a lawn-care company take care of them but before leaving she'd canceled the service. Planted on the front lawn was a realtor's for sale sign. She'd halfway expected him to buy her share but he mustn't want it, either. A realtor's lock was on the door and not knowing the combination, she didn't bother getting out of the car.

She fully acknowledged her life here was over and she wouldn't miss it, and sometime between leaving Gordon's office and now she'd reached another major decision. She wanted home to be in Jess Harper's world. Fat chance of that, she snorted at the idea, especially after the other night. He'd made his position abundantly clear but now that she was away from him and could think, part of her believed he was blowing smoke, and a lot of it. Was there another reason he'd said those horrid things? Was he only pretending to want the other woman? Suspicions swirled around in her head. Was that his game? Or did he really believe the nonsense he'd spouted? Her fingers drummed on the console. It was a front all right, but until he admitted he was wrong, admitted the dark-haired woman meant nothing, she wasn't sure what she'd end up doing. Her mouth pursed. The man had her twisted up in so many knots she was dizzy, but she decided to give him until after the holidays to come to his senses. If he didn't then she'd throw the pieces of her broken heart in the trash and move on down the road. Twice she'd given her heart and twice it had been stomped to pieces. Her chin lifted defiantly. It was high-time she did some stomping of her own! And she'd had enough of the house, the demons were gone and she bid it a heartfelt good-bye.

Lighter in heart and spirit, she headed for the highway, ignoring the prickly sensations in her neck. Approaching the turn-off, she considered stopping to see Ethel but instinct said no. It was a good thing she drove on for Robert Ford followed discreetly behind her. He followed her to the hotel, heard her floor and room number then inquired if there were any rooms available on the same floor. Luck was still in his favor.

She made her call to Cora. "It's me. I'm checked in and other than dinner I'll be here the rest of the evening. I've already seen Gordon and taken care of things."

"That's a load off your shoulders but you sound tired." Cora detected weariness and something else. "Are you okay?"

The woman must be psychic to pick up something in the tone of a voice so far away. "I'm fine, just tired, probably from being up so early." Cora wasn't convinced, but there wasn't anything she could do. "How's my girl?" She asked, fingering the locket around her neck containing Katy's picture.

"She's fine. After we got home we took a nap then baked some cookies. Right now she's at Inez's. Her grandkids are there and she thought Katy might like to have some playtime with them. I didn't think you'd mind if I let her go."

"I'm sure she's having a blast and she needs to spend time with kids her own age. Plus, it gives you a little break. Just give her a kiss and tell her I love her." Raine hesitated for the merest of seconds before asking, "Is everything else okay?" It was her back-handed way of asking if she'd seen Jess.

Cora thought her about as transparent as a piece of clear tape. Exasperated, she fairly snorted the answer. "No. I haven't seen hide-nor-hair of that stubborn man. I think he's afraid to come here. So, what the heck went on between you two? I thought when you went down to work on Katy's dollhouse you two might get on the same page. Instead you've been all Gloomy-Gus and moping around. You two are avoiding each other like the plague and I happen to know neither of you has been exposed to it. I'm thinking you both should have your heads examined."

Raine rolled her eyes in exasperation as Cora went on. "I heard his truck startup not long after we got home this morning but I haven't seen hide-nor-hair of him since." And she wanted to. It was high-time she gave him a good blistering.

"I don't care what he's doing or where he's going. It's none of my business!"

Liar, liar, pants on fire, Cora thought. When Raine got back it was time for a meeting of the minds. "Do you know when you're coming back?"

"In a couple of days, I want to make arrangements to put things in storage." She also wanted to see Detectives Green and Collins and get their take on Addison's early release rumor.

They chatted a bit longer then ended the call.

Next door Robert Ford made notes on a yellow legal pad listing everything she'd done that day and thought of his client, he ought to visit him before heading back to that frozen tundra of a state. Why couldn't the ex-wife have picked some place like sunny Florida to hide out? Taking in the furnishings, the hotel room was quite nice but he'd rather be at his own place, sleeping in his own bed, but that was entirely out of the question. No way could he keep an eye on her from his apartment.

Later, hearing Raine's door close had him peeking out to see her heading for the elevators. He took the other elevator, arriving in time to see her enter the hotel's dining-room. Finding an end seat at the lounge's bar, he ordered a scotch and kept an eye on her having dinner. A while later she paid her check and headed for the elevators. Figuring she was in for the evening, he settled back and ordered another drink.

Raine spent a restless night wrestling with her two problems—Jess and Addison. With Jess, she needed to know if there was any reason to stay. As for Addison's early release, it was going to take some thinking outside the box to stay ahead of him.

Tuesday, she found a storage company and made arrangements to have the house packed up. Gordon agreed to coordinate everything. Wednesday found her rising as early as the day before but sometime during her fitful sleep she'd come to a decision. She wasn't finished with Jess by a long-shot. She wanted that man heart-and-soul and by damn she was getting him. She was going to make him eat every hateful word he'd said to her, and then he was going to love her. As for Addison—she was done running, she would meet him head-on.

Calling the precinct, she was told it was the detectives' day off. After another call to Ethel, she decided it was useless staying any longer. Crossing her fingers, she called to see if any flights were leaving that day for St. Louis. Elation filled her when told she was in luck, a flight was leaving at two-thirty that afternoon. She packed her suitcase and called Cora with her flight information. It took only a couple of minutes to check-out then she was headed for the airport.

Excitement raced through her when it came in sight. She was going home—wait, to Missouri, oh who cared! She was going home to Jess, for home was wherever he was. She'd just have to do everything in her power to convince the stubborn man they were meant for each other.

Robert Ford, shadowing her every move, was also on the return flight.

CHAPTER TWENTY-FOUR

The midmorning air held a crisp snap and pristine white snow sparkled like a blanket of diamonds. Jess had already mucked out the stalls and given the horses some much needed exercise, their pleasure evident as they frolicked and whinnied, their breath making foggy clouds in the air. From time to time they jostled him as he pitched fresh hay to them. Though his shoulder had a slight twinge, it was great to be doing physical activity again.

"You guys are cruising," he said as he smoothed a hand down first one long face then the other.

From habit his gaze strayed to the cabin visible through the leafless trees. Driving past it earlier he'd had an unsettling feeling, as though something wasn't quite right but he couldn't put a finger on what was making him twitchy. Miserable since the night he'd done the unthinkable, he was haunted by memories that wouldn't leave him alone. Now that unsettling feeling grew stronger. Something sure as hell didn't sit right where his tenants were concerned but he'd be damned if he'd stop to find out.

Sliding behind the wheel of the old truck, Jess headed back to the house. Approaching the cabin, an inner voice coached, "Just keep going. Stay focused, chump. You got what you wanted. You used the one weapon you knew would tear her to pieces and drive her off. You had her purring like a kitten then you dumped the milk dish. Your loss will be someone else's gain. Just forget her." Forgetting was a lot easier said than done, Jess conceded.

He'd been trying for days but the blasted woman haunted him constantly.

Believing the urge conquered he was nearly past the cabin when it hit him what he'd been missing. He'd seen Cora and Katy over the past couple of days but not Raine. Throwing the truck in reverse he whipped in behind the SUV and in quick strides was rapping on the door.

Immediately, Cora opened it, her eyes flashing. She'd been waiting and her exasperation-filled words took him by surprise. "What the heck took you so darn long? I was beginning to think you really were missing a few marbles after that knock on the head. It's about time you came to find out what's going on." She opened the door wider, ushering him inside to the warmth.

At once he detected the delicious smell of bread baking and his taste buds jumped back to life for the first time in days. Keen eyes swept around the cabin. "Okay. Where is she?" He demanded, not seeing the object of his search. "Where is she?" He barked again.

Demanding devil, but he could hold his horses. "Sit!" She ordered, giving him a stern look. "And don't use that tone with me, young man." Pouring a mug of coffee, she set it in front of him with a loud thump before settling herself in the chair across from him. "You're not blind. You can see she's not here." She took a sip of her coffee, eyeing him over the rim of the cup.

"I can see that." He snapped. Cora reminded him a lot of Inez, both possessing the knack of making him feel like he hadn't a lick of sense. "It just hit me she's not here. It's been nagging at me for the last couple of days that something wasn't right but I couldn't put my finger on it. Then it finally hit me—I hadn't seen her for days. So, where the hell is she?" He demanded again, his flinty eyes drilling holes in her.

Across the table, Cora studied him. He looked bad, haggard-eyed and deep grooves rutted either side of his mouth and his broad shoulders sagged as though carrying a heavy load. For a brief moment there was a flicker of pain in his dark eyes but just as quickly it was banked. No doubt about it, the man was hurting as bad as Raine and if she didn't step in to help them she'd never forgive herself. Taking a deep breath, she waded in with both feet.

"Raine doesn't think it's any of your business where she's goes, especially after the other night. That girl went to have an honest talk with you, even used Katy's dollhouse as an excuse to get a foot in the door but instead of coming back here happy, she was miserable and crying, and you're the reason for it. You've got that girl twisted up tighter than a bread tie. So just what in tarnation did you do to her that night?"

So Raine hadn't told her the sorry details. He went hot with schoolboy guilt, squirming under her glacial stare. It was the same way he'd felt back in third grade when the teacher had caught him pulling Nancy Clay's pigtails. "She's not the only one all twisted up!" He snapped, meeting her evil-eyed stare.

So he had done something to run her off. "Oh, don't worry. She hasn't uttered one word about what went on but my instincts are telling me something awful happened, something bad enough that she's ready to..." Cora stopped short, not quite ready to tell him Raine was leaving.

His head shot up, his dark eyes clashing with hers. Ready to what . . . what had Cora been about to say? What was Raine ready to do? Another wave of guilt-ridden flush stained his face darker. He knew exactly what he'd done because he relived it every waking moment and it filled his sleep at night. The horrible accusations were burned in his head forever and every time he recalled the rotten things he'd uttered he wanted to cut his tongue out. "Cora I . . ." he started to speak but she cut him off.

It was time to take this bull by the horns and throw him. The worst that could happen was they either appreciated her interference, or be mad as hell at her. "If you must know, she's in Phoenix. Her attorney needed her, and if you two weren't circling each other like rabid dogs you'd have known it." Her eyes were steady, never wavering. "You should be acting like two people in love." His heightened color confirmed her hunch. He was in love with Raine but some inner demons were fighting it.

"You know, Jess, I don't know what kind of games you're playing but ever since the other night she's not been herself. She puts on a good front, and I know she's a very good actress. For years she pretended everything was hunky-dory between her and Addison when the whole time he was using her as a punching bag. And, somehow, she's managed to keep up a happy front for Katy when I know she'd love to scream until she's hoarse, but she won't. She's not like that. Raine's a fighter, a survivor, otherwise she wouldn't have made it this far. Even when Addison left a threatening message the day after Thanksgiving she stayed strong." His surprised look confirmed he knew nothing about it and she didn't elaborate.

"Her only problem now is you, big boy. So, what do you have to say for yourself?" Jess looked at her but remained silent. "Sometimes talking clears the head. I know I feel better already." She grinned. When she'd spoken her piece, she'd halfway expected him to jump up and stalk out. The warring emotions on the face of this very private man were a good indication of the turmoil he was in. "Anything you tell me stays between us. I promise never to utter one word of what you tell me to her."

Closing his eyes, Jess rested his tension-filled head against the back of the chair. Talking would be great but hell, what could he say?—Hey Cora, I figured out a sure fire way to run her off. Since I refuse to become involved with a married woman, no matter how much I love her, I found the deadliest way to get right to the heart. I told her I understood why her husband had done those things. If she ensnared every man within mile of her and got them all hot and bothered . . . His eyes jerked wide open and found himself staring into a set of eyes spewing outrage, loud cursing, and a fist pounding the table. God in heaven! He hadn't meant to utter anything aloud. He'd been trying to arrange the words in his head.

"You did what!" She was thunderstruck. Whatever she'd expected, it wasn't this. She smacked the table again. "I ought to kick your behind up between your shoulder blades. Please tell me you didn't say something that stupid to her! You've got to be out of your blasted mind blaming her for what happened, especially when you know absolutely nothing about it."

Jess went on the defensive. "Well maybe if I'd known I could have handled it differently! But no, not once since she's been here has she broached the subject with me. Thanksgiving I got a few tidbits and we ended up arguing because of it. Why is she so closed mouth about it?" he yelled back.

Cora's eyes narrowed. "I seem to recall she went looking for you the Monday after Thanksgiving to explain everything but that apparently went to hell in a hand-basket for she came back madder than a thundercloud. And it only got worse when she saw you out with that woman. That's when she decided it was healthier staying away from you than ending up one of your conquests in your little games. From the very start you let her know you wanted to be left alone yet you're the one always showing up on her doorstep playing your games. No matter what you may be thinking in that crazy, mixed-up head of yours, Raine is a one-man woman. She won't share you, or any man, with another woman. And she will not be another notch on your bedpost!" Jess started to bluster that he was no womanizer, that he had no notches on his bedpost, fence post, or anything else but Cora was mad and on a roll.

"What were you thinking?" She slammed the cup down on the table hard enough that coffee sloshed over the side onto the table. "No wonder she's upset. Now I understand why she's avoiding you. I'd avoid you, too, you idiot. You really need your behind kicked and I'm about to do it. What in the world ever made you say something so stupid? If you didn't want her there all you had to do was say so. Shoot, she was down there a long time so the two of you must have been getting on just fine for a while."

Misery coated his face. He was hurting, too, and that was a good sign but she wasn't sure there was anything to salvage now that she knew what had happened. No wonder Raine was ready to leave. If she'd been in her shoes she wouldn't wait until after Christmas to go.

Jess heaved a sigh that sounded so miserable she almost felt sorry for him. Almost—but not quite. Wearily, his fingers raked through his black hair. "I know I've been acting one way then doing the complete opposite ever since you guys got here. From the moment I laid eyes on her I was hooked. She got under my skin and burrowed in. I might have acted all cranky and cantankerous but that was just an act. Raine's not the only one good at fooling people. I figured if I kept a safe distance then what I felt would eventually go away, but it hasn't. And that's part of my problem," he paused, staring at her, "in a nut shell, Cora, as much as I love Raine and would love to spend the rest of my life with her, I can't do that. She's still married." He grunted. "You'd have thought she'd hate him after what he did but she told me she still loves him."

Cora's mouth became a fine line. Raine's little ploy certainly had come back to bite her. Heaven help her, why did they have to play games? Now it was up to her to fix them.

"You're kidding, right? You're telling me she came right out and said she was still in love with Addison? I can't believe that. That doesn't sound like the woman I know. Her still love Addison—absolutely not! Hate him would be more like it, yet I doubt she even feels that for him. In a way, deep down, she probably pity's the man he's become. And knowing Raine, I'm sure she feels blame for not being able to help him."

"Well you can believe me or not. She didn't deny it when I ask . . ." Comprehension lit up his face and he swore softly. "Damn her . . . damn her . . . she didn't deny or confirm it one way or the other so like an idiot I took it to mean she was still in love with him."

"If you ask me, you both are idiots and need your heads examined." She commented dryly.

"It still doesn't make any difference. I know she's attracted to me, wants me, but she won't do anything to go against her wedding vows, even if it is frustrating as hell." He hadn't realized he'd said the last bit aloud either until Cora chuckled. Again, heat scorched his cheeks.

"What makes you think she's still married?" Obviously, he didn't know the divorce was final. What in the world had those two been doing . . . never mind. They'd been doing the same thing she and Ben would have been doing at their age. Shoot, if he was still alive they'd still be frisky as little kittens.

"She's still wearing her wedding ring, isn't she? And if she were divorced why wouldn't she tell me?" An eyebrow shot up accusingly.

Indignation filled her. "Hell and damnation! You've got to be the most obtuse man I have ever come across!" She sputtered disgustedly, "Of course she's still wearing her wedding ring. It hadn't occurred to her to take it off. Her divorce was only final since the Monday after Thanksgiving," she paused, letting the words to sink in. When they did it was like watching the proverbial light bulb flash on and his face turned a ruddier shade of red even as it lit up. "I don't know what the heck happened after you two met up but when she came back she was not the happiest girl in the world, and she should have been. Finally free of that monster, she wanted you, the man she'd entrusted her wounded heart to, to know she was free for you."

Feeling seven kinds of a fool, Jess closed his eyes, remembering that scene in the stable and it hammered home what a complete jackass he'd been to her. And that didn't count his hurtful ruse, carrying his punishment even further by involving Belle. If he could reach behind, he'd kick his own ass. Worse yet, was the abominable way he'd treated her the night she'd come to see him. The dollhouse had been her excuse and once again he'd acted like a complete moron. Instead of giving her a chance to explain, he'd gone on the attack, tearing her to pieces. No wonder she'd left without telling him. But hope rose inside him. She was coming back. Katy and Cora were still here and by-damn he was going to be at the airport when she stepped off the plane. Even if he had to hog-tie her to make her listen, he was going to apologize and right the wrongs he'd so ignorantly done.

Wearily, he scrubbed calloused hands over his face then looked at her. "Oh Cora," he sighed, "I did and said some awful things to hurt her. She knocked me for a loop from the very first time I laid eyes on her and ever since then I keep having these Jekyll and Hyde moments. One moment I want her so badly I can hardly stand it and the next I'm shoving her away, trying to convince myself its nothing more than physical attraction." He shook his head slowly. "But it's more than that. I love her and as much as I keep fighting it, I'm lying to myself. I love her so much and knowing I couldn't have her made me crazy."

"Do you love her enough to do whatever it takes to make things right, to convince her you're sincere in your feelings?" Cora asked quietly.

"I'll do whatever will make her believe in me, trust in me. I want her more than I've ever wanted anything in the world. I'd walk buck naked down main street if it would convince her."

Cora's eyes lit up with pleasure imagining the hard-bodied man showing off all his fine stuff but that would have Raine beating the women off with something bigger than a stick. Chuckling, she shook her head. "I don't think you should go that far. That'd just start another fire to put out."

Jess blushed at her meaning. "Do me a favor, Cora. Let me go to the airport. Let me pick her up and bring her home."

The request made her hesitate. "I don't know if that's a good idea, Jess." Would Raine even want to see him? It was all well and good that he'd poured out his heart to her, but what of Raine? Learning what he'd done, she still thought he'd gone too far to repair the damage. However, if there was a chance for them, it had to be taken but knowing Raine's state of mind, she had to be honest with him. "She's furious with you and I understand why. In fact, she's so furious that the day after Christmas we're leaving here." She added, "For good."

Shocked, his jaw hit the floor and her heart contracted. If those two, hard-headed people were to have a chance at a future together then she wanted to help them. She just hoped Raine had enough forgiveness in her heart to get past the hurt.

"All right, go pick her up." She really was a romantic at heart. She gave him the arrival information. "You do know your work's cut out for you? You're going to have a hard time convincing her it was all silly dribble to keep from getting involved with a married woman. She's not innocent either, but in this instance you have to be the one to step up to the plate. You struck a mighty low blow blaming her for Addison's behavior. All I can say is, if you love her like you say you do, then you'd better darn well do everything you can to make her believe in you." A scheming light entered her eyes. "You know, it might take you a while to get the job done so take your time, don't hurry back. As mad as she is it might take overnight, even longer, depending on how good your skills of persuasion are." She thought she'd have to beat him on the back when he strangled on the coffee.

"Cora," he rasped, "I know I've acted like a real jerk. I didn't want a permanent relationship with her, or any woman, for that matter, but she just burrowed into my heart." He had to convince her he truly loved Raine and would no longer hurt her. It'd be just the opposite. He'd do everything in his power to love and protect her until his last breath. "Oh, I admit wanting her," he paused, a bit embarrassed, "if you know what I mean."

Cora patted his hand, knowing Raine felt the same way. It was that age-old sexual attraction that entrapped all of them, love arrived a bit later. "I know what you mean but you two have to clear the air and get on the same page. That's the only way you stand a chance for a future. And don't forget, there's Katy. That little girl adores you and if you dance in and out of her life she'll get hurt, too." Her expression was dead serious, "If you're not in it for the long-haul then don't go to that airport, don't make promises you can't keep. That girl's already picked herself up and dusted herself off from one man. Thank God it hasn't jaded her about life and men. But if you hurt her any more than you've already done there's no telling how she'll handle it. Remember, believing what you said, she's leaving here so if you're serious you'd better consider what this means to all three of you."

Jess understood her concerns. "You're right about everything but . . ." he trailed off, his face bleak. There were a couple of issues remaining that bothered him—the difference in their ages, and if Raine's feelings were more of the rebound type.

Cora refilled their cups. "But what, what else is stuck in your craw?"

His eyes flashed in irritation. Just like Inez, excellent at barking orders, Cora would have made a great drill sergeant. "Okay. It's the age difference. Maybe I'm too old for her."

Mother of God! The man could be an idiot at times and she told him so. "You're an absolute idiot! That's it! You win the trophy!" She threw her hands up in disgust. "Haven't you ever heard the old saying, 'love knows no age?'"

"Yeah, I've heard it," he replied with an edge of sarcasm, "I just never thought it'd ever apply to me. What if she has regrets down the line?"

"Well it does apply and I know she'll never have a moment of regret. If you love her the way she loves you then your ages won't make a difference."

Something else bothered him and she had a hunch what it was. "And Jess," she stared straight into those smoky brown eyes, "she didn't turn to you on the rebound. You just happened to be the lucky man who was at the right place at the right time."

Relief swooshed out of him leaving him weak-kneed. "Thank you, I don't know how you knew, but thank you."

"It was just simple deduction, son." She patted his hand and warmth wafted through him. It had been a long time since he'd been called son. If he'd ever had a chance for a second mom he'd have wanted her to be just like Cora. "Are we good now? If so, she's due to arrive in a couple of hours. You'd better get a move on if you're going to be there on time to meet her plane."

"Oh, we're better than good. Okay, I'm out of here." He jumped to his feet, gave her a great big hug then grabbed his coat.

Standing in the open doorway, Cora gave him one more piece of advice. "Jess, get her to open up about everything she's been through. It's something you two definitely don't need hanging between you. You must have plenty of questions and it'll do her good to talk about the terrible things Addison did to her. Shoot, I'd bet there are things she hasn't even told me that he did."

A look of understanding passed over his face. "If she's willing to forgive me for what I've done then I'll get her to confide in me, she can place her trust in me fully. She shouldn't be carrying all that ugliness inside of her. From now on all she has to think about is us and our future." He kissed her cheek again then was gone.

If Jess could regain Raine's trust he had it made. Still, a little extra help wouldn't be remiss. She said a prayer. "Please Lord let them find their way back to each other. YOU know they're meant to be together. Open her heart to forgiveness for him, he's a good man, a caring man, and has been shown the way by YOU. Now show her the way back to him."

Whistling a jaunty little tune, Jess focused on one thing—how to convince Raine he hadn't meant any of the awful things he'd prattled. His intent was to catch her by surprise, storm her defenses. If he had to get down on his knees in the middle of the airport to plead forgiveness, he'd do it.

A while later Cora was at the window. Through the leafless trees she watched him toss an overnight bag in the truck. A happy smile lit up her face that he was taking her advice. My, but she loved a good love story with a happy ending.

Chapter Twenty-Five

Raine placed a hand over her stomach to quell the butterflies skittering wildly in it. They came alive every time she flew. The clicking of seatbelts melded with the pilot's announcement of their impending arrival in St. Louis where the temperature a crisp thirty-seven degrees. In no time the landing gear was down and locked followed by a textbook-smooth landing.

Waiting to step into the aisle, that weird tingling sensation raised the hair on her neck. Scanning the departing passengers, she recognized no one. She was just jumpy. Ever since finding out Addison was being released early she'd been all spooked up. Some man was kind enough to hold up the exiting flow of passengers to let her in line. Not suspecting he was the reason for the prickling warning, she smiled her thanks to Robert Ford as she moved passed him. Following the line and looking straight ahead, she didn't see the familiar man leaning against the wall.

Seeing her, his heart jumped with excitement. He called her name. "Raine."

She started, swearing she heard Jess calling her name but her imagination was playing tricks because he'd been constantly on her mind the whole flight back. Taking another step, a strong hand suddenly gripped her arm, hauling her out of the stream of passengers. Frightened, she dropped the carry-on bag and began struggling. "What . . ." she gasped, barely getting the word out as fright gripped her throat. Dear God, Addison had found her!

Survival instincts kicked in and she opened her mouth to scream bloody murder, but a voice stopped.

"Raine! Raine! It's all right. Honey, it's me, Jess. I didn't mean to scare you to death. I'm sorry. I just wanted to surprise you." Dear God, he hadn't meant to frighten her to death.

"Well you sure as hell did!" She stormed; blue eyes wide with fright in her ashen face. "What are you . . .?"

He didn't give her a chance to finish. He had the most overwhelming need to taste her, to drink his fill of the honeyed sweetness he knew her mouth to be. And he claimed it. And her head spun. One second he had her by the arms and the next she was crushed hard against his chest, his mouth hungrily devouring hers. What little resistance she possessed vanished at the first brush of his insistent tongue against her lips. Moaning softly, she savored the taste of him, decided to make the most of it and caution be-damned. To hell with whatever reason he was there. She'd missed him so much it was like losing a vital part of her own self.

A sigh of pure bliss slipped from her and desperate for the feel of him, she burrowed into the warmth of his solid chest. Her arms twined tightly around his neck as she returned his kiss with a consuming need. Against her, she felt the out-of-control pounding of his heart even as her head screamed to stop, that he'd only hurt her again. But her heart argued just as strongly, saying this was right, that he wouldn't be here if he didn't care for her. Wisely, she listened to her heart.

He rested his forehead against hers, breathing heavily. "If we keep this up I'm not going to care if we have an audience when I make love to you right here and right now."

"No kidding. We certainly wouldn't want that." She giggled breathlessly then sobered as reality threaded through her. The suspicious glint shining in her eyes set him on edge. "And why are you here?" A bit of clear thinking called for, she stepped back. To Jess it seemed a mile. "You're the last person I expected to see, especially after making your opinion of me crystal clear."

Dropping his head, he gave her a sheepish grin. "I'll get to that in a minute. I'm here because you need a ride home and I talked Cora into letting me meet your plane." At her raised eyebrow, he tugged gently on her hair. "Believe me; it took a lot of convincing. We had a good, long talk about a lot of things just like you and I are going to have, but before agreeing she made me promise not to do anything stupid to hurt you again."

Hope gleamed in her sapphire eyes, turning them translucent. "And are you?" She asked huskily. "Going to hurt me again?"

Shaking his head, he stroked a finger down the curve of her cheek. "No ma'am. Never! I have a lot of explaining to do on why I've been acting so crazy and it probably won't make much sense. Probably sound just about as crazy as I've been acting but I hope you'll hear me out. Everything hit me like a ton of bricks this morning when I realized you were gone. It nearly killed me that you'd left and I thought I might not see you again."

Her blue eyes darkened with pain. She could relate. "I wanted to tell you about flying back to Phoenix but given your attitude I didn't think you'd care." Censure filled her voice.

"Oh, I care all right. Just ask Cora." He laughed hoarsely, tucking a silky strand of hair behind her ear. "I could act like a callous jerk and pretend I didn't care as long as you were within eye-sight but as soon as I realized you weren't just avoiding me, but actually gone, I got scared, honey. I knew I had to right the wrongs I'd done you or lose you for good. I don't want that. Not ever. The pretending stopped right then and there. I'm tired of hurting. I'm tired of you hurting. What we have is meant to be and I'm not letting it get away." He smoothed a finger down her cheek again. It trembled and tenderness melded through her as everything he was feeling showed in the warmth of his eyes. Moving closer, she linked her arms around his neck.

He drew her against him, needing the reassurance that she really was there. "I need to apologize for the crazy way I've been acting but I really don't want," he glanced around him, "to do it in front of an airport full of people. We need to talk about us and this is not the place to do it."

He was saying all the right things and she so wanted to believe him. The intensity in her eyes took his breath away, searing his soul. Lord, but he loved her. How could he have ever been so cruel to her? Her question, when it came, was riddled with doubt and it reached deep down to rip at his insides. "Is there an 'us,' Jess?"

"Your damn right there's an 'us'!" He said vehemently. "I love you!" Then his mouth was hard on hers before turning tender. He trailed kisses from her mouth to her eyes then buried his face in the silken mass at her neck. His voice was thick and ragged with emotion in her ear. "I'm sorry. I'm so sorry. So very sorry I hurt you. If I could go back and undo that night, I would."

Tears misted her eyes for she'd never expected to see this man so humble. Her heart pounded in her chest, the trembling in him was more than she could take. "And I love you, she said softly. "Let's go home. Your home, my home, I don't care. We've a lot of talking to do and we need privacy."

"Yes, we've got a lot of air to clear and I've got an idea. Just promise you'll keep an open mind when you hear me out. I've made up a lot of stupid excuses, put on a show that you might want to kick my ass for."

Grinning, she patted his cheek smartly. "No might about it, big boy. I've been itching to kick that gorgeous backside for a long time, probably since the very first time I laid eyes on you and saw what a stubborn man you were."

A gleam in his eye, he asked, "Should I be wearing body armor? Will you kiss it and make it better?" Her laughter rang out making him easier, but he hadn't cleared all the hurdles yet. "Come on, let's get out of here."

"Jess Harper, I'm making this too easy for you," she protested even as she touched her mouth to his. "You're nothing but a spoiled little boy disguised as a grown man. If I forgive you this easily I'll never stand a chance with you."

"That's the whole idea, honey. I aim to use any means I can to make you forgive me and let me back in your good graces." Catching her left hand, his joy increased seeing the gold band was gone while she thought she'd lost all common sense where he was concerned. Oh well, she shrugged, entwining her fingers with his.

In the parking garage he stowed her suitcase in the back seat, shut the door then moved to her but didn't open her door. Instead he pinned her against the side of the truck and kissed her for a long, long time.

Finally lifting his mouth, he gazed into the deep blue pools of her eyes. "I'm sorry. I'm so sorry for all the rotten things I've done and said to hurt you. In case you haven't realized it yet I can be pretty ornery. If I'd let you talk the day you came to the stable it would have saved us a lot of heartache." There was deep pain and regret in the huskiness of his voice.

Raine laid a fingertip against his lips. "I know why you did it. I did a lot of thinking while away and realized I was at fault, too. I should have made you listen to me but you made me angry so I said forget it. You're not the only one blessed with a stubborn streak, Jess Harper. I'm sorry, too." She gathered him close, pressing her lips to his, never wanting to leave him again. "Let's get out of here."

Starting the truck, Jess cranked the heater to high before turning to her. She met him in the middle, an unspoken urgency filling them both. Here in the privacy of the truck they lost themselves in the intensity of fevered kisses and exploring caresses they'd been denying themselves for too long.

The need to touch her consumed Jess and he pulled her onto his lap, locking his mouth to hers. Her arms slid around his neck, her fingers twined in the crisp black hair that curled against his collar as she returned his kiss with a heat of her own. Pent-up longing overflowed, cascading like a waterfall through them. Beneath the soft material of her sweater, he was delighted to find the rounded warmth of bare flesh, she wasn't wearing a bra. The knowledge sent another fiery streak through him as they began their new intimacy.

Molten fire radiated through her as whispered moans of pleasure filled the cab. They feasted on each other, wanting so much more. She wanted to touch him with no barriers and tore the snaps of his shirt open. Her fingers found the furrowed hair curled thick and soft on his chest then as lips nipped at his neck. His head lolled against the back of the seat, his eyes clenched tight. His sharp intake of breath, his low growl, made her smug with wanton power.

Her touch, the feel of her lips trailing over his neck before returning to his mouth, drove him beyond all endurance. His hand fumbled with the button at her waist then stopped.

"No . . . don't stop," she pleaded, excitedly.

Breathing harder than a racehorse having just won the Triple Crown, Jess tore his mouth away. It took every ounce of willpower to remove his hand from beneath her sweater and shift her off his lap to the seat. A soft groan filled the truck. Was it his, or hers?

"I don't want to stop either, but we are not making love for the first time in the front seat, or back seat, of this truck." His voice was filled with passion. "But we are definitely going to make love tonight, all night—for sure."

"Then I guess it's a good thing one us is keeping their head. Jess Harper, you have a way of making me forget everything I should be mad at you for. One kiss and I'm ready to throw caution to the wind and forgive you. I can't think straight when you look at me, then you kiss me and my brain takes a vacation—but I like it!"

"And the bad part of that is?" His heart-stopping grin had her thinking the gorgeous man was all hers and no dark-haired woman was getting her hands on him.

"You go right ahead and mock me, but I bet I can drive you out of your mind, too." She tossed the challenge, giving him a feline grin.

"I look forward to it." He accepted with a dark-eyed intensity, knowing there'd be no losers. She could stroke him and he'd roar like a lion and while making her purr like his lioness.

Jess moved back behind the wheel, watching with regret as she straightened her sweater. "I can't wait to kiss you all over." Another hot flush surged into her cheeks at his words. Right now, she was so languid and boneless if she stood up she'd have fallen flat on her face. "Fasten your seatbelt. I don't want a repeat of the last time you rode with me. I plan on sharing your bed tonight and that doesn't mean a hospital bed."

His obvious intentions turned her cheeks rosy. Using the center lap belt, she did as he bid. No way was she sitting that far away from him. She shot him a knowing grin. "I can hardly wait. But you're the one who wanted to talk first." In the dimly lit cab he saw the teasing gleam in her eyes.

"Don't get cheeky!" Jess growled threateningly then grinned as he put the truck in gear. A thrill of renewed excitement shivered through her feeling his warm possessive hand on her leg.

Leaving the airport, she stared at the twinkling of the city's lights. It was the first time she'd seen this part of it and Jess pointed out several points of interest. There was so much to see. Someday she wanted to go exploring and visit the world-famous Gateway Arch, the riverfront, and the St. Louis Zoo. Katy would love the zoo. She shook her head in wonder that she'd left for Phoenix planning on returning there permanently and here she was a couple of days later contemplating going to the zoo.

Seeing her smile, he ached for a kiss and asked. "I hope that smile has to do with me?"

"Maybe," she teased. "Actually, I was thinking about plans."

"Do they include me?" His tone went wary.

"If you want to be a part of them," she answered, waiting a heartbeat for his answer.

"I do." The hand on her thigh squeezed suggestively. "Anything you plan had better include me from now on."

"Be careful what you ask for," she teased, "you may come to regret it." For a moment, she thought of the danger lurking in their very near future. Addison being free was going to be a problem she didn't want to face alone. She shivered with apprehension.

"You let me be the judge of that." Eyes on the road, Jess didn't see her troubled expression. "I like the idea of doing things with you, and with Katy. She's a sweet kid and I hope one day she appreciates having you for a mother."

"I'm the lucky one. She's such a plucky little thing, always rolling with the flow. Just look at how well she settled into the cabin and living in "dem woods." She mimicked Katy's pronunciation perfectly.

He laughed, having been treated more than once to Katy's laments about Santa finding her in "dem woods." "I happen to know Santa will find her in "dem woods" even if I have to drive the sleigh myself." He declared.

"Careful what you promise, Jess Harper. She might hitch a ride with you." Teasing him was fun.

He grimaced. "Yeah, I guess I'd better watch it. I open my mouth and who knows what she'll be making me do. She might even try for the North Pole."

"If she has you hitching up the horses to a sleigh, look out."

Slowing for the coming exit, they pulled into the parking lot of a hotel. Though taking Cora's advice about privacy, suddenly he was nervous, his mouth full of dry cotton and he wasn't the only one with a sudden case of the jitters. It wasn't that they were checking into a hotel. They were two adults who loved each other deeply but it was the fact that no matter how much talking, eventually they'd be making love and he'd see all the ugly scars. But she wanted this time to clear the air and start all over with him, the man she wanted to share the rest of her life with, good or bad, and if a few scars scared him off then he wasn't that man.

He gave her a questioning look. She's scared, he thought. Well she's not the only one. He'd already made so many stupid blunders; he didn't want to screw up again.

Meeting his eyes, she smiled. "Go ahead."

In the minutes he was gone she gave herself a pep talk but was unable to get past that before the night was over he would see the reminders of Addison's viciousness. Maybe they could turn the lights out?

Jess was back in minutes. "We have a room on the other side." He pulled around and parked in front of it. "Let's check it out first. If it's not to your liking, we can go someplace else. Or we can go home." There was a slight hesitancy on the last words. He no more wanted to go home than she did. Inserting the key card into the slot, he pushed the door open, flipped a switch, and a soft glow filled the room.

Looking around, she gave him a shy smile. "This looks fine."

Her shyness touched him and he tilted her face up. "We don't have to do anything but talk, Raine. I'd never force you do something you're not ready for."

That he read her so well turned her misty-eyed. "Thank you."

He thumbed a tear away. "I meant what I said. I'll never intentionally hurt you again, or make you do something you don't want to do."

The quiet assurance gave her confidence the shoring up it needed. "Then I think we should stay."

While she drew the drapes blocking out the rest of the world, he got their cases out of the truck. Hoping everything would turn out the way he wanted, he'd even brought along a bottle of champagne to celebrate. A quick trip to the ice machine filled the bucket.

Finding a station on the stereo playing soft, romantic music, he drew her against his solid warmth. His lips sought the soft curve of her neck and the heady scent of her put his senses on overload. He shuddered to be holding heaven in his arms.

They swayed to the music, wrapped in the profound relief that they'd stopped acting like silly fools. She feels so damn good, Jess thought, hands trailing down her back to the flare of her hips, drawing her closer to him.

She went willingly. Though they should be talking, she preferred being in his arms. Emotion welled strong in her chest thinking how close she'd come to losing this precious second chance at happiness and vowed never to take it for granted. Caressing the strong column of his neck, her hands sought the heated, velvet-smooth skin beneath his shirt.

Threading his fingers in her hair, he blessed the heavens she'd been wise enough to see through his stupidity and give him a chance to make things right. His mouth descended on hers and just like in the airport garage, the desire flamed to a roaring inferno.

Delicious heat diffused through her. If she could, she'd crawl inside him. It was pure sin that a man could be so handsome, feel this good, and it would be pure sin not to love him with all her heart, to revel in the heated splendor he created inside her. Again, she thought of how close she'd come to losing him and her arms tightened around him convulsively, never wanting to let him go. Talking could wait. Right now, she had another type of conversation in mind.

Riding the same thought, Jess drew her even tighter against him, his own desire unmistakable as he worked the fastenings of her jeans. They gave easily and he sought the sweet heated flesh.

Reveling in the muscled hardness, a glorious thought drifted across her conscious, she wasn't afraid of the coming intimacy. Instead, she wanted to embrace it with her whole being, knowing intimacy with Jess would be wonderful. Her heart trusted him completely and she no longer dreaded him seeing the scars for it would be a healing balm.

Easing her sweater over her head, the breath caught in his chest at his first glimpse her alabaster flesh, nothing short of hell could have stopped him from touching her. Raine shivered as pleasure rippled through her. Their swaying steps led them to the bed. Jess came down beside her, his mouth claiming hers, again drinking deeply of the sweetest nectar he'd ever tasted. He kissed her cheeks, her neck, made a sensual trek across her chest. The contrast of tanned skin against pale softness sent another surge of heat through him. On a soft groan, his lips followed the same path his fingers. At her pleasure-filled moans, Jess swore to spend the rest of his life doing all he could to make her happy. His body responded to her delight, demanding that part of her it instinctively knew was his.

The wildly erotic sensations were driving her mindless. Never in her entire life had she been so aroused and so quickly. Jess shifted against her and she opened her eyes, the love and intensity glowing in his fever-darkened ones was so overpowering, it pulled her into their depths. It made her yearn for much, much more.

Gazing into the depths of her misty eyes, what he saw left him breathless and his heart slamming uncontrollable in his chest. They were the mirror to her soul and in them he saw the deepest love a woman could have for a man. He kissed the dampness away before claiming her mouth in fierce possessiveness. Another moan filtered out and she moved against him, not sure how much more she could stand of the torture he was inflicting.

"Easy, baby easy." His lips skimmed the smoothness of her chest. He chuckled richly. "I thought we were going to talk first."

"Jess Harper, I'm going to hurt you." She arched into him, twining her fingers into the softness of his hair.

His sexy growl filled the room. "I'd rather you loved me to death but I'm thinking we put talking off for a bit." Her approval came in the excited little pants coming from her. "We have all night to talk."

A long time later she lay in the darkness, her racing heart returning to normal as she pondered the inexplicable response to Jess's lovemaking. Never in all the years with Addison had she been as wanton as she'd been with Jess and in those final months she'd been repulsed by any kind of intimacy with Addison. But Jess made her feel different; he made her feel sensual, beautiful, and loved. He elicited an intense need for more pleasure and fulfillment than Addison ever had and he put her needs before his, making sure she reached the highest pinnacle of satisfaction then taking her along with him when he'd finally went up in mindless flames, soaring right along him, searing them together forever.

Jess snuggled against her, lightly tracing her arm, caught up in the euphoria of their lovemaking. He'd dreamed of this night for months and it was everything he'd imagined. This night was a new beginning for them and he hadn't wanted to rush her but one look was all it took and his good intentions got left at the airport.

Loving her was all and more than he'd dreamed. He'd wanted her to know it was his hands touching her. His every intention had been to give her the greatest pleasure she'd ever experienced, and erase every trace of Addison's cruelty from her memory.

Raine couldn't believe the work-calloused hands could touch her with such infinite tenderness and she fell more in love with him. This was what it was all about—giving and taking, caring and loving.

"Are you all right?" His voice was husky, still thick with desire.

"Oh yeah, more than all right," she purred, her body still humming. "That was phenomenal." She drew his head down and kissed him deeply, shivering anew as desire wove through her again. Twining her fingers with his, they gazed in each other's eyes. This intimacy, new and profound, was unlike anything either had ever experienced. It was an intimacy that took them under into the dark hazy world most lovers never find. Their movements unhurried, the intensity grew hotter. When they reached the summit this time they slid over the precipice together, their cries echoing in unison.

Afterward, snuggling against him, Raine realized something she'd never been before. She was sated—sated in both mind and body. And smothering a yawn, she was sleepy. Making love with Jess was sweet and wonderful, she mused, and exhaustive, but she would keep on loving him for ever and ever. And one thing was a certainty; her man knew exactly what he was doing when it came to pleasuring a woman. Addison may have been her only other lover but he couldn't hold a candle to Jess.

At last he eased away to slip from the bed. At her protest, he murmured, "Be right back." Eyes half-closed, she watched him enter the bathroom. She drifted off only to be awakened by the feel of the warm cloth bathing her.

"This feels so good." She stretched, practically purring.

"It certainly does, sweetheart." He murmured. His tender ministering endeared him to her even more.

Tossing the cloth aside, he patted her backside, slid in beside her and pulled her against him. "You've plumb wore me out." He whispered in her ear.

"You're welcome," she said, siren smugness very evident in her voice. She's quite pleased with herself, he thought, giving her a firmer smack on her bottom. She yelped then chuckled seeing the satisfied grin on his handsome face.

"I know we should talk, sweetheart, but I'm too worn out right now. Let's nap a bit then talk." He traced light circles up and down her arm, raising goose bumps all over her and the light caresses started a tiny throb of desire echoing between her thighs.

"Um, that sounds good," she snuggled against him and in seconds drifted off to sleep.

Chapter Twenty-Six

She was having the most delicious dream in which a very heated body was curled against her back, however there was no mistaking the desire proving she was definitely awake. This was so much better than a dream—this was her fantasy come true. She giggled. Did the man never get tired? God, she hoped not. They'd made love several times throughout the night, talking had come after each bout of loving. And as they talked it became mutually enlightening how asinine each had been.

Jess explained why he'd been so cruel to her, that it was a built-in self-defense against her. "I wasn't getting caught up in some woman's trap. I'd been single a long time and planned on staying that way. How was I to know some long-haired, leggy blond, would come charging in like gangbusters, making me forget all about the joys and perks of being a handsome, sought-after bachelor? Hey!" He yelped when she elbowed him.

Raine explained as well. "I should have made you listen to me that day at the stable. Maybe we wouldn't have done so many stupid things to hurt each other and maybe we wouldn't have wasted so much time, either. FYI—sometimes my temper gets the better of me, too. In case you haven't noticed I can be very mule headed at times."

"Oh, I've noticed, honey." He said, grabbing the hand that smacked his shoulder and kissing the palm. "Just remember, I can be a stubborn jackass, too."

"Oh, I know. I've seen you braying in rare form!" She retorted only to be reward with a searing kiss as punishment. He understood about not wanting to start anything him until she was free. "I didn't want what was happening between us to be dirty or sordid. I'm no prude, Jess, but I couldn't have an affair with you, not while still married to Addison. You deserve better than that and so do I."

"I agree." He pulled her tighter against him. "And if I hadn't been acting like some smartass jerk maybe you'd have felt more like trusting me."

"I had to be free of Addison. I couldn't have him hanging around my neck like an albatross. If anything was to develop between us I wanted no leftover remnants associated with him." She sighed. "I sure wasn't looking for someone else when we showed up on your doorstep that day. Then bam! There you were. All steamy-hot and oozing so much sex-appeal I doubt there's any left for any other male. I watched you heading toward us buttoning your shirt and all I wanted to do was to rip it off you. I knew you were going to be trouble from the get-go. You practically knocked me off my feet with those gorgeous bedroom eyes. I never believed in love at first. As far as I was concerned that corny stuff only happened in those romance novels I edit. That's one of the reasons I love my job so much. I get to read the most fantastic fantasies. Believe me, after what I'd just gone through with Addison there was no way I was getting tangled up with another man! Then I take one look at you and wham! I'm ready to throw myself at you."

"For wanting to throw yourself at me you put up a damn good front." He scoffed sarcastically.

Leaning over him she stared into the darkness of his eyes. "That's all it was, too, a front. I'm ashamed to even admit this but there have been times I wished I was Katy. When you talked and laughed with her, I wished it was me."

Jess touched his mouth to hers. "Then I'll make sure you get plenty of attention from here on out. I'll give you so much attention you'll get tired of me."

"Not happening big boy, I love you too much for that." She snuggled back in, her head on his chest. "That first day you scowled at me so hard I thought your face would freeze permanently. But it only took one look at you and I fell so hard I thought I'd scraped my knees. But I fought and fought those feelings. After dealing with Addison I wasn't sure I could trust my judgment where men were concerned so I kept telling myself it was only physical attraction and I'd get over it."

"Not happening, sweetheart!"

"I won't argue with you." Taking his hand, she pressed her lips to the back of it. "You were so angry that day at all of us except Katy. You smiled at her and it was like a dome covered the two of you, keeping everyone else out. I think I was actually jealous because I wanted you to smile at me that way. Then I got my back up even more when you gave us fit about staying. If you hadn't I'd already decided to stay around the area. I'd have figured some way to get under your skin."

He chuckled at her tenacity. "Sweetheart, you certainly did that. I took one look at you and was a goner. And that scoundrel Inez knew exactly what she was doing bringing you out to the house. She knows me pretty well. She dealt a sure hand that day then trumped me with you."

"Yeah, but you hated being backed into a corner. I couldn't hear what was being said but you looked ready to strangle her during your little talk." She grinned at his snort. "And if you recall, I was already backing out of the drive when Inez started issuing orders. Man, the woman should've been in the service."

"Thank you! I've told her more than once she'd have made a great drill sergeant."

"We can't pick on her too much, though. If not for her I wouldn't have found you and we wouldn't be here seeing if this is going to develop into something." There was an unsure catch in her voice.

Hearing it, he rushed to reassure her. "I love you, Raine and this is definitely developing into something. You might as well get it in your head that you're stuck with me and you'd better get ready for the fun and exciting ride our future's going to be."

As far as he was concerned the future and fun had started the second she'd pulled into his driveway that sunny September day. His mind drifted to the ring on his dresser, he'd been right all along to get it. The very thought of her as his wife aroused him to the point he just had to have her right then.

When reality returned, it was Raine who padded to the bathroom, returning with a warm cloth to bathe him. He watched through hooded eyes, another flickering tingle rippling low in him. At this rate, they might make it home by Christmas.

Bathing him, a fierce possessiveness took hold. He was her man. She was his woman. Throughout the night they'd taken turns ministering each other. It felt so right, so intimate, and his assurance of a future echoed round and round in her head. She was about to slide back in beside him when the lamplight caught her back at just the right angle showing the faint silvery markings all over it.

Seeing them, Jess shot up. White-hot fury engulfed him. "What the hell happened to your back? What are those scars from?" He demanded. "What did that son of a bitch do?"

His anger wasn't directed at her but she was caught off-guard, he'd totally made her forget about the scars. And how had he missed them before now? Tears burned her eyes that Addison was already intruding.

"Sweetheart, it's all right. You can tell me." He pressed his lips to a patch of silvery-white scars before wrapping a strong arm about her urging her between his legs. He pulled the sheet over them, positive this was what Cora had been talking about.

Jess deserved to know the whole sordid story of what Addison had done to her. Settling against his solid warmth, the reassuring beat of his heart was comforting. Only one question tormented her—would he really want a future with her after finding out the kind of trouble Addison could wreak? She stiffened with fear.

Reading her like the small print in a contract, he ordered firmly. "Stop right there! There's absolutely nothing you're going to say that will make me want you less. Not happening. You're mine, I'm yours, and it's going to stay that way. We've put each other through enough these last weeks. Now that we're together absolutely nothing's tearing us apart. Nothing you tell me will send me running in the opposite direction. Now what caused those scars?" He commanded even as he pressed his lips to her shoulder.

The reassurances gave her courage. She gave him a bleak smile. "Okay, but it's not a pretty story." Jess nodded, already consumed with a rage that needed venting. Wisely, he remained silent.

Starting with before the party, Raine explained Addison's flipping out that she wasn't wearing the dress he wanted, of his ripping the dress to shreds before jumping on her, that it wasn't the dress that made him angry so much as the fact she'd chosen something else. She told of fighting back but it'd made Addison even more furious.

Jess muttered a curse and Raine covered his hand soothingly as she on with the story; that Addison finally stopped, figuring he'd better leave her in some shape to go to the party, that he stormed out threatening she'd better not make him late or there'd be more where that came from. "I didn't doubt it for a minute, either. I pulled myself together and I must have done okay because no one said anything, and the jacket covered the bruises on my arms. Absolutely no one at the party knew the mess I was."

Jess was getting angrier and sicker by the second hearing the living hell she'd endured. The killer-instinct was rising in him and he ached to get his hands on the bastard. He'd squeeze the life out of him with his bare hands, and take the greatest pleasure watching him struggle for his last dying breath. "Your ex is a dead man!" He growled. "He deserves to burn in hell!"

Raine cringed. This angry now, he'd really go off the deep end by the time she was finished. She told what a good act Addison put on, that no one would've believed what he'd done to her, that he had two personas that night—the evil one with her—and the good one with others. He was so smooth no one would believe him capable of such violence.

"But the evil Addison was still angry with me," she closed her eyes, "and as the evening wore on the more he drank, the angrier he got. Then right before leaving the party he started disappearing for periods of time. When he'd return I knew he'd been snorting cocaine. Someone brought it to the party and Addison thoroughly indulged himself."

"No one noticed the change in his behavior?"

"No. Addison's sly. He's very good at fooling people but I knew all the signs."

Addison Andrews is an alcoholic, a junkie, and a sadistic wife beater. The ache to squeeze the life out of him grew stronger. The snake better pray he never crossed paths with him. He wouldn't leave alive.

Next came the frenzied drive home; Addison's accusations that she was flirting with other men and his attempt to wreck them. "Jess, I never flirted with anyone."

"I believe you. You don't need to convince me." He hugged her, trapping her tighter against him. Not that she wanted to get away anyway.

She told of regaining control of the car then losing her temper, not caring anymore. If Addison was taking both of them out, then she had nothing to lose.

"I'll kill him. I swear to God, I'll kill him." Images of what she'd gone through on the frightening drive filled his head. Pushed over the edge, she'd lost all fear of him. A person did that when backed into a corner. There was more, of that he was certain. So just where did the shooting come into play?

"Addison was still ranting but he didn't go for the wheel again. And don't ask me why he didn't smack me for screaming at him but right then I wasn't afraid of him."

She continued on, telling about reaching home trying to get inside first and lock him out, but Addison was faster than she'd given him credit for. She shuddered remembering the terror of what happened next.

Guilt riddled Jess for making her relive the hellish nightmare. "Don't. Don't say anymore, honey. I can guess what happened next. Addison being bigger and stronger, you had to protect yourself and shot him. I'd have done the same thing and I'm a hell of lot bigger and stronger than you. But one thing I want you to always remember is that you did nothing to deserve his treatment of you."

"That's just it, I didn't shoot him. And no, I didn't deserve what he did and that's why it cut me into a million pieces when you sided with him." A sharp thread of hurt tainted her voice.

Okay . . . she hadn't quite forgiven him for that bout of stupidity and cursed himself seven shades of hell for inflicting the wound running ragged and deep, but he vowed to make it up to her. Then her words sunk in. She hadn't shot the bastard? He puffed away a stray hair that tickled his nose. "If you didn't shoot him, how did he get shot?" Then he changed his mind. "No! I don't need to hear any more."

"Yes, you do! If we're starting fresh, then you need to know everything. No woman deserves what Addison did to me. Who knows, maybe if I'd caught on sooner he wouldn't be the monster he is. Maybe if I'd stood up to him more, hadn't let him use Katy as leverage threatening to take her away from me, things might have turned out differently." No, she decided, everything would have turned out the same. Those times she'd stood up to Addison she'd paid a hefty price.

"Did he ever hurt Katy?" Just the possibility made his stomach churn.

"I've questioned her quite a bit and she says no." She worried a strand of hair. "I still feel so guilty that he snorted coke while she was with him and I had no clue. I should've been more alert."

He gave her a scolding squeeze. "Don't blame yourself. You said he was sly. It sounds like he was long past helping by then. That stuff makes a person do things they normally wouldn't. It turns a sensible individual into a burned-out junkie and they go off the deep end with the slightest provocation. It's powerful stuff; it changes a body and eats at the brain. They try hiding it but eventually they don't care."

"That describes Addison to a tee. He was able to maintain a semblance of normalcy. In the early years, I believe his mother and father were the only ones to fully know how bad his habit was yet they kept protecting and glossing everything over." Talking felt so good. If this had been Addison, he'd have been on her in heartbeat accusing her of making things up just to start trouble. "If I'd known he had a substance abuse problem I'd never have even gotten involved with him. But I didn't and he was so charismatic. He swept me off my feet and soon we married. It was this last year that his temper really got out of control. Sometimes I think if I just breathed it set him off."

Jealousy ripped through Jess hearing even the littlest praise for the bastard who'd marked her so savagely. "There are no excuses for what he did to you. He was your husband, your partner, your protector. He was supposed to keep you safe, even from himself. But he must have stayed straight for quite a while before things went south."

"He did. At one time he was totally different man, so kind and considerate, then little things started setting him off. If I didn't have dinner on the table at a certain time he'd get upset. I'd begun freelance editing so there were times things would run a little behind schedule. At first he was very understanding then that changed."

"Sounds like he couldn't control the drugs and booze so he found something he could control—you."

"You're right and I'm still amazed he kept up with the construction company the way he did. Probably still is, even from his jail cell. It's a shame too, because Addison was one of the brightest architects and contractors. There were times he'd bid jobs even though he had no crews free. He'd always tell me not to worry, that by the time the bid came through he'd have one ready. He would, too," She shook her head sadly. "What a waste of talent, of a man, but it's his fault. No one else is to blame."

"That's right. He made those choices and one of these days he'll have to look Katy in the eye and explain why he's the reason you had to take her and leave." Raine closed her eyes in dread. Jess had no idea how soon that time would come. "Losing you would kill me. Finding out you were leaving nearly did it." His voice was rough with emotion as he nuzzled her neck. "I can't even imagine raising a hand to any woman let alone one I've vowed to love and cherish." His breath against her neck sent tingles peppering over her making her shiver deliciously.

Jess smiled at her reaction then frowned at the silvery scars on her shoulders. What had put those marks on her, he wondered again? And did he really want to know after all? That her ex-husband had kicked her like a dog and used her for a punching bag fueled his murderous desire to mete out retribution.

Warmth curled through her. "That's comforting but I already knew that. You're nothing like him. Even when backed into a corner ready to tell everyone to go to hell, you didn't get violent." She was referring to Inez.

"That all depends on the situation and who's doing the backing. I'd never lay a finger on a woman but a man—that's a whole different matter. I don't normally start fights but I sure as hell won't back down from one and if someone hurts what's mine there'll be hell to pay. Your ex-husband better be glad I wasn't around when he was kicking you all over the floor. He'd had more than one bullet hole in him, I can promise you that!" He gritted with barely controlled anger. "He'd better never show his face around here or he'll find out how it feels to get stomped to pieces." She still hadn't explained about the scars on her back. "What else did he do to you?"

Raine didn't doubt Jess would do exactly as he said. Already upset, how much more incensed would he become learning what else Addison had sadistically done to her. Given what she'd learned in Phoenix, there was very good chance Addison would find them and when he did he wouldn't just stop at beating her and if Jess tried to help her he could get hurt. Addison was a formidable foe out for blood—her blood.

Sensing her reluctance, he reassured her. "Sweetheart, I'm not going to make you tell me. If you're uncomfortable talking about it then I don't need to know."

"No." Raine turned her head to gaze up at him. The tenderness in his eyes vanquished her concerns. "This is our fresh start and you should know the rest of the whole sordid story of what happened that night."

With Jess protecting her from the horrible memories, she exorcised the demons of that night. Enmeshed in the memories, she relived it in vivid clarity how she'd fought back for all she was worth, especially when he'd dragged her to the bedroom, that he meant to hurt her worse than ever before, that there'd been no doubt he meant to kill her. She told of Addison knocking her out, stripping her clothes and tying her to the bed. A snarl erupted from him and she patted his hand. She told of coming to with Addison standing over her with a leather belt in his hands, of his having already used it then of his whipping her again, that he just kept on hitting and hitting until she couldn't stand it anymore lost consciousness.

Though he remained silent, any second he thought he'd explode. The urge to kill Addison was overwhelming and lying there with her in his arms, not saying a word was the hardest thing he'd ever done. He ached to scream at the top of his lungs and hit something very, very hard. He could actually taste the bitter black rage roiling inside of him.

"That no good son of a bitch!" He spat. "I'll kill him. I swear to God if he shows his face I'll kill him." His threats weren't idle ones, either. Shivers raised the fine hairs on her arms. "That's not the end, is it? What else happened, what about the shooting?" She moved restlessly and he pressed his lips to her shoulder, murmuring. "It's okay, baby, he can't hurt you anymore."

She continued that coming to and thinking Addison gone and knowing she had to get away, she was to the front door when he caught her. Instead of leaving, he'd been sitting in the dark drinking and waiting.

"Somehow he must have known I'd try leaving and had the gun to stop me. Anyway, he kept knocking me down and I kept getting back up. He wasn't expecting that, not after all the beatings and whippings he given me. Truthfully," she grimaced, "I was surprised I still had it in me. I guess it was survival instincts."

Crazy as it seemed, Jess suffered an intense ineptitude for not being there when she'd been fighting for her life. Clearly, he had no idea the extent of the things she'd endured living with the monster. Now he hated himself for insisting on hearing it. "Sweetheart, you don't have to go on. I really don't need to hear anymore."

"Yes, you do. You can't imagine what it was like. Or maybe you do. I don't even know what you did in the Marines. Having no one to help me gave me the strength to get away. I couldn't give up and knowing Addison had the gun the whole time we were fighting, that he was hell-bent on using it was a pretty good incentive, especially when he's screaming over and over that he was going to kill me. We ended up on the couch with the gun between us. That's when it went off."

The memory of the loud crack, the sharp echo of the pistol firing was as real as if happening that moment. Jess wrapped her tighter in his arms. "I thought he'd shot me. I waited for the pain and the blackness but it didn't come and I realized Addison was a dead weight on top of me." She laughed coarsely, "Ironically, he'd shot himself. He was unconscious and bleeding heavily so I used my shirt to try to staunch the blood." She chuckled with relish. "Actually, it was his shirt." The crimson blood soaking the shirt was still vivid in her mind. Had she any clue of Addison's plans for revenge, she'd have let him bleed out.

Jess stroked her arm. What a dilemma she'd been faced with—to help him or let him die. "You must have had a tough decision. Me? I'd have let the bastard die. But you couldn't. You could never intentionally hurt anyone or let anyone die. You don't have it in you."

"Don't kid yourself." She traced a path in the hair on his wrist with the tip of her fingernail. "The thought crossed my mind, but you're right, I couldn't live with my conscious if I didn't help him," then she added drolly, "Little did I know when he came round he'd accuse me of shooting him!"

"You're kidding, right!" His brow shot up in disbelief. "You should have let him bleed out!"

"I'm not kidding." A flush reddened her cheeks remembering her state of undress. "I was such a mess, Jess, I wasn't even aware I didn't have a shirt on." Jess knew this woman, the one who wouldn't break her marriage vows though the marriage was dead, would never willingly be seen that way. She must have been mortified. "Anyway, when Addison regained consciousness he accused me of shooting him."

"I know I'd like to shoot him in several places," he said vehemently.

Raine chuckled, knowing full well what places he was referring to. And he might just get the chance and that thought turned her fiercely protective. No way in hell would Jess go to jail because of Addison! If anyone did any shooting it'd be her.

"At first I thought the police might believe him and arrest me but they didn't. I guess I looked a sorry enough mess with Addison's blood all over me and being so beat up. And they were positive from the start I didn't shoot him. They knew he was lying. So did the paramedics."

"Did they arrest him right then?"

"They wanted to but it was his word against mine. After all, he was the one with a bullet hole in him. It was the bindings on the bed that gave them a pretty good insight to what he'd done." She chuckled at the memory. "Man, I thought Detective Collins was going to go shoot Addison herself."

"I already like this detective and I don't even know her," Jess said. "Like I told you honey, just give me the chance to come face-to-face with the bastard! There's not one judge or jury around here that will give me any grief for doing away with the scumbag."

Careful what you wish for, Jess Harper, you just might get your wish. "Anyway, while Addison was in the hospital the fingerprint results came back and mine weren't on it. They charged him with felony domestic battery and attempted murder. He went from the hospital directly to jail. The detectives said if he'd left the gun locked in the safe no one would have been shot."

A horrible angst rose up inside Jess that Raine could have died that night and he would never have had the chance to fall in love with her. Then another horrible thought occurred—where was Katy while all this was going on, surely not in the house?

"Where was Katy when this was happening? Please tell me she didn't see what he did to you?"

"She was with Cora and Ethel. If I'd had to protect her and fight Addison, too, I doubt I'd have made it. Anyway, they transferred him to jail to await trial. Bail was denied and I refused to drop the charges so he stayed behind bars. In the meantime, everyone suggested I take Katy and leave town. And bless her, Cora refused to let us go off alone, even insisted we use her vehicle in case Addison tried to have us followed. We left Phoenix and just drove, figuring when we reached a place that felt safe we'd stop. I give thanks every day that we ran into Inez. Without her I wouldn't have met you."

"And to think most of that time I've been a jackass." His voice was low against her ear. "You caught me totally by surprise, honey. I wasn't looking to get tangled up with anyone, let alone one gorgeous little blond that had been beaten to within an inch of her life. But I didn't have much choice in the matter. Inez is a force to be reckoned with when she wants something. Part of me was so attracted to you I wanted you right then and there, while the other part said to keep my distance, that you'd be trouble. I tried to discourage you, but every time I looked at you my heart said 'go for it.'"

"Trust me. I know exactly what you mean. I felt the same way about you. That's why I let you think I still loved Addison though sometimes I literally wanted to knock you to your knees and tell you the truth and get you to admit you cared for me.

And just when I'd decide to do it you'd be in one of your snits, grouchier than an old bear when I got close."

"I do not get into snits," he protested indignantly.

She shot him a dry look. "Sure you don't! You were in one the first time I saw you. I've come to know those looks quite well." She loved the warning glittering in his eyes.

"I'll show you another kind of snit I can get into." He rolled over until they were lying heart to heart. In her eyes he saw the lingering shadows of the past. He had a feeling she'd suffered even more than she'd told him. The kiss he gave her was meant to comfort but soon turned to soul-bearing passion.

"Now I love this snit you're in," she chuckled against his mouth, running a barefoot up and down his hair-roughened leg. His body responded immediately. "Maybe you should be in this kind of snit all the time."

Jess pulled his mouth away, shaking his head. Her eyes were sultry with mischief. "I knew you'd be trouble the first time I laid eyes on you. But now you're mine and I think you need a little punishment."

"Bring it on, big boy. I can take it," she chuckled as his lips covered hers at the same time their bodies joined.

CHAPTER TWENTY-SEVEN

The midmorning sun shone brightly as they drove toward home. Wrapped up in each other and all being right between them, neither paid any attention to the car following them. Robert Ford had tailed them from the airport, spied on them all night, and was behind them at the fast-food drive-thru when they got coffee—even getting one for himself.

And he had decided to err on the side of caution and would move from his current hotel to a different one. He wanted nothing traceable connecting him to Andrews when he finally met up with his ex-wife. Despite his conscience, he was proud he'd gotten the kind of dope Andrews wanted against his ex-wife. And thanks to some hi-tech photography equipment, he'd caught the couple in several of the most passionately intimate moments a man and a woman can share. And even if he said so himself, he was damn good at getting pictures from the slightest openings and angles. Though the photos were bought and paid for, he still had everything on a USB drive. Sold to one of the girlie magazines, he'd get a fortune. There was no telling what opportunities might come his way once things died down.

"Do you want to stop off any place before we go on home?" Jess asked, giving her thigh a light squeeze where his hand rested.

"No." His touch put a hitch in her voice while stirring her blood. Geez, after making love nearly all night you'd think you'd be sated by now. She was just looking at him but that set the embers of desire burning and now there was more than just the physical attraction. Her thoughts drifted to yesterday at the airport. She'd definitely been surprised but all her prayers had been answered. Admittedly, theirs hadn't been a true courtship but sometimes life just didn't work that way. Anyhow, whatever was meant for them, she was in it for the long-haul. Her eyes misted that she loved this man with all her heart then a determined gleam filled them. Addison no longer an obstacle, it was time to get rid of the brunette. She refused to believe he'd profess his love for her if that woman really meant anything to him.

"I sure do love you Jess Harper." Heart soaring, he closed his hand around her left hand, delighted her wedding band was no longer there. He thought of his own ring and fantasized slipping it on her finger.

"I love you too, honey. I just hope I'm not rushing you if you're not ready."

She smacked him on the thigh. "Jess Harper, I'll have you know I've been crazy about you since the day I followed Inez to your house. I fell in love with you even though you were wearing your cranky-pants."

"I fell for you, too, even though I put up stumbling blocks along the way. But let me tell you," he chuckled, "as quick as I put one up you'd blast through it with your magical laser gun. I'm a stubborn cuss, but I just had to quit being the world's biggest jerk and admit I'd fallen in love with you."

"Thank God you did." The glow on her face was testament of how breathlessly happy she was, like a kid on Christmas morning anxious to find out what Santa had left. That Jess loved her was the most cherished gift she could receive. The agony of the past weeks had been for nothing. "Let's go home."

In town, Jess took the shortcut past several stately old homes. Raine couldn't decide which one was her favorite. On the left, amid a sweeping snow-covered lawn stood a large two-story Victorian. Its wide wrap-around veranda had several white cane-back rocking chairs on it. Children played in the yard; some were building snowmen while others tossed snowballs at each other. She pointed to a little girl about Katy's age packing a snowball that she sent flying at a bigger boy. It smacked him square in the face and he went chasing after the giggling culprit.

Someday, she dreamed wistfully, she'd have that with Jess.

"That little gal's got a pretty good arm," Jess chuckled. Glancing at Raine, he saw the wistful longing. If he hadn't wanted to surprise her at Christmas, he'd propose right then but he had a plan. Watching the kids again, he hoped someday their children would be having fun like that. The thought started desire flaring in him again and he shifted in his seat. He better put his mind to something else or he'd never be able to face Cora and Katy.

Driving on, they passed a forlorn looking three story log house that had fallen into sad neglect. If that cabin were mine, she thought, it'd shine so bright you'd need sunglasses. She knew the cabin's history, having pumped Inez. It, and the one further down the road, had been built around 1850. Brothers had bought up a huge chunk of land, built the log homes then a feud drove them apart. One sold out to strangers while the other stayed on. Descendants of the brother who'd stayed now occupied the well-kept cabin while the other one had been used mostly as a hunting lodge, even a lover's tryst, then nothing. Raine wished it could talk. It must be chock-full of secrets and she'd bet a ghost or two haunted the old place. It would make a perfect shelter for battered women. Someone should see if it was for sale. It gave her something to think about.

The second they stopped, the kitchen door flew open and Katy came barreling out, launching herself into her mother's arms. "Mommy's home, Mommy's home, I missed you Mommy!"

Raine scooped her up. "I missed you, too, baby girl, bunches and bunches." Raine counted her blessings. She had Jess and the sweetest daughter. Life was great. Maybe she'd been destined to go through hell with Addison in order to reach this level of happiness and nothing, or no one, she vowed, was tearing her world apart, she'd fight to the death to protect it. "Were you a good girl for Cora?"

She nodded vigorously. "I was, and Cora let me play at Ms. Inez's house with the kids."

Observing the tender reunion, a boulder-size lump swelled in his throat and he blinked several times at the moisture in his eyes. And, to think he'd almost missed being a part of their lives. Well, he was going to do something permanent about that very soon.

Wiggling out of Mommy's arms, Katy went to Jess extending her arms in silent command to be picked up. Obliging, he settled her on his hip. "I'm glad you brought my mommy home, Mr. Jess." Rosebud lips rewarded him with a smacking kiss on the cheek. Considering himself the most fortunate man in the world, the lump in his throat grew bigger. To hide his misty eyes he nuzzled her neck, making her giggle. A heartbreaker now; he could only imagine how many hearts she'd break when grown, and yes, he planned on being right there to see her grow into a beautiful young woman. After all, a girl needed a dad to make sure the boys behaved themselves.

"I'm glad I brought your mommy home, too, sweetheart." He whispered huskily.

"Come on in." Cora smiled from the doorway. "Katy and I have been making Christmas cookies and there's a pot roast with all the trimmings in the oven. I figured you two might have worked up an appetite." She turned to the oven but not before they saw the triumphant gleam in her eyes. Jess looked like a man in love and there was a rosy glow on Raine's face, and a whisker burn on her neck she probably wasn't even aware of. Obviously, they'd worked through their misunderstandings. It was as plain as the noses on their glowing faces they were besotted with each other.

"Jess, you're joining us for dinner this evening, right?" Shutting the door, she removed the lid on the cookie tin, setting it in the middle of the table. "Help yourselves. Katy and I baked our fingers to the bones, didn't we kiddo?"

"I'll be here." He sat, balancing Katy on his knee. Peering inside the cookie tin at all the festively iced cookies, his mouth watered. He selected a gingerbread man and bit into. It practically melted in his mouth. "That is if I don't fill up on these cookies first."

Raine poured mugs of coffee and set them on the table. She opted for a Santa-shaped sugar cookie.

His next cookie was an iced one in the shape of a snowman. In no time, without realizing it he'd eaten half-a-dozen of the brightly iced treats while the conversation centered on Katy's visit with the McCullen grandkids.

"Those are the best cookies I've ever eaten." Katy beamed while Jess shook his head when Cora shoved the container at him again. "I want some of that delicious smelling pot roast. Any more cookies and I won't be hungry. Now," he scooted the chair back, dropping a kiss on Katy's head before setting her on her feet, "I'd better go check on things. I'll be back in time for dinner." He reached out to squeeze Raine's hand. What he really wanted was to cover her in kisses.

Passing Cora, he kissed her cheek. "Thank you." Then he was out the door.

The second it closed Raine was out of her chair twirling and giggling. She threw her arms around Cora. "I should have known you'd have something up your sleeve. I'm so glad you had Jess meet me at the airport. Everything is wonderful."

Raine's eyes shined so bright Cora thought she'd have to get her sunglasses. "I had to do something to get you two mule-headed people together. You were driving me nuts with all the mooning then pretending you couldn't stand each other."

"I'll have you know I don't moon," she said haughtily.

"Oh, sure you don't," Cora scoffed. "You most certainly do! Anyway, the stubborn man stopped by yesterday when it finally sank in he hadn't seen hide-nor-hair of you for days. I was beginning to think I'd have to spray paint it in the snow you were gone. When he found out you weren't here he got all bent out of shape, like he had a right to know what you were doing."

Raine nodded. "Yeah, he got his message across about that. But I told him the same thing; that given his attitude I didn't think he cared. You can't imagine how many times he apologized last night."

"Oh, quite a few times I'd imagine," Cora's said smugly. "After telling him where you'd gone we had quite a chat. You can't imagine the ton of nonsense swirling around in that handsome head. We talked about your effect on him and why he'd been acting like an idiot. Claimed it was some kind self-protection against you. He was putting walls up around his heart, but just as fast you tore them down. I thought you had some silly notions but he beats you all to heck." She looked at Raine expectantly. "So, I'm assuming all went well and you got everything all worked out?"

"You could say that. We talked the whole night . . . now what are you smirking at?" She demanded at the look on Cora's face.

"I may not be young anymore but I know talking sure didn't put those whisker burns on your neck." Cora chuckled. "Look in the mirror."

"I don't have anything on my neck!" A hand to her neck, she marched to the mirror. To her consternation sure enough there was a red rash. Fingering the marks, she grinned. Well . . . maybe we did take a little break from talking." A rosy blush stained her cheeks. She was in love and for the first time in a very long time, happy.

The only dark cloud marring the horizon was Addison's impending release. As soon as he was free, he'd find a way to track her down and make her pay for her imagined sins. The little voice inside her head screamed to get prepared. And she would, starting this evening she'd tell Cora and Jess about Addison's impending release, but only after Katy was in bed. The less she knew about her father the better.

From time to time she'd asked about him. What was he doing? Was he coming to see them? With childlike understanding, she accepted the explanations that daddy was still working and couldn't come see them. Raine fervently prayed he would never show up. But she was only kidding herself. Instinct told her it was only a matter of time before he found them. And if he got to Katy, she was his ace in the hole for bait. It wouldn't be the first time one parent used their child to coerce the other. Just look at the woman in Florida whose ex-husband fled with her child. That incident had turned out okay because an observant citizen saw their pictures in the news and alerted the authorities. She swore to do everything in her power to keep Katy safe from Addison, even if it meant killing him.

When Jess arrived for dinner her heart did a happy pitter-pat dance that could have put Fred Astaire to shame. His gleaming midnight hair was damp from a shower and her fingers curled remembering its softness and a delicious heat wafted through her. Looking into her eyes, his heart started pounding like a racehorse. If he'd had any remaining doubts, which he didn't, the look in them would have vanquished them. The love glowing in those gorgeous sapphire pools pulled him into their mesmerizing depths.

It was Katy tugging impatiently on his pant leg that brought him back to earth. "Mr. Jess! Mr. Jess!"

"Sorry Katy-bug. I zoned out for a minute." Caught dreaming, Cora's snicker reached his ears, making him grin like a love-struck teenager.

"Is that for me?" She eyed the chocolate soda in his hand. "You know that's my favorite," she informed him matter-of-factly, dainty hands on either side of her little waist.

Jess tugged her pigtail. "It's my favorite, too. We're like two peas in a pod." He lightly tipped the end of her nose with his finger and was rewarded with a coy giggle.

"Are we celebrating something special?" Cora asked.

"No ma'am. No special reason at all. I just thought we might enjoy a glass of wine with dinner and perhaps toast the holiday season." He said innocently, setting the wine on the table.

"Unh-huh, if you say so," she grunted, pouring the wine and soda. He wasn't pulling the wool over her eyes one bit. They were celebrating, all right, celebrating the fact that two very hard-headed people were finally on the same page. "So," she looked at Raine, "you haven't said how your trip went. Everything go okay?" She passed the platter of succulent pot roast to Jess. He was curious, too. That subject hadn't come up during the night. They'd talked, made love, talked and made love, but they hadn't talked about her trip to Phoenix.

Sipping the rich burgundy, feeling it slide smooth as silk down her throat, Raine glanced at Katy busy tearing her crusty dinner roll into bite size pieces for dipping in the brown gravy, just the way Jess had taught her.

"It went fine. Everything was ready to be signed and filed and then we discussed a new matter that's come up, something that will require strategizing." She met Jess's smoky look over the rim of her wine glass, getting lost in those dreamy eyes. "You know, Phoenix didn't feel like home anymore and I couldn't wait to get back here. This is home to me."

Despite her smile, the haunted look in her eyes sent a feeling of trepidation up his spine. She's holding something back. Did it have to with that new matter she'd mentioned? Last night they'd worked through their feelings, loved one another, and locked the outside world away. And just as he'd promised, whatever was happening, they'd get through it together. One dark brow lifted inquiringly. Seeing it, she looked at Katy then back at him. He got the message—little ears were listening. Cora also detected something was going on that had Raine spooked. Meeting Jess's quizzing eyes, she shrugged her shoulders.

Dinner was a lively affair with Katy chiming in on every other breath about Christmas and Santa Claus, her two favorite subjects. Picking up that she was still worried about Santa finding her, Jess promised to put guide lights on the roof so Santa and the reindeer could land the sleigh.

Afterward, they cleaned up the kitchen while Cora put her feet up. "It's only fair." Jess shooed her away. "You cooked; we do the clean-up."

Lifting Katy from the booster chair, Raine grimaced while deliberately ignoring Jess's inquiring look. Her ribs were the least of her problems.

The flicker of discomfort made him frown. They'd been very active in their lovemaking last night. Their need for each other had been so overwhelming intense that everything else had faded into the background. Had he hurt her? God, he hoped not. That was the last thing he ever wanted to do. Intimacy with Raine had been like receiving a gift from heaven. "You okay?"

"I'm fine, just a twinge. It happens every now and then if I move the wrong way or pick up something heavy. It's not as bad as it was right after the accident, and it's nothing I can't live with."

"Have you done a follow-up with the doctor?" Now his tone was stern.

To stave him off she went on the offense. "You haven't either, I bet. I must say though, that knock on your head knocked some sense into you." She tapped his cheek, delighting in the fire that sprang to his eyes but knowing him she wouldn't put it past him hauling her straight to the nearest medical center.

Warning glints filled his eyes. "Watch it, woman! I've always been in my right mind. It just took a little vacation for a bit. Now be serious. I'm not the one that's had the sh . . ." he trailed off at the warning shake of her head and nodded to Katy. Ah yes, little ears. "Oh, never mind. It wouldn't do me any good anyway."

"You do catch on fast, Mr. Harper. I'm telling you, you set a fine example for the male gender." She teased, but in an attempt to appease him added, "If it'll make you happy I'll make a follow-up appointment."

"It will. So, get on the horn and make it soon." He opened his mouth to say more, then thought better of it, quitting while he was ahead. Hearing Cora's snicker, he ignored it.

Katy dashed to the bedroom. "I'm coloring Mr. Jess a picture," she tossed over her shoulder. She sprawled in child-like abandon on the bed to watch one of her favorite cartoon shows and color at the same time. Soon she was lost in her own little world.

The dishes done, Raine sent Jess to watch the news with Cora while she set a fresh pot of coffee to brewing. It always seemed everything discussed was done over a pot of coffee. It had to be a form of comfort food and right now she needed all the comfort she could get. This was certainly a matter of gigantic importance in need of serious attention.

Coffee brewing, she leaned against the counter, studying Jess. At the moment, he was perched on one arm of the leather sofa listening intently to a report concerning government security breaches occurring around the country. She noticed that even when relaxing he was on alert. It had to be all the years in the military. Though he hadn't said much about what he'd done, she had seen the scars. Obviously, it'd been dangerous. Those experiences had influenced his installing high-end surveillance devices like the ones employed at sensitive facilities. It also explained his concerns about the surveillance of his property. It made her feel safer than she had in a very long time. But knowing Addison, if he wanted to get his hands on her nothing would stop him. That safe feeling slipped a little.

Intuitively, Jess looked up. The worried expression on her face got his attention. Forgetting the news, he joined her at the counter, kissing her gently. She leaned into his warmth. The strength she so badly needed flowed from him into her as she breathed in the scents of him—the combination of the subtle spice of his cologne and the fresh air that clung to him.

Feeling the tension gripping her, he whispered, "Are you sure you're okay? Nothing got knocked out of whack last night, did it? We did get a little rambunctious."

Chuckling softly, she whispered, "No, last night was wonderful. I'm fine and I promise I'll call for a checkup, but there's something we need to discuss, I just didn't want Katy hearing us."

Worry lines etched deep grooves on either side of his mouth now. "What's got you so spooked?"

Cora, hearing him, looked at Raine. Jess was right. She was spooked, and that meant something was wrong. A sick feeling hit the pit of her stomach as the answer came to her— Addison. "What'd you find out in Phoenix that's got you looking so worried? What's you-know-who up to now?"

Glancing into the bedroom she saw Katy had dozed off, and she picked up her colors and put them away. Katy had finished the promised picture for Jess. "Let's have some coffee and I'll fill you in."

They gathered at the table, silent and watchful as she poured the steaming coffee into mugs. Cora's brow knit in a frown, that bad feeling growing ten times worse than before.

Jess was impatient, shifting restlessly. He hated waiting. Then a shiver of dread crawled up his spine realizing this was about her ex-husband. When she sat down he reached across the table giving her hand a reassuring squeeze.

Clasping it, she looked at Cora. "You're right. It's about Addison and some interesting information Gordon gave me." How could she sound so calm when she was quaking inside?

"What did he say that's got you so worried? Whatever it is, we'll handle it together. You're not in this alone and if I have any say so you'll never be alone again."

Cora nodded in agreement. "He's right, honey, we're in this together so tell us what shenanigans Addison's pulling."

Raine looked to Cora then Jess. "You're right about shenanigans. Jesus!" She blasted. It came out loud. Cringing, she made sure Katy hadn't woken up and closed the door. "I could just scream. It seems Addison, slick as always, managed to finagle an early release and will be getting out in the not too distant future."

The explosions she expected weren't long in coming. Cora's was loud and vocal. Jess's was a silent rage that rolled off him in thick waves. "What do you mean, he's getting out early?" Cora slammed her mug on the table sending coffee sloshing over the sides. "That no good piece-of-you-know-what should be locked away forever. After what he did to you and he's getting out early? Give me a break. They should've locked him up and thrown the key away!" She grabbed a napkin out of the holder to sop up the spill. Angry eyes flew in Jess's direction. "You should see what he did to her. You should see how evil this man is."

"I did see." Jess muttered, not sure if the heat flooding his face was due to Cora's knowing grin or the fury building against Addison. Actually, it was a little of the first and a whole hell of a lot from the latter.

Seeing the smug look Cora shot her, heat crept into Raine's face too. Drat that woman for making her blush like a school-girl, especially after having a baby. And heaven only knew; that experience left you with no modesty whatsoever.

The hard set of his jaw and the dark look on his face were good indications of how upset Jess was. "How can your ex be walking free in such a short time? I thought he was behind bars for years." His growl sounded like an angry lion. "And why the hell didn't you tell me this sooner?" His glare was accusing.

And that sparked Raine's temper. Momentarily forgetting they had an audience, she spoke before she thought. "Excuse me? You weren't worried about talking last ni . . ." She stopped dead at the chuckle Cora couldn't hold back. Jess bit the inside of his mouth. "Oh, never mind." She snapped then pointed a stern finger at Cora. "And you can stop laughing! As for you," that same finger was now pointing at him, "you can stop glaring at me. It's your fault I got sidetracked." And his wide grin showed that she'd just stroked his already too large ego. She shook her head in exasperation, but smiled.

"Anyway, I gather Addison is being released sometime in April. A judge believes he's just so remorseful. I swear if I'd known this would happen I'd have never agreed to anything. Instead I'd have dug my heels in and gone through a trial." Gripping the coffee mug until her fingers turned white, she wished it was Addison's neck.

"Am I safe in assuming Gordon will keep you in the loop?" Cora asked.

Raine nodded. "He'll make sure I know everything that's going on. The second Addison steps outside the jail he'll be on the phone to me. Addison blames me for all his troubles and he's not bashful about telling anyone who'll listen. Even his former attorney is concerned he'll do something crazy. He told Gordon it'd be wise if I stayed away. And Gordon made no bones about it either and was emphatic we stay away from Phoenix." At that a loud snort drew her attention to Jess.

His dark eyes were flinty-hard. "You're not going anywhere, not now, not later, so you might as well get used to the idea. Whatever trouble Addison is cooking up we'll handle together. You're safer here with me than anywhere else. I do not want you leaving here. In fact, I'm not ever letting you leave here. Got it?" He told her forcefully.

Despite the seriousness of the conversation, she grinned. "Got it. Besides, I'd already made up my mind I wasn't leaving; especially not now that we've worked through our stupidity." She shot Jess a hesitant look. If there was ever a time for him to turn tail and run this was it.

Jess shook his head. "You're not getting rid of me. You three are my family now. And even if he does try tracking you down he has no idea where you are. This far off the beaten path, it'll take him a long time to find you and you're a lot safer here than off God knows where alone."

Had Jess any idea Addison knew exactly where Raine was he wouldn't have been so confident. And had Raine known, she'd have packed them up right then and there and disappeared into the night. Though he made a convincing argument, doubts riddled her. Where Addison was concerned, no one could be sure of anything. The difference between her and Jess—she knew first-hand how Addison's cunning mind worked and that he wasn't above using any means to hunt her down. He had the determination and the resources and anyone who helped her could pay a mighty high price, too.

Seeing her so worried after their bliss-filled hours infuriated Jess. Maybe it was just as well he didn't know where Addison was being housed. She hadn't told him of the location but with his connections it'd only be a matter of hours before he had it.

He was seriously considering a quick covert trip to get rid of the bastard. That would be the best gift he could ever give his future wife.

A sudden flush tinged his cheeks thinking of her as his wife. Seeing it, an inquiring brow lifted. What had put that adorable blush on the man's face? He winked at her. For now, he'd stay mum. He had a plan that he needed to enlist Cora's help with. In the meantime, he refused to let Addison Andrews intrude on his happiness. They were going to enjoy Christmas and leave the worrying for later; at least that's what he wanted Raine to believe.

"Quite honestly, until we're sure he's out, there's no sense worrying ourselves sick." He hoped he sounded convincing.

Cora saw through the smokescreen and championed him. "He's right. Christmas is right around the corner. We've got kids coming, things to do, and I refuse to let Addison ruin it."

Raine agreed. Letting Addison ruin the holidays would be like giving him an invisible club to beat her with and she'd be damned if that was happening. They deserved to celebrate. Her warm gaze encompassed them both. "You're right, but I won't lie. I'll worry, but having you two makes it a lot easier to deal with." Her voice went rusty and her eyes misted up. "Darn! Here I go again with the water works!" She dabbed her eyes with a napkin.

"You can cry on my shoulders all you want, sweetheart. Besides, I'd be crazy if I didn't think you'd worry." He squeezed her hand. "I'll put in extra safety measures and in case you haven't noticed, I'm not exactly what they'd call a "snowflake" either. I can, and have, held my own with the best of them. Like I told you, I don't start fights, but I don't back down from them, either."

Never expecting to have this kind of happiness again, her eyes blazed with love for him. Seeing it, Jess swallowed hard against the boulder threatening to choke him. No woman had ever looked at him that way and he swore he'd do everything in his power to keep her safe. But it was time to get off this serious subject and on to something more pleasant, otherwise he'd be crying right along with her.

"Okay, this business is settled, now on to more urgent matters. I really could use your help. I've got three cabins needing decorated inside and out before the weekend." He affected the best innocently pleading look he could muster, and his most engaging smile.

Raine swiped at her still streaming eyes. "Don't use that innocent look on me, bud. You already knew we'd help you get them ready."

Jess grinned sheepishly. "Yeah, I did. I just wanted to make sure I hadn't ticked you off too much with my stupid actions."

Cora reached across the table and patted his large hand. "You're all right in my book. You've redeemed yourself."

Eyes dancing with merriment, Raine said, "And Katy will love helping you string lights on the cabins. In fact, I've a feeling she'll fight you for the ladder."

Jess grimaced. "Oh man, that little scamp will be up the ladder faster than I can get down. I can see her, little hands on her hips, arguing that she can do it. I've a feeling she's just a little hard-head like her mother." Seeing her brow shoot up in warning, he added, "But that's just fine with me."

Yes sir, he couldn't wait to have that adorable little girl and her beautiful mommy in his life forever. The ring on his dresser had been calling to him that day in the mall, as though knowing he would ask the woman sitting across from him to be his wife.

Just before midnight, Jess checked his watch. "I didn't realize it was so late. I'd better be heading home so you two can go to bed." His eyes were sending an entirely different message saying, I really don't want to go. I want to kiss you, hold you. I want to make love to you. I want to share your bed with you. Permanently.

The unspoken message set her senses to tingling. She wished for the same.

Cora took the hint. "I'll leave you two to lock up. Night, Jess." She couldn't resist peeking before closing the bedroom door. The tall, broad shouldered man and the petite woman were wrapped in each other's arms.

She grinned, quite pleased with herself. All they had needed was a push in the right direction. And no matter what the coming months brought, they'd get through them—together.

ABOUT THE AUTHOR

Tina swears she was bitten by the writing bug probably further back than she can remember, attributing it to the tales and antics she recalls as a youngster growing up amongst a whole passel of aunts, uncles and cousin. Now with her own family there are even more stories to inspire ideas, even collaborating with granddaughter Harmony for a poetry contest and finishing second.

Though a Missouri girl, a graduate of East Central College in Union Missouri with a degree in Criminal Justice, she, her husband Tom and family have resided on the Florida Gulf Coast for twenty-five years, arriving the same month that Hurricane Andrew. Among the many hats she wears is office manager at a local law firm and now has donned a new one with the plunge into the literary world with her first release of You'll Come to Me.

Besides her love of travel and history, Gatlinburg Tennessee being one of her favorite places to go, Tina loves family vacations and reunions, doing genealogy, reading, crocheting, baseball and soccer. A lover and spoiler of animals she unabashedly admits her little Morkie Marshmallow absolutely rules the house.

If you enjoyed reading this first book in the new

DUSK *to* DAWN SERIES

be sure to let the author and publisher know
by leaving your comments on Amazon.

Stay connected with Tina on Facebook
and be the first to know about her new
releases and Raine's continuing saga.

Facebook: tinamarienicholsauthor
Website: www.tinamarienichols.com

www.ingramcontent.com/pod-product-compliance
Lightning Source LLC
Chambersburg PA
CBHW031316280626
47169CB00019B/1727